Scot Under the Covers

Scot Under the Covers

SCOT UNDER THE COVERS

SUZANNE ENOCH

THORNDIKE PRESS
A part of Gale, a Cengage Company

LIBRARY OF CONGRESS CIP DATA ON FILE.
CATALOGUING IN PUBLICATION FOR THIS BOOK
IS AVAILABLE FROM THE LIBRARY OF CONGRESS

ISBN-13: 978-1-4328-7898-6 (hardcover alk. paper)

Published in 2020 by arrangement with Macmillan Publishing Group, LLC/St. Martin's Publishing Group

Printed in Mexico
Print Number: 01   Print Year: 2020

SCOT UNDER THE COVERS

Scot Under the Covers

CHAPTER ONE

"I said he was in the doorway," Aden MacTaggert stated, eyeing his older brother on the great black Friesian warhorse Coll rode. "He walked in, opened his gobber, and started yapping like he always does, and I threw my boot at him."

"And cracked him in the head," Coll MacTaggert, Lord Glendarril, finished, scowling. "With ye being still half drunk, woke from a sound sleep, and nae more than a peep of light in the room? I think maybe ye did throw yer boot at him, and it scared him when it hit the wall or someaught, so he fainted."

"I knocked him cold," Aden protested, slowing his chestnut thoroughbred, Loki, as they reached Grosvenor Street and the front of Oswell House. "Ask Oscar. He'll even point ye to the lump he says he still has on his skull."

"I'd nae admit to fainting in fear, either,"

Coll grunted, swinging to the ground. "Ye cannae throw a boot with any accuracy."

"I cannae speak for ye, but ten pounds says *I* can," Aden returned, dismounting to hand Loki's reins over to Gavin, the groom they'd brought with them when they'd all been ordered down to London.

Had that only been five weeks ago? It seemed a century had passed since Lady Aldriss, their estranged mother, had revealed the existence of that damned agreement she and their father, Angus MacTaggert, had signed back when the three MacTaggert sons had been bairns. If they didn't wed English ladies before their only sister — Eloise, the youngest — married her own beau, Francesca Oswell-MacTaggert would cease funding Aldriss Park — and thereby the lives of all the cotters, farmers, shopkeepers, servants, and her own sons.

"And how do ye mean to win that wager?" Coll retorted. "We're in damned London. Ye cannae go about hitting valets with boots, or the pretty people will frown at ye."

Aden looked around. "Gavin, go take that bucket down the street."

The groom eyed him. "I'll nae have ye pelting me with boots, Master Aden. Oscar claims his eyes still cross when the weather turns foul."

"I'll wait till ye're clear. Go."

With a sigh the groom picked up the bucket and went trotting up the street. Twenty or so feet away he stopped and looked back at them. "Here?"

"Nae. Keep going."

When Gavin had to wait for a carriage to pass before he continued up the street and then motioned at them from fifty or so feet away, Aden nodded. "That'll do. Get out of the way."

Beside him, Coll sat on a mounting block and pulled off his boots. "Ye'll go second," he said. "And if I get closer, ye owe me *twenty* pounds."

That had escalated quickly, and predictably. "Then throw it, before ye end up losing yer hide." Leaning back against the wrought-iron railing that enclosed the front drive of Oswell House, Aden crooked a leg and yanked off his own Hessian boots. Their mother would no doubt be dismayed to see her two oldest lads walking about the streets of Mayfair in bare feet and kilts, but then she'd demanded they hie themselves down to London for no damned reason but to find wives. There were consequences to such rash orders. "And likewise. Twenty quid when I thrash ye."

Standing again, Coll hefted a boot in his hand, cocked his arm back, and hurled it toward the bucket as if the finely crafted leather footwear were a rock. A horse carrying its dandy of a rider up the road skittered sideways as the boot bounced beside him and then skidded to a halt about eight feet short and two feet wide of the bucket.

"I say!" the rider chastised, trotting toward them. "This is not how —"

"Move, ye peacock," Aden said, taking Coll's place. "Dunnae get in the way of a Scotsman's wager."

With a squeak the dandy paled, yanking the gray's reins sideways. "Heathens!" floated back on the breeze as the fellow vanished down the side street.

"He's wearing more colors than a stained-glass window," Coll observed.

"Aye. That's a lad ye could spy in the dark." Aden took his own boot by the top, letting the heavier heel hang. Swinging it back and forth, he opened his fingers and let fly near the top of his arc. The Hessian boot did a slow loop end-over-end, clanging against the bucket before landing straight up and down directly beside it.

Whistling, Gavin stopped an ice wagon. "Go around, ye fool," the groom ordered. "We've a wager to settle here."

10

"Why are people shouting in front of my h . . . Oh," Francesca Oswell MacTaggert, Lady Aldriss, began as she descended the short, half-circle drive. "Barefoot? Really?"

"I cannae throw a boot while it's on my foot," Coll grunted, shouldering Aden out of the way to line up his second throw.

"Why are you throwing your boots?" the countess asked, a faint line furrowing between her brows.

"Coll claims Oscar fainted and hit his head when I tossed my boot at him, and I'm proving that ye can hit a valet from across the room well enough to knock him cold."

"You — I will not have you hitting servants, Aden."

He kept his attention on Coll. "It was eight months ago. And he might've ducked. I did warn him."

Beside him the oldest MacTaggert brother had adopted Aden's underhand swing. Coll was nearly six-and-a-half feet tall, all muscle and no subtlety, though, so Aden wasn't surprised when the boot sailed up toward the clouds and past the bucket, past the curve in the road where Grosvenor Street turned up Duke Street, and landed in the shrubbery of the Duke of Dunhurst's hedgerow.

11

"Ha!" his brother chortled, slapping his hands together. "Beat that."

"The wager was over whose throw is closer to the bucket, ye lummox," Aden reminded him. "Nae who can fling their footwear all the way back to Scotland."

"Bah," the viscount growled. "Give me another throw, then."

"I willnae. Two feet, two boots."

"Then yer second boot has to land closer than the first."

Aden lifted an eyebrow. "I've already won twenty pounds. I may as well put this boot back on my foot."

"Yes, please do," their mother muttered from behind him.

He grinned at that, keeping his face turned away from her. "Unless ye'll double the wager," he went on. "Forty quid that this boot lands closer to the bucket than the first one."

"Ye're on," Coll said on the tail of that, as if he thought Aden might change his mind. "Since ye'd have to get it inside the bucket to win."

So be it. Half closing one eye, Aden swung the boot once, waited for a trio of bairns to cross the street with their nanny, swung again, and let go. The boot's heel hit the rim of the bucket, tipped it over, and landed

12

half inside as the thing rolled in a slow half circle. "Forty pounds," he said, straightening and keeping his own surprise to himself. A time or two he'd benefited from luck over talent, but only a fool counted on the fickle lass.

"Gavin, bring my damned boots back here," Coll bellowed.

As the groom dove into the shrubbery, a knee-high black dog dodged around him into the street and grabbed up one of Aden's boots. Aden scowled. *Damnation.* That wouldn't do. Those Hessians were his only pair of boots fit for wearing in proper Sassenach company. Stepping forward, he whistled before Gavin could give chase.

"Here, laddie," he said, opening his sporran and pulling out the biscuit he'd stolen from the kitchen earlier. "Do ye favor a trade?" Squatting, he held the biscuit out in his hand.

The long-snouted dog edged forward, tail down, pointed ears flattened, and boot in his mouth. Whoever he was, he hadn't been treated kindly on the streets of London. Aden could sympathize with that.

"Grab him, Aden," Coll urged.

Aden ignored his brother. Coll always favored a scrap, even when a gentler hand would serve a situation better. The dog

13

dropped the boot, stretching forward with a slightly sideways cant, one eye twitching as if it expected to be struck. "Only cowards beat animals," Aden soothed, holding his hand and the biscuit steady and outstretched. "Ye've nae a thing to fear from me."

Ears lifting a little, the dog clamped its teeth over the edge of the sweet and skittered away, disappearing around the corner in the direction of Hyde Park. With a sigh Aden stretched out to pick up his boot and stood again. Poor wee lad.

When he turned around, Lady Aldriss had her green gaze on him. The woman was clever and knew it, and because she'd managed to get the youngest of the three MacTaggert lads married already, she thought she had them all figured out. But he wasn't amiable, goodhearted Niall. He was three years older than his twenty-four-year-old brother, and ten times more cynical. He remembered quite well the day their mother had left them behind in Scotland, and how empty and . . . idiotic he'd felt for months afterward. That was the last time he'd been caught unaware. Hell, he hadn't led matters with his heart since then.

"What is it ye think ye've deciphered, Countess?" he asked aloud, catching his

14

second boot when Gavin tossed it to him and turning for the Oswell House front door.

"I don't know," she returned, following him. "I continue to observe."

"Observe all ye wish, then," he countered. "I reckon ye'd gain more insight doing that with me in my natural surroundings, which isnae here in London."

"From the way you and your brothers speak about you, I thought your natural surroundings would be anywhere you might find a table and some cards or dice."

"Aye. Ye've the right of that, then. Ye've deciphered me."

"Aden, d—"

"Nae," he interrupted, not slowing his retreat. "I'll do yer bidding and find a wife, because ye've nae left any of us a choice. But I'm nae going to sit down for a heart-to-heart chat with ye over tea, *màthair.*" Over his shoulder he caught sight of Coll's interested expression. Always looking for trouble, the viscount was. "Forty quid, ye behemoth."

"I'll pay ye in a damned minute."

Padding barefoot into the foyer, Aden passed an affronted-looking Smythe the butler, who'd likely never seen any of Oswell House's residents without footwear before.

15

Heading upstairs, he freed a necklace made of paste pearls from his coat pocket and hung it over the antlers of Rory, the stuffed deer they'd brought south with them and left on the landing of the main staircase for every exalted Sassenach guest who stepped through the front door to see.

The red deer had been a part of the ridiculous amount of luggage they'd toted from the Highlands with them, because as far as they'd known, all traveling English had a ludicrous number of trunks and bags accompanying them. And they'd wanted to make a ruckus, to demonstrate that they wouldn't be ruled by some Englishwoman they barely remembered just because she had gold in her purse. When the countess had declared that under no circumstances would Rory be allowed to live in the library as he had up at Aldriss Park, Aden and Coll had set him down on the landing out of pure contrariness.

In the weeks since then the deer had acquired a cravat, a beaver hat, a blue satin skirt, a lambskin glove over one antler tine, earbobs, and various other knickknacks hung over his impressive rack of antlers and muscular frame. The lad looked less than dignified now, but the amusement of dressing him like a disheveled Sassenach had kept Aden, at least, from punching several actual Sassenach.

"Where did you get that?" a female voice asked from the landing above him.

"Rory?" he replied, glancing up at his sister, Eloise. She was the youngest of the MacTaggerts, and the only one of them raised English. She was also the reason her brothers had allowed themselves to be dragged down to London. The eighteen-year-old had gotten herself betrothed, an act that had set their father on his deathbed — where Angus MacTaggert still remained better than a month later according to his frequent letters warning his sons of the treacherous females lying in wait in London — and her three brothers with pretty, English-bride-shaped nooses around their necks.

"No, the necklace," she corrected, descending the steps to join him. Eloise removed it from the deer's antler and held it up to examine it. "Oh, they aren't real, are they?"

"Nae. A lad lost a wager and had to give over whatever he carried in his pockets. I dunnae if they were to be a gift for a lass, or if he tried and she refused them, or if he nicked them from some unsuspecting lady or other."

"That's sad, any way you put it." With a sigh she hung them back on the antler. "Even so, Rory is quite well dressed."

"Aye. All the other deer in the Highlands would be jealous if they could see him now." Kissing her on the cheek, he continued up the west-side stairs toward the group of bed-chambers given over to him and his brothers. Whatever bother she'd caused them, Eloise was their bairn of a sister and a MacTaggert. She was to be loved and protected, English-raised or not. She'd lost her heart, and hadn't known about the agreement any more than her three brothers had.

Behind him Eloise cleared her throat. "Thank you for returning in time to attend my luncheon," she said, and he could almost hear her grimace. "I know you don't like the idea of having young ladies thrown at you. But they are all my friends. And it's just food, which you like. There's no harm in you and Coll joining us."

Aden slowed. Women were always flinging themselves at him, but since they'd arrived in London it seemed like someone had loaded a catapult full of skirts and bosoms and launched it at his head. Aye, Francesca demanded he wed an English lass, and aye, he'd been looking now for five weeks. Well, not looking as much as he'd been observing with growing cynicism. Fluttering eyelashes and discussions of the weather bored him to tears, but as far as he could tell that was the sum of female Sassenach conversation. Eventually, though, he would have to choose one of them, empty-headed and dainty or not. He did recognize that. The future of Aldriss Park depended on it. But he didn't have to like it. And he did not. At all. Even Eloise's friends — the ones he'd met, anyway — had seemed very, very . . . young. Naive. Dull. Full of naught but polite chatter and lace.

He couldn't put into a sentence what it was he wanted in a lass, but a bit of fire and boldness would have been nice. Or not nice, which was what he preferred. A lass who wouldn't lie on her back, wide-eyed and stiff, while he did his "husbandly right" or whatever the proper set called fucking here in London. As for the rest . . . well, he needed to marry. All he required, he supposed, was a woman who didn't make him wish to drown himself in the nearest loch.

Perhaps the difficulty here was that Niall, the youngest MacTaggert brother, had not only found a lass within a day of arriving in London, but he'd found one he loved. And Amy adored him. Hell, they'd barely left

Niall's bedchamber in the six days since they'd returned from Gretna Green. Love was a sticky proposition, and any man aiming to find it was a fool. Niall, to his credit, hadn't been after the damned thing, which apparently *was* the only way to find it. A bloody conundrum, and one Aden wasn't certain he would ever trust, anyway.

"Aden? You're to respond by saying you appreciate my efforts and that you'll behave yourself."

Blinking, he turned around to face Eloise again. "I'll behave myself," he agreed. "But I suggest ye remind Coll of that, too. He's the one more likely to put a lass over his shoulder and stomp off with her."

"Yes, but he said he wants a dull, fainting lily he can leave behind here in London. That wouldn't seem to require kidnapping."

That made him grin. "Ye're half Scottish down to yer bones, *piuthar*. Ye've the right of it. Just prop some half-dead flower up beside him, and he'll thank ye for it."

"But what about you?"

"Me?" Aden feigned surprise. "I keep thinking any lass will do, but then I reckon I'd prefer nae to be bored. So nae a boring one. And mayhap a lass who wouldnae faint at the sight of her wedding bed."

"Aden," she said, blushing.

He lifted an eyebrow. "Do ye mean to faint when ye see yer wedding bed, Eloise?"

"Well, no, but —"

"That's because ye've a backbone. Someone nae boring and with a backbone, then, if ye mean to find me a match."

Eloise tilted her head, her nearly colorless green eyes assessing him. "Weren't there any lasses in the Highlands who could stand up to you, Aden?"

Was that how she interpreted his request? A fighter? It didn't much matter, he supposed, if such a lass didn't exist. Flashing a grin he didn't feel, he turned up the stairs again. "If there were, I wouldnae be here, *piuthar*. I'd be in the Highlands, a married man and free of Lady Aldriss's claws."

There had been lasses aplenty in the Highlands, aye, and he was well acquainted with a fair share of them. At seven-and-twenty he'd begun to contemplate marriage even before he'd learned about Lady Aldriss's decree, but he'd yet to encounter a lass whom he cared to wake beside for longer than the stretch of a single morning or two. They didn't call him the elusive MacTaggert brother for no reason.

"My friends will be here in an hour. And you must have on shoes, for heaven's sake. You're fairly pleasant-featured, I suppose, but a prospective bride wants to know that her prospective husband is able to dress himself."

He grinned. "Aye, Eloise. I'll wear someaught to cover my nethers as well, even without ye reminding me."

"Mm-hm. One hour, Aden."

As he reached his bedchamber something crashed downstairs. Several voices began yelling, and he turned around yet again. Coll had been in a fine enough mood during their ride, but that had been all of five minutes ago and he'd lost forty quid since then. Or mayhap Eloise had reminded the viscount that they were to attend a proper luncheon with proper lasses.

Before he'd managed two steps back toward the stairs something black and smelling of wet and cabbages hurtled up the hallway and crashed into his legs. Staggering, he grabbed the wall to keep himself upright. "What the devil?"

The filthy thing wound around his legs, muddy paw prints all over the tops of his bare feet and patterning the green carpet runner around him. Finally it sat on his left foot and leaned hard against his knee.

Smythe the butler came into view, a walking stick raised in one hand and his generally bland expression locked into one of shocked affront. "Have you . . . There you are, you little piece of filth. Off with you! Out of this house!"

Tilting his head, Aden blocked the downward swing of the stick with his forearm. "I reckon ye'll have to go through me before ye hit this wee beastie," he drawled, catching and holding the butler's angry gaze.

The man subsided. "It ran in past me, the wretched thing. And it's ruined the carpet, I'll wager. If you'll wait here, I'll get a rope and —"

"Nae," Aden interrupted. "Ye willnae. This is my dog, Brògan," he decided, settling on the Gaelic word for "boots" since the lad had attempted to steal one from him. "He's come all the way from the Highlands to find me, and ye'll do naught but put a bucket of warm water and some rags out in the garden so I can clean him off after his long journey."

"That is not — I saw you giving it a biscuit in exchange for your boot not five minutes ago!" the butler exclaimed.

"Aye, because he brought it back to me," Aden returned coolly. "He's a fine beastie."

"That . . . thing walked all the way from Scotland," Smythe countered skeptically. "And found you here, at Oswell House."

"Ye see him with yer own eyes, do ye

23

nae?" Aden said, nodding at Coll as his brother topped the stairs. "Coll, this Sassenach butler is near to calling me a liar. Tell him, will ye, that this is my dog Bròganan, all the way from Aldriss Park? I told ye the lad had a fine nose."

His oldest brother's deep-green eyes narrowed as he took in the scene, then he pinned the increasingly alarmed-looking butler with his gaze. "Were ye calling my brother a liar, Smythe?"

"I . . ."

"Because I'll swear it to ye if ye insist, and I barely recognized him beneath the mud, but that's Bogan."

For a second Smythe looked like he'd swallowed his tongue. "I thought his name was Brògan," he forced out between his teeth.

"Oh, aye," Coll drawled easily, his expression shifting to amused. "Good lad. Dunnae let him anywhere near me while he's that filthy, Aden. And I changed my mind, brother. I believe I dunnae owe ye any blunt."

Hiding a grin, Aden nodded. "I believe ye to be correct, bràthair."

"Aye." With that Viscount Glendarril vanished into his borrowed bedchamber and shut the door behind him.

"A bucket of water and some rags," Aden said again. "We'll be down in five minutes."

"I . . . Yes, Master Aden. As you wish."

Hm. All the antics of the past month hadn't seemed to trouble the butler overly much, but a muddy, flea-ridden dog might have just broken him. Grinning, Aden leaned over and shoved open his door. "In there, lad," he said.

Thankfully the dog stood, removing his arse from Aden's foot, and ambled into the bedchamber as if he'd been inside it a hundred times. Shutting them in, Aden made his way to the overlarge wardrobe and pulled out an old work shirt and his most faded kilt. He wasn't even certain why he'd bothered to bring them south with him, except they'd added to the general mass of nonsense they'd loaded into that pair of wagons. The work clothes and pair of well-worn boots were here because of that, as was the large, stuffed boar's head Aden had placed above his bedchamber door.

When he turned around, the dog had his front paws up on the bed and looked like he meant to jump onto the soft mass of pillows and blankets. "Nae!" he bellowed.

With a yelp the black mutt ducked beneath the bed and disappeared. Aden frowned. If he'd had a previous master, the

25

man hadn't been kind. But for the moment the dog could stay where he was. His own generally restless sleep wouldn't benefit from a battalion of fleas added into the bedsheets.

Pulling off his proper Sassenach coat and waistcoat and yanking his fine, soft shirt over his head, he dumped the clothes over the dressing table's chair. His kilt followed, while he tossed his road-scuffed boots over by the door. Then he dressed again, immediately more comfortable in his old work clothes and heavy work boots and a simple white shirt that had seen better days.

"Come along, lad," he said, crouching by the door. "Brògan."

Toenails tapped beneath the bed, but the beastie didn't reappear.

"Brògan. Come on, lad. I'll nae have ye in here flinging fleas onto my things. If ye mean to stay, ye need a bath."

Whether it was his words or the tone of his voice, Brògan seemed reassured enough to stick his nose from beneath the coverlet, then crawl into the open. Tail tucked and wagging slowly, he crept forward until he could stuff his nose into the palm of Aden's hand.

"I dunnae ken who ye were, lad," Aden murmured, "but ye've annoyed the butler.

That's good enough for me. Let's see what kind of companion a Sassenach stray can make for a Highlander who'd rather be back in Scotland."

Straightening, careful to keep his motions slow and unthreatening, he opened the door and walked down the hallway. A moment later the dog followed, leaving more smudges along the bottom two feet of wallpaper as he sniffed from one side of the hallway to the other. At the top of the main staircase Aden paused, eyeing the very clear set of paw prints trailing up the steps and the two maids with buckets and brushes already attacking the bottom-most stairs. Cursing under his breath, he squatted down to put one arm under the dog's neck and the other beneath his hindquarters. Annoying Smythe was one thing; making more work for the lads and lasses of the house was quite another.

The fellow weighed forty pounds or so, light enough for a man accustomed to hauling about sheep for shearing. Up this close the beastie's scent nearly made him gag, but he locked his jaw shut and descended the stairs. Continuing on through the rear of the house, he juggled the dog so he could open the back door and then went outside.

As usual Smythe had exceeded his orders,

providing both a bucket and a tin trough that must have come from the stable. Both already contained water, and a generous pile of rags sat a few feet away. For a broomstick-up-his-arse Sassenach, Smythe wasn't so bad, Aden supposed.

With a glance to see that the garden gate was closed in case the beastie decided to make a run for it, and not bothering to question why he'd decided BròSan would be staying on at Oswell House, he set the dog down in the half-filled trough. "Let's see what we can make of ye, lad," Aden grunted, and went to work with the bucket and the rags.

Five more buckets of water, some scissors, cursing, splashing, and a good brushing later he had what looked to be a black English springer spaniel and another curious development. "Lad, I'm sorry to be the one to tell ye, but ye're a lass," he commented.

Brògan wumphed and buried her face in the rag he'd been using to dry her.

"Och, ye knew that already. Ye've been using yer feminine wiles on me all along, have-nae?" He looked at the dirty, furry carnage they'd left on the garden steps and at the same stuff caking the front of his shirt and his kilt. "I'd be more swayed if ye hadnae left half of London on my front."

A male throat cleared from the direction of the top of the steps behind him. "Master Aden," Smythe intoned, "I'm to remind you that you gave your word to Lady Eloise that you would attend her luncheon."

Aden turned his head to eye the stone-faced butler. "Aye, I said I would, and so I will. What's got her bonnet full of bees?"

"The luncheon began twenty minutes ago, sir. Your brother Lord Glendarril is in attendance, as are Master Niall and Mrs. MacTaggert."

"Niall got himself vertical, did he?" Aden intoned, straightening. "Tell Lady Eloise I'll be down in ten minutes. Come on, Brògan."

"Did I hear you referring to that . . . Brògan as a female?" Smythe queried, his expression unchanged.

"Nae, ye didnae. I'll be needing a bowl of scraps for the lad; he's had a long journey."

The butler craned his neck sideways, clearly trying to see Brògan's undercarriage. "I'll see to it, sir. Lady Eloise did stress that you were already late, however, and that she would not be pleased if you broke your word."

She wouldn't, would she? Well, when a Highlander gave his word, he kept it. "I'll still need the scraps," he said, patting his damp thigh as he headed up the shallow steps back into the house.

Luckily the dog kept right on his heels; no doubt she'd sensed that he remained her best chance for a meal and a safe place to sleep. They'd somewhat reversed roles now, since she was damp but clean, and he was slathered with mud. But Eloise seemed to doubt that he meant to make an appearance, and that he meant to keep his word. And buried beneath that, the idea of walking into the small dining room looking as he did, especially when by now most every female of his sister's acquaintance knew he needed to find a wife, appealed to him more than a little.

"Behave," he muttered over his shoulder, half to Brògan and half to himself, and he pushed open the double doors of the small dining room.

A wall of high-pitched chatter hit him like a smack to the face — and then all at once dropped into silence.

"Ladies," he drawled, sketching a loose bow. "I've nae had a —"

"Is that Brògan?" Eloise interrupted, leaving the table and hurrying past Aden to crouch in front of the damp dog. "Oh, he's darling! Why didn't you ever say you'd left him behind in the Highlands?"

Immediately a herd of females shoved past him to form a circle around Bròganm, all the cooing and baby talk nauseating. At the same time, it fascinated him, like watching a worm eat its way through an apple. When a hand patted him on the shoulder, he jumped.

"What do ye expect?" Niall muttered, clearly amused. "The beast's clean. Ye look like a pigsty."

Aden half turned to view his younger brother. "Ye look a bit disheveled yerself, *bràthair*. Almost as if ye havenae worn clothes in nearly a week."

"Shut yer gobber, Aden," the newlywed returned, his expression darkening. "I'll nae have ye embarrassing Amy."

That made sense. Niall wasn't just Niall any longer. He was Niall and Amelia-Rose — Amy, for short. At the moment the young lady with the golden hair and forthright manner was ruffling Brògan's ears, but Aden nodded anyway. "Aye. She has enough of a burden, being married to ye."

"That's more like it," his brother commented, grinning again. "So is that the dog Coll said tried to steal yer boot?"

Of course Coll would have told their youngest brother the actual story — or part of it, anyway. "Aye. Did he also mention he lost forty pounds to me because he throws with all the finesse of a bull?"

Niall glanced over to the table where Coll still sat, devouring half a baked chicken and helping himself to a good portion of the hot rolls. "He must've forgotten that bit. Is that why ye were throwing boots about?"

"Aye. He questioned my word about Oscar."

"Aden," Eloise said, prancing up hand in hand with a lass in a yellow-and-green gown, "Bròganは is not a male dog."

Aden sent a glance at the pair of pretty brown eyes and an upcurved mouth standing beside his sister. If this was the lass Eloise had selected for him today, his sister at least knew how to find a bonny one. With a few exceptions most of her friends were bonny, though. It was the tittering, the unwavering commentary on the weather, the sighs and giggles that made him shiver. And almost without exception every one of Eloise's friends he'd met so far suffered from that disorder.

Stepping between his sister and her bonny friend, he lowered his head. "I gave Brògan a biscuit in exchange for my boot, and she followed me into the house," he murmured. "Smythe wanted to toss her out, but I dunnae hold with turning away guests. So I told a wee white lie about Brògan being my dog from Scotland. A boy dog. As far as Smythe knows, that's what she is. Ye ken?"

"Aye," Eloise answered. "And you ken that I'm trying to help you find a wife, and that making an appearance at my luncheon looking like the inside of a chimney isn't at all helpful, aye?"

"Aye," he returned, hiding his scowl. Eloise, sister or not, was English-raised, and a bit of mud and fur was no doubt enough to overset the stoutest Sassenach.

"Good." She lifted on her toes to kiss him on the cheek. "I've always wanted a dog. But Smythe will figure out eventually that you've bamboozled him, you know."

"I'm not so certain of that, Eloise," her friend put in. "People see what they want to see, and that is generally what's most convenient for them."

Aden straightened. Insightful, and not a thing about the weather at all. That had only been one sentence, though. How would she fare with two, this lass with the dark eyes and dusky-brown hair? "And who might ye be, lass?"

"Oh, I'm sorry," Eloise exclaimed, squeezing her friend's hand. "Aden, this is Matthew's sister, Miranda Harris. Miranda, my middle brother, Aden MacTaggert."

Now that he knew the lady was related to Eloise's fiancé, he could see the similarities. The dark-brown hair with its hints of sunset gold, the eyes dark as liquid chocolate. Miranda's face was narrower than her brother's, her features more delicate, and while she didn't have Matthew's height, the top of her head did come to just above Aden's shoulder. She was a tall lass, since he stood an inch above six feet himself. And he was the short brother.

"Miss Harris," he said, remembering enough of his manners to incline his head. It wasn't that he was struck by her. It was just that she'd surprised him a little. He'd still be willing to wager that weather would enter the conversation within the next two minutes, though. Aye, Brògan was the most promising lass in London so far. All she wanted was food and a blanket, and she didn't pretend to be after anything but that.

The lass — not the dog — curtsied smoothly. "I'm so pleased you and your brothers are here," she said, her accent very cultured and very English. "Eloise has been telling stories about you for ages."

Since the stories had apparently come to Eloise via their father, Angus, Aden had to doubt their authenticity. Lord Aldriss did like a good tale. He should have come down to London with them and seen his daughter for the first time in seventeen years, but Angus had decided he was about to perish from the shock of learning of his wee bairn's engagement. Or more likely, he was too scared of Francesca Oswell-MacTaggert to leave the safety of the Highlands. "I reckon she told ye tales about Coll mostly, a handful about Niall, and nae a one about me."

Miranda Harris tilted her head. "Only if the story about you starting with a shilling, going wagering, and ending up with a horse a day later is false."

He grinned. She hadn't fainted or blushed, or mentioned the chill in the air. Yet. "I'll give ye that one, then."

Eloise released her friend. "I'll be right back," she said, sending Aden a swift wink that clearly said she thought she'd found him his future wife. With that she dove back into the dog-petting circle.

"If ye kept straight which tale was about which brother," Aden commented, "I have to give ye credit for paying attention. Here in London I'm at best 'a MacTaggert brother,' and at worst I'm 'one of those Highlanders.' "

She folded her hands primly in front of her. Miranda Harris had long fingers, he noticed. Gambler's hands, some called them. And those dark-brown eyes, her lips slightly pursed now in either a stifled grin or an escaping grimace, he could tolerate. More than tolerate, as long as her next sentence wasn't about the damned weather — as if a soft Sassenach even knew what weather was.

"I did pay attention," she said in her proper tones, "especially because of the wagering. I detest gambling. And gamblers."

That straightened him up a little. Nothing much caught him flat-footed these days. Miss Miranda Harris had just accomplished that feat. "That was admirably direct," he drawled. "Well done, lass."

Her grimace deepened. "I was not offering you a compli—"

"I know ye didnae intend to say anything I'd admire," he cut in, taking half a step closer and setting aside the inner question of why he was bothering to verbally fence with a woman who'd apparently set herself against liking him before they ever met. Perhaps it was because he generally made a point of being fairly likeable. And because even if he didn't like the words, she'd bothered to speak her mind — when most of the Sassenach in London wouldn't dare spit out a direct insult to save their own lives. He'd seen fewer twists in a snake. "Ye need to keep in mind that I'm nae some wilting English dandy. In the Highlands we like to disagree with our fists. What ye said almost sounded like flirting to me, Miss Harris."

For a second she looked like she wanted to give the fisticuffs a go. "You don't seem to be obtuse," she returned, her voice clipped, "so I will assume you are deliberately misreading my statement. I shall be more clear, then. I know what Eloise was about, and I have no interest in a match with a gambler, a wagerer, someone who views the inferior skills of others as an invitation to rob them."

Aden kept the loose grin on his face — mainly because it seemed to annoy her, but also because he'd never expected to cross paths with such a sharp-tongued lass in this soft country. A bit of fire. "That's a shame, lass, because wagering is about patience and finesse, about intimacy, and about having hands that know how to do more than shuffle cards."

The fine color of her cheeks darkened just a shade. "I could say the same about being a rat catcher. And he doesn't trick people into poverty."

He could argue that rat catching didn't have shite to do with intimacy, but he could also certainly make better use of his time by finding a woman who wouldn't spew vitriol at him. It was a shame, really. One lass who'd dared a direct word with him, and it was to proclaim that she wanted nothing to do with him. "I've been ordered to wed an English lass. I reckon I dunnae need to spend my time convincing one who doesnae see past the gossips. I'll leave ye be, Miranda Harris."

And she still kept her feet beneath her. Looking a wee bit relieved, as if she'd expected him to toss a deck of cards at her or something, Miss Harris nodded. "As long as we understand each other, Mr. MacTaggert."

"I understand *ye*. The rest isnae my concern."

CHAPTER TWO

Miranda Harris sipped a glass of Madeira, her attention on the pairs and trios of guests as they emerged from the crowded hallways of Gaines House and flooded into the ballroom. Thus far no one else wore the same deep-yellow chiffon with light-green lace and trim she'd acquired just yesterday, but even if it didn't happen tonight it wouldn't be long before she set eyes on her apparel twin. The color was simply too vibrant to pass by, and Mrs. Allen the dressmaker had confessed that she'd acquired a great quantity of the very expensive material from Paris.

Her friends strolled into Gaines House in drips and droves, favoring her with waves and smiles and motions to join them for conversation. For the moment she put them off; the soiree would last well into the wee hours of morning, and she very much enjoyed watching the newly arrived guests.

Not that she looked for anyone in particular, though it would be fortunate if she noted when Aden MacTaggert arrived.

It had been bad enough when she only knew him by reputation; now that they'd met — and with silly Eloise actually trying to make a match of them, for goodness' sake — she found him even worse than she expected. He didn't look at all like an inveterate gambler should. Not a hint of narrow, suspicious eyes or the odor of cigars and alcohol, no stringy, unkempt hair or rumpled clothes. His accent seemed intended to be charming rather than menacing, not that she found him to be anything other than . . . just someone to be avoided.

"Could I fetch you a glass, Mia? They have an orange punch that looks passable."

Sighing as a deep-yellow chiffon trimmed with peach glided into the ballroom on the frame of Lady Caroline Mays, Miranda faced her brother. One evening of being complimented as shining like the sun would have been lovely, but she did still adore her new gown. "That's the third time you've offered me a beverage, Matthew. Why are you my shadow this evening? Why aren't you lurking about the doorway, waiting for Eloise?"

"It's already dreadfully warm in here and

I thought you might be thirsty, Eloise sent over a note earlier that she won't be arriving until half nine, and I'm your brother. Why shouldn't I dance attendance on you? Or would you rather stand beside Mother and Father as they get their ears talked off by the Applethorpes?"

Miranda grimaced. The last time she'd spied her parents by the library door, the Applethorpes had still been chatting at them. "Very well. I concede I am perhaps a little grateful not to have to listen to Mr. Applethorpe's tales of fighting those upstart Colonials again. Orange punch, if you please."

With one of his affable grins her brother bowed and disappeared in the direction of the nearest refreshment table. She might have found his information about the expected arrival time for the MacTaggerts helpful, but he had no cause to know that. At least she could put Aden MacTaggert from her thoughts now, though she had no idea why she kept conjuring him, anyway. Perhaps it was because he should look as odious on the outside as a gambler was on the inside, and he simply didn't. Annoying man.

A group of her friends had begun forming at one end of the room, but for the moment she remained content to observe, and to look for more yellow chiffon gowns. At least Mrs. Allen had cut the two dresses differently. While Lady Caroline's boasted half sleeves and a straight neckline, her own had a gathered waist, short, puffed sleeves, and a deep, rounded neckline her mother had deemed "nearly scandalous." Miranda liked being in the "nearly" category. It made her feel a little daring while never earning her more than the occasional raised eyebrow from the powdered wig-wearing set of elders.

"Here you go," Matthew said, handing over the brimming glass of orange-colored liquid.

"Thank you." She took a sip. *Oh, good heavens.* Lady Gaines had clearly been experimenting with her culinary creations again. Orange and . . . Oh, crushed marigold? Miranda put her hand over her mouth to keep from spitting it out. The marigold explained the dark, vibrant color, but in that concentration, it was unbearably bitter. "Sweet angel of mercy," she gasped. "That would curl the wallpaper."

"Would it? Hand it over," her brother demanded.

Giving it back to him, eyes watering from the bitterness of it, she pulled a handkerchief from her reticule and dabbed at her eyes. Lady Gaines must have decimated an entire field of marigolds. No doubt their hostess had been attempting to find the perfect orange color rather than bothering over the taste of the concoction.

He tasted it himself, because of course he would. With a grimace he put it on the tray of the nearest passing footman. "With a pint — or a gallon — of vodka added, I imagine it would be nearly tolerable," he commented, then cleared his throat. "You are dancing this evening, aren't you?"

"Of course. I missed the last three grand balls tending Aunt Beatrice and the babies. They are darlings, and I don't begrudge them a moment of the weeks spent away from London, but it is nice to be back again. And to not find dried porridge in my hair."

When Matthew didn't respond to that she glanced over at him, to find his attention on the doorway. Lord George Humphries stood giving his greetings to Sir Eldon Gaines and his wife Lady Harriet, but her brother's gaze was on the tall man in the naval captain's uniform beside Lord George.

"Who is that?" she asked, taking in the deep-set eyes beneath a prominent brow, the narrow, thin-lipped mouth, and the long, straight, down-angled nose in between.

With short, upright brown hair to complete the ensemble, in profile he looked rather like a crested bird of prey, a blue-dressed falcon grown too large for perching in trees.

"Hm?" Matthew started a little as he turned to look at her.

"Who is that with Lord George?" she repeated.

"Oh. It's his cousin. Captain Robert Vale. He's been in India for a time."

That would explain why she didn't recognize him. Lord George and her brother practically lived in each other's pockets, after all, and at three-and-twenty this was her fifth Season in London — yet her first sighting of this species of falcon. "Is he here on leave, then, or —"

Matthew offered his arm. "Come on. I'll introduce you."

"That's not nec—"

"Come on, Mia."

When she put her hand over his sleeve, he seemed . . . stiff, his muscles tight. For her easygoing brother to be tense about anything immediately seemed odd. He'd recently been introduced to his fiancée's three towering Highlander brothers, after all, and Father said he'd barely batted an eye. And they'd suggesting drinking and brawling as a get-acquainted ritual. "Matthew," she muttered, "what is —"

"Captain Vale," he said over her protest, stopping before the two men. "My younger sister, Miranda. Mia, Captain Robert Vale. George's cousin."

The captain, hat beneath his arm, swept a bow before he took her hand and bent over it. "Miss Harris. I've heard a great deal about you. So glad we could finally meet."

He had a falcon's eyes, as well, light-brown with a hint of amber, and a direct, unblinking gaze — almost as if she were a rabbit he'd just spied. Of course, his predatory appearance wasn't his fault, and he spoke mildly enough, but even so she retrieved her hand the moment she could politely do so. "Captain. Matthew says you've been in India," she said anyway, because her brother seemed to like him. "Are you here on leave?"

"No. I've retired," he returned. "I'm deciding my future, as it were. I have friends and business connections in India, but it's a very . . . warm place. I prefer a cooler clime."

"I imagine it *would* be quite warm. Were you not on the water, though?"

He lowered his head a little, eyes still on her. "It's warm on the water, as well. Not quite as hot and humid as it is inland,

45

however."

"Mia, give Vale a waltz, won't you?" Matthew put in abruptly. "Help welcome him home."

She would have preferred not to, and Matthew needed to have his foot trodden upon for even making the suggestion, but she'd been trapped into it now. "Certainly." Summoning a smile, she retrieved her dance card and pencil from her reticule and handed them over to the captain.

"The third one's a waltz," Matthew pointed out helpfully, reaching over her shoulder to gesture at the appropriate line.

As the captain wrote *Vale* in a neat hand on the appropriate line, Miranda abruptly wished she'd joined her friends when she'd had the chance. All the dances on her card would have been taken, or at least the two waltzes, but instead she'd decided to look for yellow dresses. Dash it all.

Hopefully Captain Vale could dance adequately, because she didn't wish to have her toes crushed. And hopefully he could carry on a polite conversation, because nothing was worse than standing face-to-face with someone and attempting to carry on a chat by herself. Still smiling, she retrieved her card. "I'll leave you three to chat," she said, giving a shallow curtsy. "I see my friend

Helen, and I promised her a moment."

It was a lie, of course, but Vale clicked his heels together. "There is nothing more important than honoring a promise."

That sounded very straightforward, or it would have if he hadn't been gazing at Matthew when he spoke. An abrupt chill went through her even in the warm, crowded room. It took some effort not to hurry her steps as she joined her growing circle of friends. "There you are, Miranda," Rebecca Sharpe said, clasping Miranda's hands in hers. "This is a sad crush tonight, isn't it? There are so many people my elbows are trapped against my ribs."

"There's a rumor Prinny might appear," skinny Frederick Spearman commented, lowering his voice a little. "No one will admit wanting to be seen with him, but everyone wants to make certain they are."

As much of a disruption as even the rumor of Prince George's presence caused, the flurry of mixed sycophancy and scorn fascinated Miranda. With his gout the Regent wouldn't be dancing, but he did have a refined eye for art and fashion. Perhaps he might admire her yellow gown.

"Speaking of seeing," Helen Turner commented, "I'm saving a spot on my dance card for one of the MacTaggerts. Hopefully

Aden. Did you see him yesterday? Muddy and wet, with that hair of his? If he wasn't a Scot, I would think him a poet."

"By 'that hair of his,' I assume you mean the way it's nearly long enough that he might consider braiding it," Miranda returned. For heaven's sake, queues had gone out of style better than a decade ago. And wearing it loose, the black strands whipping about in the breeze to artfully frame his lean face and whisper against his shoulders — yes, Helen was correct: It was poetic. Too poetic. A wolf trying to convince everyone that he was a harmless sheep.

"Miranda, you shouldn't say such things," Rebecca countered, her tittering giggle saying otherwise.

Perhaps she shouldn't, but Aden MacTaggert gambled. Apparently quite often and quite well, according to the snippets of conversation she'd heard from Matthew and Eloise — and lately, some of her other friends, as well. She glanced across the room at her brother still in deep conversation with Lord George and Captain Vale. For every gambler who played well, there were two dozen who played poorly. And of those poor players, half risked more than they should, or were overly confident or desperate or prideful or . . . naive enough to think they could beat the odds. The professional gambler didn't care about them, that their squandered money had come from rent or food or university funds. And yet in her opinion, being naive certainly didn't seem a crime that a man should have to pay for with his future.

An image of her uncle John crossed her memory, a laughing Aunt Beatrice on his arm. John Temple had been amiable and charmingly confident, and not nearly as skilled as he'd believed himself to be. At least the holder of his debts had been a so-called friend, willing to allow John the chance to pay off the sum he'd gambled away — though seeking his fortune in the wilds of America didn't seem anything a married man with two young daughters should have been attempting. It had been nearly a year since Aunt Beatrice had had any word of him at all, and privately Miranda had begun to think she never would.

She scowled. Matthew had idolized Uncle John, and her brother had confidence enough for a king. Lord George had never been the steadiest of friends for Matthew, but the third son of Lord Balingford at least possessed enough sense to know when to walk away from a table or a wager. And it had been two years now since the last of the angry speeches Matthew had used to earn from their father. Being forced to sell his own horse to pay off his debts, swiftly followed by the disastrous lesson of Uncle John, seemed finally to have made the truth of his shortcomings sink into his stubborn head. Thank heavens for that, because she didn't think her heart would be able to survive losing him to the Americas — or worse.

"Miranda, Helen's broken my heart and turned me away from the quadrille," Lord Phillip West drawled as he moved between her and her view.

"You were simply too late, Phillip," Helen protested, putting her gloved hand on Frederick's arm. "I told you I meant to dance every single dance this evening."

Shaking herself out of her unexpected gray cloud of memories, Miranda smiled and imperiously held out her hand. "I shall dance with you, my lord," she enunciated, dropping into a deep curtsy.

The Marquis of Hurst's younger brother took her proffered hand in his, bowing in return. "Thank you. I do admire the way you always keep back a dance or two for us poor, late-arriving unfortunates."

Actually she had only one name *on* her card at the moment. That wasn't like her.

But she seemed to be busy worrying over gowns and sharp-eyed gamblers and nebulous, unnamed, unarticulated dreads this evening. Hopefully a quadrille with the charming Lord Phillip would settle her so she could enjoy the evening again.

Ten minutes of twirling and quick-stepping did make her breathless, and she grinned as the music stopped. *Ah, much better.* Together with Phillip she returned to her friends — stopping her approach only when a broad chest appeared directly in front of her.

She looked up. A strong chin, a mouth turned down at one corner and up at the other, clearly amused, high cheekbones and a straight nose, gray-green eyes that abruptly made her conjure secluded, mist-covered pools in some ancient forest, and a fall of black hair framing the portrait and hanging in slight waves almost down to broad shoulders.

"Good evening, Miranda Harris," Aden MacTaggert said, catching the r's of her name in that deep brogue of his.

She drew in a breath, blaming her accelerating heartbeat on startlement. "Mr. MacTaggert. Has your sister arrived? Matthew has been practically pacing, waiting for her."

"Aye. She's here." He tilted his head, a lock of hair falling across one eye. "Ye're to be my sister-in-law. I reckon we shouldnae be unfriendly."

"We're not unfriendly," she countered. "We simply have nothing in common. That happens quite often, I believe."

"Even so," he pressed, ignoring Lord Phillip and evidently anticipating her response, "I've some curiosity. Most lasses who decide they dunnae like me have at least conversed with me first. Do ye have a dance to spare for me this evening? Then we can chat and ye'll have a reason to loathe me."

Rather than argue over her degree of dislike and whether it was warranted, which was undoubtedly what he wanted, she smiled. "I'm afraid not," she lied, glad her dance card lay safely in her reticule. "It's such a sad crush this evening, and I haven't one single free spot on my card."

The tall Highlander inclined his head. If he was disappointed or simply oblivious to the snub she couldn't tell; his expression remained one of mild amusement. But then he was a gambler, and knew how to disguise his thoughts. "I'm nae a cat. Curiosity willnae kill me." Inclining his head, he strolled off, pausing to speak with the absurdly

52

nervous Sarah Tissell. A moment later the poor thing held out her dance card, and he wrote down his name.

Well. Good for him, then. Sarah rarely danced, so she had the unfortunate tendency to become so concerned over making an error that she inevitably tripped or misstepped. He likely didn't know that, but Sarah's fingers twisting the strings of her reticule were difficult to miss. He was looking for a bride, as everyone knew, and Sarah would likely expire on the spot if he asked for her hand.

The music for the country dance began, and as Lord Phillip hurried off to collect his next partner Miranda abruptly realized she didn't have one. *Dash it all.* Twirling, she spied the short, balding Francis Henning holding a glass of whisky and gazing about the ballroom absently. "Mr. Henning," she said grandly, taking the glass from his hand and setting it into a potted plant, "would you do me the honor of a dance?"

"What? I — oh, well, dashed splendid," he stammered, letting her half drag him onto the polished floor. "Certainly. Sterling. Far side of the floor, if you don't mind. Want my grandmama to see me socializing."

Miranda stifled a smile. Mr. Henning's grandmama was famous for being ridiculously difficult. "Of course."

That had been a near one. No one liked to be caught in a lie, and especially not three seconds after uttering it. Of course, now she had seven more partners to find for the evening. Perhaps she felt a little less annoyed with Matthew and Captain Vale after all. They'd saved her one search, at least.

Francis's request put them in the group of dancers also occupied by Mr. MacTaggert. She danced down the line, pairing briefly with him and making a point to meet his gaze as they brushed hands, but he only lifted an eyebrow at her. Perhaps he *was* merely curious why she disdained gambling and gamblers, then, but Matthew was very nearly a part of the MacTaggert family. If her brother wanted them to know about his previous recklessness, or the better-known tale of their uncle, he could tell them himself.

As the dance ended, she escorted a panting Mr. Henning to the refreshment table and fetched him an awful orange punch, which he gulped down. Pulling her fan from her reticule, she waved it at him. "Thank you, Miss . . . Harris," he wheezed. "Been spending too much . . . time sitting about holding yarn . . . for my grandmama."

"And how is your grandmother?" she

54

asked dutifully.

"Oh, she's fit as a country horse, don't you know. If you'd care for a chat with her, I'd be happy t—"

"Miss Harris," a low, precise voice uttered from directly behind her, so close she could feel warm breath on the back of her neck.

Jumping a little, she turned around. Captain Vale gazed down at her with his bird-of-prey eyes. "Captain. Is it time for our waltz?"

"Yes." He held out one hand.

Stifling an inward sigh, she set her gloved fingers into his bare ones and they walked onto the dance floor. Ah, well. She required a partner for this dance, and he was one. He also appeared to be more fit than Mr. Henning, which boded well. When he put a hand on her waist, she put hers on his shoulder, resting her fingers on the gold braids and epaulets that adorned all captains in the British navy. Even retired ones.

She looked up to realize they were the first ones on the floor, which left them poised like anxious statues as the rest of the couples gathered around them. "Are you enjoying your evening?" she asked, to break the silence.

"Yes."

"How long has it been since you were last

55

in London?" There. That would require at least two words to respond, doubling his total thus far.

"It's been seven years since I was last in England."

Oh, ten words at once! "You never even returned for leave until now?"

"No."

And back down to one-word answers. Before she could summon another query for him, the orchestra began the waltz. He knew the steps, wherever he'd been, and he danced precisely and neatly. What he didn't do was smile, instead continuing to gaze at her until she rather desperately wanted to look away. Deliberately she slid one foot a touch sideways, at the same time tightening her grip on his fingers and looking down toward her feet. Swiftly she blinked a few times before she lifted her gaze again, this time angling her head to view the dancers around them rather than him.

"Has your brother spoken to you about me?"

Drat, now she needed to look at him again and pretend he didn't remind her of a hawk. "No, he hasn't," she returned, managing to focus on his left ear.

"I thought not. As I said, Miss Harris — Miranda — I have been away from England

56

for quite some time. Now that I've returned, I wish to establish my place here among the peerage. The most efficient way to do so is to marry someone whose place and reputation are already both established and unblemished — as are yours. A marriage between us would be efficacious, and we should proceed without delay."

Her feet kept moving, but Miranda couldn't quite hear the music any longer. *Of all the* — what — how was she supposed to reply to that? Matthew might have warned her that his new friend was softheaded. She meant to kick her brother in the shin the moment they returned home.

"I admire your logic," she said slowly, choosing her words with care, "and your determination to succeed. That said, I am not looking to wed a military man, retired or not. Thank you, though, for your complimentary words."

They did another circle of the room while he continued to look at her. "You are in an inferior position without realizing it," he stated in the same tone with which he'd proposed — outlined — their marriage. "Speak with your brother."

A frown pulled at her mouth, and she fought to suppress it. "I don't need to speak to anyone. Again, I thank you for your interest, but I simply do not return it. Now, let us be civil until the end of the dance."

"I am always civil. Nor do I wish in this instance to play the villain. Speak to your brother."

"I don't —"

"An argument now is pointless. I shall call on you in the morning at ten o'clock and we shall proceed once you are in possession of all the facts." Around them the music hit a crescendo and echoed into silence. They stopped moving, but he kept hold of her hand and her waist. "As I said earlier, I believe in promises. And in keeping them."

Letting her go, he turned on his heel and strolled off in the direction of the garden doors. Perhaps he was hungry and meant to go swoop down on a mouse or a hedgehog outside. Whatever the devil Captain Vale might think he'd heard from Matthew, this could not be allowed to stand. She would not tolerate hearing the gossip that some too-long-at-sea ship's captain had declared that he meant to marry Miss Miranda Harris.

Matthew stood with Eloise and the giant MacTaggert brother, Lord Glendarril, and she set off toward them. When her brother spied her, he actually took half a step backward. Since he couldn't possibly be reacting to her careful, composed expression, something else was afoot. That idea alarmed her to her toes. Still, he was an affable young man, her senior by only a year, and he might well have said something in jest that the captain took seriously.

"Might I have a quick word with you, Matthew?" she asked as she reached his side.

"Eloise and I were about to take a stroll in the garden, Mia. Could it wait?"

"Nae," the viscount countered. "Ye'll nae be strolling in any garden in the dark with my wee sister, Harris."

"Coll," Eloise protested, her cheeks darkening. "It's just a bit of fresh air."

The big Highlander took his sister's hand in his great paw and set it around his forearm. "Then I'll take ye. Harris's sister wants a word with him."

"Coll, y—"

With Eloise still protesting, the two MacTaggerts headed off toward the garden. Miranda didn't wait to see whether they went outside or not. Instead she took Matthew by the arm and pulled him into the nearest corner. "Your new friend Captain Vale just declared that he and I should marry," she stated, keeping her voice down. "He said I should speak to you about it, intimating that the scheme has your approval. I don't know what you might have said to him, but you need to go make it very clear that there's been a misunderstanding and there will not be a wedding."

Her brother opened and shut his mouth. "He's not a bad sort, Mia. A bit direct because he knows what he wants, but —"

"You are jesting," she cut in, the sharpness in her voice making him flinch. *Good.* "I know you generally like everyone, but you cannot allow some addle-pated lunatic to go about making such declarations to your own sister simply because he's George's cousin."

"That's not . . . You shouldn't call him addle-pated. Vale's a sharp stick. He . . . I —"

"Matthew Alexander Harris, stop stammering and tell me what the devil is afoot." Miranda dug her fingers into his forearm. "I do not like where my suspicions are taking me." Actually, her heart had begun hammering fast as a hummingbird's wings, and something like horror crawled with cold fingers up her spine.

He scowled. "Don't make it so dramatic. You mean to marry eventually, don't you? And you haven't found anyone in the five years you've been out. Why not —"

"It took you six years to find Eloise," she pointed out.

"Yes, but she only came out this year."

"What does that have to do with any —"

"I can't even count the number of completely acceptable men who've tried to court you. Well, Vale's not one of the horde you've already rejected. He —"

"Don't be ridiculous." She curled her fists. The lengths to which Matthew would go to make himself seem like the reasonable one were maddening. "I am *not* marrying him."

"You have to, Mia."

That stopped her tirade cold. "And why is that, pray tell?" she whispered.

"Because I owe him nearly fifty thousand pounds."

The amount . . . Even in her worst nightmares she'd never imagined such a sum. *"Matthew!"*

"It didn't begin that way," he protested. "I lost a few quid to him at the tables, and then I won it all back and more — I was up by five hundred quid, Mia, so I knew I could best him — and then when I went under again, he kept giving me chances to win it back. The odds that two horses would pull up lame in the same race last week — any sane man would have wagered against that."

"No, Matthew, any sane man wouldn't wager more than he could afford to lose. And for you that number is nowhere near fifty thousand pounds. Good heavens! You know better."

"I was already under by twenty thousand. A chance to wipe that out all at once . . . And it was a sure bet. A sure bet."

"Evidently it was not. For God's sake." Miranda took a breath, trying to quiet the roaring in her ears. Fifty thousand pounds. She couldn't even imagine. And yet, there it was. "I thought you'd stopped with all the gambling after you had to sell Winterbourne. And Uncle John — his debt wasn't even a quarter of what you've managed to acquire."

"I did stop, mostly. But Vale was fresh in London, and wanted George to take him gambling, and I didn't want to look like some bumpkin just sitting there." He looked down, his expression one of abject despair. "It's only been six weeks. I don't know how that amount . . . I don't know how it happened."

She did. Captain Robert Vale had seen precisely who Matthew was, and he'd dug in to bleed him dry. To accomplish that in six weeks told her everything she needed to know about the man. He was a gambler. A very proficient one. "How did my name come into this?" she made herself ask, however clearly she could see it happening.

"Two days ago, he said he'd decided to remain in London and wanted to purchase a house in Mayfair, and he required the blunt I owed him. When I admitted that I could pay him only two hundred quid, he said I should go to Father — or he would. I can't — Father would disown me. Or I would bankrupt the family. Or both." Matthew shut his eyes briefly. "So, I asked if we could reach some kind of agreement for repayment. That's when he said he required a wife, and that he would forgive the entire amount in exchange for your hand in marriage."

"We've never even met. How —"

"We saw you walking on Bond Street right after he arrived in Town. He said you showed very well. Mia, I —"

"Don't you dare try to apologize to me. I am so angry with you, Matthew. I can't even . . ." Miranda took a breath. "Does Eloise know how much debt you're in? That you've agreed to barter your own sister to clear a ledger?"

His already-pale countenance grayed at the edges. "Of course I haven't said anything. Lady Aldriss would call me a fortune hunter and order the engagement ended. Her brothers would murder me. I would deserve it, of course, but I can't bear the thought of being without her."

"But you can bear the thought of your sister marrying to settle your debt," she snapped. "Thank you very much."

"What should I do, then? Throw myself off a bridge? Run off to America and vanish? The debt would still be owed. He has my promissory notes, my signature. And he's not likely to take pity on us, as Lord Panfrey did with Aunt Beatrice. My life, my future, is in your hands, Miranda, and I don't know what else to do. I owe the man the money."

She wasn't so certain about that; Matthew seemed more a victim than an unlucky equal in this equation. What, then, did that make her? "Just to clarify," she said quietly, looking at him until he met her gaze, "you expect me to give up *my* future in your stead."

"I —"

"Stop," she cut in. "Just stop." He couldn't give her advice or aid; Captain Vale had left open only one road for her brother, and reluctantly or not, he saw no choice but to walk it. She, however, was not Matthew.

When she turned around, he grabbed her

arm. "You can't tell Father or Mother, Mia. Please."

Miranda shrugged out of his grasp. "I won't. Not yet, anyway. For their sake. Not yours."

"Then you'll agree to marry him?"

The idea made her clench her jaw until her muscles creaked. "I am not as much of a fatalist as you are. And it is far too early to give up hope."

She'd experienced life with a poor player who thought himself the equal of every card-counting scoundrel in London. That view, that perspective, would not help her. No, she didn't need more bleating from the sheep. She needed a word with one of the wolves.

CHAPTER THREE

Aden liberated a glass of whisky from a
passing footman's tray and downed a good
third of it. Beyond him couples gathered for
yet another quadrille — the hostess of the
party, he'd learned from her niece, thought
the quadrille showed a lady at her most
elegant and refined. The woman had sched-
uled five of the damned things.

At the side of the room a handful of lasses
stood, the desperation with which they were
avoiding a single glance at the dance floor
only making more obvious how much they
yearned to be out there. To one side of them
were the so-called damaged lasses, standing
or sitting alone or with a mama, each one
convinced that her lisp or limp or whatever
flaw she'd settled on as most devastating
stood between her and any chance of a good
match — or even a partner for a single
dance.

Finishing off his drink, he set the glass

aside, pushed away from the wall, and made for a plump, spectacle-wearing lass in an expensive-looking green silk gown. A man who had her same nose and eyes but much less girth said something briefly to her that had her sinking lower in her chair before he walked away to claim the hand of a pretty blond lass.

"Mr. MacTaggert."

People didn't slip up on him much, but in the noise and shuffle of the ballroom he hadn't noticed Miranda Harris approaching in her pretty yellow dancing slippers. She was a bonny thing, with her brunette hair and chocolate eyes and soft-looking lips that seemed highly kissable even turned down at the edges in a frown as they were, but the lass claimed genuinely to dislike him — on principle, he supposed, since she'd declared it within one minute of their acquaintance. "Aye?"

She folded her arms across her bosom, pulling the low neck of her yellow gown down a bit to where he could see the curve of her breasts, before she lowered her hands again. "I . . . spoke harshly earlier. I would be happy to dance this quadrille with you."

He folded his own arms, shoving back the unexpected desire to take her up on her offer. What better way to prove a lass wrong about his poor character than to make her fall for him? With a marriage noose hanging over his neck, though, he didn't have the time or the inclination to dash some woman's heart against the rocks for frowning at him. "And why is that?"

Her face folded into a brief grimace before her brow smoothed again. She thought she was being generous, no doubt, and hadn't expected to have to explain herself. "I would like a word with you," she finally stated, clasping her restless hands in front of her trim waist.

"Ye've already had a few of those with me," he returned. "I reckon that even if ye've a mind to bite at me some more, I've had enough." Resuming his walk, he stopped in front of the plump, green-garbed lass. "I've nae partner for this dance," he said, watching as she jumped and then whipped her head up to stare at him, light-blue eyes enormous behind her spectacles. "Would ye tell me yer name and come prance about beside me?"

She shot to her feet, grabbing onto his outstretched hand. "Phillipa," she said. "Miss Phillipa Pritchard. And yes."

"Aden MacTaggert," he returned, and led her into one of the circles just as the music began.

While Phillipa beamed, nearly twisting herself inside out to catch her brother's eye with every rotation of the dance, Aden took a gander at Miranda Harris, still standing where he'd left her. Evidently her claim that she had a partner for every dance had been a lie, though he had no doubt she could make it a truth with a snap of her elegant fingers.

She kept looking about the room, clearly searching for someone who wasn't there, while her fingers tapped together in a nervous, impatient rhythm. Mayhap some lad had forgotten to claim her for the quadrille, but he didn't feel inclined to step in and be her rescuer after she'd insulted him. Twice now.

At the end of the dance, though, she hadn't moved except to send him frustrated glares every couple of seconds. This wasn't about a missing dance partner, then. When Eloise and Matthew walked close by her and Miranda turned her back on the two of them, Aden nearly gave in to his mounting curiosity. Something had shifted, sent a breath of unease through the soiree, or at least the part of it where he happened to be paying attention. And now he could claim curiosity instead of whatever else it was that made him keep her close in his thoughts.

Once he'd returned Miss Phillipa Pritchard to her gawping brother, Aden paused. He wasn't a man who let himself get punched twice. Or thrice, in this instance. And while his curiosity often served him well, he didn't allow it to overrule his common sense and logic.

"Mr. MacTaggert."

Damn, she was stealthier than a wild cat. "Miss Harris," he drawled, turning around.

She took in a breath, mouth pinching. "Please allow me a word with you."

"Mayhap if ye didnae look like ye've scented shite when ye speak to me, I'd be more inclined to converse with ye," he returned.

"I don't *want* to speak with you," she countered. "However, I require some insight that I believe you can best provide." She paused, her gaze aimed at the floor. "I need your assistance."

Behind him another damned quadrille began forming. "But ye didnae need my assistance earlier when I asked ye for a dance."

"No, I did not."

"Well, I dunnae need anything from ye at the moment, Miss Harris, so I reckon I'll decline."

"You — you are a horrible man," she sputtered.

"Now, then, I didnae say anything disparaging about ye when ye turned *me* down." Sending her a swift grin mostly because he knew it would annoy her further, he walked away to claim Miss Alice Williams, who lisped but knew a great deal about their host and hostess and how the ball was especially extravagant this year because Sir Eldon had made a pair of bad investments in the Colonies and they didn't want anyone to know just how badly off they were.

A few feet back from the dance floor Miranda Harris still stood, and still glared at him when she wasn't looking toward shadows at the edges of the room. A pretty lad approached her, and she smiled as she sent him away — and the smile dropped from her face again.

At the end of the dance he parted from Miss Williams and then ducked into a side hallway. Working his way around to the other end of the ballroom, he slipped up behind Miranda Harris. As she glared about for him or some other menace, he leaned in a breath and caught the scent of her hair. Lemons. That suited her: bitter and decisive. Of course, it was also a lovely scent, fresh and clean against the warm oppressive smell of the ballroom.

Aden stood still for a moment. It would

serve her right, to demonstrate that he wasn't nearly as charmless and despicable as she'd thought him before they'd ever met. To make her feel a little of the disappointment that touched him when he thought of never kissing her, never turning that scowl of hers into a laugh. He could damned well have done that, if she'd bothered to give him half a chance. So. Let the games begin. "Miss Harris."

She flinched, then turned around. "Mr. MacTaggert."

"I've nae partner for this waltz. Since ye want insight and I want to dance, I reckon a waltz is a fair solution." He held out one hand. "Agreed?"

Squaring her shoulders, she set her white-gloved hand in his. "Agreed."

"Ye look as if ye've just decided to stand in the street and let a coach run ye down," he commented, noting that both Miss Pritchard and Miss Williams had partners for the waltz; the Sassenach bucks might call him a barbarian, but they were eager enough to follow behind him.

"Thank you," Miranda returned crisply. "Very flattering. Just what a young lady wishes to hear when she's at a grand ball."

"If ye want compliments, ye're going to have to be nicer to me. Fair is fair."

They took a position on the dance floor close by where Niall and his Amy stood, and a few feet from Eloise and Matthew. Coll, as usual, wasn't dancing, but had taken command of a table covered with breads and cheeses.

As the music began Aden put his hand on Miranda's waist and stepped them into the dance. She had a grace about her, a confidence that made her movements fluid and seemingly effortless, a skill that most of his other partners for the evening had lacked. For once he didn't have to keep himself poised, ready to catch a lass before she hit the floor if she should stumble.

"I don't want compliments," she finally said.

"Nae. Ye want insight, ye said. To what?"

"A man who wagers."

"We're all different, lass. Some of us arenae even particularly villainous. Ye'll have to be more specific."

"A man who is very skilled at wagering." She took a breath, her gaze briefly lowering to his cravat. "One who might select a particular person, and intentionally work to put that person into a difficult position for a reason."

The query surprised him. "That's fairly specific. And still a wee bit vague. Who's the target? What's the difficult position?"

She shook her head. "None of your affair. I want to know what sort of man does this, and whether he can be reasoned with."

With a brief frown, he considered. Clearly, she didn't intend to give him any further information. Even so, her description was precise enough that she had a specific scenario in mind. And luckily enough for her, whatever he thought of her insults, he did enjoy a good puzzle.

"The sort of man who'd lure another man into ruin to get someaught he wants," he mused aloud. "I reckon ye've answered yer own question, lass. What anyone else wants or needs doesnae concern him. Another man's situation and pride doesnae concern him. He has a goal, if I'm hearing ye straight. As far as he's concerned, he's worked toward it, put up with someone whose skills dunnae come close to his own, spent his valuable time leading the fool into temptation, and he means to collect."

As he spoke, Miranda's fair complexion took on more than a hint of gray. None of this discussion was supposition or fancy, then. Someone she knew had gotten in too deep, and she wanted a way to get them out. "But reasoning with this person?" she countered. "It can't be as pointless as you're suggesting."

Turning her in his arms, he shrugged. "Ye gave me two sentences, Miss Harris. In my experience, which is all I can go by, this lad wants whatever it is he played for. Find someaught else that interests him and convince him how that thing will benefit him more. Offer him a prettier prize, or one ye can convince him is more valuable."

Her grip on his hand tightened, and she leaned into him a little. If not for her stated dislike of him and the blood gone from her face, he might have thought the move flirtatious. But this woman didn't do flirtation, evidently; she remained direct. If she ever decided she liked him after all, she'd likely simply state that very thing to his face. Aden shortened his steps and firmed his grip on her hand and waist, keeping her secure until she got her feet beneath her again.

She lifted her face to look at him. "Thank you."

Well, that was unexpected. He wasn't about to let her know she'd surprised him, however, or that it hadn't occurred to him not to support her. "I've a wife to find. I dunnae need to be known as the MacTaggert who makes lasses faint. I'll leave that to Coll."

"Even so."

The dance ended, and since she still didn't look quite steady on her legs, he carefully transferred her hand to his forearm so she'd have something to hang on to. "I like wagering," Aden said, not certain whether he'd be better off confessing his sins or denying he had them. "I'm good at it. I've nae brought anyone else to ruin by it, and a time or two I've walked away from the table to keep from doing just that. If my insight helped ye then I'm glad of it; as I said, ye're to be my sister-in-law, after all. But if ye want to hate me, I'm nae overly troubled by that, either, except to note that I did give ye my best dance just now."

"Why *did* you waltz with me, then?"

"Curiosity," he answered smoothly, because that answer made more sense than him admitting that perhaps her loathing did trouble him just a whit. Or that in general he admired a lass who could stand toe-to-toe with him in a conversation, and one who looked like a sultry goddess while she did it. Or that he could imagine her eventual apology, and that it would be spectacular.

On the tail of that thought he stopped near a line of chairs so she could take a seat if she needed to. Freeing his arm, he gave her a nod and turned away.

"You've given me some things to consider," she said from behind him. "Thank you for that. As for causing someone's ruin, even if *you* walked away from the table, you left someone desperately unskilled in the hands of others. Don't expect praise for that. Not from me, at least."

Aden kept walking. Arguing with a pile of rocks didn't budge the stones. She'd made up her mind about who he was before they'd ever met, and nothing he said would alter her opinion. Whoever it was who'd gotten into debt with some talented swindler, with that tongue of hers she likely had as fair a chance as anyone of negotiating a settlement.

He generally liked a sharp tongue on a lass, a bit of fire to warm a chill night. And Miranda Harris had that aplenty, with a touch of flame in her brunette hair and a smolder in her deep-brown eyes to match. It was a shame she didn't seem to want to warm up to him as much as she wanted to burn him to a crisp and shovel him into the ash bin. But then tonight he'd asked her for a dance, and whatever the twisting path was they'd traveled, he'd danced with her.

By the time the clock in the foyer had edged past half nine in the morning, Miranda had thrice put on and removed her bonnet and shawl, begun and abandoned two pointed letters, and contemplated simply announcing to her parents that she'd tired of London and meant to spend the remainder of the Season at home on their small estate in Devon.

Her brother had put her squarely in the middle of his troubles, and her flight, her rebuke, would do nothing to remove the debt he'd incurred. And while she'd several times decided that his stupidity in no way obligated her to do anything but tell their parents, she'd known that to be a lie even as she was thinking it.

Matthew was her brother, and she would not allow his ruination — or her family's — if she could do anything to prevent it. And he'd been correct when he'd worried what their parents would do if they discovered he'd been wagering again. It would take more than selling his beloved horse to settle this debt. It would take more than selling Harris House here in Mayfair and its entire contents, she imagined. It would take more than the lot of them fleeing to the Americas to find their fortunes, because acquiring that much money in any of their lifetimes seemed beyond impossible.

The knocker swung against the front door, and a shiver rattled through her as Billings answered it. She'd kept to the morning room since an early breakfast; the last thing she wanted was for the butler to have to come looking for her and arouse everyone else's interest about who might be calling.

She glanced at her maid, who sat in the corner mending a stocking. "Remember," she whispered. "No matter what, you do not leave this room."

Millie nodded. "I would never."

Billings rapped on the half-open door. "Miss Harris, a Captain Vale is here to see you."

"Please show him in, Billings." With a hard breath, clenching her hands together behind her back both so he wouldn't touch her and so he wouldn't see them shake, she took up a position between the end table and the window. It was a flimsy piece of furniture, but this morning it was the best shield she could manage.

The butler stepped aside and Vale walked in, still neat and precise in his naval blues, his hat tucked beneath one arm. "Miss Harris," he said, inclining his head.

"Captain. That will be all, Billings. Please shut the door."

Sparing her a curious look, the butler did as she asked. Both Matthew and her father had already left the house — Matthew fleeing like a cat with its tail on fire — but her mother remained abed. Balls always did her in until at least noon, and hopefully today would be no different.

"You've agreed to see me," Vale said into the silence, "so I presume Matthew has spoken to you."

"Yes, he has. The subject of our conversation made me curious, however. As you wagered with him, surely you realized that you encouraged a debt far beyond my brother's ability to repay. Absurdly so."

"I will point out that your brother also knew his own . . . budget, shall we say? And that he passed by that number with his eyes open."

"I understand that, though I might compare the two of you to a snake and a mouse. The only reason the mouse doesn't flee is that he doesn't see the snake — until the snake's jaws clamp down over him. Once beyond a certain point, the debt became so absurdly large that playing deeply to extract himself was undoubtedly the only thing that made sense to my brother. But my question to you is why keep playing when you could not possibly hope to receive ten thousand pounds, much less fifty?"

He tilted his head a little, the gesture making him look even more falconlike. And today she was definitely the rabbit. "Because he might think himself capable of repaying five thousand or even ten thousand pounds. At fifty thousand — well, to be succinct, I own him. There is no escape but the one I suggest."

The statement reminded her of what Aden MacTaggert had speculated — that Vale had had a goal, and he'd reached it regardless of any harm it might cause to others. "And you suggested a union with me."

"Just so."

She forced a chuckle. "Frankly, Captain, I am not worth fifty thousand pounds. But you did say you were thinking of purchasing a house in Mayfair. I imagine my father would be willing to assist you in that. He is also on the boards of several clubs, which could bene—"

"Why would I accept a discounted house and a membership at Boodle's over fifty thousand quid, which would gain me all that and more?"

"Because you'll never receive fifty thousand pounds from Matthew. It simply doesn't exist."

"But it does. I'm looking at it. The fact of whether you're worth that amount of money isn't the point. The point, Miss Harris, Miranda, is that to me you are worth

81

enough to convince me to make the trade: you for your brother's debt."

"But why?" she burst out. For heaven's sake, none of this made sense. Logic. She wanted logic. That, she could argue against.

"Your brother pointed you out to me one day shortly after I arrived. I recall it quite clearly. 'That's my younger sister, Miranda,' he said. 'Half the bucks in London are after her, the ones with taste, anyway. She's a smart one, knows everyone, and never makes a misstep.' You are what I require. Anyone can purchase a house. You are Society. Everyone knows you and, more important, likes you. And a love match between us grants me all those things, as well. Therefore, an imaginary fifty thousand quid in exchange for a lifetime of chances at investment, of dining with dukes and princes, of being admired and feted — I must disagree with my previous statement. You *are* worth every shilling of your brother's debt."

Miranda stared at him, the edges of her vision darkening and a dizzy swirl of lightheadedness pushing at the back of her eyes. "You . . . you dragged my brother to ruin just to avoid . . . courting me?"

"He went along quite willingly. I didn't drag him anywhere. And courting is a gamble. I prefer a sure bet."

"And yet you are a gambler."

"A very good one."

The words she wanted to say would prevent her from calling herself a lady ever again. She weighed them anyway, then chose the one her mind kept shouting the loudest. "No!"

"That is what a child says when asked to give up a toy," he stated. "You are three-and-twenty. Men have chased you for five years. I am a stranger with unknown prospects and a pension from the navy to recommend me. In an otherwise level playing field, why would you choose me?" He held her gaze for a dozen hard heartbeats as she tried to conjure an argument against what was actually some very logical mathematics — from his perspective, anyway.

"I wouldn't," she answered. "And I won't. You don't want me; you want my reputation. Your chosen course of action relies on the cooperation of a woman with whom you never bothered to speak until last night. You want my honor, and yet you have cheated and connived to steal it. No, Captain Vale. Choose another prize."

The falcon assessed her, unblinking. Then he pulled a piece of paper from his pocket and set it on the back of the couch. "These are the dates and amounts of promissory notes signed by your brother. A carriage and I will be here at one o'clock tomorrow to take you to luncheon. If you do not get into the carriage, I will send an identical list to your father."

"He —"

"If I do not like the response I receive from him, I will bring legal action against your brother. A well-respected family with such a reckless wastrel of an heir . . . Especially with the barely contained tale of your uncle still hanging in the air. John Temple, isn't it? I imagine your friends will be shocked. As will the family of Matthew's fiancée. The Oswell-MacTaggerts, I believe. All that is an aside, however, to your family being stripped of all its property and your father and brother, and quite possibly you and your mother, being thrown into debtors' prison."

Miranda wanted to scream. She wanted to punch him in his beak of a nose. "You will face repercussions as well, Captain. You have done nothing honorable."

"True, but I have no stake in London. Not at the moment. And distasteful or not, a debt is a debt. My plan to settle this is simpler and much less messy, but the next step is yours. I shall respond accordingly."

He flicked a glance toward Millie, who sat openmouthed with her needle in the air. "And with equal discretion."

"So you would wed someone who loathes you? What an unpleasant future you've imagined for yourself." The argument was weak, but most of her mind simply wanted to wake up from this nightmare.

For the first time he smiled. His teeth were small and even, except for a gap where the left upper canine should be. The expression rendered him less like a falcon, but somehow more sinister — as if all the polite polish he showed on the outside was just that. Beneath a very thin layer of gentleman he stood there full of black, gaping holes.

"I have been places and done things you couldn't imagine," he said matter-of-factly. "Your displeasure matters as much to me as a single drop of water does to the ocean." With a crisp motion he set his hat on his dark, short hair. "One o'clock tomorrow. And this will appear to be a love match. I suggest you act accordingly."

With that he turned on his heel, opened the door, and left the room. When the front door opened and shut a moment later, Miranda sat down hard on the nearest chair. She'd spun this in every direction she could think of, searching for something else he might want, and he'd never even blinked. How . . . What . . . What could she do? Because this . . . horror could not be allowed to happen.

"Oh, my," Millie whispered.

Miranda sat upright again, twisting around to face her maid. "You must not speak a word about any of this, Millie," she said, trying and failing to keep her voice steady. "Not to anyone. Promise me."

"I . . . Yes, Miss Harris. I promise. Not a word. But what will you do? He . . . I had the shivers just seeing him standing there."

He had given her the shivers, too. And a sick feeling in the pit of her stomach that made her want to vomit. Aden MacTaggert had figured Captain Vale's character nearly to perfection without even knowing the man, and with only a few vague sentences from her. She expected gamblers to be . . . nefarious. Perhaps it was silly of her, but she'd simply been flailing for help. She hadn't actually expected Mr. MacTaggert's insights to be useful, much less sharply on target.

She stood up, reaching over to retrieve her bonnet from a chair. "Millie, put that mending aside. I have a call to make."

Clearly she was in well over her head. She recognized that, even if Matthew hadn't

86

until far too late. She couldn't afford to wait that long.

CHAPTER FOUR

Smythe the butler pulled open the front door of Oswell House before Miranda could do more than touch the brass lion's-head knocker. "Miss Harris," he greeted her. "Lady Eloise is not in presently, I'm afraid. Nor is Mrs. MacTaggert."

Yes, Eloise and Amy had gone to shop for hats this morning. She'd planned to go with them, until Captain Vale had demanded an audience this morning. "I actually had a query for Aden MacTaggert," she said, keeping her chin up. She had no reason to be embarrassed, of course. She wasn't some debutante throwing herself at the Highlander; just the opposite. If not for some desperately needed advice, she wouldn't have been anywhere near Oswell House this morning.

A grimace ruffled one side of the butler's mouth, but he stepped aside to allow her entry. "You'll find him in the billiards room,

I believe. Do you know the way?"

"Yes. Thank you." Since Matthew's engagement she'd visited Oswell House perhaps a dozen times, though only for Eloise's luncheon since her older brothers had arrived from Scotland and Miranda had left to care for her ill aunt Beatrice and baby cousins in Devon. If she hadn't gone, would Matthew have confided in her that he'd stepped in over his head with this Captain Vale? Would she have been able to stop his foolishness before he decided that sacrificing her was his only recourse?

As she stepped through the foyer today, she still half expected to see clan Ross tartans hung on the walls and men playing bagpipes in every corner. Aden had definitely made a stir at Eloise's luncheon, and his sister had previously mentioned that a large degree of chaos had arrived in conjunction with the MacTaggert men. Instead, though, the grand house looked as neat and well appointed as ever — until she reached the main stair landing where the grand staircase split off in two directions. There, close by the back wall, stood a full-grown stag, his antlers wide and impressive, and his personage adorned with a bonnet, a beaver hat, and a pearl necklace hung from one tine. An earbob sparkled beneath one alert ear, while the beast boasted a wilted cravat around his neck and a green lace and satin skirt around his waist and hind legs.

"Good glory," Millie whispered from behind her.

"The poor thing looks like it crashed through a party and took half of it away with him, doesn't it?" Miranda whispered back, and the maid giggled.

She hadn't noticed the deer when she'd attended the luncheon two days ago, but then she'd remained downstairs had been busily and stupidly thinking she didn't have a care in the world. Today that seemed like ages ago. Taking a breath, she paused in the billiards room doorway, eyeing the pair of men seated across from each other at a small table set beneath a window in the blue-and-red-wallpapered room.

"I'll do it for ye one more time," Aden was saying, shuffling a stack of cards. "Pick the one ye want, show it, and shove it back in the deck."

His younger brother, Niall, the one who'd just returned from a supposedly planned elopement to Gretna Green where he'd married Amelia-Rose Baxter in spectacularly romantic fashion, selected a card and flipped it over in his fingers. "Seven of hearts," he said.

"Ye certain that's the one ye want?" his brother asked. "Nae an ace or a diamond or someaught? The king of hearts? I can wait while ye decide."

"Shut up, ye *skellum.*"

"I'm only trying to make this as simple as I can for ye, *bràthair.*"

"Aye, and sheep grow coats of satin," Niall intoned, and stuffed the card back into the deck his brother still held.

Aden shuffled again, his fingers sure and quick. No fumbling, no stacking, just a blur of cards flitting effortlessly together. Even from the doorway it mesmerized Miranda a little, and she detested it all the more for that reason. She wanted to detest him, as well; after all, she'd as much as said so at luncheon the other day. He gambled, and apparently very well. That made him unacceptable.

Everything about him — his careless black hair with its long, straying strands and the way it seemed to always be stirring in some mysterious, otherwise unfelt breeze, his hard, lean frame and grace, that handsome face and the way she wanted to sigh every time she looked at him — it all seemed designed to disarm her, to keep her from seeing a man with very questionable morality. And now that she knew he had some

91

wits about him, he seemed even more dangerous.

Setting the deck down, Aden cut it, putting the lower half on top. "Turn it," he said, moving his hands away from the cards.

His brother reached over and turned over the top card. The seven of hearts looked up from the table. With a scowl Niall flipped the entire deck faceup and spread them out. "I didnae see it, damn it all."

"So ye reckon I've an entire deck of naught but sevens of hearts?"

"I'd nae put it past ye." Picking up the card, he examined it. "Tell me how ye do it."

"Nae. I showed ye four times just this morning, Niall. Figure it out yerself." He took the card back, danced it through his fingers, and put it back into the messy stack before he straightened the pile. "And do it elsewhere; I've a lass come to see me." Turning his head a little, he caught Miranda's gaze with gray-green eyes.

His brother turned as well, his eyes a startling light green very like his sister Eloise's unusual ones. As he stood, she noticed the medium-sized black dog curled beneath Aden's chair. Brògan, who wasn't at all a male dog, whatever Aden claimed, and whomever he chose to fool. "Ye're Matthew Harris's sister, aye?" Niall asked as he reached the doorway.

"Yes. Miranda. I didn't mean to eavesdrop; I didn't wish to interrupt."

"Have at him. I'm grateful ye appeared before I started losing blunt to him." With a nod and a loose grin, he moved past her into the hallway and toward the stairs.

Aden remained seated, a king in his own well-appointed domain. Hiding her scowl at his very unsurprising lack of manners, she went over to sit in his brother's vacated chair. "I'm not a lass who's come to see you. I am a female acquaintance who would like to speak with you on a particular subject."

"And I'm a male acquaintance all aflutter over what ye want to say to me. An unmarried lass coming to call — to speak with — an unmarried lad. Ye'll have so many Sassenach tongues wagging, we'll all feel the breeze." He shuffled the cards again, this time using only one hand to do it.

Miranda supposed he could imply whatever he liked, as long as he did end up helping her. And the fact that for a moment she thought him clever — well, she was not some fickle female who changed her opinions simply because she required some assistance. "If it flatters you to think I'm setting my cap at you, then indulge yourself. I only ask that you answer my questions."

He chuckled. "Relentless, ye are. If ye're nae here because our waltz made ye swoon, then, I reckon ye're here for more free advice. An angel seeking out the devil for help with another demon, aye?"

"Your insights last night were useful," she admitted, ignoring the fact that he'd called her an angel and suggested she made a habit of swooning. A man like him wouldn't mean either one as a compliment. In his world no doubt angels served only to spoil all the devil's fun. And swooning in his presence could be . . . precarious. It was beginning to seem, though, that he had more than a keen insight into fellow reprobates. No, he seemed to have taken her measure and decided he could stand toe-to-toe with her. And though she hated admitting it even to herself, he'd managed to do so — for the moment, at least. "My difficulty, however, remains unresolved. I require more information."

His gaze assessed her, though she had no idea what he looked for, or what he saw. Worry? Fear? Frustration? Anger? They'd all been taking turns with her for the past half hour. "I'll make ye a bargain," he offered. "Ye tell me how I produced that card for Niall, and I'll give ye all the insight I own."

Miranda's jaw clenched. The nerve of this Highlander continued to astound her. No, he wasn't poetical at all. Devilish, yes. "You're actually wagering me."

"Aye. Ye insulted me. Climb down into the mud for a damned minute if ye want help from a man ye called a pig." He held out the deck in one hand. "I'll even show ye once."

"I never called you a pig, sir."

"Ye did; ye were just more polite about it. I may nae sound like ye, but I do speak English."

Very well, he did have a point. At the same time, he hadn't precisely disproven her original assessment of him. Pride pushed at her to refuse, to stand up, fling the cards at his face, and walk away. At the same time logic refused to budge, insisting on reminding her that having a little familiarity with this world into which she was being dragged might actually prove helpful. Clenching her jaw, she picked up the top card between her gloved fingers. "The queen of clubs," she stated.

"If I were a superstitious lad," he commented, lowering the remaining cards in his closed fist as he spoke, "I'd say I reckon ye've chosen the card that most resembles yerself. Regal and confident, and ready to whack at me with a solid weapon."

Under other circumstances she might have found that amusing, and even slightly complimentary. "No doubt you arranged the deck precisely so you could make that comment. Let's get on with it, shall we?" She gestured for him to produce the deck.

Opening his hand, he held the stack of cards out, and she removed a good two-thirds of the deck, set the queen into their spot, and placed the rest back on top. He tapped the cards against the table and began shuffling with nimble fingers. Then he set down the deck and cut it. Reaching over, she turned over the exposed card. The queen of clubs again.

Looking at him through her lashes, she picked up the queen and turned it over, examining the back for a cut mark, the edges for a bend or a sign that he'd marred it with a fingernail. Nothing. She rubbed it against the soft white kid of her glove. No ink came off against the material.

If his brother hadn't already suggested he had a deck full of the same card, she would have demanded to see them all. It was a trick of some sort, but what was the trick? What wasn't she seeing? Had he secreted it up a sleeve and only returned it as he cut the deck? She'd been watching carefully, but she wasn't accustomed to deviousness.

"Do ye give up, lass? Should I wish ye good day so I can go find someaught to eat? I'm feeling a bit peckish. Or do ye have someaught else ye're of a mind to offer me in exchange for my insight? Someaught more personal might suffice, I suppose."

Miranda scowled. Everyone wanted something from her, apparently. Every man did, anyway. At least this one was thus far only annoying and arrogant. "May I touch you?"

"That was swiftly decided," he returned, his gray-green eyes amused and, unless she was greatly mistaken, a little surprised. "Well, I'm a man of my word. Do ye want to do it here, or somewhere more private?"

What? "Oh, for heaven's sake. May I touch your damned arm, Mr. MacTaggert. To decipher your card trick." There. And she'd spent barely a second imagining herself kissing him, as if she would ever wish to do such a thing. Just because his appearance was likely to set other, more naive women swooning didn't mean she was the least bit tempted by him.

His grin only deepened at her rejoinder, and if her clarification disappointed him, he didn't show it. "Oh, aye, then. Such language, Miranda Harris. Ye'll make me blush."

She very much doubted that, though she couldn't recall ever cursing in a man's presence before. Well, this one deserved it for being so aggravating and handsome and more complex than she'd expected. Sitting forward, she reached for his right hand. He had large hands, with calluses across the palm and several fingertips — marks of someone who labored. That surprised her. Gamblers gambled. That was their occupation and their means of support. They didn't do whatever hard work it would take to make calluses.

"Do ye reckon I hid it inside my skin, then? That's a worse guess than any Niall's ever made."

"I'm not finished." When she glanced up at him, his gaze was on their joined hands, his palm up with one of hers holding it there and the other touching his fingertips. His hand did have an elegance to it despite the calluses — a sculptor's or a wood carver's hand rather than that of a common laborer. And his skin felt warm, even through her gloves.

Mentally shaking herself, she felt up along his sleeve to the elbow. This wasn't a seduction, and it wasn't simply about trying to solve a puzzle; her future might well depend on whether he would answer her questions or not. No springs or wires lurked beneath his coat sleeve or the superfine shirt beneath; no sign that he'd hidden a card away.

"Are ye finished now? Ye can check beneath my kilt if ye like, but I can promise ye there's nae room for a spare deck of cards down there."

"I will not be rattled, Mr. MacTaggert," she stated, even as her cheeks heated. "Not by your crassness or your lack of empathy." She couldn't afford to be dissuaded; she didn't know where else to go for advice that wouldn't tear her family apart and break several hearts in the process.

The idea of trying to find a way out of this disaster all on her own left her cold. Thus far Captain Vale had had a ready answer to every argument she presented. It felt like he'd already been there, seen all the paths she might use to escape, and laid out snares and dug pits, and now just waited for her to realize she had nowhere to turn.

On the outside she felt chilled as well, but then half the windows in the room were open to the overcast outside. Clearly that didn't trouble Aden and his warm hands, but then he was from the Highlands and likely accustomed to a much colder clime.

Miranda blinked. Releasing his sleeve, she sat down again, reviewing the trick in her mind — him shuffling one-handed, his fingers closing over the deck as she selected her card, his chat about queens and clubs as she held the card in her gloved fingers in the cold room. Could it be that simple? And that clever?

She took a slow breath. He'd wanted her to wager her mind against his skill, but how far was she willing to trust his instincts? Could she trust him at all?

"I require your advice and quite possibly your assistance," she said, tapping her fingers against the tabletop as she spoke. "And in order for you to be of the most use to me, I also require your discretion, your word that whatever I tell you will not go beyond the two of us. Will you agree to those terms?"

He lifted an eyebrow. Then a slow smile touched his mouth once more. "Ye reckon ye've figured it out, then, do ye? And ye're confident enough to double yer wager? Aye, I'll accept those terms. If ye're wrong, though, ye have to leave and nae trouble me again. But before ye go, I'll require a kiss from ye. Yer mouth to my mouth, right here at this table."

She'd already been looking at that smile

of his, an amused, cynical temptation to sin, an expression that dared her to trust what she thought she knew and place a value on that decision. If he hadn't just proven once again that he was nothing but a game player who twisted people about to suit his own whims, she would have noted that he had an attractive smile, that altogether he made for an astoundingly well-featured man. That only made him worse, that he had the means to lure someone in with a pleasant, compelling countenance and then ruin them. At least her eyes were open, thank goodness, and she was already under threat of ruination. "Agreed."

Leaning back, he folded his arms across his chest. "What is it, then? How did I find yer queen?"

"Temperature," she replied, mentally crossing her fingers. She needed to be correct. Everything depended on it. "You keep the room cold, the cards in your hand warm, and when a card is chosen you distract your victim with chatting about something or other until the air cools it. Then you feel it as you finish shuffling and cut the deck appropriately."

For a long moment he gazed at her, gray-green eyes still assessing and measuring for something she couldn't guess. "I've been fooling Niall for three years and he's nae come close to guessing. Ye did it in one morning, with one shuffle. I am impressed, Miss Harris."

She was rather impressed with herself, and with how sensitive his callused fingers must be. That, though, was neither here nor there. "You gave me your word that you will not speak of what I'm about to tell you."

"Ye are a single-minded woman, Miranda Harris. Ye've my word. What's sent ye running up here to find me, of all people? Because after that dance last night and now ye coming to me here, I'm beginning to think mayhap ye're smitten with me, after all."

"I am most certainly not smitten with you. I'm somewhat amazed your swelled head could even fit through this doorway."

Aden laughed aloud at that, watching as she gathered her thoughts together. The lass was desperate about something, or she never would have sought him out — twice, now. He'd watched these lunatic Sassenach over the past few weeks, though. A sideways look from the wrong man, some bread crumbs on a waistcoat — anything might send one of them spinning off into ruin. This had something to do with wagering and a man who wouldn't forgive a debt, he'd surmised; had she done a bit of wagering and lost a bauble? That might explain her dislike for the whole enterprise.

At the same time, her swift dismissal of every flirtatious word he spoke was less amusing. Because despite his own logic and the knowledge that at least a bevy, and perhaps even two bevies, of eligible females lay ready to throw themselves at him, not a one had caught his interest. With one exception.

"Millie, please shut the door," she said, and her maid hurried over to comply. Then Miranda folded her hands together on the tabletop. "My brother in the past has gotten a bit . . . tangled into wagering. His skill does not match his confidence. We thought — my family thought — he'd learned his lesson several years ago and had stopped these nefarious pursuits. We were wrong."

That was interesting. If this was about a man of four-and-twenty stepping into gaming halls over the disapproval of his family, she might as well have stayed home, though. He made a full pocket on the confidence of well-born dim lads twice a week, here in London. It didn't hurt that everyone who dwelled south of Hadrian's Wall thought him an ill-educated, brogue-spewing simpleton who couldn't count to ten. That was *their* mistake. He attempted not to make any of those himself.

"Nothing to say?" she prompted.

Aden shrugged. "He's a man with blunt and nae enough chores to keep himself occupied. I'd be surprised if he didnae spend some evenings at the tables."

"Men," she muttered beneath her breath, but he heard her reply quite clearly.

"If that's all there is to the tale, Miss Harris, ye risked kissing me for nae good reason." He'd made the wager on a whim, more or less, to see if the lass who claimed to detest him would turn tail. She hadn't, which meant either that her troubles were worse than he'd assumed, or that the idea of a kiss wasn't quite as off-putting as she'd let on. The contrary, challenge-loving part of him hoped it was the latter.

"He lost four hundred pounds and Father made him sell his hunter, Winterbourne, as punishment. Matthew adored that horse. He'd trained him from a colt."

"I ken ye have sympathy for yer brother, but actions have consequences, lass. I reckon yer da did the right thing."

She sent him a sharp look. "Yes, I'm aware of actions and consequences. I thought Matthew was, as well. For three years he's stayed away from the tables. And then six weeks ago, I learned just last night, he made the acquaintance of a Captain Robert Vale, newly retired from His Majesty's Navy."

A shiver went down her shoulders, almost imperceptible, but enough for him to see. Aden sat forward a little. She'd reached the important part, then. This was where her distress came from. And she was a clever, bonny lass who'd already turned his head more than he cared to let her know. Miranda had come to see him out of pure desperation. She wouldn't have bothered, otherwise.

"Do you know him?" she asked into the silence.

"The name doesnae sound familiar."

"But he's a keen gambler, evidently, and you've been in Town for nearly the same amount of time."

"Do ye reckon every soul who wagers belongs to the same secret club or someaught?"

Her delicate brow furrowed. "How the devil should I know? All I do know is that he began as the cousin of a dear friend of Matthew's, and six weeks later — as my brother informed me last night — he holds notes worth nearly fifty thousand pounds."

Aden blinked. He'd known lads who played deep, well above their means, but even by those standards this was bloody extraordinary. "Are ye certain of that amount, lass? He didnae say five thousand pounds or five hun—"

"Of course I'm certain, Mr. MacTaggert."

Aye, she would be. He'd known her for but two days, but nothing he'd seen led him to believe that Miranda Harris was the least bit foolish. "Fifty thousand, then. But if ye ken the debt, why do ye need more advice from me? If yer brother cannae pay, find someaught else this Vale will take as compensation. I reckon he's aware he'll nae see the entirety of the money. Most gamblers would be."

"Captain Vale did find something he is willing to accept as compensation." Her folded knuckles showed white, she had her hands knitted together so hard. "Me."

His jaw clenched. Something hot and angry scratched down his spine. A dozen bits of conversation from last night and this morning fell into place, pieces of a puzzle now made whole. This, he hadn't anticipated. And he didn't like it. At all. He didn't like that some stranger had built a trap against her brother and then demanded her in ransom.

Aside from being wrong, it was unfair to her. Her conversation was quick and sharp, alternately striking blows and showing

106

gratitude — the dance of a clever mind. That was her problem now, he realized. She saw a trap, knew it to be a trap, hadn't even stepped into it herself, but now she couldn't find a way out of it.

There were other things, as well, that she hadn't mentioned directly but that he could surmise — why this captain had pushed the debt so far, why she hadn't learned anything about Matthew's wagering until the trap had been sprung. "Ye reckon this Captain Vale has been after ye from the beginning," he stated.

She nodded. "After my meeting with him this morning I have come to believe that, yes. I don't know why; evidently, he saw me on the street six weeks ago when Matthew pointed me out to him. He wants instant respectability. The purchase of a respectable house in Mayfair and the acquisition of a respectable wife who might otherwise not have accepted his suit. His entrée into popularity and high Society, through me."

"Did he tell ye all that, or did ye surmise it?"

"He told me. In well-considered detail. The only thing I don't know is why he settled on me." She stood up, for once abrupt and graceless, pacing to the billiards table and back again. "I offered him introductions to Society's bastions, to my father's clubs and friends, assistance in purchasing a house — anything I could conjure. He would not be swayed."

As she spoke, an additional thing occurred to Aden. He and Coll were still required to wed before Eloise married Matthew, or their mother would cut off all funds to Aldriss Park. With what he'd just learned, a few carefully placed words would end his sister's engagement faster than a cat could climb out of a water bucket. He and Coll could return to the Highlands, perhaps find lasses who hadn't been raised in hothouses like delicate flowers. He'd taken their mother's measure, now — she wanted to be a part of their lives. At the time she'd left the Highlands, requiring that they take Sassenach brides had seemed the surest way to do that.

Now, though, they and Francesca Oswell-MacTaggert had had some time to become reacquainted. The countess wanted them to like her; to love her the way they had when they'd been wee bairns. He imagined it wouldn't take much persuasion to convince her to allow them to marry whomever they wanted, as long as they gave their word to visit London once or twice a year.

So Miranda Harris had been trapped, and that trap could ensure *his* freedom. Except for one thing. In the back of his thoughts, teasing at him since their first conversation and growing in volume since their verbal and literal waltz last night, crept the feeling that he'd found his lass. If she genuinely disliked him he'd turn elsewhere, but beneath the sparring between them, perhaps even because of it, he felt . . . something. A slow, brewing lightning storm that made the hair lift on his arms and had him anticipating things he couldn't yet put a name to.

Miranda seated herself in front of him again. "I won your wager. I expect something helpful from you."

Her deep-brown eyes weren't nearly as calm as her tone. Given that her dislike of wagering had likely tripled since yesterday, the fact that she'd sought him out spoke of several things, including just how worried she must be. Aden restacked the cards and shuffled them idly. "I'm guessing yer parents dunnae know any of what's afoot?"

"No. They would disown Matthew. And the debt would remain." She lowered her head briefly. "Captain Vale insists it look like a love match. He plans to take me to luncheon tomorrow, at precisely one o'clock. He's very precise; that must come from his naval background."

Mayhap it did. He wasn't as willing to

make convenient assumptions himself, though. Aden blew out his breath. She'd asked for advice rather than a rescue, and he admired that. Given what she'd told him, however, providing either one of those seemed a very distant hope. "He's told ye why he wants ye. My advice to ye, lass, is to either pay yer brother's debt, or see to it ye're nae longer what this Vale requires."

She stared at him, her eyes widening a little. Saint Andrew, she had long lashes and expressive eyes. Did she know that? Was she in some way using her wiles to sway him? That would make him an idiot, considering that she'd already announced that she didn't care for him. Unless she did, and that was part of the lure.

All the Sassenach lasses he'd encountered during his time in London baffled him. They giggled at his accent, thought his kilt quaint or barbaric or scandalous depending on the setting, and claimed to find him attractive — and marriageable — despite his being a Highlander. *Despite.* Being a Highlander wasn't a flaw to be overlooked or excused. It was him, his blood and his heart.

"You're suggesting I ruin my own reputation," she said, breaking into his unexpected reverie.

Aden shrugged. "If ye're nae useful to

him, he'd have nae reason to wed ye." Shifting in his chair a little, he regarded her. She was bonny, and he couldn't place the word "dull" anywhere in her vicinity. Aye, she claimed to dislike him, yet there she sat, two feet in front of him, alone but for a maid and a stray dog. "I could assist ye with that, if ye like. If ye mean to be ruined, ye may as well do it right."

Her fair cheeks darkened. "I need your assistance, not your . . . scandalous offers." Miranda's gaze flashed down to his mouth and up to meet his eyes again.

He grinned, because he wasn't going to let her know that he was disappointed. "It was only a suggestion."

She grimaced. "A useless one. Whatever my status, he would still hold my brother's papers. I'd only be putting this trouble back on Matthew, and on my parents."

"It's Matthew's trouble to begin with, if ye'll recall," he countered. "What's *he* doing to get ye out of it?"

"He tried, I think. But he's so deep in a hole that all he can see is the rope Captain Vale offered him."

Despite all this landing on her shoulders, she could still see it logically, and from her brother's point of view as well as her own. Her clearheadedness was admirable, even though it no doubt gave her a fairly accurate view of what lay ahead for her. And yet she'd sought him out, anyway — looking for what, a miracle? That didn't quite fit with her firm hold on reality, but he supposed even he looked better in comparison with certain doom. Thank Saint Andrew for small favors.

"I dunnae ken what other advice or answers I can give ye, Miss Harris," he made himself say, looking down to shuffle again. "Ye'll nae return yer troubles to the man who caused 'em, and I dunnae have fifty thousand quid to give to ye, lass."

With a slow sigh she stood. "No, I don't suppose you would have anything useful for me. No doubt you gamblers have some sort of code against interfering in each other's schemes and traps."

Well, that hit a bit close to home. "I've nae done a thing to ye, lass. Snap at me if ye wish, but I've nae as much as played a single hand of whist, much less faro or vingt-et-un, with yer brother."

"True enough. I apologize for bothering you." Turning her back, she walked to the door where her maid waited. With one hand on the handle, she faced him again. "If we were friends, would you have given me the same advice and sent me on my way?"

"I could offer to kill him for ye, I reckon," he returned, trying to sound offhand even if the idea held a great deal of appeal.

"I try to avoid murder over gambling debts."

He shrugged. "And I'd ask ye what else it is that has ye hating card players, because a brother selling a horse doesnae seem enough to make a proper lass go stomping about claiming she hates a lad the moment she's set eyes on him."

Her jaw jumped. "I do not stomp. And we are not friends. I don't owe you any confidences."

There was something more to it, then. Well, he'd figure it out. "There's nae secret handshake I know of that I could give ye. I wish . . . I wish there was, Miranda Harris."

Miranda looked at him for another handful of seconds, then left the room.

Aden blew out his breath. She might not condone murder over gambling debts, but he'd seen men ruined and dead with deep play before. One had fled to America rather than face the consequences of losing his estate and his fortune. Another had joined the Sassenach army as the only way to keep himself fed. A third had rowed into the middle of a loch and shot himself in the temple. Aden hadn't had a hand in any of it, but he'd watched, and he'd learned a good lesson about not playing beyond his own means.

What none of those lads had done was sell a sibling to settle the debt. Then again, he didn't recall that any of them had been given that option. As an older brother to Eloise — who happened to be engaged to a lad who'd just handed over his sister to satisfy a wager — his primary concern was whether he needed to take steps to protect his sister or not. Matthew Harris had been reckless, and after he should have learned his lesson.

Unfortunately, he'd promised his discretion. That would make him the awful man Miranda had accused him of being if and when he did pass on to his brothers or to Lady Aldriss what he'd just learned. For the moment, though, he wasn't willing yet to be the villain in his sister's eyes. Or in Miranda's, truth be told. She might dislike him, but he hadn't yet given her an actual reason to do so. Well, until he'd told her just now that he couldn't do anything more to help her and sent her on her way, that was.

Beneath his chair the black mop of hair known as Brògan thumped her tail, and he reached down to scratch her behind the ears. Another bold female who'd stormed her way into his protection, who had him lying about her for no damned good reason. "Ye'd nae make more trouble for me, would ye?" he asked her, and her tail thumped again.

Straightening, he reshuffled the deck and flipped over the top card, holding up the queen of clubs. Miranda Harris had piqued his interest, and then she'd thrown cold water over him just when he'd been contemplating whether the insults were genuine or her way of flirting. He'd begun to think he could end his search for an English bride, and then learned she'd been bartered away.

He didn't want to turn his back on all of it, on her, even if that might have been by far the easiest course of action. Beyond his own attraction to her, there remained one ironclad point. Miranda Harris was being forced into a marriage against her will, because of someone else's actions.

Well. He'd been handed an opportunity, then. A lass he fancied had asked for his help. That at least gave him a bit of time to see if this attraction was one-sided, or if she felt that damned lightning, as well. Captain Robert Vale needed to be dealt with, regardless. But if Miranda had felt that spark between them, then fifty thousand quid, the

115

King of England, and all the Highlanders in Scotland wouldn't stop him from winning her.

"Smythe, who was at the door?" Francesca, Lady Aldriss, asked, as she handed over her morning's correspondence to the butler.

"Miss Harris, my lady," he answered.

She glanced up from the evening's dinner menu. "Miranda? I thought she'd begged off going shopping this morning. Did you tell her where Eloise and Amy went?"

"She actually inquired after Master Aden. I directed her to the billiards room. Should I not have done so?"

"No, that's fine. Is she still here?"

"She left just a moment ago."

Well. A young lady calling on her second, exceedingly elusive, son. Francesca handed over the menu and made her way upstairs, conjuring an excuse as she went. Aden was tricky; he smiled and spoke with a degree of amused sarcasm, but it all seemed like a mask. He frequently disappeared after dark and didn't reappear until after dawn, and she didn't think he was in pursuit of some woman or other. She wished he had been; he and Coll still needed to fulfill their part of the agreement she'd made with their muleheaded father.

"Am I interrupting?" Francesca asked as she strolled into the billiards room.

Aden balled up another playing card and tossed it, watching as his dog scampered after it. "Nae. What is it? Or should I guess? Ye want to know what Miss Harris was doing here, aye?"

So much for inventing an excuse. "I am somewhat curious, yes. Is her family well?"

"I've nae idea."

He threw another wadded-up card for the spaniel. Brògan was a pretty thing now that he'd washed and trimmed her, but Francesca had to wonder what it was that had prompted Aden to rescue the little thing. It seemed a great deal of trouble to go to if the only goal was to antagonize poor Smythe. "Is Miranda well?"

"Ye could likely catch her if ye want to find out. She only just left."

So he could match her in vague questions and responses. How would he respond to directness, then? "Miranda Harris is a lovely, accomplished young lady. Are you pursuing her?"

Another card crumbled. "Do ye recall when I wagered dinner against Coll one night and I won, and ye told me that my brothers would always be my best allies and that if I took his dinner he'd be less likely to trust me the next time I needed him for someaught?"

Francesca hid her frown. Good heavens. He'd been what, seven years old? And Coll, ten? "I recall. The wager was over who would catch more fish, I believe."

"Aye. I gave Coll back his dinner. I didnae break his trust." Another card went flying. "Ye broke mine, though, and I reckon that I dunnae need ye for anything, and I dunnae trust ye. So ye'll know if I've found a woman when I tell ye I'm marrying one."

He stood, walking over to crouch down and pick up the scattered, ruined cards and ruffle the fur on Brògan's head, then straightened and strolled out of the room with the dog at his heels. Francesca stood where she was for a moment.

She'd tried to explain her reasons for leaving Scotland to her sons, back when she'd first fled back to London. Faced with boys aged seven, ten, and twelve, she'd talked about what she thought they would understand — arguments and being far away from where she'd grown up and wanting Eloise to have the best life possible. She hadn't attempted to explain what happened when an overwhelming passion driving two people together began tearing them to pieces, and she hadn't told them that she'd tried to bring them back to England with her. Angus had had the final word, and when he'd refused to relinquish them, she'd granted him the favor of not making him another villain. Her boys needed a parent, and she'd let them keep one.

Stirring, she walked over to close the open windows, shutting the chill out of the room. Niall had forgiven her, in large part because she'd turned half of Mayfair upside down to enable him to give Amelia-Rose — Amy — the life she wanted. When she'd asked him for insight into his brothers, though, he'd been less forthcoming. A suggestion that she figure them out for herself answered the question over whether the MacTaggert boys were still the closest of allies, but it didn't help her understand the men they were now.

"Smythe?" she called, heading back toward the main staircase. "I will need a footman to deliver a note for me." If Aden wouldn't talk, perhaps Miranda's mother would. Knowing one way or the other if the two of them had a connection would tell her whether to focus her attentions or turn them elsewhere.

"Of course, my lady."

She would figure the MacTaggert brothers out, though, with or without their cooperation. Her sons were in London, beneath her roof. Relinquishing them again, without knowing they would return willingly and without her making more threats to their future, would destroy her. Aden might not trust her, but she hoped he realized that she would do anything for him. For any of them. Even if she had to resort to underhanded means to do so.

CHAPTER FIVE

"Who is this Captain Vale?" Mrs. Elizabeth Harris asked, looking up from the dinner menu she'd been plotting for the past twenty minutes. "He seems to have made an impression, because you haven't been able to sit still since yesterday morning."

Miranda looked away from the front window, even though she remained half convinced that Vale would appear the moment she did so. "I told you, Mother. He's Lord George Humphries's cousin. He's been serving in India."

"He doesn't mean to drag you across the ocean, I hope," her mother returned. "I won't have it."

"We've just met, Mama, for goodness' sake, and Matthew says he's retired from service. If I care to join him for more than a single luncheon, though, I will certainly make a point of asking where he means to settle." She knew that already, actually, but

121

if this was going to be a love match, she meant for it to proceed as slowly as possible. The longer it took, the greater her chance of finding something — anything — to help her escape it.

Oh, she hated lying to her mother about this. Playing along seemed the wiser choice, though, at least until she found a way to escape. So as far as her parents were concerned, she and Vale were barely acquainted. Nor did she intend to pretend to be easily smitten. Every one of her acquaintance knew she was not some doe-eyed debutante wearing her heart on her sleeve.

She'd been foolish yesterday to place her hopes in the hands of horrid Aden MacTaggert. He might claim to be a gambler, but Captain Vale's play seemed to be completely beyond his ability to comprehend, much less to contribute anything useful toward countering. *Ruin herself.* That was laughable and selfish. She couldn't imagine him simply giving in if someone presented him with an untenable choice. She couldn't imagine him falling into that sort of trap in the first place, actually, though of course she had very little idea of his level of skill in anything but clever card tricks and evasive conversation. Even so, she would eat her bonnet if he would ever even consider handing over his sister to settle a debt.

Or maybe that was just all fanciful thought, a wish that she had found herself in different circumstances. Miranda shook out her hands, trying to warm her cold fingers. She might have stayed upstairs and fretted more openly, she supposed, but at the moment she preferred to have Millie sitting quietly and hemming her riding outfit rather than loudly lamenting the death of chivalry and decency in the world.

The front door opened. Miranda jumped, every nerve already stretched nearly to breaking point, and shot a glance at the mantel clock. Blast it all, he was twenty minutes early. She hadn't managed to circle her thoughts back around from self-pity to useful plotting yet.

Billings knocked at the open morning room door. "Miss Harris, a Mr. Aden MacTaggert has requested a brief word with you."

"Aden MacTaggert? One of Eloise's brothers?" her mother asked, setting aside her menu and rising. "Show him in, Billings."

The butler moved sideways to allow the tall Scotsman entry. "Shall I fetch tea, ma'am?"

"That won't be necessary," Miranda

interjected, pushing away the sudden flutter of hope and . . . warmth that jangled through her at Aden's arrival. He'd offered nothing but witty repartee and some suggestions of scandalous ruination yesterday. Today he might well be there simply to posit that not all professional gamblers were blackhearted, and that perhaps she should give Captain Vale a chance to win her affections.

"Mr. MacTaggert," her mother said, a wide smile on her face. "Matthew told us Eloise's brothers were impressive sorts. I see he was not exaggerating."

The Highlander inclined his head, strands of his poet-length black hair falling across one observant eye. Perhaps his appearance wasn't as poetical as Miranda had originally thought; poets didn't have that alert, coiled sense of alertness surrounding them, sinew and muscle and a keen awareness of . . . everything. Or perhaps she'd simply become delirious from lack of sleep.

"Ye'd be Mrs. Harris. I see ye in Matthew and Miss Harris, here," Aden commented.

He'd worn his kilt and a pair of Hessian boots, which together with his proper blue jacket, cravat, and black waistcoat actually looked rather dashing — half civilized and half wild. Not that it mattered, because he was still the same man he'd been yesterday. Physically perhaps he could make a Greek god jealous, and mentally, well, he seemed to be a great deal sharper than she'd first expected, but morally . . . she didn't want to quite equate him with Vale for reasons she couldn't fathom, but neither could she tell where the difference might be.

But there he stood chatting about the weather and clearly charming Elizabeth Harris while he held a very large secret that could decimate the entire Harris family. However useless he'd been, she had given him a degree of trust, which put her in his hands. Miranda shook herself, hoping that she'd been correct in doing that, at least. "I only have fifteen minutes or so to spare, Mr. MacTaggert, as my afternoon is spoken for. What was it you needed?"

Aden faced her, six-foot-one of formidable, unreadable Highlander. "Ye'd mentioned that book the other night. I wondered if I might borrow it."

Well, he could be discreet, then. A believable, innocuous reason for his presence and the suggestion of a location where they could speak in relative private. She nodded. "Of course. I'll show you. Millie?"

As she left the room, her mother reached over and squeezed one elbow. "He's delicious," she whispered, grinning. "Whoever this Captain Vale is, he must be perfection to outmatch this Highlander."

No, he wasn't anywhere near that, and yet his appearance didn't even signify. It was Vale's black heart that troubled her. And Aden's mysterious-colored one.

Miranda brushed past Aden and Millie to lead the way down the hall in the direction of the Harris House library. Once the three of them were inside the large, well-lit room she closed the door. "Have you thought of something after all?" she asked, facing him. "Or are you here to suggest that I surrender?"

"Do ye always go directly to the bleakest explanation, or is that just for me, lass?" he countered, walking over to peruse the contents of one bookcase.

"My world has become a bit bleak over the past few days. Don't expect me to apologize for not showering you with compliments for whatever it is that's brought you here. Yesterday you suggested I ruin myself, after all."

Leaving the books, he returned to her, stopping close enough that she had to lift her chin to meet his gaze. "Ye're a sharp-tongued woman."

She imagined she was, or she could be,

126

though no one had ever dared say such a thing to her face before. "And you are a mannerless gambler."

His mouth quirked, as if her insults had once again amused him. "And I didnae suggest ye ruin yerself. I suggested that I ruin ye. It's more fun that way."

How in the world was a lady supposed to respond to that? "I'll take your word for that." *Good heavens.* They certainly made them bold in the Highlands.

For now, aye." He regarded her for a few hard beats of her heart.

Arrogant, insufferable or not, he was a very fine-looking man. Deliciously so, as her mother had said. It would have been silly to pretend that he wasn't physically tempting, the stuff of heated dreams. But she didn't have the luxury of dreams right now. "You still haven't said why you're here."

"When ye go to yer luncheon with Captain Vale, ask him a couple of questions for me."

"Ask him yourself."

Aden tilted his head at her. "I have a different set of questions to ask him. These are better coming from ye. If ye say a couple falling in love would be learning things about each other, and that yer parents already have questions, ye can likely get him to chat. Ask about his parents, brothers or

127

sisters, why he purchased a commission in the navy, what he thought of India, how he kept himself entertained, the name of the ship he captained, clever things he's done — and anything that might give me some insight, a place to begin studying him."

She looked at him, something very like hope stirring in her heart. "You mean to help me, then?"

"I'll take a gander at him. Men wager for all kinds of reasons, but a man deliberately destroying someone in order to steal a lass and a position has someaught wrong with him. *I'd* wager this isnae the first time he's ruined a man to gain an advantage. But he's been in India, ye said, and I've been in the Highlands, so I need to know where to begin looking for the skeletons following him about."

Miranda nodded, her heart giving a hopeful little hop. She had no idea if he could actually be of assistance or not, but if he could be, and if he'd suddenly decided to be her ally, she'd be foolish not to do as he suggested. "I'll find out whatever I can."

"Be a wee bit cautious, lass. I reckon he has a high opinion of himself, but an idiot couldnae have orchestrated all this. That makes him a villain, but nae an idiot." Aden brushed a straying strand of her hair off her forehead, the gesture seemingly innocuous except for the slight, pleasurable shiver it caused along her scalp. "Were ye pleasant to him yesterday, or did ye talk to him the way ye talk to me?" he went on, as if he hadn't even noticed that he'd rather intimately touched her.

The caress didn't mean anything, Miranda reminded herself. He must be proficient at distracting people, and he'd just attempted it with her, whether he realized it or not. Well, she would not be distracted. And in all honesty, she didn't think she'd ever spoken to anyone else with the same . . . vigor she exercised in her conversations with Aden MacTaggert. "I was polite, I think," she said aloud. "I did attempt to reason with him. Why?"

"Go at him in that same way. Polite, looking for an escape, but also hoping to be impressed by him if ye cannae see a way out of this. If ye're too fawning ye'll make him suspicious, and if ye're too hostile ye may convince him to do someaught ye'll regret."

It all made sense, even if the idea of a long conversation with Captain Vale left her feeling distinctly queasy. "While I'm convincing him that I'm reluctantly amenable to a match, and when you've learned who he is, what do you mean to do, Mr. MacTaggert? This would all seem to rely on me trusting you, and on you being trustworthy."

"Aye, I reckon it does." He took half a step closer so that she had to lift her chin to keep her eyes on his face. "Ye keep batting at me, and I keep returning for more. Mayhap I see a kinship with a lass being pushed to marry against her wishes, or mayhap I like ye more than ye like me." He shrugged. "Or mayhap ye won a wager and I'm paying ye what I owe ye."

She held his gaze. What she'd heard about him, specifically his wagering, hadn't impressed her, because nothing about wagering did anything but dismay her to her bones. The man himself, though, wasn't nearly as easy to dismiss. A sharp-eyed poet or a Highlands warrior, Aden MacTaggert made an impression. She didn't feel uneasy or threatened in his presence, but she did feel more . . . aware. Alert. Exhilarated. His wit, his insight, kept her on her toes. That bit of him, at least, she almost enjoyed. And of course his face, his attire, his physique, even his careless hair, only added to his appeal. The fact that at least the part of it he could control might be deliberate just made him seem more dangerous.

Taking a slow breath, she nodded. "As

you've given yourself a trio of possible explanations, I have a trio of responses. I am hopeful, cautious, and willing to attempt just about anything if it helps me escape this trap. I'll even put a small degree of faith in you, if you give me your word that you won't wake up tomorrow feeling less generous and abandon me."

"I give ye my word, then," he returned without a trace of hesitation. "I'll nae abandon ye without making a fight of it." He stuck out his right hand.

He couldn't promise success, of course; that would be ridiculous, and she wouldn't have trusted it. Matthew hadn't promised a fight, or even an argument, with Captain Vale. In fact, he'd hurried off this morning again before she could even set eyes on him. Miranda reached out and grasped Aden's hand, large, callused, and steady. In response something warm and electric trailed slowly up her spine. "Thank you, Mr. MacTaggert."

"We're allies now; ye'd best call me Aden," he drawled, keeping hold of her hand for a good dozen seconds before he released her again.

"Miranda," she returned. "Thank you, Aden."

His name on her tongue felt intimate,

almost as if they'd kissed. That thought then made her cheeks heat, because she certainly had other, more important things to consider than what it would be like to kiss Aden MacTaggert — who either felt some empathy, owed her for a lost wager, or . . . liked her.

"Miranda," he said, heading for another bookcase.

Her name in his brogue, with the soft, rolled "r" and the elongated first "a," sounded rather splendid, but he likely knew that, just as he knew his large-muscled, soulful appearance made people, players across the table, underestimate just how keen-eyed he truly was. She shook herself. For the moment, at least, he and his surprisingly acute perception were her allies. "Which book am I lending you, then?"

He pulled one down from the shelf and opened it. "I reckon this one'll do. I've been meaning to read it."

Approaching, she looked at the tome he held. "*The History of Tom Jones, a Foundling,*" she read aloud, and blushed again. "I'm fairly certain I would not have recommended such a scandalous book to anyone."

With a grin that made her insides feel bubbly, he tucked the Henry Fielding book beneath one arm. "If anyone asks, then, I wanted to read about being a Sassenach, and ye were being sarcastic." He pulled a pocket watch from his coat and clicked it open. "Vale will be here soon. I reckon I'll say hello to him on my way out."

The unexpected warmth tingling through her cooled into ice. "No!"

Aden lifted one eyebrow. "And why should I nae? Ye and I are nearly in-laws, aye?"

That was true, yes, but he was her secret. The thought startled her a little. First of all, he'd agreed to assist her. Therefore, she should be following his advice and whichever plan he'd begun to lay out, at least until she had her own ideas regarding strategy and battle. "Vale thinks I'm alone in this," she said, choosing her words as she deciphered them in her mind. "Isn't it to our advantage for him to continue to believe that?"

"Aye. And he will. I only want a look at him." He took a step closer, his gaze lowering for just a second to her mouth before he lifted it again. "I gave ye and yer ma my reason for being here. That's why I'm here. Dunnae lie about me; he'll likely ask yer brother, and Matthew's bound to say I'm known to gamble."

Miranda found herself nodding. If she couldn't trust him to be helpful, it seemed best to discover that now, rather than after she'd begun relying on anything he said or did. "Very well. On your way out."

"I may embarrass ye a bit, but then I'm a mannerless Highlander."

His swift grin was the only hint that he might be jesting with her. Or not. "I still wish I knew why you decided to help me," she said in a low voice, opening the library door.

He put his hand out to stop her and half closed the door again. "So do I. But I reckon we both ken it wasnae the wager."

That left two remaining choices: empathy or affection. As Miranda watched him lean back against the wall, his gaze through the cracked-open door in the direction of the foyer, she didn't know which she preferred. Empathy seemed more reliable, if he saw his own situation mirrored in hers and wanted at least one of them to be able to escape.

The other one . . . Well, he'd only said that perhaps he liked her more than she liked him, and four days ago she had declared to his face that she detested him. "Like" was therefore a very broad category in this circumstance. In truth, she liked him a bit more than she had yesterday, because he'd bothered to come see her. It didn't mean anything romantic, even if everything about him seemed pure sin.

A large shadow passed by the window panels at one side of the front door and stopped. He was here. Miranda's hands clenched before she was aware of it, and she forced her fingers to uncurl as Billings pulled open the front door to admit Captain Vale. They exchanged a word or two, and the butler turned to approach the library.

"Now," Aden said quietly, pushing away from the wall and reaching past her to pull the door wide. "If I'd any idea I was being scandalous," he went on in a normal tone, "I'd nae have announced the book I was after in front of my mother this morning. Ye should have told me ye were being sarcastic, Miranda."

She rushed her thoughts to catch up to him, taking a second to note how unusual it was for her to be behind in a conversation with anyone. "I didn't think you would actually turn up asking to read it," she returned aloud, flashing him a smile as they headed toward the front of the house.

"Ye mean ye didnae think I could read." Glancing ahead of them, he slowed. "Och, someone's let a vulture loose inside the house. Ye, butler. Get me a broom."

Because she was looking directly at him,

135

she saw Captain Vale's raptor eyes narrow just a little. And just for a moment, she wanted to utter an unladylike snort. A villain who horrified her, and now, for a few seconds, she felt like laughing at him. Thank God or the devil or whoever had delivered Aden MacTaggert to her.

"Aden, this is Captain Robert Vale. Captain, my almost brother-in-law, Aden MacTaggert."

Aden inclined his head just a little. Regally, almost. With him in his kilt and semicivilized clothing, it somehow suited him. "Vale."

"MacTaggert," the captain returned. "I've an engagement with Miranda."

"This is what's dragging ye off to luncheon, lass?" Aden drawled, his brogue growing even thicker. "I'll nae understand ye Sassenach, I reckon." Before she could conjure a retort to that, Aden leaned down and kissed her on one cheek. "Thank ye for the book, Miranda. I'll nae let my dog chew on it."

Her cheek felt scalded, and it took all of her will not to touch her fingers to the place where he'd brushed his lips. "Thank you for that," she managed, hoping it at least sounded like she was referring to his assurances about Brògan, and not about that surprising kiss.

He smiled at her. "I'll be by to return it to ye soon enough." With a last, dismissive look at Captain Vale, he patted the butler on the shoulder and headed past them out the open front door.

She watched after him for a moment. When she belatedly returned her attention to the captain, Vale had his bird-of-prey gaze fixed on her. Even though his expression hadn't altered, she had the definite feeling that he was most displeased. And that made her exceedingly pleased.

"Who was that?" he asked in his level monotone.

"I introduced you. Aden MacTaggert. One of Eloise MacTaggert's brothers."

"The Scottish ones."

"Yes." That seemed a rather obvious observation for him to make. Perhaps Aden had managed to rattle him a little. Even if he hadn't, she didn't feel the same angry hopelessness with which Vale had left her yesterday. She wasn't entirely alone in this any longer. She had an ally of sorts, and a plan of sorts. Yes, she definitely liked Aden more than she had yesterday, and by a rather large margin.

Aden stopped Loki just short of the corner.

137

Edging the chestnut in between a stopped coach and a cart brimming with coal, he dismounted to stand in the shadows. At six-foot-one and wearing a kilt he wasn't precisely invisible in the middle of Mayfair, but at least he wasn't obvious.

Less than a minute after he found his hiding place, Captain Vale and Miranda in her bonny green-and-gray gown topped by a jaunty green bonnet, her maid trailing behind her, left the house for the waiting barouche. That vehicle boasted a yellow-and-white coat of arms in the shape of owls and what looked like a spade. After only a few weeks in London, Vale likely didn't have a coat of arms or a barouche, so the birds and shovel would belong to his cousin Lord George Humphries.

According to Miranda the man had left the naval service, but today he'd worn a crisp blue uniform together with one of those tall, fan-shaped hats that would have him breaking his neck in a stiff breeze. The naval uniform was there because it looked impressive. Because it meshed well with whatever plan Vale had concocted.

Vale looked fit and fairly tall for a Sassenach, even if Aden would have preferred him to be a short, twisted hunchback. His walk was just a drumbeat short of a march, his shoulders and back straight enough that he could well have a broomstick shoved up his arse. What he *did* have up there was another question entirely, because while Aden could understand what Vale had done, and how he'd done it, the why still had no answers.

For that he needed to rely on Miranda, at least for now. If she did as he had suggested and got Vale to chat about himself, it would provide at least a starting point for some additional digging. Whether he *should* be doing that or not was a slightly stickier dilemma. Because while gamblers didn't have a secret club as Miranda had implied, there were some rules. One man did not go after another's target, or interfere in someone else's game. A man who did that could find himself uninvited from a table or a club at best, and with a knife through his innards at worst.

He knew all that — and he still fell in behind the barouche as Miranda Harris and Captain Vale drove off for their luncheon. Since he'd set Miranda on a particular course of action, if something went wrong he had an obligation to make certain she stayed safe. Or that was what he told himself as he trotted down the street, anyway.

Because he didn't believe in deluding

himself, he also had to acknowledge that he in part felt indebted to Vale. The greedy bastard had given Miranda a reason to call on Aden, and had given Aden a reason to be in her presence. How that might end he had no idea, but he intended to find out.

Miranda had perfected the art of conversational repartee and brought it to the very edge of the precipice. She'd sharpened her tongue to a razor point, and slashed and cut with the skill of a champion fencer. She not only knew how to navigate Mayfair, she shone among the glittery aristocracy. Aden could likely learn a thing or two from her. At the same time, he could conjure a thing or two he wanted to teach her.

That served to remind him that he hadn't shared a bed with a lass since before he and Coll had left London to shadow Niall and his Amy on their flight north to Gretna Green. And while the young widow Alice Hardy had been enthusiastic enough in bed, he couldn't think of any man who, before he'd even caught his breath, wanted to be subjected to questions over whether he preferred white or red roses at a wedding. Saint Andrew, he'd barely paused long enough to collect his boots before he'd fled.

But then there was Miranda Harris, who, however desperate the situation, remained levelheaded and circumspect. It made her initial assessment of his character sting a wee bit more than it would have otherwise, because he'd known from the first minute they'd met that she wasn't a lass who spent her days cooing over roses. He admired her — perhaps *because* she'd bothered not to flutter her eyelashes at him. The fact that she had eyes the color of dark, sweet chocolate and a mouth that seemed to miss its smile didn't hurt, either.

The fancy barouche turned the corner ahead of him, and he shook himself. Waiting until a pair of riders and a trio of wagons passed him, Aden sent Loki up the street after Miranda and the captain. If they knew what he was up to, both of his brothers would be laughing at him right now. A lass had declared her dislike of his character, and because he didn't like that, he'd jumped at the first opportunity to charge to her rescue and thereby prove her wrong.

Actually, that made for a fair explanation. It would save him from having to confess that he had fallen for her at first insult, and that all this was an excuse to become better acquainted with the lass before he made an idiot of himself by declaring his infatuation when she did, in fact, dislike him.

The barouche turned south now toward

141

Bond Street, and he kneed Loki into a trot so he wouldn't lose sight of the vehicle. He'd spent the last few weeks — in between shadowing Niall and Amy on their flight to Gretna Green and now avoiding Alice Hardy — learning the streets of London. Going out at night as he tended to, knowing where he was and where he was headed could mean the difference between arriving back at Oswell House and being dead in an alley somewhere. Parts of London were proving more bloody dangerous than even the wildest bits of the Highlands.

Vale seemed to be staying in Mayfair, which made sense. The captain was after respectability; he would want to be seen by his would-be peers while he wore his dashing uniform and had Miranda Harris on his arm. That fact also provided her with a measure of safety, since Vale would have to behave like a gentleman in public. Still, punching and yelling weren't the only ways to hurt or frighten or injure a lass.

When the barouche stopped in front of the Kings Hotel, he frowned. An establishment that large featured a great many places where a lass could find herself in trouble not of her own making, and it was too fancy for a tall, broad-shouldered Scotsman in scuffed boots and a work kilt. He wouldn't have minded the coincidence of them all dining at the same establishment, but getting booted out on his arse wouldn't help his plans.

Even so, he wasn't about to leave until he knew for certain that she was safely dining and not being dragged into some room upstairs. Dismounting, he led Loki up the street, slowing to look through the first of a quartet of windows spanning the ground floor of the three-story building. Tables and well-dressed diners, but no Miranda.

"No gawking at your betters," the doorman said as Aden drew even with him. "Move along."

Aden stopped, looking over the man's head as the door behind him opened. There she was, seated toward the back of the room across the table from the captain. He could only see her profile, but her back was straight and her hands folded in her lap. Attentive and unwilling to risk Vale touching her. To Aden her posture shouted suspicion and discomfort, but no doubt the captain expected that from her. Hopefully the only thing Vale hadn't anticipated was that the Highlands barbarian he'd just met was more than a potential romantic rival, and that someone else was advising her on the direction of her conversation.

It took more effort than it should have to turn his attention to her dining companion. Now that the captain wasn't eyeing him in return, Aden took a good look at the short brown hair and long, hooked nose — in profile the man even more resembled a damned vulture. No wonder Vale had reckoned he needed to resort to threats and blackmail to get a lass like Miranda.

"Did you not hear me? Move along. You'll get no handouts here."

Aden blinked, returning his gaze to the black-, yellow-, and red-liveried doorman. "Do I look like a man who's missed a meal, Sassenach?" he asked, taking a step closer. Loki at his shoulder snorted.

The doorman's jaw jumped, but he kept his chin up. "What you look like is someone not attired to dine at the Kings Hotel, or to take rooms here."

An argument might have been amusing, but he didn't want to be attracting the attention of the diners inside for no good reason. Aden put a smile on his face. "I cannae argue with that, wee man. Good day to ye." With a nod he tugged on Loki's reins and continued up the street.

Once he was clear of the windows he swung back into the saddle. He couldn't do much here without throwing the little bit of strategy he'd conjured into chaos, but if Captain Vale was as proficient a gambler as he seemed, men at the tables hereabouts would either have played against him or at least know of him.

The problem with that was that Vale had a lord for a cousin, one who was more than likely a member of all the best gentlemen's clubs. Aden had a lord for a brother, but Coll wasn't a member of any London club. Nor was he likely to become a member even if they would have him.

Matthew Harris had several memberships, but he seemed a poor choice for a sponsor, especially under the circumstances. Aden blew out his breath. There were other places he'd found, other, less savory men with whom he could talk. They would do for a start.

Sooner rather than later he would have to have a conversation with Matthew, though. The lad was worse than a fool to put his own sister in harm's way. If there was *any* chance of his poor behavior continuing, he and Eloise needed to be parted. At this moment Matthew was an enemy in the middle of MacTaggert territory, but Aden had the feeling that the lad would also be necessary to solving this disaster.

All that was aside from the fact that stopping Eloise and Matthew's wedding remained the simplest way to get him and Coll back to the Highlands without Sassenach brides. That was a topic for later. First, he needed to figure out a way to rescue this lass, and to convince her that he wasn't a villain simply because he enjoyed playing cards.

He did have a reason not to speak up — Miranda would never trust him with anything again, and for good reason. But he worried about Eloise. His sister, the youngest MacTaggert, had been less than a year old when she and their mother had left the Highlands. Seventeen years later they had her back in their lives, and the idea of risking their newfound relationship didn't sit well with him at all. Neither, though, did he intend to allow her to marry a man who was proving to be both reckless and a poor judge of character — not to mention a poor gambler.

Eloise would not be put in the same perilous position as Miranda. That was a fact, as unalterable as the Highlands. As was the fact that he wasn't going to allow any harm — any further harm — to come to Miranda Harris. Every conversation he had with her impressed him more, left him more convinced that he'd found his English lass. It

146

didn't matter that she had another man trying to force her into marriage; there were several ways around that, only a few of them bloody.

The one thing that could alter his plan was both simple and supremely complicated — did she like him in return? Once he had that bit answered he could decipher whether it was him or his offer of assistance that had lured her in, and whether that made him a hero or a fool.

CHAPTER SIX

Aden's suggestion that she pretend reluctant curiosity seemed to be working like a charm, though Miranda remained uncertain whether she could believe anything Captain Vale told her. A man didn't suddenly decide to become ruthless and heartless, and it seemed that a milder sin like lying would come first and that he therefore would be proficient at it.

Something had sent him down this path, but she refused to feel any sympathy. If he were simply an injured party, then yes, she could empathize. But he had already made it clear that he meant to injure her, and that made him an enemy.

"What is the next soiree you attend?" Vale asked, finishing off his tea and sugared biscuit. At least he hadn't mastered the art of reading minds, however much he might prefer to give that impression.

He had selected a very respectable estab-

148

lishment for luncheon, she had to admit, but then he was looking to acquire a respectable reputation — by stealing hers. "I would have to consult my appointment book," she returned.

"Then I will accompany you back inside Harris House and you will tell me there."

She cocked her head at him, half hoping he could see just how perturbed he made her. "If you were more pleasant and less threatening, you might find your pathway less full of ruts."

"There are no ruts, my dear. There is only you digging in your heels. You know you have no recourse, so flail about if you choose to do so. You'll lose."

If this was the end of their more pleasant, informative conversation, she had no further reason to prolong the encounter. "The Darlington ball, then, day after tomorrow," she stated. "Bully."

"Speaking of bullies," he said smoothly, "tell me more about Aden MacTaggert."

A chill went down her fingers. "He likes to read, and he called on me this morning because I mentioned a book he hadn't yet read."

"Where did you mention this book to him?"

"At the Gaines soiree. I was being sarcastic

149

when he asked if I knew of any books about English life, but I don't think he realized it at the time." There. She wondered if Aden had realized all those little seeds of information he'd planted in their earlier conversation would be so useful to her. She hoped so, because that made him exceedingly clever in addition to handsome and . . . aggravating. Miranda pulled the ties of her reticule back over her wrist. "You're becoming intolerable, so please see me home."

"Smile when you speak to me. We're falling in love, after all."

She would sooner fall in love with a toad, but she smiled anyway. For every smile he ordered her to show, she would find a way to stab him in his nonexistent heart. Perhaps she was mad to put any faith at all in Aden MacTaggert and his so-called assistance, but at this moment she clung to the idea of having a partner in this, of not being so very alone and on her own.

Since Aden had said he needed information, she'd gotten as much as she could for him. Now, though, if this encounter continued much longer she couldn't guarantee she wouldn't begin either vomiting or, worse, punching this vulture in his beak of a nose. Miranda deepened her smile at that pleasant thought. "Take me home, please."

Captain Vale smiled back at her, the expression going nowhere near his amber-brown eyes. "As you wish." Standing, he walked around behind her to hold her chair. "I do hope you'll permit me to call on you again," he said, loudly enough for the diners at the neighboring tables to hear.

She nodded, trying not to flinch at how . . . vulnerable she felt with him behind her. "I would not object to that, Captain," she forced out, motioning to Millie where the maid sat over by the kitchen.

Outside he summoned his borrowed barouche, making a show of pulling open the low door and handing her inside. Once she'd settled herself, he sat beside her, leaving Millie to clamber in on her own and take the rear-facing seat. "Back to Harris House, Tom," Vale instructed the driver.

"I still don't understand why you require me for any of this," Miranda ventured. "Lord George is your cousin. You have a pathway toward respectability, though I've yet to see anyone so much as look askance at you."

"How many people greeted you as we drove here?" he asked, sitting back to light a cheroot.

Miranda feigned a cough at the acrid smoke he blew into the air. "I don't recall.

151

Half a dozen or so?"

"Seven," he corrected. "Which is seven more than greeted me."

"That hardly signifies. You're a stranger here. Once George has introduced you about, the —"

"Two points, Miranda. First, George Humphries is an amusing, bombastic fellow whom no one takes too seriously. While his initial introductions and living at his residence have proven helpful, I don't wish to be paired in people's minds with a fool for a moment longer than necessary. Second," he went on, taking another pungent puff of his cheroot, "he isn't my cousin."

Her mouth opened, but no sound came out. If Millie's stunned expression mirrored hers, they both looked like gawping fish drowning in the air. Clamping her jaw shut again, she sent a quick glance forward at the driver's perch. Tom was Lord George's usual driver, but he didn't so much as flinch at the revelation of this stunning bit of information. "How —"

"A debt considerably less significant than that of your brother." Vale's mouth curved into that brief, humorless smile again. "I didn't decide on this course of action on a whim, Miranda. I found George Humphries first. He gained me entry into your very elite circle. At the moment that is a façade. Marrying you ensures that I remain here. A marriage renders the façade real."

She wanted to fling open the low door of the barouche and run. In an odd sense she'd hoped he'd somehow become infatuated with her personally. If he liked her — and wanted her to like him — she could perhaps reason with him, convince him to leave Matthew and her alone. This, though . . . this water was far above her head, and she already felt like she was drowning.

"Mention me to your parents this evening," he went on coolly, as if he hadn't just flipped everything on its head once again. "Mention that you enjoy my company, and that I'm looking for an appropriate residence in the immediate area, one suitable for raising a family. Ask your father if he has any ideas — and if he might be willing to assist me in making connections, as I am newly returned to London and he's no doubt aware of Lord George's frivolity and will understand my reluctance to rely on my cousin. Emphasize that you would be quite happy to have me nearby, and would detest the idea of me having to rejoin His Majesty's Navy and sail away to parts unknown."

"I will not bring my parents into this mess.

I'm here in this barouche in order to avoid precisely that."

"You will do it, unless you'd rather inform them that the Harris family owes me fifty thousand pounds. I know your family is comfortable, but not drowning in wealth. What the lot of you are is well connected. That is your value to me." Vale blew out another smoky breath. "If you do something to devalue yourself, I'll still have fifty thousand pounds to collect. If you were considering doing something so foolish, that is."

Ruining herself was precisely what Aden MacTaggert had suggested. He'd even volunteered to assist her with that particular task, in a way that had made her insides feel jangly. Did all men think a woman's best course to avoid an unwanted suitor was to be ruined and left forever unmarried?

It made for an interesting line of thought — but one she didn't have time for at the moment. It was more significant that she now had some proof that Captain Vale and Aden MacTaggert thought in similar ways, and as long as Aden remained helpful, she would consider that an advantage. She'd guessed a card trick. How much assistance did that earn her? How much difficulty would he be willing to face before he decided he'd done enough? What, in short, was in this for him?

Her, of course, but though he'd said he liked her, that might only have been because she'd made a point of saying she didn't like him. That had been stupid — though she hadn't known at the time that her brother had been in the midst of selling her to cover his debts. No, it had been stupid because he wasn't just a gambler. She'd judged one of the parts of him, and had decided that nothing else mattered. And in a few short days she'd already begun to realize that she had been both narrow-minded and shortsighted.

"I have no intention of ruining myself, Captain, and certainly not to spite someone else. Even you."

Vale flicked the remains of his cheroot onto the street. "You do appear to have a logical bent that I didn't expect. Matthew said you kept a level head, but he hasn't precisely proven an exceptional judge of character. Or of the odds."

No, Matthew had horribly misjudged several things, and she was the one paying the price. For every escape she imagined, Vale had already anticipated and countered it. Once again, her thoughts trotted down the path to the Highlander who'd unexpectedly given her the tiniest bit of hope, and a few other things to ponder. Aden's involvement might well be the one thing Captain Vale *didn't* know about and hadn't anticipated. She intended to keep it that way.

The carriage rolled to a halt outside Harris House. *Thank goodness.* She'd survived her first outing with this awful man, and she had two days to prepare for their next encounter. Just the idea of that next meeting made her heart shudder, but she hid her reaction as she stood and stepped to the ground.

"I'll meet you at the Darlington ball," he said, descending behind her. "Turn around and offer me both of your hands."

She would rather have offered him both of her fists, but any brief satisfaction punching him might give her would be drowned out by the ruin that would likely befall her entire family. Miranda turned around and held out her hands to him.

He closed his fingers around hers, favoring her with his unsettling smile once more. "You will save me two dances. One of them will be a waltz." His grip tightened just short of the point of pain before he released her. "Now smile as you walk into the house. Tell your parents how unexpectedly interesting you find me, and whatever else convinces them that you're looking forward to

156

seeing me again."

"I will," she said, though she wasn't certain whether it was worse to have to recite the lies he'd provided, or to have to make up her own.

Once safely inside the house she just resisted the urge to wrench the door out of Billings's grip and slam it shut, followed by dragging all the house's furniture into the foyer and piling it against the entrance. But even here she had to keep up the ruse that she found Captain Vale interesting. If she couldn't manage that, her parents would become suspicious. Once that happened, protecting them — and herself — would become much more problematic.

"I hope you had a pleasant afternoon, Miss Harris. You have a note from Lady Eloise," the butler said, lifting a salver from the hall table.

Willing her fingers not to shake, Miranda took the missive from the tray and unfolded it. The handwriting inside looked nothing like Eloise's looping, round hand. Neat, spare, and precise, it said only, "Go for a walk this afternoon at five o'clock. A.MT."

Aden MacTaggert. Her hard heartbeat eased into a steadier rhythm. Aden hadn't simply been paying lip service when he'd said he would help her. She'd half trusted

him, and half thought he was merely looking to amuse himself. Instead, he'd already
figured out how they would next meet, and
without arousing Vale's or anyone else's
suspicions. And she would damned well go
out and meet him. Because as much as she
disliked the idea of it all, Matthew owed
that money. It wouldn't take much of a
nudge from Vale to induce her brother to
report on all her comings and goings.

"Good news, I hope?" Millie said, as the
maid trailed her upstairs.

"Yes. Good news." One man, at least,
seemed to be on her side, even if it was
because he fancied her. Miranda paused on
the steps. Was that the only reason he'd
decided to help? He certainly hadn't given
her a straight answer when she'd asked.

He didn't seem the sort of man who followed a lady about, holding her parasol or
fetching her punch. But if encouraging him
would help ensure his assistance, she'd be a
fool to keep snapping at him. Hmm. Leading a man — any man — on made her feel
dirty, whatever the reason. Could she do it,
though? Would she be leading him on if part
of her enjoyed the way he kept her on her
toes, or the way other women eyed her jeal-
ously when she waltzed with him?

But then Uncle John had charmed Aunt

Beatrice into marriage, and Matthew had charmed Eloise into accepting his proposal. Charm and attraction might be influencing her reaction to Aden MacTaggert, but as long as she knew it, as long as she kept that firmly in mind, no one would be leading her astray. Dragging her, yes, but she wouldn't be going of her own volition.

For now she would settle for deciding that Aden wasn't as intolerable as she'd first believed, and that she'd won his silly wager so he owed her some assistance. Yes. That would do. Until it didn't.

Aden fed an apple to Loki, leaning a hip against the chestnut's haunch as he munched on another fruit himself. Miranda hadn't responded to his note, not that she could do so without stirring up trouble. Pretending to be Eloise had seemed the least suspicious way to communicate with her, even if it did leave her no simple way to answer. He therefore might well be lurking down the street from Harris House for no good reason, but at least he'd thought to bring snacks.

But then his reason for lurking emerged from Harris House, and he forgot what he'd been thinking about. She and her omnipresent yellow-haired maid walked down the

159

short drive, pausing there as Miranda looked up and down the street. Aden straightened, his pulse speeding in a combination of anticipation and lust. When she spied him, she gave a subtle wave of her fingers and turned in his direction. The streets of Mayfair stood fairly empty at the moment, since most of the bluebloods would be home now dressing for dinner or the theater or whichever distraction they'd planned for the evening. That all made the two of them more obvious to anyone who might be passing by, but as long as Matthew didn't leave the house to follow his sister, it remained the best option.

"Aden," Miranda said, as she reached him.

"Miranda." He handed Loki's reins to the startled-looking maid. "Dunnae fret; he's a well-behaved lad."

"I —"

"We cannae stand here chatting," he pushed, falling in beside Miranda. He wanted to touch her, so he offered the lass his arm — which any gentleman would do. Her gloved hand sliding around his forearm felt somehow significant, but then she was a proper lass and more than likely wouldn't slight him in public. "I followed ye to luncheon, but I left once I saw ye settled into a chair at the Kings Hotel."

"You followed me?"

Aden shrugged. "Ye said the vulture wants respectability, but there's more than one way for him to gain yer cooperation, I reckon."

She nodded. "I had my reticule in my lap for the entire ride so I could beat him with it and flee if necessary. Thank you."

"Ye dunnae owe me thanks, lass. I lost a wager to ye." He hadn't done a damned thing other than trot his horse after Vale's carriage. And insult the man to his face, hopefully giving the captain something to think about for a moment other than Miranda. No heroics, ill conceived or not, had been necessary.

"Several people are aware of my present circumstance. You — and Millie — are the only ones who seem concerned." Her mouth quirked. "And I believe you mentioned you weren't aiding me because you lost that wager."

Aden studied the brief humor in her eyes. *A remarkable lass, she was.* "I did say that, aye." Whether that made him an idiot or not, he couldn't yet guess. "I can make ye one promise, Miranda: I'll nae stand aside and allow ye to pay for someone else's mistakes." He wanted to declare himself, to inform her that he'd found his English

161

bride, but at this point she'd only laugh at him. Aside from that, she already had one villain trying to force her into something. He didn't wish to be another.

It had also struck him that the most interesting lass with whom he'd crossed paths in London might well be the one who could ensure that he was able to return to the Highlands without a Sassenach bride. He'd hold on to that for later, because he never let go of a good playing card even if he meant never to use it. If she'd been a three-eyed gargoyle, aye, he might — likely would — have been tempted, but she was a two-eyed bonny lass with a sharp wit, and he liked her. "Like" seemed a simple word for the vast tangle of questions hovering around her and poking at him, but he'd make use of it for now.

"And that is why I thank you," she said, clearly unaware of what he was thinking.

Aden shook himself. He could have his mental dilemmas over entanglements and duty to family, but she was in the middle of a field of thorns. Very real ones. "Save yer appreciation; I've nae done a thing yet. Were ye able to get any information out of Captain Vale, then?"

"Yes. The last thing I learned may be the most important, and in all honesty, I discovered it completely by accident. Lord George Humphries is *not* Captain Vale's cousin. They are not related at all."

He scowled, noting the satisfaction on her face at flummoxing him. And she'd done a damned fine job of it. "The hell ye say."

"He told me straight to my face. Lord George is in debt to him, as well, and that is how he chose to collect. By fashioning himself into Lord George Humphries's cousin and staying at Baromy House with him."

Up front the lie was so outrageous that he had to wonder why Vale would attempt it. Proficient gamblers could be surprisingly cautious lads. On the other hand, who would question the truth of it once Lord George declared it to be so? It did turn a tangle of misinformation he'd gathered about Lord George's cousin into something that made more sense — in that nothing made sense, because none of it was true. "So, he's used Lord George Humphries to open the door, and means to use ye to keep himself in Society. At some point later on if anybody asks him about being cousins, he can say the lot of ye must have misunderstood him or someaught."

She nodded. "That's what he said. The first part, anyway." She sighed, and he tried not to lower his gaze to her very distracting bosom. "I do find it rather unsettling that you seem to understand him so well," she went on. "You have said you're not alike, after all."

"If ye mean to keep pounding at me for enjoying a hand of cards here and there," he retorted, "I reckon I could be elsewhere, chasing down a less testy lass for me to marry in the next four months."

"If you mean to tell me you only play a hand of cards now and again, I'm going to call you a liar. Both of us are here precisely because you are reputed to be a formidable opponent at the gaming tables."

A dim lass would have been easy to manage, he reflected, but a dim lass wouldn't have caught his attention. Unmarried young ladies had been pelting him with handkerchiefs and fluttering eyelashes and glimpses of ankles for weeks now. This one clubbed him over the head with her wit, and he was panting after her like a buck after a doe.

"Aye," he agreed after a moment, "but only one of us dislikes my reputation."

"I dislike your reputation out of principle, and your choice of hobby or distraction or whatever it is because it affects other people's lives," she returned. "*You* are harder to quantify."

"Well, thank Saint Andrew for that, anyway." Aden tucked her in closer against his side. "I'm carrying yer secret with me, ye ken, whether ye like me or nae. So ye decide either to trust me with it, or to go look elsewhere for a man who'll agree to partner with ye."

" 'Partner,' " she repeated. "I like that. But what, pray tell, do you get from this partnership? There must be something you want."

You. "Aye. Ye . . ." He searched for something to say that wouldn't start her panicking that she had two inveterate gamblers hunting her down. "Ye ken the ways of London Society. Coll and I had a good laugh when some fool set out three forks and two knives for dinner one night, and then we used them all for a venison pie with some odd sort of white sauce and wee sliced potatoes, and we'd nae forks left for cake. Help me navigate this sea of nonsense, and I'll call us even."

Miranda lifted one curved eyebrow. "That's what you want in return? Lessons on the order of forks?"

If that was all he wanted, he wouldn't be standing there, imagining kissing her. Imagining her in his bed, and him inside her. "Nae, but I reckon that'll do. For now."

For a moment she walked silently beside him. "Considering that aiding you will help keep Vale away from me, I would be a fool not to agree."

"Ye're nae a fool, so shake my hand. Partners."

Stopping, he freed his arm from hers and stuck out his hand. Her gaze on his fingers, she nodded as if to herself and closed her smaller hand around his. Even through the gloves her fingers were warm, her grip firm. Aye, she was a practical lass. Practicality said she needed to accept his help, and therefore she'd done so. Wondering abruptly if that practicality was why she flirted and didn't slap him for his less-than-proper suggestions, he decided it didn't signify. It was likely his own well-honed sense of self-preservation stepping in. He'd keep his eyes open anyway, because he generally wasn't a fool, either.

Aden glanced up and down the street, to find it temporarily empty. Before he could decide he was being an idiot, that no amount of stealth or practical experience would be able to extricate him from this, he leaned down and touched his mouth to hers.

She had soft lips and tasted faintly of tea, and something . . . undefinable shuddered through him. He allowed himself a long moment of heaven, less gentle than he could have been, and less thorough than he wanted to be, before he straightened again. Even the devil must have missed harp music now and again — and he'd just heard it loud and clear. "That's how we seal a bargain in the Highlands," he drawled with a nonchalance he didn't feel.

For a moment he thought he'd finally earned a slap after all, but then she took half a step back and he realized she'd gone up on her toes to kiss him back. And whatever else he might discover today about plots and villains, *that* seemed the most significant. She'd met him halfway.

"I, um, I very much doubt that you kiss everyone with whom you make an agreement," she stated, her chocolate gaze lowering to his mouth and her color high. "It's not done, Mr. MacTaggert."

"Is that so?"

Miranda nodded. "As your tutor in things English," she continued, "I should tell you that it's improper for you to go about kissing women under any circumstances."

Amused now, he lifted an eyebrow. *"Any?"* he repeated.

"Well, wives and such. But not in public." Visibly shaking herself, she placed her hand back over his forearm. "But you didn't come here this afternoon for kissing lessons."

"I dunnae need kissing lessons, Miranda. I can prove that, if ye like."

"I believe you just did."

"And do ye object?"

"I . . ." Her shoulders lifted. "I believe I would have told you if I objected."

He chuckled. "True enough. Ye've nae been shy about expressing yerself, lass."

She didn't object. Not exactly a stirring expression of enthusiasm, but enough for today. Every kiss, every glance, every word exchanged with Miranda Harris had significance. He damned well didn't want to make a mistake. His parents had made one, had found fire and passion and then realized that beneath that, they were utterly incompatible.

They managed a few steps during which he took the time to study her profile, or what he could see of it around her straw bonnet. His fingers twitched with the abrupt desire to untie the green ribbons from beneath her chin and pull the silly thing from her dusky hair. Those wishes, though, were for a lass who didn't have a man attempting to force her into a marriage. He could be poetical later.

"Did Vale tell ye anything else useful?" he asked, when he realized he'd forgotten about that. Stupid. He couldn't afford to miss anything here. Anything could mean the difference between victory and disaster.

This time a grimace touched her face. "Yes. Back to that, then."

"It's important, but if ye'd rather chat about the weather, I'll walk beside ye all the way to Dover."

"I'm not wearing the shoes for that." She took a breath. "After hearing that last bit about George and him, I fear that everything else he told me may well have been a lie."

"Even a lie means someaught. Tell me."

"He said he originally purchased a junior lieutenant's commission in the navy some fourteen years ago. Then he implied that powerful people owed him favors, and that that was the reason he so quickly rose through the ranks to become a captain with his own ship."

It wouldn't have to be powerful people, as long as it was the right people. That, though, didn't make for as good a tale. "Did he tell ye the name of the last ship he captained?"

"Yes. It was the *Merry Widow.*"

"That gives me someaught to look into. Anything else? Where he grew up? Brothers or sisters? Parents?"

"I didn't want to sound like I was digging for information, but he did mention dreary

Cornwall winters and a never-sober uncle John. Nothing about immediate family."

"That sounds like a bit of truth, or it could be someaught he made up a long time ago because his family embarrasses him," Aden mused. "Or he embarrasses them."

That elicited a dark smile from Miranda. "I hope it's the former, and they're so horrid they would ruin his chances of joining the aristocracy," she put in. "Perhaps they're drunken smugglers who spied for Bonaparte."

"That would be grand, but I dunnae think it'll be that simple. Even if he becomes a laughingstock, he still has yer brother's notes."

"I could well end up married to him even if he's actually a smuggler or a farmer and pretending to be related to an aristocrat, you mean. So I could be a smuggler's wife, or a milkmaid."

"The prettiest one in Cornwall, but aye."

She glanced up at him, her dark eyes catching his and color returning to her cheeks before she looked away again. Miranda cleared her throat. "He's thirty-two years old, or so he said," she went on, "and he claims to have spent the last ten years in India. Or off the coast of India, I suppose. According to him, he frequently captured smuggling vessels, taking a percentage of the goods as a bounty and working closely with the East India Company."

Aden frowned. "I cannae sail to India to verify any of that." The fact that the idea had occurred to him at all demonstrated just how soundly he'd come down on her side in this mess. And he generally didn't get involved in messes at all. Coll called him slippery, and he preferred that to Niall's depiction of him as calculating. He liked stealthy, or wily, even more, but the epithet didn't really matter. He was the MacTaggert brother that fathers weren't chasing about with swords and pistols — not because he hadn't dallied, but because he made an effort not to be caught at it.

In this instance, though, it might well be his wily — or calculating — nature that best served Miranda. His Miranda, hopefully, after he rescued her from the ogre. "I dunnae suppose ye're acquainted with anyone from the East India Company who happens to be based in London."

"I think my father might be. Or perhaps Matthew."

"Nae. I'll ask elsewhere, for now at least."

"You don't trust Matthew not to go running to Captain Vale, do you?"

"Nae, I dunnae." Aden narrowed his eyes.

171

"Yer brother's a menace, lass. And while I'll keep yer secret, I'll tell ye to yer face that if he's willing to toss his own sister to this vulture, I'm nae certain how safe *my* sister would be in his company."

"Which is why we are going to resolve this, after which I will convince Matthew that if he so much as looks at another deck of cards or pair of dice I will break all his fingers. And you *will* continue to assist me in resolving this, yes? If it can be resolved. We have an agreement."

A tremor ran through her fingers where they rested on his sleeve. Aye, she kept logic and a certain sarcastic view of her fellows wrapped about her like a blanket, but she knew precisely how deep a hole she'd landed in. And he was beginning to realize himself that Captain Robert Vale was no novice. "I keep my word, lass," he said evenly. "I do mean to have a word with yer brother, though, when I reckon it's safe." And most useful. He took a breath, mentally shaking himself. "I asked around a bit this afternoon, but my kind, as ye say, tend to come outside after dark. What —"

Behind them the maid touched her mistress's shoulder. "It's getting late, Miss Miranda."

Dusk had settled into the nooks and crannies of the houses around them, the sky a chalky blue-brown edging into black at the east. When had that happened? "I'll walk ye back. Or close by, anyway," he said, reversing course and escorting her past the maid and a bored-looking Loki.

As they passed back behind the overgrown length of hedge, she put her free hand on his shoulder, went up on her toes, and kissed him on the mouth. "Thank you for this, Aden," she said, resuming her place at his side and abruptly hurrying her steps before he could wrap his arms around her.

He accelerated a bit to keep up with her. Even more this time, the warmth of her mouth, of her breath against his cheek, lingered on his skin. *She'd* kissed *him.* That meant something. "Ye're welcome, Miranda," he returned. "But I'm nae running down the street because ye're embarrassed that ye like me."

She stopped in her tracks, nearly sending him stumbling into the street. "I'm not embarrassed. I'm . . . surprised. And somewhat alarmed. You aren't nearly as dastardly as I imagined, but you still give me pause."

That made him grin. "If ye keep flirting with me like that, I'm likely to swoon."

Her color deepened, but she only wrapped

173

her hand back around his arm and yanked on him. "I'll keep that in mind," she said.

CHAPTER SEVEN

Aden glanced down at his cue sheet to make another mark by the number four. Only one four remained in the deck now, amid a mix of twenty or so other cards. It made sense to bet against the four, but siding with the bank barely netted a lad enough to stay even. All the sevens remained in the deck, though, which explained why each of the other three men at the table had placed bets on a seven coming up the next winner.

With a sigh he moved his wager to the queen; not as sure a bet, but that made it more interesting. Then he sat back, watching as the dealer turned a seven, making it the loser card, then a deuce. Well, he hadn't lost, anyway.

"Damnation," the bony older man to his left grunted, cradling another pair of chips in his hand before placing them on the rectangle marked HIGH CARD.

"Do ye reckon that's enough to keep ye

175

entertained, Crowley, or would ye rather have me buy ye a beer?" Aden asked, leaving his chips where they were.

Generally, he excelled at faro. Generally, he didn't require a cue sheet to remember which cards had been dealt and which remained with the dealer. But then tonight he wasn't playing because he enjoyed it. He was playing because a lass with big brown eyes and a dislike for his kind had asked him for a favor, and he'd decided he'd met his bride. Somehow that had sent him out hunting for a man who looked like a great vulture.

Crowley chuckled. "A beer's the most profit I'll see tonight. Buy me a beer, MacTaggert. Hell, if you buy me two of 'em I'll be back in the black."

"You can't leave in the middle of a game," grumbled one of the other players, a diminutive, shrewlike man who went by the name of Basker.

Aden stood. "I'm nae leaving. I'm shifting over to a table where I can keep my eyes on ye. Ye keep my wager on the queen."

"And I'll be watching you, too, Basker. Clintock, he'll steal your whiskers if you blink your eyes."

The wee man scowled more blackly. "As

if anyone would want that tangle of gray fuzz."

Hiding his impatience, Aden waited while the two men baited each other, then followed Crowley to a scratched, stained hardwood table a few feet away. The Round Cow tavern was his fourth stop on a long, frustrating evening, and unless he could get some useful information from Crowley, it wouldn't be his last.

"I've seen you here and there for a few weeks now," Crowley said, as two full mugs splashed onto the table and Aden flipped a shilling at the barkeep. "Never seen you use a cue sheet before. Or waste your time on three-shilling games."

Aden shrugged, unsurprised that Crowley had noticed. Gamblers — fair ones, anyway — were reasonably observant. And Crowley, he'd discovered a fortnight ago, had good reason to like figures and to be proficient with wagering. "A friend recommended using the sheet. I dunnae think it's worthwhile, though, especially with the other lads at the table looking over my shoulder at it to place their own wagers."

"Is that why you mismarked four of the cards?"

With a grin, Aden lifted his mug. Amusing himself had seemed the best way to

177

endure the evening, and having a bit of fun with the cue sheet masked the fact that he was having the damnedest time keeping his mind on task tonight. "If they cannae count on their own, it's nae my fault."

"But if they lose, it's not to you. It's to the bank."

"I'm only here for the fun of it."

That made the old man snort. "Fun would be Jezebel's, where all the dealers are pretty young women and they don't top off the beer with water from the Thames. Or so I've heard. That place is too rich for my blood, never mind that my Mary would wallop me if she found out I'd been there."

"Aye. Jezebel's is a sight to behold. I cannae argue with that." He'd been to that particular gaming den a handful of times. The play was good, but the establishment made money mostly because its members were so distracted by the lasses only one in ten of them even knew which cards they were holding. The mix of disdain and lust wafting off the men of the upper classes as they beheld lasses for whom they generally wouldn't spare a second glance on the street was fascinating, but he preferred stiffer competition.

"How are you finding London then, MacTaggert? The rumor is that you and your brothers have been ordered to find English brides."

"We have been. My younger brother, Niall, found himself one already. Coll and I are more stubborn." Aden took another sip of the weak, tasteless beer. "You wouldnae happen to know any likely lasses, would you?"

Crowley chuckled. "Not a one whose papa doesn't work for a living."

"Ye have any bairns yerself? Ye're a banker, aye?"

"I am. For the past thirty years. And yes, I have a daughter. She's been married for eight years now, to a butcher who sees us with a nice fat pork roast twice a month and who's given me two grandsons."

"I reckon I might marry a lass if she came with a good pork roast." Swirling the beer in its tin mug, he set a thoughtful look on his face. "I'm acquainted with more than one lad who lost his fortune at wagering. With ye being a banker, ye must have seen that from behind the desk, aye?"

The banker's expression sobered. "I have, at that."

"And yet ye wager, yerself."

"There's a reason I spend most of my wagering time at establishments like the Round Cow, my boy. I may not win much, but I don't lose much, either. Believe me, some of the stories I hear from men, young and old, who've just sold their last bit of property, or who bring other, harder men with them to the bank and simply sign over horses, carriages, houses — if I ever lose more than a pound in one evening, I take my leave."

"Ye're a wise man, Crowley. There's the other side too, though, the harder lads who willnae forgive a debt made at a weak moment. Do ye see the same ones over and over, coming to collect their winnings?"

"I have seen several of them more than once," the banker admitted, his comically forlorn gaze lowering to his empty mug.

Aden signaled for another pair of beers. "I've heard of one lad, nae here in London for long, who's leaving naught but destruction in his wake. Looks like a hawk or a vulture or someaught, and likes to wear a naval captain's uniform. Ye run across him? I'd like to know where I shouldnae be."

"I have seen him. Distinctive-looking fellow. He and a round man, a Lord Something or other, came into the Bank of England a few weeks ago. I'm generally in the back doing paperwork, but I felt the need for a cup of tea. Have no idea what they were doing there, but the younger man, the round one, looked decidedly . . . unhappy."

The round lad would be Lord George Humphries. So either Vale enjoyed tagging along while his blackmail victims did their banking, or Lord George had given the captain blunt in addition to claiming him as a cousin. Aden wasn't certain yet if that was a useful bit of information, but it was damned interesting, anyway. "Ye've nae seen him gaming, though?"

Crowley snorted. "My boy, I play for shillings. This hawk fellow and I do not move in the same circles. I did see him walking in the direction of Boodle's a week or so ago." He sent Aden an assessing glance. "You're a viscount's brother, are you not? You would likely have better luck than I would at finding him — or if you mean to avoid him as you said, you're doing so quite well by being here."

The banker had realized that this wasn't a casual conversation, then. Aden had been fairly certain that Crowley and Vale did not travel in the same circles, though, or he would have approached the banker more cautiously. Sometimes finding someone who knew *about* a man was more useful than finding someone who *knew* a man. A certain distance lent itself to honesty. Taking an-

181

other swallow of horrid beer, he shrugged. "I like a challenge," he said with a half grin.

"I may not have sat across a table from this man, MacTaggert," the banker said, lowering his voice and leaning forward a little over the table, "but I do have ears, and I do cross paths with the occasional lordling such as yourself. I don't know you well, but you seem like a decent fellow. This other man, this captain, though . . . Well, you might be wiser keeping your distance . . . as you claim to be doing."

"Highlander, you've lost your four shillings," wee Basker chortled. "And so've you, you damned cross patch."

"That would be me," Crowley commented, finishing off his beer and rising. "Time to call it an evening. My Mary will be expecting me home anyway."

Aden had spent some time reading through Grose's *Dictionary of the Vulgar Tongue,* and it had proved to be invaluable at interpreting what the blue devil most of these Sassenach were talking about. He'd have to look up "cross patch" again, but he was fairly certain it meant peevish — and would better describe Basker than Crowley.

He finished off his beer and left the tavern, as well. From the church bells it was just past midnight, still early for partygoers and gamblers, but he clearly wasn't going to find what he sought in the cheap taverns and inns on the fringes of Mayfair and Knightsbridge. If he wanted to learn how Vale played, who he targeted, which games he favored, he needed to get closer before he was ready to sit across the table from the man. And that meant true gentlemen's clubs — places where his father had vowed never to set foot even if they would have him. Places Coll would detest, with all the pretty lordlings pretending to be consequential.

How, then, did a Highlander with blue blood but no high-ranking English relations of the male persuasion manage to get through the doors of Boodle's or White's or Brooks's club?

He blew out his breath, which fogged in the chill night air. Slipping in and out of places suited him. Frequenting ratty gaming hells like the Round Cow barely earned him a glance or two. A club, however, meant introductions, exposure, and speculation. Entanglements. Owing favors. Obligations. Then again, he'd chosen his path. He would set Miranda free so that he could claim her for himself.

Collecting Loki, he patted the chestnut on the withers and swung into the saddle, heading north and east toward Oswell House. It was nearly scandalous to see himself returning this early in the evening, but clearly he wasn't much in the mood for another gambling hell tonight. Not unless he wanted to lose his shirt and kilt because he couldn't pay attention to anything but how damned fetching Miranda Harris had looked earlier, and how something warm and soft had woken in his chest when he'd kissed her. He'd tasted her, and he wanted more. He wanted her.

Like Robert Vale, he'd found a prize he wanted. Unlike Vale, he wasn't willing to ruin lives to steal it. Well, one life, aye. But Robert Vale deserved it.

"There ye are," Coll said, straightening from one of the gateposts as Aden and Loki trotted up to the Oswell House stable.

"Why were ye waiting out here?" Aden asked, swinging out of the saddle and handing the chestnut over to Gavin. "Ye ken I'm nae generally back here till much closer to dawn."

"I had a thought."

Aden lifted an eyebrow. "Well, I can see how that would render ye senseless and send ye out wandering into the dark after midnight, then."

"A clever tongue willnae keep me from

leveling ye, Aden." Coll moved between him and the side entrance of the grand house. "What if we convince Matthew Harris that he doesnae wish to be part of this family? He's young yet, and I imagine if he has any sense, he's half ready to piss himself at the sight of us anyway."

"Ye'd break our sister's heart, then?" Aden returned, regardless of the fact that he could currently end Eloise and Matthew's engagement with half a dozen carefully chosen words.

"If we can convince *him* to break off the engagement, she willnae be blaming us."

"Her heart still gets broken, Coll."

"Ye're suddenly a romantic, then? Did ye get hit in the head?"

"Someaught like that," Aden said. "I've nae wish to marry an English lass at someone else's command," he returned, unable to keep from conjuring a twinkling pair of dark-brown eyes. "But I'd rather reason with Francesca than risk Eloise's heart because I'm nae willing to risk mine."

The viscount blew out his breath. "It's nae about *my* heart. Every damned lass I've met here would blow over in a stiff breeze. I'll nae be hung for murder if I try to kiss one."

"Ye said ye meant to wed one and leave

185

her behind anyway, so what does it matter if the wind or your mighty kiss topples her?"

"I suppose it doesnae, but —"

"Ye've changed yer mind." Aden squinted one eye.

Coll frowned. "Nae. I —"

"Aye, that's it. Ye've seen how doe-eyed Niall and Amy are, and ye ken ye could make do with being in love. A shame, then, that all the London lasses reckon ye're a giant boulder-hurling demon."

"I'm a tall man with shoulders wide enough to hold me up," his brother retorted. "And I'm a Highlander. I could say the same about ye, and lasses arenae running from ye."

"Ye were cruel to Amy on the first night ye met her. I dunnae think she's spoken about it, but there was an entire herd of Sassenach around ye."

"I didnae want to marry Amy. I apologized to her. And she found Niall, so there's nae harm. Hell, we're all living under the same bloody roof." Coll's frown deepened. "Even surrounded by lasses, ye're as far from being married as I am. I smell the cigar smoke and beer on ye. Ye've nae been at some fancy soiree dancing the quadrille. Ye've been at one of yer gaming hells, and there's nae a marriable lass in one of those."

Aden jabbed a finger into his giant of a brother's shoulder. When he was ready to discuss Miranda Harris, he would do so. But that wasn't tonight. "Ye're the one least likely to wed, and so I'll nae be bothering to find a bride until ye've secured one. No sense me ruining my life when ye're going to break the agreement and render us and all of Aldriss destitute."

"One of these days ye're going to clever yerself into someaught ye cannae escape, *bràthair*," Coll muttered. "Ye'll nae be so amused when it's ye on the gallows with a rope tight about yer neck."

"Mm-hm."

They walked into the house through the servants' quarters and the kitchen. Aden paused to request some food be brought up to his bedchamber. Generally, he ate out; at the least he was rarely home while the oven was still warm.

"Coll, have any of the lords here offered to sponsor ye at a club?" he asked, trying to sound just on the near side of bored, as if he were only trying to make conversation.

"Aye, one or two. Matthew's da, Albert, said it would be his pleasure to sponsor me at Boodle's club, or even White's. I turned him down. I reckon I'll be gone from London once and for all by the end of summer, one way or the other. I'm nae keen to make a fool of myself so I can pay to be a member of a place I'm likely nae to see ever again." He paused as the two of them reached the main staircase at the front of the house. "Why do ye ask?"

Aden shrugged. "The play at most of the hells I've found isnae much of a challenge. I just wondered if there were better players in the clubs, and better games to be had."

"Deeper games, ye mean. That's it, aye? Ye're nae happy unless ye're risking yer hide?"

"I like it better when there's half a chance I could lose, and when the prize for winning is more than a copper. I can admit to that."

"Well, I hear the play at some of these clubs is deep enough to drown ye. Thousands of pounds changing hands. Firstly, ye dunnae have thousands of pounds to lose, and secondly, I'm nae sure what would happen if ye discovered there were people better at someaught than ye are out in the world. Ye might have an apoplexy or faint like a Sassenach."

"Ye keep roaring, giant. Me winning a few rolls of the die at hazard might be the only thing keeping Aldriss from falling to pieces, if ye cannae find a wife and the countess cuts us off."

"I could find a damned wife tomorrow. Just nae one I can tolerate. Ye look to yer own impending nuptials, Aden."

I am. "Aye."

Coll was both more clever and less barbaric than what he'd shown so far in London, but he'd begun on the worst foot possible. The Sassenach saw him as a hamfisted suitor, a great bear amid the delicate flowers of Mayfair. It wasn't entirely his fault, but the big man had a stubborn streak a mile wide. Rather than admit that he'd felt angry and trapped by the fact that after seventeen years of being as far away from Lady Aldriss as Britain could manage his mother had decided she knew him well enough to select a bride for him, he'd chosen to accept the consequences for his behavior that night at the theater.

His brother headed down the hallway toward the library, but Aden continued up toward the front of the house. Reading, billiards, cards — none of it held much attraction for him tonight. He needed to think, and he needed to stop imagining Miranda Harris beside him for long enough to figure out how to save her.

On the main staircase's landing Rory stood there in his usual regal pose, a new

189

yellow bonnet replacing the green one the deer had boasted this morning. He knew Eloise had taken to decorating the stag, as well, but unless he was mistaken that bonnet had belonged to Jane Bansil, Amy's cousin and former companion who'd been living with them at Oswell House since she'd aided Niall and Amy's elopement to Scotland.

"That's Jane's, isn't it?" a female voice said smoothly from the top of the stairs.

Cursing silently, he faced his mother as the countess descended the steps to join him on the landing. "That's what I reckon."

"If the girl wasn't so shy, I imagine I could find her a husband by the end of the week." His mother sighed. "At least she's taken with Rory. That's a first step, I suppose. And speaking of marrying, how is your hunt proceeding?"

"If Coll manages to make it down the aisle, I'll throw a flower and marry whichever lass catches it," he said, starting past her.

"No one has caught your heart, then?" she countered. "Miranda Harris, for example?"

As Brògan trotted down the stairs to meet him, he crouched and scratched the spaniel behind the ears. "I reckon there are two lasses in England who've caught my heart. That's enough for any man."

"Ah. I assume you're referring to your sister and your dog, there. But then you've declared that Brògan is a male, so perhaps you're referring to Jane Bansil? My, that would be something."

"Dunnae ye try matching me with that lass. She's got courage, aye, but if I look at her the wrong way it'll likely kill her."

"I would have to agree with that. You might have included me in your list, though. I am your mother."

Straightening again, Aden faced the diminutive countess. "Ye helped Niall, so ye've won him over. I'm nae as bighearted. Or peace-minded. I recall the fights ye had with Da, and I definitely remember ye nae sending any letters in seventeen years."

"I di . . ." She trailed off. "As you will then, my wild son. The agreement stands. Find yourself an English bride. I will help you if I can. You need only ask."

With a nod Aden turned up the stairs, Brògan on his heels. As he reached the second floor, though, he turned around. He didn't want her damned assistance, but he had a partner out there, and finding excuses to see her and speak to her was complicated at best. "Have ye considered having the

Harris family over here for dinner? We've all met by now, I reckon, but nae officially. Especially with Mrs. Harris and Miranda being gone from London until last week."

Francesca tilted Rory's bonnet forward a little. "That is a splendid idea. Tomorrow might do; it's very short notice, but there are no soirees of which I'm aware. You will attend, then?"

"I'll attend. For Eloise's sake." That sounded brotherly, even if it wasn't his sister's face refusing to leave his thoughts.

It wasn't just Miranda he wanted — needed — to see. He needed to speak to one of the Harris men. Miranda could teach him about being a gentleman, little as he cared about that, but she couldn't get him into Boodle's club. This Season in London, which he'd imagined would be torture ending in a disastrous union made only to keep Aldriss Park funded, had become something else entirely. Something enticing and hopeful and centered on a young lady with a great deal of sense and a very large problem not of her own making.

For a moment he paused before his bedchamber door. If he'd been a young, poetry-minded whelp he likely would be contemplating riding over to Harris House, climbing through a window, and finding

Miranda's room so he could satisfy this annoying, arousing need to be with her.

Even practical, and at seven-and-twenty not so very young, it tempted him mightily. Squaring his shoulders, he opened his door and went inside, the dog rushing in between his legs to jump on his bed. He and Miranda had a partnership, an agreement. And when he saw her tomorrow, he wanted to be able to give her more than a tale about how Vale followed his victims to the bank to collect his earnings.

Ideally, he wanted to tell her that the villain was gone, never to be seen or heard from again. Short of that, he wanted to have a plan, something she could feel safe with, something that could actually set her free. And not just because they were partners.

The maid dragged the hairbrush through a tangle of Miranda's hair. Then she did it again.

"Millie, please!" Miranda said, wincing. "I have no wish to be bald."

"Oh! Oh, I'm so sorry, Miss Miranda. I just can't help — he . . ." She leaned down, putting her mouth next to Miranda's ear. "He kissed you," she whispered, "and now you're to see him again tonight. Your mother said that Lady Aldriss said that the dinner was his idea."

Miranda glanced toward her bedchamber door even though she knew for a fact it was closed. Catching her maid's gaze in the dressing table mirror, she put on a deliberate frown. "You've been on about this for nearly a day now. Once and for all, Aden MacTaggert did not kiss me," she stated.

"But —"

"He plays games," she cut in, pushing away the memory, the eruption of heat and desire when he'd kissed her, the sensation of odd, heightened excitement she'd felt when she'd dared to kiss him back. "He wanted to see if I would remain in his little game," she said aloud.

"But he offered a partnership, and you agreed."

"Because I didn't want him to be able to walk away if he decided this was all too difficult for him," she returned, though even as she said it she had to admit that she couldn't see him backing away from anything. "Now we are aiding each other. It makes much more sense."

Millie resumed brushing. "As you say, then." From the maid's tightly compressed lips, upturned at the corners, she didn't believe a word of it.

Her skepticism made sense, because Miranda wasn't all that certain what the kiss had actually meant, either. It had felt electric, and she was still clubbing herself on the head for giving in to that surprising jumble of emotion and sensation and kissing him back.

Her supposition could well be correct, after all, and Aden had begun looking for a way to make a swift exit before he had to risk anything more than his time. That kiss said something else entirely, but then he was proficient at shuttering his thoughts.

She hadn't been able to come up with a reason he continued even to offer his advice, except for his statement that he liked her more than she liked him. Him asking for instruction about how to navigate London had eased her mind somewhat; heaven knew he hadn't demonstrated much in the way of propriety in the short time she'd known him. He'd actually admitted, aloud, to a desire to read *The Adventures of Tom Jones,* for heaven's sake.

This bargain made their partnership feel . . . more like a partnership. Like it didn't rest on him liking her, or on her realizing Aden MacTaggert was much more complicated than she'd thought. At the same time, he'd kissed her. And she'd kissed him, dash it all.

She couldn't stop thinking about it even an entire day later. In a way, though, and completely aside from how worrisome it was, she was grateful for the unexpected gesture; for nearly an entire day that silly kiss had claimed more of her attention than her troubles with Robert Vale.

That couldn't continue, though, because while Aden was confusing and troublesome, Captain Vale terrified her. The idea of Vale kissing her, of him in her bed, made her stomach roil and her head pound. She needed to find a way to escape.

And if that meant making a bargain with the troublesome Aden MacTaggert — and if that bargain kept him from ruining Matthew and Eloise's upcoming nuptials — it was worth it. And it gave her an excuse to have him about without admitting that perhaps he was intriguing. And that his too-long hair suited him. And that of the half a dozen clandestine kisses she'd had in her life, only the last pair had given her goose bumps.

"What if Mr. MacTaggert tries to kiss you again tonight?" Millie asked, setting aside the brush for a pair of silver hair clips. "In order to further test your resolve, I mean."

"I do understand sarcasm, Millie. Please desist. This is to be a family gathering, and he's to be my brother-in-law. Everyone, especially the MacTaggert brothers, will be on their best behavior. Eloise said having them here with her in London is like suddenly adopting three very large, overly protective lions. They adore her. And she'll wish for them to make a good impression. We haven't all met formally until now, Harris and MacTaggert."

"Of course, Miss Miranda. I apologize for being forward. He's just so very . . ." The maid sighed. "Pleasant on the eyes."

Yes, he was that. "And dangerous to everywhere else," Miranda finished. Oh, he had confidence in spades, to borrow a gambling term. But she needed to remind herself at every moment that charm and confidence only meant that it would hurt more when he reached beyond his grasp. Or if he wasn't as skilled as he thought himself. In her experience, no one ever was. "Now, what do you think? Will the silver shawl or the brown one go better with the green?"

"Oh, the silver one, definitely."

"I agree. Will you fetch it for me? I can hear Father rumbling about in the foyer already."

At least Millie hadn't commented on the green gown Miranda had chosen to wear this evening. Yes, it was lovely, trimmed with silver beading and a frivolous and exceedingly delicate silver lace overlaying the emerald skirt, but it was also much more fit for a formal evening of twirling about the dance floor and rubbing shoulders with the grandest of the grand. But if she didn't wear it tonight, she would no doubt be urged by her mother to wear it tomorrow, and she simply didn't want to debut it on an evening when she would be forced to waltz with Captain Vale. This gown wasn't for him.

Squaring her shoulders, she informed Millie that the maid wouldn't be needed until morning. Then she opened her bedchamber door and made her way down to the foyer. "Good evening, Papa," she said with a smile, leaning up to kiss him on the cheek.

"Ah, the one other Harris who knows how to keep time," Albert Harris commented, returning the kiss. "I understand your mother wishing to look her finest, though she always does, but I have no idea what's taking Matthew so long. I believe by now all three of Eloise's brothers have met and threatened to murder him, have they not?"

She laughed. "I believe so. Niall may only have mentioned removing a single limb, though I can't be certain."

He nodded. "It's your first time meeting

all of them together, though. Your mother's as well. Separately they are blunt-speaking in a rather refreshing way. Together they are . . . a force I should be happy not to have to face across a battlefield. And I include Lady Aldriss in that assessment."

Just facing one of them across a table was turning out to be quite tricky enough. "Eloise says they are quite unruly," she put in, shifting to make room as her mother joined them.

"That, they are," Elizabeth Harris agreed with a smile. "But oh, so handsome. Don't you think?"

"Yes," Miranda answered. 'There must be something in the water in Scotland."

"They should bottle it." Her mother narrowed her eyes. "I thought you meant to wear the green silk tomorrow," she said, straightening Miranda's silver necklace and its depiction of a perfect silver rose.

"Yes, but I couldn't help myself. It's so pretty."

"It's also made for dancing. Perhaps I could inquire if Francesca or any of her offspring mean to attend the Darlington ball tomorrow night. If not, you could wear it again. Your father and Matthew and I would certainly keep your secret."

Ah, to own no secret but that of wearing a

dress two nights in a row. "I think Eloise does mean to attend, but Matthew would know that." As she spoke, Miranda turned to look up the stairs.

She had barely set eyes on her brother since he'd handed her over, literally and figuratively, to Captain Vale, and she had more than a hunch that she was the reason he delayed coming downstairs now. His discomfiture was of his own making, and she meant to do nothing to make him feel more comfortable. His idiocy, after all, affected her far more than it did him.

The only good thing at all about it, in fact, had been her unexpected friend, if she could call Aden that. And perhaps a few of her conversations with the Highlander. And that . . . lifting feeling in her heart when he grinned, because that meant he'd figured out something helpful. Her only ally, Aden MacTaggert was, and for that reason could she admit that she looked forward to seeing him again tonight.

A moment later a door slammed upstairs. "On my way," Miranda's brother called. "Couldn't find one of my boots."

As he appeared at the top of the stairs, Miranda abruptly wished her older brother had made up an excuse to be elsewhere. They'd always been close; growing up with only a year separating them had meant interest in ponies, reading, dancing, and the idea of marrying had hit them at nearly the same time. For all of her twenty-three years she had known Matthew to be amiable, good-humored, and well liked. She'd also thought him to be trustworthy, someone who would look after her as she looked after him. Now, though, she felt as if she needed to reexamine her beliefs. Had she merely been lucky on those occasions when he'd steered an unwanted suitor away from her? Or had he been truly on her side until the moment he'd fallen beneath Vale's influence?

She preferred that it be the latter, that he'd been led so far astray so quickly he hadn't even realized he was lost until it was far too late for him to find his way back. But since he wouldn't talk to her, and since the last time he *had* spoken to her he'd actually tried to convince her that Captain Vale would make her a good match, she had no idea what to think.

"We are a fine-looking group," her father said, nodding at the butler as Billings opened the front door for them. "And I have little doubt you'll end the evening with most of your limbs still attached, Matthew."

"Such violent things you say, dear, and

yet I remain amused." Their mother wrapped her arm around Miranda's as they walked outside to climb into the Harris coach. "I've always liked Eloise, but I have to confess that I find her even more delightful knowing she has three mountainous brothers. Two of them yet unmarried."

Matthew's chuckled sounded uneasy, but that might have been Miranda listening too hard. "Haven't you heard, Mama? Mia's taken with a certain naval captain."

"Just as well," her father put in. "I've heard that Aden, the middle brother, has been seen frequenting Jezebel's and other less . . . acclaimed establishments." He banged on the ceiling, and the coach lurched into motion. "Gaming hells. You don't need to become fast friends with him, Matthew, or think that you need to go out wagering with him to earn his respect."

"I know that, Father," Matthew returned, his voice clipped, as he took the rear-facing seat beside Miranda. "He hasn't yet asked me to join him, and I haven't offered."

"Good. If his ship sinks, you don't need to be aboard it. Neither are you to be drilling holes in your own ship."

Her brother shifted in his seat. "I understand the metaphors, Father. I have learned my lesson."

"I believe Aden is also a great reader, though, and that's always attractive in a man." Elizabeth Harris leaned forward to straighten Miranda's skirt. "He was here just the other day, asking after a book Miranda had mentioned to him."

"Yes?" Albert lifted an eyebrow. "Which one was it?"

Blast it all. Miranda cleared her throat. "Someone had spoken of it as a jest, and I commented that we owned one. That's all it was."

Even Matthew looked at her sideways. "But which book was it?"

She sighed. "*Tom Jones.*"

"What?" Elizabeth Harris blushed a bright red.

Matthew burst out laughing. "And you had to fetch it for him?"

"I had no idea we still kept one about," their father mused. "Haven't read it in ages."

"Well, you won't be reading it again," his wife countered. "Good heavens. Tell him he may keep it, Miranda. But quietly. I don't want anyone else knowing we own such risqué things, much less go about lending them to people."

And now she had an excuse to speak to him in private once again. *Tom Jones* was proving to be far more useful than she ever would have expected. Her suddenly speeding heart was only nervous that he'd changed his mind or that he hadn't found anything helpful, she told herself. Not that she looked forward to seeing him. Exchanging a few words with him. Kissing him. "I'll tell him tonight. Don't fret. I think he was only curious."

As they stopped in front of grand Oswell House, Eloise pranced outside to meet them before Smythe the butler could do so. The genuine, obvious affection between her and Matthew was heartwarming — or it had been, before Matthew had decided that selling his sister to a gambler was a better choice than allowing rumors of his debts to end his engagement.

A hand touched Miranda's cheek, and she started. "I'm sorry?"

Her mother's smile faded. "I only asked if you mean to sit out here in the coach all evening. Whatever is wrong, my dear?"

Yanking her scattered thoughts back in, Miranda hurriedly stood and made her way down to the cobblestones. "Nothing's wrong, Mama. I was just daydreaming."

"About anyone in particular? A Highlander? Or a retired naval captain, perhaps? You've always had men in pursuit, but if I'm not mistaken this is the first time you've returned their interest. And two of them at once." Elizabeth Harris grinned, a bit of cheeky amusement in the expression. "You are very nearly scandalous."

"I would like to meet this Vale fellow," her father put in. "He'd best not be too modern to ask my permission for ma—"

"Don't embarrass her, dear," Elizabeth interrupted. "She is cautious with her heart, and I applaud her for being so."

That was her. Cautious with her heart. That was why, even after receiving nearly a dozen marriage proposals over the past five years, she remained single. That one drank too liberally, this one was short, the next one seemed more taken with Matthew than with her, and the one after that . . . She couldn't even remember. More than likely he'd been a gambler. She'd turned away several of those.

Perhaps if she'd been less cautious with her heart, if she'd taken a chance that the man asking her to share a life offered something more than he showed on the surface, she wouldn't be in this mess now. Matthew would be, but she might have been blissfully unaware that he'd ruined himself — and their parents — over a short six weeks. At least until it was too late, because she would have had no action she might take to prevent the disas—

"If ye dunnae pay heed to where yer feet are taking ye," Aden's low brogue came from directly in front of her, "ye may end up somewhere dangerous."

Chapter Eight

Miranda looked up to find that she'd wandered past the Oswell House drawing room doors and on down the hallway halfway to the kitchen. Well behind her noise and laughter emanated already from the large, brightly lit room, but she didn't feel a part of it. The future she faced wasn't anything she could discuss, and it made her resent the happiness of Eloise and Matthew. It wasn't right, and she certainly didn't want to reverse the punishment to hurt them instead of her, but their joy made her pain seem more vivid.

"Lass, did someaught else happen?"

Aden stood to one side of the hallway, his back against the wall and one long leg bent with his boot bottom flat against the hard surface behind him. He was in a kilt again, as if he was determined not to fit in among the so-called Sassenach. "Why haven't you told your family about this mess?" she asked, continuing forward until they stood toe-to-toe and she had to look up to meet his gaze.

"Ye asked me to nae say anything," he returned, not moving.

"You don't know me. In fact, all you *do* know about me is that I don't like you." That wasn't true any longer, but she was making a point. "Why would you do as I ask when your sister's future could well be at stake?"

His eyes narrowed just a little. "I challenged ye to a card trick, and ye guessed it. We have an agree—"

"No. That's not sufficient."

"Ye made a bargain with me. Ye show me how to act more like a Sassenach, and I'll help ye navigate a gambler's mind."

Miranda shook her head. "I am navigating a gambler's mind. Yours. Are you playing a game? Do you mean to dabble in my life, stir up more trouble, and then walk away when you don't see an easy solution? Will you ruin things for Matthew and your sister when you can't snap your fingers and fix everything?"

"I dunnae mean to snap my fingers and surrender, but aye, if I'm nae satisfied that yer brother can be trusted, I will tell the rest of the MacTaggerts what I've learned.

I'll nae risk Eloise."

Down the hallway someone cleared his throat. "I've been sent to ask where you are, Mia," Matthew commented, looking uncomfortable as she turned her gaze to him.

"I'm having a private conversation, Matthew," she snapped. "Tell them . . . I'm discussing literature, and I'll be in shortly."

"I . . . It's not seemly, you know, for you to be out here with a man."

She put her hands on her hips. "Really? It's not? Are you worried over my reputation, brother? Over my future prospects?"

"Mia, don't —"

Miranda took hold of Aden's lapel and, leaning up along his chest, kissed him full on the mouth. *Ha.* That would show Matthew.

Then Aden's mouth softened, molded with hers, and while none of the rest of him moved, she felt encircled, heated, and wanton. Oh, God, he could kiss. Tangling the fingers of her free hand into his lanky hair, she leaned harder against him. Then, before she could decide to sink down onto the floor with him right there in the hallway, she broke the kiss and looked over at her gaping-jawed brother.

"Well? Aren't you going to tell Mother and Father that I'm a wanton harlot or something? No, you won't, because you're far worse. I'll join you shortly." Waving a hand at him, she returned her glare to the clearly amused Aden. "Go away, Matthew. I can look after myself." She jabbed a finger into Aden's hard chest. "And you. Stop laughing."

"I'm nae laughing," he countered, in the same low voice he'd been using since he'd appeared in front of her. "I'm standing here being flayed and burned all at the same time."

Once Matthew had backed down the hall and vanished back into the drawing room, she shook herself. "I apologize for using you to make a point."

"The only thing ye need to apologize for, Miranda, is if ye didnae mean that kiss. Because otherwise I'm feeling fairly magnificent this evening. And that's even with ye flinging yer insults at me, and doubting that I mean to finish what I began."

Oh, yes, she had been doing that, hadn't she? "You are very upsetting to my equilibrium, Aden MacTaggert. I like things to make sense. You don't make sense."

"Why, because I'm a gambler and I'm honest all at the same time?"

"Because I don't think you care about fitting in here at all, and yet you agree to a partnership that balances my entire future against you knowing which fork to use at dinner and are willing to call that an even trade."

"I didnae say it was even," he countered. "I said I'm satisfied with the arrangement. So tell me someaught I need to know about Society, and we can get on with our conversation."

Miranda narrowed her eyes. "You're not fitting in on purpose," she stated. "You cannot wear a kilt to proper functions and not expect people to look at you sideways. Highlanders, especially, are . . . well, very nearly feared in some quarters, even now."

"Good."

"No, it's not good. You claim to be looking for a bride. A young lady needs her father's permission — and likely her mother's — to wed. A father-in-law doesn't wish to be frightened of his son-in-law. Or intimidated by him."

"Och. Mayhap I'll find an orphan lass, then."

"You are so exasperating!" she exclaimed, thudding a fist against his chest and trying to set aside the thought that she might as well have been trying to beat a stone wall into submission. "Why is this satisfactory to you? I will not allow my future to rest on

211

someone who thinks I'm a hobby to tease and toy with until something more interesting comes along."

He pushed away from the wall and straightened. She was tall for a woman, she knew, but he still managed to loom over her. "If ye dunnae wish my help, Miranda," he murmured, "tell me so. But between ye and me I've nae done a thing for ye to keep insulting me. I ken that ye came to me because ye reckoned I'm the same sort of villain as Vale. I'm telling ye now, again, that I'm nae a villain."

His words made sense, but knowing that didn't ease the heat rising through her, the feeling that she needed to do something — anything — to stop the sensation that her life was completely out of her own control. "I have to point out that a villain would say precisely that."

He tilted his head, his dark, wavy hair falling across one gray-green eye. "Ye're the one who's taken to conspiring with gamblers, carrying secrets, and looking for a way to outwit someone to whom yer brother owes a legitimate debt."

"Are you actually suggesting that I'm in the wrong?"

A slow smile touched his mouth, and her breath caught. Damn him, anyway. No man had the right to be this . . . devilish and look so damned handsome. "I'm nae suggesting. I'm . . . supposing that ye dunnae hate gamblers because yer brother lost a horse. It's more, and I'd like to know what it is."

And he'd surprised her again. "We don't talk about it," she said, trying for a dismissive tone.

" 'We'? A family matter, then. Someone who got in over his head, and the rest of ye had to pay for it, I reckon."

Whatever second she'd spent thinking this Highlander had more bravado than brains had been seriously misguided. His insight was ridiculously keen, to the point he could likely draw blood. Miranda looked at him for another few heartbeats. She'd already trusted him with her reputation, and that was beginning to seem quite possibly the smartest thing she'd ever done.

"My uncle, John Temple, lost everything. The man who held his debt declined to take away the family home, but insisted that Uncle John repay him. The last I heard of my uncle, he was somewhere in America attempting to make his fortune. My parents are paying the taxes for his house, to support my aunt Beatrice and her two little girls. And that is why I don't like gambling.

Or gamblers."

He tilted his head a little. "I dunnae know yer uncle, lass. I didnae take his money. I didnae send him to a club or put cards in his hand. Or is it ye worry that every man who picks up cards *is* yer uncle? If I had a lass and bairns at home, I'd nae be risking my fortune on luck."

"So you say."

"Och. Ye're nae so above it all, yerself, Miranda Harris. When ye were getting answers out of Vale, ye liked the idea that he didnae ken what ye were about, didnae? Ye like the idea that ye're planning to outsmart the bastard."

Was he intimating that she liked the risk of it all? *Humph.* "You're mistaken. I don't like being in this situation at all, and I don't like that while you've tasked me with finding out more about Captain Vale, I have no idea what good that will do me. All I do know is that I absolutely do not want to marry him."

"I dunnae want ye to marry him, either." He shrugged. "Mayhap it's that simple."

She looked at him for a swift moment. Nothing was simple where Aden MacTaggert was concerned. And yet he hadn't even blinked at learning about Uncle John. Whatever he did want from her, he didn't seem to mind carrying her secrets. And she continued to trust him with them, for some blasted reason. "So you only want me to be free from Vale's machinations? You have no stake in —"

Cupping her face in his hands, he kissed her. She thought her attempt at kissing him had been bold, but this . . . Heat speared through her, sparking along the inside of her scalp until she felt scalded to her bones. Oh, good heavens she wanted . . . *this*. Whatever it was, she wanted it. Digging her fingers into his shoulders, she leaned up along his taut body to kiss him back.

He moved her backward until her spine bumped against the opposite wall of the hallway. Lips, teeth, tongue, nipping, sucking, the parts of her that could still think wondered if she could be consumed entirely. If it all felt this . . . electric, she wanted to be devoured. She wanted to climb inside him, feel him all around her, wild and wanton and desperate for his touch.

When he moved one hand over to fumble at the door beside her, she moaned, shoving at his shoulders. "No."

Aden made a sound deep in his chest, then took half a step backward. Leaning his forehead against hers, he shifted his hands to her shoulders. "As ye say," he murmured, "but I'm going to require a minute before I'm presentable again."

She required a few moments, herself. "Is this because you like me?" she asked, still holding on to his shoulders. "Is that why you're helping?"

With a chuckle he kissed her forehead and straightened. "It's nae because I *dis*like ye, ye sharp-tongued lass. Ye've been stepping closer to a dark place where candles gutter and men wager their lives on a turn of the cards. Where a man sees a way to get someaught he's always wanted and doesnae care whether his wishes coincide with anyone else's or nae. Where yer daytime Sassenach rules dunnae apply."

"But I don't want to be there."

He cocked his head a little, something that might have been disappointment crossing his gaze, but so swiftly that she couldn't be certain she hadn't imagined it. "Are ye certain of that? It doesnae appeal to ye that ye could be the one to decide which rules ye want to follow, and that it's nae but yer own wits that might win or lose the night for ye? Do ye reckon that your polite rules are keeping Vale awake at might?"

Miranda hadn't looked at her dilemma that way before. Matthew, and Uncle John — could it be that they simply hadn't

216

understood the rules? That didn't explain everything, and it seemed like something a gambler would say, but at the same time she had to acknowledge that Vale played by his own set of rules, and she'd been playing by Society's. Rules she hadn't made for herself. Of course that gave the captain the advantage. What did it mean, though, playing by her own rules? She still had to function within Society — or she would if she meant for her life to resume as it had previously once they'd dealt with the awful man in the naval uniform.

"Why wouldn't I wish to follow Society's rules and principles?" she asked, half hoping he had an answer for that question. "This is where I live."

"First of all, Society's rules say yer brother lost fifty thousand pounds, so ye're to abide by whatever terms he and Vale settled on. It says yer parents arenae to be distressed, and there cannae be a scandal, so ye're to marry the bastard and pretend to be happy for the rest of yer life."

That was a bit simplistic, but it also felt . . . true. She'd seen her share of unhappy marriages where the couple clearly detested each other but stayed together because of convention or because one side or the other had a benefit in doing so.

"I can't run away."

"Lass, I'm nae suggesting ye go anywhere. I'm wondering whether ye're willing to get a wee bit muddy — dirty — to rid yerself of Robert Vale." He shrugged, his gaze lowering to her mouth in a way that made her insides heat all over again. "What I'm suggesting is that ye might find ye like doing things yer own way."

She knew he wasn't just talking about her dilemma with Vale. Miranda swallowed. "And you would be willing to show me this . . . dark side? To be my guide, as it were?"

That smile touched his mouth again. "Aye. I'd be willing to be yer guide through the darkness. And ye can guide me through the light. Mayhap we'll each of us learn something of value."

Oh, just thinking about this conversation was going to keep her awake for the next hundred nights. "I still don't think that makes this an equal partnership. And I can't pay you, but when Matthew and Eloise marry, we will be brother and sister of a sort. If —"

"I will end this partnership if ye ever call me yer brother ever again," he interrupted, scowling. "Ye ken I want ye. Say someaught about that before we take one more step."

For a Highlander barbarian gambler, Aden MacTaggert seemed to have quite a wide streak of . . . honor running through him. "If I asked you to stop kissing and flirting with me, you would do so?"

He drew himself up a bit straighter, seeming to retreat from her in more than just physical distance. "Aye," he said, his voice flat and toneless.

"And you would continue to aid me?"

"I gave ye my damned word, Miranda. I couldnae call myself a man if I didnae keep it."

"Let's go join our families then, shall we?" She willed herself to release her grip on him and turned up the hallway.

His hand closed on her shoulder, stopping her forward progress as effectively as a wall. "Are ye asking me, then? To stop?"

Blowing out her breath, trying to appear more courageous than she felt, Miranda faced him. "I believe I've made it clear that I am proficient at saying what I mean. Oh, and if anyone asks what we were discussing, my mother is mortified that we owned a copy of *Tom Jones* for you to borrow, and I've secretly given it to you and told you never to mention that it came from the Harris household."

His fingers tightened momentarily on her

shoulder, and then his warm mouth brushed against the nape of her neck. "Ye may just undo me, lass. I look forward to that."

In a breathless, terrifyingly giddy sort of way, so did she.

Something over the past hour had tilted sideways. Perhaps Miranda's kiss, when she'd stomped up and put her mouth on his just to make a point to her brother, had addled his brain. Because she hadn't said she liked him, and she hadn't said that she didn't, and yet if he'd been a man who sang a tune, he would have been singing. Aden kept up his light banter with Mrs. Harris while the conundrum of the woman's daughter continued slowly to drive him mad.

He did feel like he'd been unleashed to a degree. Miranda understood that appealing to Vale's honor, or relying on hope that the captain would act counter to his own self-interest, was as useful as a cat herding sheep. Her sense of propriety had all but assured Vale of a victory. She couldn't do anything with the confines of polite Society to stop him.

Now, though, she'd realized that they might well have to resort to doing something — several somethings — that Society would consider underhanded. And in theory, at least, she seemed willing to step out of her rosy, comfortable, proper life and help do what needed to be done. Whatever that happened to be.

That meant he needed a plan now other than simply being visible to Vale and perhaps sparking a few questions. He needed to be a threat. A large one. Luckily, he came by that fairly naturally. When the conversation in the room dropped for a moment, he sat forward. "Mr. Harris, Coll says ye offered to sponsor him at Boodle's. I wonder if ye might do that for me, since Coll willnae ever be civilized enough to walk through the doors of a gentlemen's club."

"I've nae reason to dispute that," Coll stated.

Aden had asked a favor of Harris, a marquis's grandson, in a way no true Sassenach gentleman would do, but being presumed to be a Scottish clod with no sense of propriety had served him well on several occasions now. Sometimes being precisely what other people expected was the most useful thing a lad could do. If Miranda wished to instruct him on proper etiquette later, well, he had no objection to that.

Albert Harris took a drink of brandy and

smiled. "I would be honored. I'm meeting some friends there for luncheon tomorrow, in fact. You're welcome to join us."

And that was how a blackguard used other people's good manners to get what he wanted. Except that in this instance he was working toward being heroic, for the sake of a sharp-tongued damsel in distress who had just more or less intimated that he was welcome to continue paying her attentions. Ones that at the very least included kissing.

Aden nodded. "Thank ye. What time shall I come by?"

"Ah. I'll come by Oswell House with my coach at one o'clock, shall I? And . . . dress is proper daytime attire."

"He means ye cannae wear a kilt," Coll supplied with a chuckle, clearly amused by such blatant Englishness.

"I ken what he means," Aden said aloud. "And I ken how to dress like a Sassenach."

"I wish I could go see that," his sister, Eloise, commented, grinning. "A MacTaggert at Boodle's. Good heavens, White's could be next."

Aden didn't care which club it was, except that the stories he'd heard put Captain Vale at Boodle's. Once he had a way to gain entry there, he could attack from two points — personal, and business. Because for Vale gambling would be a business.

Previously he'd disliked the man on general principle; ruining Matthew Harris in order to dig his claws into Miranda Harris and take what he wanted of her life like a flea on a dog was just despicable. Now, though, with desire for the lass running hot and thick through him, he didn't want any other man panting after her for any bloody reason. Aye, he wanted her for himself, and damn any man who got in his way.

Knowing that she'd shied away from him because of her uncle actually reassured him a little. The family had been bitten twice, and there he came, looking like another dog. Except that the MacTaggerts didn't breed dogs. They bred wolves.

"I nearly forgot to ask you, Francesca," Mrs. Harris said as Miranda walked over to sit beside her mother — and directly across from Aden — "are you attending the Darlington ball tomorrow night?"

That was the party where Vale had already demanded two dances with Miranda. Aden had no idea whether his mother would be attending, or if any of her sons had been included in the invitation. He needed a way into that ball.

He looked at Miranda as she laughed at something Amelia-Rose — Amy — said, a comment about the delight in suddenly becoming part of a large family. *His* family, which had grown larger by three lasses in the past six weeks. Seventeen years ago, he'd lost a mother and a bairn of a sister, and now he had them again, along with a wife for Niall. He adored Eloise, all lace and giggles and an immediate understanding of how to wind her brothers about her wee finger, but Francesca he still didn't trust. If he allowed himself to be hurt by her again, it would be his own fault.

Miranda's dusky hair, bound up at the back, flowed free at the ends in a symphony of riotous curls that swayed and bounced as she turned her head. Long lashes framed dark-brown eyes that hid most traces of the dilemma facing her, far more than he would have expected from a proper English lass. But then he seemed to have been favored with more insight into her character than even her dearest friends. And he liked what he'd been permitted to see, liked that she trusted him even if it had been because she considered him more villain than hero.

Aye, he had a mind to marry her. What he wanted to do with her in the meantime damned well didn't seem heroic. Just because she hadn't caught him gazing at the curve of her hips and the swell of generous breasts beneath the low-cut neckline she favored in her pretty gowns didn't mean he hadn't been looking, hadn't been imagining his hands stroking her in all the places that fancy green silk didn't dare hug too closely.

But he was the elusive MacTaggert. No one knew where, exactly, he might be at any given time. He left a lass satisfied, but not certain whether he ever meant to come calling again. His brothers could guess at, but were frequently wrong about, who or what had his interest at any given time. Anything else made him feel like an insect on the end of a collector's pin — exposed, categorized, and finished.

Whatever he'd decided in his own mind, if he stood up with Miranda in public, if he pushed himself into an argument with Vale over her, there wouldn't be any slipping away. He would be declaring to his entire damned meddling family that he'd set himself after her, that she was the one. If she disagreed with that, which seemed likely despite her eagerness to kiss him in the shadows, everyone would know he'd made a play for her and failed. Miranda was the one with the established reputation in Society, after all, which was why Vale required her hand in marriage.

Arms wrapped around his shoulders from

behind, and Eloise leaned around the back of his chair to kiss him on the cheek. "Stop staring at Miranda," she whispered at the same time. "I thought you two might suit, but it turns out she has a beau."

"Dunnae wager any money on the captain," he muttered back, hiding his deep breath.

"Are you serious? Or are you jesting with me again?" his sister demanded sotto voce.

"The answer to one of yer questions is aye. Ye figure out which one."

"Aden."

"Go away, ye wee elf."

Aden turned his gaze to a potted plant. *Bloody Saint Andrew.* He'd been worrying over how trapped into his decision or whim or flight of fancy he might be if he danced with Miranda over another man's objections. Apparently, he couldn't even refrain from staring at her, and lustfully enough that his younger sister, lovestruck and planning her own nuptials, had noticed it.

What the devil was he doing? Miranda had asked him for a damned favor, for a bit of insight into a blackguard. It had taken a single sentence from her to make him understand that she was not a lass to be trifled with. She was a lady, and he couldn't bed her without ruining her. If he stepped onto that ballroom floor tomorrow, it would be with the idea of forever. He knew that, but after the Darlington ball, everyone else would know, as well. Miranda would know for certain. No more teasing about his motivations.

Generally, the faintest whiff of forever sent him fleeing into the night, as it had with Alice Hardy and her postcoital cloying. He glared at the potted plant, willing the familiar loathing, the imagined years ahead when he would be consumed with regret, boredom, and dissatisfaction, but the palm fronds remained unmoved. His heart remained . . . not hopeful, because the devil knew he wasn't the sort of lad who relied on hope, or luck — but interested. Excited. Engaged. Things with which he wasn't entirely comfortable. After all, he'd stopped putting faith in the idea that a lass could be trusted with his heart after his mother had fled Aldriss Park when he'd been ten years old.

He risked another glance at Miranda, to find her already looking at him. With a slight smile she turned to reply to something Amy was saying. That movement shook him free from his thoughts a little. After all, he could torture himself into deciding whether he felt trapped by this or not, but ultimately

227

none of that would matter unless she came to the same conclusion. And that, as they said in wagering circles, was not a sure bet.

"Is the gaming that much better at Boodle's?" Coll asked, kicking his great black Fresian, Nuckelavee, into a full gallop. "Worth a herd of nose-in-the-air Sassenach blowing cigar smoke at ye, I mean?"

Aden kept Loki to a trot; Eloise said galloping was perfectly acceptable as long as they stayed on Rotten Row in Hyde Park, especially this early in the day, but he was more in a thinking mood than a galloping-into-hell mood. Or it could be that if he set off at a run, he and Loki wouldn't stop until they reached Scotland. Him, aiming to do heroic deeds to help, and to impress, an English lass.

Coll dragged the stallion back around to circle his brother. "I asked ye why ye're suddenly so keen to be a Sassenach, *bràthair,*" he intoned.

"Ye asked about the gaming, then went flying off like a great bat before I could answer ye," Aden retorted. "But aye, I hear it's better at Boodle's. Less chance of me taking a knife through the gut when I leave the establishment, too."

"That makes sense. And I reckon I need

228

to show better than I have been. I'll go with ye to luncheon."

Bloody Saint Andrew. "Nae, ye willnae."

Coll hefted one slash of an eyebrow. "And why is that? What are ye up to?"

"I'm nae up to anything," Aden lied. "Ye'll nae like having to dress for it, or having to make polite conversation, or nae being able to have a drink. And ye ken that already, so I reckon ye've an idea toward making trouble."

The viscount pulled up his horse, blocking Loki. "I dunnae like being here. I dunnae like that I have to find a wife here. And aye, I was damned rude to Niall's lass when I didnae have to be, and now I reckon I'm cursed for it. If *ye* want to fit in here, I'll nae stop ye. I dunnae understand the attraction, but ye're my brother and I want for ye whatever it is that makes ye happy."

"Ye're nae cursed."

Coll snorted. "Ye soak in gossip like a cat in a patch of sunlight, Aden. Are ye trying to tell me ye've nae heard that Niall went behind my back and rescued Amelia-Rose out from beneath my heartless, ham-fisted clutches? I'm nae about to argue otherwise; the devil knows I owe the lass a good turn. But I've become the bogeyman of London, a great lumbering ox with naught between my ears but violence and haggis. And I still need to find a damned wife."

Aden started to retort, but thought better of it. Aside from the fact that it might earn him a fist to the jaw, Coll had begun the trip from Scotland angry, and in the seven weeks since then, that hadn't changed much. "Ye've nae precisely been subtle about looking for a lass with nae a brain in her head. That makes every English lady ye do approach reckon ye're insulting her before ye've ever said a word."

"Aye." With a slight shift of his knees, Coll sent Nuckelavee sidestepping to fall in beside Loki. "The Highlands isnae a subtle place. Nae for me. Everyone in shouting distance of home knows I'm Laird Glendarril, set to be Laird Aldriss when Da turns up his toes. Any lad who wants to prove himself comes at me with fists clenched, and every lass worth marrying has her cap set at me."

Aden had never really thought about it that way, but it made sense. They all liked a good brawl, but Coll had a black eye or bruised knuckles almost weekly. Not even the oldest MacTaggert brother could cause all that trouble on his own. No, it came looking for him, and he met it head-on. "Shouldnae that make it easy for ye to find a lass here? Amy's ma sent her after ye, sight unseen."

"The ones coming after me now are shrivel-hearted and sharp-tongued, pretending to be empty-headed, thinking me empty-headed, and waiting for the first chance to put on my ring and then dance circles around me." He gave an exaggerated shudder.

"Nae to start a fight, but when we came here, we all meant to find lasses we could leave behind in London while we trotted back to the Highlands," Aden ventured. "What does it matter if ye like her or nae, or if she's some title-seeking shrew?"

Coll shrugged. "It shouldnae matter. But Niall seems so bloody happy. And that lass adores him." He took a breath. "I want to do right, I suppose — by me, by her, and by Aldriss Park. I'll be chieftain one day, and we've plenty of cotters and farmers and fishermen and peat cutters relying on me being a good one. A competent, well-bred lass with a good heart by my side doesnae sound so bad, I reckon."

"It sounds bonny." Narrowing his eyes a little, Aden glanced around them. Thanks mostly to giant Nuckelavee and his rider, the Sassenach out riding this morning had given them a wide berth. "Since I ken ye're

231

nae an idiot, why dunnae ye go about convincing the lasses here of the same thing? Go to dances and book readings and dinner parties where ye'll have a chance to converse. Go to the damned theater."

"I'll consider it." Coll slanted him a sideways glance. "As for how ye're spending yer days here, there arenae lasses at Boodle's. And the ones serving drinks at some of yer gaming hells arenae precisely the sort Francesca would approve of." He chuckled. "Though her damned agreement doesnae say a bride cannae be a lightskirt. Only that she has to be English." They reached the end of Rotten Row and swung back around again. "But what I mean to say is, ye'll nae find yer own bride at the places ye've been visiting. And that's why I'm still of a mind to join ye at luncheon today. To figure out what ye're up to."

Aden held secrets that weren't his to divulge. At the same time, after tonight his family would likely be coming up with their own stories to fill in the very large gaps he left. And there remained the very slight chance that he might need some assistance here and there, at least until he figured out how best to be rid of Vale. He pulled in a breath as he mentally crossed his fingers. "Ye cannae go to Boodle's with me because

I've a mind to impress Albert Harris."

"Ye . . ." Coll opened his mouth, then shut it again. "I'll be damned. Miranda Harris." They rode in silence as they reached the next corner and turned east in between the two towering cliffs of stately homes.

"Dunnae be gentle now, giant," Aden said. "We may be in London, but I grew up with ye in the Highlands."

Coll cleared his throat. "She's the one for ye, then? The one lass in London who looked ye in yer soulful eyes and saw yer clever smile and told ye to go to the devil?"

"That's nae got a thing to do with it."

"How so?"

"I've chatted with her since then. She's clever and doesnae detest me as much as ye might think."

The viscount actually laughed. "That's a fine reason for wanting a lass. She only hates ye a wee bit."

Aden reflected that he should have kept his mouth shut, after all. "This is why I did-nae want to say anything to ye, giant. Leave be."

"Aye." Coll narrowed one eye, even his profile amused. "But isnae she nearly be-trothed already? Her ma kept mentioning some navy lad she's mad for."

"I amnae saying anything else. And for a

man who wants to be seen as more subtle, ye tramping yer big feet all over territory that's nae yers doesnae become ye."

Coll slowed Nuckelavee to a walk. "Ye dunnae go into anything blindly, *bràthair*. I know ye. Ye've a plan, a game, and ye're half a dozen moves ahead of everyone else. So convince me ye're nae pretending to have a yen for this lass because she insulted ye and now ye mean to break her heart."

That sounded like him. Aden couldn't deny that. This, though, was different. If he admitted it all to Coll, though, even the part that he worried Miranda was only tolerating him because she needed his help, his brother wouldn't believe it. Him, putting himself in the position of being dragged about by his cock. Him, about to step into the middle of a battle that would likely earn him nothing and where the odds were good that not only would he lose, but the lass would laugh at him even if he won.

"I reckon we'll find out," he said aloud, though Coll's statement was the one thing he already could answer. Because no, he wasn't planning on breaking Miranda's heart. And no, he wasn't pretending that he'd become damned fond of the lass. He'd already become so fond of her that he was apparently willing to risk his own reputa-

tion at the tables in order to save her —
whether she actually liked him in return, or
not.

CHAPTER NINE

Matthew knew Captain Vale had demanded two dances of her this evening. He had to. Otherwise Miranda couldn't explain why her brother had both hovered close by her all through the family's light dinner, and managed at the same time to make certain the two of them were never alone so she could kick him even while they climbed into the coach afterward. It was quite a feat, but she didn't admire it in the least. No, it only added to the throbbing swirl of trepidation, anger, frustration, and dread pounding in her skull. For the first time in her life her brother was not an ally, at a time when she sorely needed a few of those.

"Papa," she said, interrupting her brother's prattling over why Eloise preferred white roses over pink, "you haven't said how your luncheon at Boodle's went today."

Albert Harris, seated opposite her in the cramped coach, rubbed his chin. "Your mother said you were taken with Aden MacTaggert as well as Captain Vale. Very roguish of you, my dear."

"Not Aden," Matthew put in, frowning. "She and Robert are well suited."

She forced a chuckle, even though hearing Vale's name said aloud made her want to vomit. "Come now, Papa. A Highlander practically invited himself to your favorite club, in your company. That is not something that happens every day. I'm perishing of curiosity."

And it happened to be supremely important to her possible escape from that awful hawk-faced man who also frequented the club, at least according to Matthew's ramblings. Because although Aden had done more kissing than talking last night, she gathered that she — and Vale — were the reason for his sudden interest in being admitted to a gentlemen's club. She hoped that was so, anyway.

"Very well. I take your point." Her father grinned. "If you must know, it went quite swimmingly. That Aden has his wits about him. I'd forgotten that Eldridge has holdings in Scotland, but the earl began spouting his poor opinion of cotters and Scottish whisky before we'd even managed to take our seats."

237

"Oh, dear," their mother intoned, shaking her head. "Lord Eldridge is too old to be stomping on the pride of young men. However did Mr. MacTaggert react to being insulted?"

"He lifted one eyebrow and said — in that accent of his — that Eldridge's land must be in the bad part of Scotland, and what a shame that was. The next thing you know, Eldridge is defending his property and the entire countryside." Albert Harris laughed. "If there's one thing a landowner can't tolerate, it's having people think his holdings are no good."

"Hm," Miranda offered, realizing she wasn't at all surprised that Aden had managed to turn the conversation on its head, "no punching at all? The wags must be terribly disappointed."

"More than likely," her father said with a chuckle. "But Eldridge must have been relieved to see Aden brush off the insult like a dog not bothering with a flea. That is to say, you've all met Eldridge. Aden MacTaggert could likely break him in half with one hand while he kept hold of a mug of beer in the other. And still not spill a drop."

"Oh, please, Albert," Elizabeth countered, her own expression amused. "Mr. MacTaggert looks far too poetical to break people in half. It's more likely Lord Eldridge would trip over one of the numerous young ladies swooning over this Aden and bloody his own nose."

Well. Other women might swoon over Aden and his stormy green eyes and his overgrown wavy black hair and that straight, cynical mouth and that strong chin and hard, lean, imposing figure, but they would be risking their virtues if they did so. He was far too clever by half for most of them, anyway.

Miranda took a quick breath, surprised at the dark, squawking raven of her thoughts. She sounded jealous even to herself, and she certainly knew better than that. He might kiss with a heat and intimacy that curled her toes, but she had no idea if she was the only one he was kissing. He'd said he wanted her, but that didn't mean he wasn't going about bedding every female who caught his eye.

It wasn't any of her affair, really, except that he'd promised to help her and that he was nothing like the stereotypical heartless, soulless gambler she'd expected. No one would approve of the idea that her partner's attentions were divided. Miranda nodded to herself. That had some logic to it. She wanted his undivided attention because it would take at least that to extricate her from this mess.

"I'm going to ask Captain Vale to join us for dinner on Sunday," her father announced.

She swallowed down the bile rising in her throat. "That's not . . . Please, Papa. Don't look for things — or encourage things — that aren't even there. We've only just met, you know."

"And what sort of father would I be if I waited until you completely lost your heart before I bothered to meet your beau and decide whether he was worthy of your hand in marriage?"

"Marriage?" she repeated, her voice squeaking. "That is precisely what I mean. Mama, please tell Papa that he's being silly. Don't force an outcome that we have no idea might otherwise be in the offing. For goodness' sake."

Elizabeth Harris narrowed her eyes. "I'm afraid I have to agree with your father in this, Miranda. I want to meet this man and learn his character before hearts are entwined — or broken. We've met Aden MacTaggert, whether you'll admit to liking him or not, so it's only fair we take a gander at your other possible beau."

She would have to do it. She would have

240

to invite Captain Robert Vale to her home, to meet her parents. He would no doubt charm them, much as Aden had charmed her father, and they would be a bit baffled that she, who'd remained single despite numerous offers of marriage, had ultimately chosen such an . . . unspectacular man. Not just his peculiar looks, but he would more than likely work very hard at seeming ordinary. Or as close to that as he could imagine, anyway.

"I'll ask him, if you like," Matthew piped up. "He was my friend first, after all."

If you like him so much, you can have him, Miranda thought, but kept her mouth firmly shut. Nothing positive she said would be believed, because her tongue would blacken and fall out of her mouth if she tried to say anything nice or flirtatious or complimentary about Robert Vale. "Ask him, then," she managed. At least it would be fewer words she needed to speak to the man.

Aden had advised that she be more . . . worldly in her outlook, and it made sense that she couldn't fight Vale's underhanded ways by fluttering her fan at him. But Aden had also said that she might enjoy certain things about living her private life as she chose. That should have appalled her; she'd been raised to be a lady, and was well known to be such. The idea that she could be as cunning and bold as she pleased while the face she showed in public would be the same one she'd always presented, however, had an appeal to it that she'd never expected. Aden had an appeal to him that she'd never expected. Was it as simple as saying that he wasn't like those men who had ruined her uncle and driven her brother into debt — twice, now? Was that logic speaking up, or her heart demanding another excuse to kiss him?

How did one go about being cunning and bold, anyway? She hadn't the faintest idea. If it would aid her in escaping from Captain Vale without publicly ruining herself and her family, she meant to figure it out. "Did you ever learn if Eloise and her family will be attending tonight, Matthew?" she asked, attempting to sound unconcerned.

"She's attending. I didn't think to ask about the rest of them."

"Lady Aldriss told me that she means to at least make an appearance," her mother took up. "She said so after dinner last night. Do none of you listen to polite conversation any longer?"

That must have been during one of the times she'd been lost in thoughts of heated kisses and Aden. "They are a rather raucous group," she put in. "I couldn't hear every bit of every conversation."

"They are a very handsome family as well," Elizabeth countered with a grin. "I'm certain that had nothing to do with your being distracted, though."

Miranda's cheeks heated. "Of course not."

"Then you heard the exchange between myself and Francesca where I invited her and Eloise to join you and me for luncheon in the garden tomorrow?"

"But I have a b—"

"Ladies only," Mrs. Harris broke in, before Matthew could finish. "So go to your boxing match."

Did that mean Captain Vale would be at this boxing match, as well? Miranda would make certain to inform Aden, just in case. That thought led her to more questions — would Aden be in attendance tonight? Now that she'd agreed to learn some of his devious ways, when would he begin instructing her? And how? She swallowed. That statement of his had contained some rather intimate bits, but admitting that those intrigued her would seem both premature and naive. She had other, more pressing troubles that should have been taking up her entire attention.

In addition, she had a task of her own to

perform. They'd made an agreement, after all, and she refused to let it just be lip service, something he'd conjured so she wouldn't feel as vulnerable to his whims as she actually was. And if anyone could stand to learn proper behavior, it was the MacTaggert brothers.

The coach made a turn and stopped, and a moment later a footman in bright-red-and-yellow livery pulled open the door. Her father stepped down and turned around to offer his hand to his wife. "Be cautious, my dears. Evidently the entire Horse Guards has been trooping up and down the street."

Matthew had once said that the success of a ball could be measured in the amount of horse manure covering the street in front of the house. Going by that logic, the Darlington ball was thus far the crush of the Season. Hiking her skirts up to her ankles and deliberately ignoring Matthew's proffered hand, she followed in her mother's careful footsteps.

"Mia, don't be like that," her brother whispered. "Our parents *will* notice."

"Perhaps," she returned in the same tone. "I shall leave it to you to explain why we are at odds."

"I had no choice."

She stopped just short of the doorway and

faced him. "You had a choice seven weeks ago. Now another man owns you. You might consider delaying your wedding, to ensure that he won't also own Eloise. Because while no one defends *me,* you may find that the MacTaggerts don't care about consequences when one of their own is threatened."

The look he gave her spoke volumes. She was to save him, save his impending marriage, save his reputation. He'd had a week to consider, and he still had no better plan than one that would ultimately keep him under Vale's sway for a lifetime. They would be brothers-in-law, after all, if the captain had his way and put a ring on her finger and a shackle around her ankle.

As she considered all of that, the butler announced the Harris family and she found herself ushered into the main ballroom. The Darlingtons had removed the folding wall that divided the ballroom from the music room, doubling the space and creating what amounted to a double-tennis-court-sized ballroom. And though the evening was early and the first dance hadn't yet begun, the room, the surrounding hallways, and the adjoining library and drawing room — now turned into a gaming room — were full to the rafters.

"I'm off to see if Eloise has arrived yet," Matthew declared, and promptly vanished into the crowd.

"What of you, my dear?" her mother asked, taking Miranda's hand. "I imagine we won't see you again until the party is over."

She wanted to stay close by her parents, be the young girl who knew her mother and father would never allow anything to happen to her. But if she remained there, Captain Vale would speak with them when he arrived to claim her for the dance. He'd insinuate how deeply he'd begun to care for her, and he'd say how much he hoped she returned the sentiment.

"Oh, I'll swoop in for a kiss on the cheek now and again," she said aloud, sending them a smile before she did kiss her mother on the cheek and then allowed herself to be swept away into the crowd.

A group of her friends had gathered close by one of the balcony windows, and with a deep breath she headed in their direction. If she could lie to her parents, then she could lie to her friends. If this was Aden's idea of being more free, though, she didn't much like it. Lying to everyone felt exhausting, and supremely taxing. All those different tales to keep straight.

Now that she'd thought about Aden, she looked about to see if he was in attendance. He more than likely would prefer to be at some dark, dirty gaming hell, but Captain Vale was to be here tonight. If Aden meant to help her, she could certainly use some of his wit and guile this evening.

"Ah, Miranda, my dear."

Her spine tightened in a spasm so hard that her back arched a little. However many times she'd thought about how she would feel the next time Captain Robert Vale appeared, the fact of it was that he terrified her. "Captain," she said, and continued walking. Friends, twenty feet in front of her. They couldn't know what was afoot, and a second ago she'd dreaded having to dissemble in front of them, but now their mere presence might aid her.

He drew even with her. "The second dance of the evening is the waltz. I'll have that one, and the following dance. The quadrille."

She kept her gaze on her friends. On silly Helen Turner and her twin brother, Harry. Surely nothing sinister could happen in Helen's presence. "Two dances in a row could invite scandal."

"Then I'll have both waltzes."

"No."

247

"Yes." His left hand grabbed hers, and he placed her fingers over his right forearm. "Both waltzes. That's fitting for a couple falling in love."

"I am much sought-after, Captain. If you take both waltzes, you will earn the animosity of several of my would-be beaux."

"I have very good information that I will triumph over them in my pursuit of you."

"You manipulated my brother into owing you money. Does that truly give you license to be arrogant here?"

His free hand closed over hers. Hard. "I manipulated a great many things to pave a way into Society for myself. Those things I've done give me leave to have you do precisely what I want, when I want. Your supposed beaux who've failed to win you in five years of courting all entered into this game knowing only one of them would win. Even the latecomer Scotsman who thinks he can gamble. That winner is me."

"You're a horrid man. I detest you."

His thin mouth curved into a thin smile. "Do so silently. And smile."

She smiled.

"Hand me your dance card, my dear."

Oh, she wanted to crumble it up and throw it at his head. If she meant to misbehave, though, she wanted to select something more useful than throwing a public tantrum. "Take all the dances," she said, remembering to keep her voice low. "Let everyone see how you're attempting to lead me astray. I'm certain that will make you a very popular guest at highbrow parties."

He glanced at her from beneath the shelf of his brow. "Flail and wail, Miranda. I find it rather intoxicating. You are prey worth capturing. The lone rabbit still flicking its ears in defiance at the wolf."

That made her want to be ill all over again. Avoiding his fingers, she snatched back the dance card and pencil once he'd finished scrawling his name beside the two waltzes. "You're not a wolf," she countered. "You're a vulture."

That earned her a brief, humorless smile. "Either way I shall have my prize. Make yourself available on Friday at noon. You're accepting my invitation to go on a picnic."

Now he wasn't even asking when she might be available. He simply expected her to scuttle her other plans — and of course it would look to the outside world like she was canceling engagements in order to spend more time with him, damn it all. More than anything she wanted to inform him that she was not a lone rabbit, that she had a wolf of her own in the shadows, waiting for an opportunity to strike. That Aden might have come late to this game, but he knew how to win. Aside from the fact that that wouldn't do anything but forewarn Vale, however, firstly she wasn't entirely certain this wolf *was* hers, and secondly she had no idea where he might be this evening.

"You may go," Captain Vale said. "Go tell your friends I'm taking you on a picnic, and how romantic you think it is that I've claimed both waltzes with you tonight."

She would not be doing that. Rather than telling him so, she turned her back and walked away. She had no desire at all to go and lie to her friends about this horrid man and the affection she supposedly felt for him. Nor did she want to go stand beside her parents and have to answer their questions.

Vale's actions had cut her off from friendship, from family. She didn't know if that had been his intention, but if not for Aden she *would* have been that lone rabbit desperately trying to avoid being eaten. As she walked over to the roaring fireplace to pretend to warm her hands, she could admit that she wanted to see him. As . . . challenging as he could be, he made her feel protected. He also made her feel giddy and off-kilter, in a way she could easily see herself craving.

What did that mean, though? They were the definition of incompatible, she and Aden MacTaggert. They agreed about almost nothing. He gambled, frequently. Unlike Vale, Aden didn't seem to care a whit that she had a reputation for propriety and sophistication — in fact, he teased her about it. And while he was clever — remarkably so — cynicism and amusement wouldn't help him navigate the drawing rooms of Mayfair any more than they would help her make her way through the Scottish Highlands.

"Last door on the left down the hallway is for chair storage," a low voice murmured behind her. "Reckon ye can meet me in there in five minutes?"

She nodded, the sudden wish to turn around and look at Aden stronger than she anticipated. He'd come, and so she wasn't alone. She knew something that Vale did not, and for the moment that, and Aden's warm, solid presence at her back, meant everything.

Miranda kept an eye on the gold mantel clock, but only made it to minute three before she turned around and wandered out of the ballroom. It was frightfully easy to slip away; everyone preened and twittered like birds in a bright-colored flock, and no one noticed anyone else except to find fault. She made a point of not exhibiting faults.

The door at the back of the hallway stood closed, but with a quick glance behind her she pushed down on the latch, slipped inside the small room, and shut herself in. She could see thanks to a single candle set on the uppermost chair in a stack of three, while Aden had freed another chair and sat there, ankles crossed, a book across his thighs.

He'd forgone his usual kilt tonight, opting instead for dark-gray trousers, a gray waistcoat with purple and green thistles embroidered across it, and a dark-green coat that deepened the shade of his eyes. Only the simple knot in his cravat gave away that he might not have been born to the blue-blooded English aristocracy.

"Like what ye see, do ye, lass?" he asked, closing the book and setting it aside.

"You look very proper," she offered, her cheeks heating.

Aden climbed to his feet and pulled down another chair, righting it and setting the heavy thing down facing his. "Ye said I shouldnae wear a kilt or I'll frighten all the lasses away."

252

"That's not exactly what I said, but I think you know that."

He answered her with a swift grin. "Did ye see the knots in that Lady Penelope's hair? She'll have to cut them out to be rid of them."

"They're a wig," she returned, taking a seat as he resumed his.

"Aye? She *chose* to look like a hedgehog?"

Miranda's lips twitched as she tried to keep from laughing. "The rumor is that Lady Penelope had to cut off her hair early this spring when a trio of her precious cats decided to have a fight over who got to sleep on her head. I heard that at one point she had two cats hanging in her precious golden locks, both of them trying madly to escape the tangle."

"Ye Sassenach are all mad, so how did that nae become the latest fashion?"

She shrugged. "It's quite difficult to find matching cats, you know."

His short laugh warmed her to her toes. Perhaps they could simply spend the rest of the evening in this storage room, and Captain Vale could go hang himself. That, though, smacked of cowardice, and given that she'd already given Vale a piece of her mind, he might well decide to inform her parents about everything — and that would not bode well for anyone.

"What are we doing in here?" she made herself ask. "I cannot simply hide from that rat."

"I'm here and he's here," Aden replied. "It seemed wise that we should have the same story about why that is."

A shiver ran up her spine. "Aden, I will not have you making a mess simply because you enjoy chaos."

To her surprise, he grinned. "Do I enjoy chaos, then? I'd nae thought of it that way. I suppose I do, a wee bit. Especially when I've caused it."

"Do not cause it tonight." She caught his gaze, determined to stare him down. "My reputation, my family's future, too much is —"

"I'm nae an idiot, Miranda," he cut in, without heat. "And whether ye believe me or nae, I mean to help ye." He sat forward, planting both booted feet flat on the floor. "Have ye told him how ye and I met?"

"Just in general, that you're Eloise's brother."

"That'll do. If ye can avoid mentioning that I wager and that ye detest me, I'd appreciate it."

Miranda frowned. "He already knows that you wager. Matthew, no doubt. And I

254

don't . . . . Our acquaintance has demonstrated to me that I underappreciated several useful aspects of your character."

That earned her another laugh. "Saint Andrew, ye're a stubborn lass," he muttered. "If Vale should ask what ye think of me, how will ye answer?"

"That it's none of his affair."

He cocked his head. "Can ye really tell him that? Or is that only what ye'd like to say?"

"Well, what would you say about me, then?" she countered, folding her arms. For heaven's sake, she might not be able to push at Vale, but she could certainly stand her ground with Aden MacTaggert. He practically demanded that she either do so or flee. And she didn't wish to flee.

"It's nae his affair," Aden said matter-of-factly. "And that *is* what I would say to Vale."

She looked down at the floor, then lifted her gaze to him again. "What would you say to me, then?"

Clever Miranda, never willing to let a chance to flay him go by without comment. What did it say about him, then, that he kept returning for more? Keeping his expression neutral, Aden stood. "I think ye're clever, that ye see far more than ye'd ever speak about in polite company, that ye use yer manners and yer politeness to be a good friend or to be a shield, depending on who ye're with. I think ye're lovely, and elegant, and I want to hear ye laugh more."

Miranda stood up, her movements a little too rushed to be graceful. "What else?" she whispered, closing the short distance between them.

He frowned, deciding he'd picked a poor time to decide he had a conscience. "I reckon I'm nae willing to say more when ye require my help. As we say in wagering circles, ye've got a weak hand, and ye reckon ye need me to win."

"Do they actually say that in wagering circles?" Miranda asked, putting her palms flat against his chest and then sliding them up over his shoulders.

Saint Andrew and all the angels. "If they dunnae, they should. I like ye, lass. A fair amount. For now, that'll have to do."

"Well, I may like you a fair amount, myself," she returned, and lifted up on her toes to touch her lips featherlight to his.

He'd wanted her to know that she wasn't alone here, tonight. He'd meant to do that with words, though kissing and other, more carnal things were never out of his thoughts where Miranda Harris was concerned.

Before she could back away he caught her hips and dragged her harder against him, catching her mouth in a deep, hot kiss.

Aye, he had the advantage in this relationship, and he knew her to be desperate to escape another man's clutches. That should have meant that he couldn't trust her mouth, her kisses, her gazes, her hands, or anything else about her. Because he was aware of all that, though, did kissing her back, wanting her, mean that he could be taking advantage of her? It was damned confusing, and he intensely disliked moral conundrums for that very reason.

Beneath his cynicism he trusted her, trusted that she kissed him now because she did like him, did . . . crave him in the same way he craved her. "Lass," he murmured, pulling away a breath, "ye're scattering my wits about on the floor."

She nodded, her fingers digging into his shoulders. "I'm rather scattered, myself. You did say I might enjoy living a bit more freely, though."

"I'm definitely enjoying that," he commented.

With one last, swift kiss she stepped back out of his arms, and he let her go. It nearly broke him in two, but he let her back away until she'd put a stack of chairs between them. "I need to return to the party."

"Aye. I'll follow ye out shortly." As soon as he apologized to his cock and explained that one of them needed to be patient.

"What are your intentions, Aden MacTaggert?" she asked abruptly.

They were brave words, but he noticed that she didn't move from behind the chairs. "I intend to have ye," he returned, because saying anything else would have been a lie. "Beyond that, I —"

"Stop there," she interrupted. "It gives me something . . . secret to think about tonight. Something Captain Robert Vale can't touch. Something that's just mine."

"It isnae just yers," he countered, clenching his jaw to keep from saying some very flowery things that would leave him too embarrassed to ever allow her to set eyes on him again. "But ye hold it close, use it how ye like. Just ken that it's nae some metaphor, Sassenach."

He heard her slow breath. "I ken that, Highlander. Now come here and make certain you haven't ruined my hair so I can go dance with that . . . bastard."

Aden grinned, both because she wanted him to, and because he admired her courage. "Och, Miranda. Such language. Ye'll make me faint."

"Very unlikely."

One hairpin had come loose, and he carefully pushed it back into place, using the moment to run a finger along her soft cheek before he stepped back again. "Whether ye like me or nae, when Vale asks again what ye think of me, tell him I'm interesting, or unexpected, something that's nae an insult. And if the conversation turns the right way, ye might mention that I've given up wagering, or so I've told ye."

She gazed at him, eyes narrowed suspiciously. "And why am I to make more trouble for myself?"

"Think of it as making trouble for me, lass. If we can divide his attention a little, that'll help us more than it does him."

"What are you pl—"

The fact that she was still in a mood to argue reassured him even as he half pushed her out of the room and shut the door on her. Then he spent the next five minutes pacing while he considered whether he'd gone mad or not, and why that prospect didn't trouble him as much as it would have a few weeks ago. He'd just set her on a course, and that obligated him to take the voyage with her.

Aden stopped pacing. However this had begun, it wasn't a sense of obligation pushing him now. No, he wanted Miranda Harris for himself, and Captain Robert Vale was in his way. One of them needed to go, and he didn't mean for it to be him.

CHAPTER TEN

"Where the devil have ye been?" Coll grunted, hooking an arm around Aden's shoulder and guiding him toward a table laden with cakes and biscuits. "I've near been killed by all the lasses hurtling themselves at me tonight. Ye might have helped me fend them off, or at least divided their attention."

Aden shrugged out of his brother's grip. "Stop fending them off and try dancing with one or two of them," he suggested. "Ye might even find one ye like."

"Dunnae advise me unless ye intend to do that yerself. Ye spend more time with the squinters and fainters than ye do the pretty ones."

"I'm looking for an interesting lass. Doesnae matter where I might find her." Although the most interesting lass he'd ever found would seem to be among the so-called pretty ones, pursued by another man she couldn't afford to reject.

261

Coll snorted. "Ye cannae bamboozle me, *bràthair.* Ye're after information, though where ye put it all, and what ye use it for, I've nae idea. I do see ye've nae pranced over to say hello to Miranda Harris, though. Ye scared of her?"

Not much of the information he'd uncovered would be of use to anyone other than gossips. He simply enjoyed knowing what lay beneath the expensive clothes and polished silver, who had a grudge against whom, which family desperately needed a wealthy daughter to marry into the family, which family's façade of perfection was about to be shredded by a wayward son or daughter. "Aye, terrified."

Not a single one of those interesting conversations, though, had provided him with any news about a family named Vale, and at this moment he would have given a great deal to alter that fact. For Saint Andrew's sake, he didn't even know if Vale was the captain's true name, or if he'd assumed it somewhere along the way to India or back again. At home there would be a minister who would know which man belonged to which family. Here, with churches on nearly every street, he had no idea where he might even begin. Cornwall, he supposed, though he was loath to leave London

— and Miranda — for anything while she remained threatened.

"There's Matthew's sister now," Coll announced unnecessarily, because Aden had had his gaze on her from the moment she walked back into the ballroom.

"Aye," he returned, keeping an eye on her until she'd joined a group of her friends before he pulled from his pocket a dance card he'd pilfered. She'd said Vale had wanted both waltzes, though he'd neglected to ask if he'd actually claimed them. Two waltzes with Miranda seemed a fine idea to him, but he'd heard enough of Eloise's lecturing to know that waltzes were rare and absconding with both of them bordered on scandalous. It also made a statement about possession, which was no doubt what Captain Vale had had in mind.

"Are we supposed to have dance cards as well, now?" Coll asked, scowling. "Ye might have told me that."

"Nae," Aden answered, pocketing his again. "I just wanted to know where the waltzes were."

"Ye dance every dance at these horrors," his brother pressed. "I reckon ye do need a card, so ye dunnae give the same quadrille to two different lasses."

Evidently Viscount Glendarril meant to

stick like honey to him tonight, which wouldn't be at all convenient. Aden blew out his breath and gestured the big man closer. "When we arrived in London, ye had yer back up, and ye made a mistake or two. And now ye're tiptoeing about like ye're worried ye're going to break someaught. Th—"

"Ye might consider yer next words carefully, Aden." Coll hadn't moved, but Aden knew him well enough to take the warning seriously.

"This is the way I see it," he continued, shifting just a little so he could see his brother's hands from the edge of his gaze. If fists appeared, he was going to have to decide whether to dodge or take the hit. "Ye had lasses throwing themselves at ye in Scotland. The only difference was, it was home. Ye knew who they were, and ye knew what to say, who ye could bed, and who ye shouldnae even cast yer eyes upon."

"Aye," Coll said, his eyes still narrowed. "So far ye're making sense. What of it?"

"So use yer imagination. Ye're a man with a title, bound for a grander one. Ye'll be a chieftain of clan Ross one day. Ye've a damned fine estate in the north, and nae a one of those lasses needs to know ye're only marrying to keep it funded. As far as they ken, ye're marrying at yer mother's request, which makes ye a dutiful son. All the Sassenach reckon we're savages and they dunnae expect perfect manners or that ye can even read. That gives ye a step up right there. Ye're nae ill featured, and if ye do spy a lass who interests ye, the odds are that she'll want ye right back. Pretend ye're still in the Highlands, at a grand party, and ye're on the hunt. Just be . . . Coll MacTaggert. He's a fine man, and I'm proud to know him."

"I'm nae a fine man. I'm a rugged man. I know my way about a tavern, and a woman. I dunnae like the way everyone talks behind their lacy fans or their hands here, trying to be fancy and looking down their damned beaks at anyone who willnae play their game."

"That's what I'm telling ye. Play *yer* game. Then at least if ye dunnae find a lass, it willnae be because ye didnae try. Could be even Francesca might excuse ye, then."

"I bloody well hope so." Still grumbling, Coll clapped Aden on the shoulder, his way of showing appreciation, before he stalked off toward a group of young females.

Aden might have spent a moment reflecting that a miracle had occurred, except that the hawk-faced Captain Robert Vale appeared from the direction of the gaming room. If he didn't care about the consequences, it would have been fucking tempting to go punch the man in the face until his nose took on a more flattering shape. But he did care about the consequences, because they affected Miranda. And so he watched.

When Matthew made his appearance from some nondescript hallway, Aden was fairly certain Eloise's betrothed had been in the gaming room as well, and didn't want his family to find him out. Harris could pretend whatever he pleased, but this damned wagering needed to stop. If it didn't, Aden would have to stop the wedding, and that would upend everything — including his own plans.

He liberated a glass of wine from a passing footman, then slipped into the crowd to arrive beside Matthew Harris. "There ye are," he said with a nod. "I've a question for ye."

"What is it? I'm on my way to claim Eloise for the country dance."

"Yer sister," Aden went on, matching Matthew's pace. "She's a fine lass."

He could practically feel the abrupt tension roll down his companion's spine in response to what should have been a mildly interesting comment. Matthew had already proved willing — reluctantly or not — to use his sister to protect his own reputation. Whatever he said next would play very heavily into how Aden proceeded from there.

"Mia?" Matthew returned. "She has a beau, I think."

"Some naval captain," Aden said dismissively. "I reckon I'm willing to take my chances. What do ye think, though? She's a stubborn woman, and I'd appreciate it if ye'd put in a good word for me."

"I . . . try to stay away from Miranda's business," her brother put in, his words clipped and clearly chosen very carefully. "And she dislikes wagering, so I'm not certain I could honestly vouch for you."

"She dislikes wagering, but I hear ye still make the odd bet, aye?"

Matthew Harris's face grayed. "No, I don't. Not for some time."

"Ah. So the rumors I've been hearing are all lies, then? That ye and this Captain Vale play deep, and ye've gotten in over yer head?"

"I — You cannot —" Coming to an ungraceful stop, Matthew clamped his mouth shut. "You aren't from here, so I'll overlook the . . . insult to my character, but here in London we generally do not barge into

267

other people's private affairs."

Hm. He hadn't lied about it, at least. Not yet, anyway. Aden nodded. "I'll give ye my apology, then. And ye're right; I'm nae from here. I'm from the Highlands, from clan Ross. That's a place where family and honor mean everything. Where if a lad needs help, he says so, and his clan does whatever needs doing. Even if it gets bloody." He caught Matthew's gaze and held it. "Eloise says ye're to be her husband. That makes ye my *bràthair* — my brother. So if ye need someaught, ye tell me."

"That's very nice, Aden, but I assure you that I don't —"

"I told ye a truth. Now ye nod to show ye understand what I said," Aden interrupted. "We dunnae lie to each other, so when ye decide ye want to say someaught to me, ye make damned certain it's the truth. Aye?"

The younger man swallowed, then gave a stiff nod. "Aye."

"Good. Now go dance with my sister. Ye ken where to find me if ye've a need to chat. And I do expect that we will be chatting."

There. Aden watched as Matthew hesitated again, then hurried away into the crowd. He'd put the lad on notice, but hopefully hadn't said enough that young Mr. Harris would feel the need to wag his tongue to Captain Vale. Or he wouldn't feel the need, yet. After tonight that might just change.

Once Miranda partnered with some pretty lad from her large circle of friends, Aden made himself go pluck a wallflower and coax her onto the floor. Captain Vale hadn't noticed his presence yet tonight, but when he did so Aden meant to give him a great deal to think about. That meant doing things a bit different than he generally did them. Subtlety had its place, but it wasn't here, and it wasn't tonight.

"Give me yer name, lass," he said with a smile, taking the hand of the thin, pale young lady he'd selected.

"Regina," she answered, her high-pitched voice a near whisper. "Regina Halston."

"Good evening to ye then, Miss Halston. I'm Aden MacTaggert." Inclining his head, he moved them into position in one of the circles of other guests.

"Yes, I know. You danced with my cousin earlier this Season. She talks of almost no one else."

That caught his attention. "Who might yer cousin be?"

"Alice Hardy. I daresay seeing us together now will make her quite jealous." Regina gave a brief, painfully tepid smile. "I know she's a widow and we should be generous-minded, but she hogs all of the attention she can manage. She even says the two of you are practically betrothed."

Bloody hell. "I reckon she can think what she likes, and I'll do the same. We may nae agree on all the points, though."

The music began, and he bowed as she curtsied before they all joined hands and twirled about in their circle. Miranda did the same halfway across the room in another group, with Eloise and Matthew in yet another cluster of dancers. When he spied Coll also there, in the company of a wee blond lass, he nearly lost his footing and fell onto the floor. The two of them together looked like a giant and a bairn's doll, but at least his older brother was making an attempt to socialize.

He tried to keep his attention on what he was doing, but every time he took Regina's fingers or twirled her about it wasn't her hand he wanted to be holding, her cheeks turning a fine rose that he wanted to see. Someone had said once that the best lies were those based on the truth. If so, telling Matthew he found Miranda to be a fine lass had to be the best yarn in the history of knitting. He wanted her. He craved her. Just bloody talking to her aroused him. And if telling her to embrace the darker side of things hadn't been purely for her own benefit, he could only hope he would be forgiven.

Away from the polished dance floor stood Captain Vale, his gaze shifting between Miranda and the elderly Duke of Dunhurst, who sat close by the fire in the company of half a dozen other high-ranking lords. Those were the men by whom Vale wanted to be accepted, the men from whom he wanted recognition and undoubtedly admiration. And the captain didn't dare approach them now, because they would ignore him. No, he needed Miranda Harris first, needed her politically minded father to make introductions on behalf of his new son-in-law, needed her smile and her charm and her reputation to wrap around him so he could steal it for himself.

It was likely a nice dream for a falcon-faced man with no sense of humor and no prospects of his own, but Aden meant to see that it never came to fruition. Not for anything. Not even if Miranda decided she didn't want either of them. This all would have been easier if he'd fallen for a stupid, malleable woman — but if she'd been stupid and malleable, he wouldn't be imagining a lifetime of waking up beside her.

The moment the dance ended he escorted a blushing Regina Halston back to her tittering friends, sent a quick glance about for her troublesome cousin, then headed directly for where his brother Niall and his bride, Amy, stood feeding each other bits of cheese.

"The two of ye are sweeter than a lump of sugar, ye ken," he grumbled, and caught his younger brother by the shoulder. "If ye can manage it, ask a dance of Miranda Harris tonight," he whispered.

Niall's light-green eyes widened. "Is that who ye've been circling?" he returned in the same tone. "Ye —"

"I dunnae want a conversation," Aden cut in, already moving on to find Coll. "Do it."

"Aye. But we're having a chat later."

Coll had maneuvered himself into a large circle of lasses currently asking him to say their names in his so-called charming brogue. "Mary," he drawled, emphasizing the "r" sound.

Good God. At least Coll had found a way to be less intimidating to the females of London. "Coll, ask a dance of Miranda Harris tonight," he muttered, leaning in to keep his voice low.

"Aye, if ye're sincere about her. Nae, if ye're playing another game," the viscount

272

rumbled.

Aden stopped his retreat. It *was* a game, but not one he was playing with Miranda. "I'm sincere," he said.

"I've a few more questions before I believe ye, but I'll do as ye ask."

So now he'd backed himself into an interrogation with both brothers. If that was the price for their assistance tonight, he'd pay it. The next dance, though, was the first waltz. And however little he'd dared tell Miranda about it, thanks to Vale's arrogance in claiming both waltzes this evening, he had a plan.

Keeping his attention split between Vale and Miranda, he maneuvered around the edges of the room until only a small crowd stood between him and her. Saint Andrew she was lovely, in a deep-blue gown that glittered in the candlelight and bordered the deep neckline and short, puffy sleeves in matching blue lace. It was deceptively simple — the strategically scattered glass beads sewn throughout the gown were wee and likely very expensive, the effect subtle and eye-catching all at the same time.

Vale approached, and, snatching up a glass of something from someone who was looking elsewhere, Aden moved in just ahead of him. "Miranda," he drawled, inclining his head, knowing Vale would see her face, the abrupt flush to her cheeks, "I've been looking for ye."

"Mr. MacTaggert," she returned, dipping a shallow curtsy and pretending they were barely acquainted as her eyes demanded to know if this was the plan he'd been concocting. "I hadn't thought to see you here tonight."

"Och, yer brother and my sister cannae be parted. Someone has to keep an eye on them. I'm happy to have the excuse to set eyes on ye again, though. Will ye waltz with me, bonny lass?"

"I —"

"She's spoken for," the vulture's flat voice announced from behind him.

Aden turned around. At second glance his assessment of Captain Robert Vale didn't alter; the man had the countenance of a raptor, deep-set brown-amber eyes, and a straight, thin-lipped mouth currently showing just the slightest hint of closed-mouth annoyance. Since like any proficient gambler he would have read every second of the expression on Miranda's face, the frown would be for good reason.

"Ye again, Vane?" Aden asked, deepening his brogue just a wee bit. That was him, a mannerless, overbearing Highlander. "I thought ye'd have flown off to roost by now."

"Captain Robert *Vale,*" Vale returned, pointing out that he had a position of responsibility in the world and should therefore be respected. "This is my waltz."

Aden turned his back on the man. "That so, lass? Ye gave the first waltz to Vale, here?"

Miranda's eyes narrowed just a little as he silently urged her to play along. "Yes, I'm afraid so, Aden. He asked first."

Good lass. "He," not *the captain* or *Robert,* while he, the interloper, received the honor of having his given name used. "Fair is fair then, I reckon," he returned. "I've nae a mind to go the entire evening with nae a dance, though, so save me a spot, if ye dunnae —"

The music for the waltz began, thankfully before he ran out of nonsense to prattle on about. He shot a glance at the orchestra for effect, then hesitated a second before he moved out of Vale's way. For the moment this was up to Miranda — and to a lesser extent, her damned brother.

If that was the totality of Aden's plan to be rid of Captain Vale, he'd failed rather spectacularly. Attempting to claim a dance? As Vale put her hand over his forearm and led her into the center of the ballroom floor, Miranda risked a glance at Aden.

Generally, he made an appearance and then vanished into the nearest gaming room until required again. Tonight, however, he remained at the edge of the dance floor, a thoughtful expression on his lean face and his gaze on . . . her. He wasn't being at all subtle, or clever, and she had no idea what to make of it.

"I told you to be rid of him," Vale said stiffly, facing her and placing one cool hand on her hip.

She hated when he touched her. Stifling a shudder, she put her free hand on his shoulder. "I couldn't very well tell him we would never suit when he hasn't suggested that we would." Just because Aden had mentioned a few things she might choose to say about him, it didn't mean she meant to simply volunteer everything. As the Highlander had pointed out previously, if she made things too easy, the captain would become suspicious.

"And yet he seems to think you *would* suit, or he wouldn't be dogging your heels. I told you to do something about him. The fact that you haven't turned him away does not put me in a jolly mood."

"While I don't give a single damn about

your mood, Captain," she returned, picking her words carefully as she spoke, "that is one of the MacTaggert brothers. Eloise's brothers. My soon-to-be in-laws."

"And your point is?"

"Avoiding him, or speaking cruelly to him for no reason, would come back to me, and to my parents. He's practically family."

Vale lifted an overhanging brow. "He's also a gambler, you know. You dislike gambling. And gamblers."

For a moment it felt odd to have someone else quoting her own strictures to her, but she knew Matthew had already told Captain Vale about his own gambling misfortunes, and about those of Uncle John Temple. If Vale's plan was simply to remind her that she disliked gamblers, though, it seemed like a fairly pitiful one. The larger question she wanted answered was how Aden had known this conversation would come up in the first place. It was off-putting, almost. And yet it also provided proof that she'd sought out the perfect man to assist her.

"I said, 'you dislike gamblers,'" the captain repeated. "What is your response?"

Don't give up your information too easily, she repeated to herself. "How am I supposed to respond? You're correct. I dislike gamblers."

"Aden MacTaggert is a gambler."

She shook her head. "You are a gambler. Aden MacTaggert *was* a gambler," she corrected, sending up a silent prayer that Aden knew what he was about. Vale thought himself the smartest, cleverest man in the room, and yet Aden had guessed very nearly the exact words of his conversation. Twice. "He's given it up."

They waltzed in silence for a moment. "For you, I assume?"

"What do you care?"

"I don't. But several weeks ago, your brother said you had no serious suitors, which causes me to ask when, precisely, he declared himself?"

"Well, I'm sorry if your spy was so occupied with his own betrothal that he missed me smiling at someone, but unless you've had a change of heart and my happiness matters to you, I don't imagine it signifies."

"It does not."

"Then don't speak of it again."

The lying exhausted her. She never would have thought prevaricating took so much effort. At the same time, it felt . . . powerful. Robert Vale played by his own rules, so why the devil couldn't she do the same? Especially if it tipped the odds ever so slightly against him. But the horrible man continued to gaze at her, so she kept her expression angry rather than smug.

She had little enough reason to feel smug, anyway. If she'd sent Vale in the correct direction, she'd perhaps given herself and Aden the very slightest chance of getting in a blow. That didn't mean she'd won the war, or the battle.

"You will turn him away," Vale said again, sending a glance in Aden's direction.

"I asked you n—"

"You and I will marry for love. At least as far as everyone else is concerned. Another suitor, some interloping Highlander or not, puts the lie to that story. I won't have it."

Oh, he wouldn't have it, would he? More than anything she wanted to step on his toe, shove him to the floor, and tell him that she *would* have it. Miranda took a deep breath. "I will say something to him."

"Before the end of the evening."

"Clearly you know nothing about how people behave in polite Society," she pointed out, just barely keeping her expression neutral when a muscle in his cheek jumped. *Hah.* She'd delivered a blow. Finally. "No one turns away a suitor in public. Much less at a grand ball. Not unless he's committed murder or something."

It was mostly nonsense, of course, but she had to think that Vale wouldn't know that. He needed her to join Society, so he hadn't been in Society until now. At least that had become her theory. She hoped she was correct.

"You tried to keep something from me. I don't like that. Do not do it again."

Miranda lowered her head. She needed to watch her tongue; Vale was not Aden, and he wouldn't respond with humor or mere exasperation. Vale could hurt her — and her family — if he chose to do so. "I won't apologize," she hedged. The balance between pushing as hard as she could and still being compliant was becoming untenable, but she had no other option at this moment but surrender.

"Smile while you're sulking, then."

She smiled, but didn't mention that the pleasant thought she conjured was him on his arse with a bloody nose. Vale no doubt thought he'd just fended off a very minor threat, an inconvenience, a stone on his well-tended pathway toward Societal acceptance. He had no idea she held on to Aden's words, to the memory of his mouth on hers, like an iron cloak. The captain could jab at her, but while she had Aden MacTaggert on her side none of the blows could do more than sting.

The waltz ended, and she kept the smile on her face as he escorted her off the dance floor. "Get rid of this MacTaggert, or I will," he muttered, releasing her as Eloise and Matthew approached. "Ah, Matthew. And the lovely Lady Eloise," he crooned, his tone perfectly even and respectful. A non-tone, if any such thing existed. No doubt he thought it made him sound charming and reasonable.

"Captain Vale," Eloise said, inclining her head. Then she hopped forward and seized Miranda's hands. "You must come with me. I have questions only you can answer."

Deepening her smile, Miranda allowed herself to be led away from the two men. Thank goodness. A moment or two for her to breathe before she worried over who might claim the next dance. Perhaps Aden w—

"Miss Harris?" a low brogue rumbled from beyond Eloise.

For the barest of seconds she thought it must be Aden, but the voice was a touch lower and didn't have the smooth ease of the middle MacTaggert brother's. As she turned, she found herself looking at a broad chest and a thistle cravat pin. "Lord Glendarril," she said, craning her neck up and then offering a curtsy. "How are you this evening?" They'd barely exchanged a sentence in the two or three times they'd crossed paths, but any distraction tonight was welcome.

"Bonny," he returned. "Do ye have a dance to spare? Nae a country dance; I dunnae like hopping about like a rabbit."

"I . . . Yes. The next quadrille, if you please."

"Aye. Do I have time to fetch myself a whisky?"

"Just."

"Coll," Eloise broke in, her eyes narrowed and her tone a warning.

The large Highlander frowned. "Ye're my wee sister. I'll nae have ye telling me what to do." The corner of his mouth quirked. "And it was a figure of speech, ye ken," he rumbled. "A man doesnae like to say he has a thirst for a dainty pink punch."

His sister chuckled. "By the end of the night the punch may not be so dainty. Be wary, big brother."

"Aye. A man's a fool to trust any of ye Sassenach. Write me down on yer card, lass. Ye've a herd of pretty lads stampeding in this direction. They claim I'm a giant with nae manners, but they trudge about after me, anyway."

Miranda glanced over her shoulder. She wouldn't have termed it a stampede, but a dozen male acquaintances had gathered a safe distance away from the giant Highlander and were sending her hopeful looks. Apparently, Lord Glendarril being granted a dance had signaled that her card wasn't yet full. And thank goodness for that. The only thing worse than dancing with Captain Vale would be standing aside for every other dance with nothing else to think about.

As she wrote down names and smiled, yet another MacTaggert arrived. The youngest brother, Niall — the one who'd eloped to Scotland with Amy Baxter — stepped to the fore and somehow avoided offending the three other young men he'd cut in front of. "I'll wager Coll didnae want a country dance, aye?" he said with a grin.

"No, he didn't. Something about rabbits."

"It's nae about him looking like a rabbit. It's because when he jumps, those about reckon they've felt the earth shaking. I'll take one of 'em, though. I'm more graceful."

Chuckling, she added his name. "I have a suspicion," she said, lowering her voice, "that Aden put you up to this." Why, she had no idea, but she remained grateful, nonetheless.

"Ye're to be part of the family. I reckon we should act like it, aye?"

Miranda's heart leaped nearly out of her chest. A bare second later she realized he meant that she would be the MacTaggerts' sister-in-law once Matthew and Eloise were wed. Of course. *Silly girl.* "Of course."

"How many dances do ye still have free?"

Still smiling, she checked her card. "Not a single one." If someone, Aden, say, had claimed her second waltz instead of it going to Captain Vale, she would have been willing to call this night nearly perfect. Ifs, however, hadn't served her at all well lately.

"Then I'll nae ask ye for another one," Niall returned, nodding as he turned to claim his sister for a quadrille.

So the intent was to fill her dance card. Miranda looked down at it again. Between friends and MacTaggerts they'd accomplished just that. But Aden hadn't taken a dance at all. She glanced up, looking for him. Now that she wanted a word with him, he, of course, was nowhere to be seen.

It made no sense. He'd tried to take a waltz, knowing full well that she was already spoken for. And now, when he'd had a chance to claim one, he'd vanished. Whatever he was up to, she wished he would enlighten her, because this was exceedingly frustrating.

At another time, and in a less public place, she might also have been asking *herself* a few pointed questions. Accepting Aden's continued offer of assistance had been both a relief and a logical thing to do; she'd had no other alternative but surrender to Vale, after all. That, though, didn't explain why Aden MacTaggert had been the first person she'd gone looking for when she'd walked into the Darlington ballroom, and why her heart had practically leaped out of her chest when she'd heard his voice behind her.

She didn't believe in love at first sight. For heaven's sake, she'd been pursued by several exceedingly pleasant-featured young men over the past five years and hadn't fallen for any of them. Aside from that, she'd disliked Aden before she'd ever set eyes on him. Her opinion hadn't been entirely fair, of course, because Aden had never preyed on Matthew and her brother's self-delusional gaming skills, and he'd been up in the Highlands when her uncle John had succumbed.

Now she'd become acquainted with him, and she'd altered her opinion. Not of wagerers in general, but of him in particular. Whatever happened at the end of all this, thus far Aden had been honest, helpful, and toe-curlingly arousing both to her body and to her mind. She couldn't point to the moment when he'd become so . . . necessary to her, but there it was. And that was why she felt disappointed even with a full dance card and very limited chances for Captain Vale to approach her again tonight except for the one additional waltz he'd demanded. She wouldn't be dancing with Aden.

Letting Aden know her thoughts would be a horrid mistake; if he somehow managed to help her then she would owe him a great deal without adding in her feelings and emotions. And he'd already expressed hesitation at the idea he might be taking advantage of her, as if she'd ever allow anyone to do that ever again.

Before she could begin to decipher what the devil was wrong with her, Thomas Dennison returned to claim her for a quadrille. Next was an old-fashioned reel, followed by a very vigorous country dance with the charming Niall MacTaggert. All of the quick-stepping and hopping and turning left her breathless and with a genuine smile.

Then, as she turned to find her next partner, Aden appeared in front of her. "Ye've been a popular lass this evening," he said with a faint grin. "I reckon ye're accustomed to that, though, aye?"

"Generally, yes," she admitted. "I have a large and generous circle of friends. Honestly, though, I'd thought not to do much dancing tonight. I suppose I'm trying to avoid having to explain Captain Vale to my friends."

"Dunnae explain him, then, is my advice," Aden returned. "He doesnae deserve yer lies."

"I agree, which is why I've been avoiding my friends. So why are you trying to see my dance card filled?"

He put his palm on his chest, lifting both eyebrows. "Me?" the very image of innocence queried. "Let me have a gander at this card of yers, then."

Even more suspicious now, she handed it over. Aden perused it, a slight frown furrowing his brow. "Ye've nae a single dance free."

Miranda took back her card. "Why do I have the feeling we're in the middle of a play where you're the only one who knows the lines?"

His expression stilled for half a dozen beats of her heart, which she knew because she counted them. "If I had any assurance at all that ye'd nae punch me in the face, I'd kiss ye right now, in front of all these

Sassenach," he finally said. "I'm sorely tempted as it is."

"Considering that would give me a whole new set of problems in addition to not ridding me of the ones I already have, I think I *would* have to punch you." Of course, for a moment or two she would also have very much enjoyed it — until the moment her entire present and future came crashing down around her ears.

His gaze held hers, gray-green and holding, she decided, far more secrets than he'd yet chosen to disclose to her. "I'm still tempted."

As her cheeks heated, she abruptly realized what this exchange must look like to anyone who might happen to be watching them. "Vale told me to send you away. Are we playing out that conversation in semaphores? You frown, demand my card, I frown, I blush, you turn your serious, soulful gaze on me?"

"I —"

"You might have simply said something," she went on. "But no, you have to set your own stage and put on a play. Do you think I'm completely helpless and lost without your overlarge muscles and brain to come to my half-witted rescue?"

Aden took half a step closer. "What I

think, Miranda, is that ye dunnae like to lie, and ye arenae comfortable with it. If I can put a bit of the weight ye carry on my shoulders, I reckon I'm strong enough to bear it. And to make it clear as glass, partner, I mean to uphold my end of our agreement. If ye dunnae like my methods, or if ye dunnae trust me, find a more righteous man."

CHAPTER ELEVEN

Miranda lifted a hand to touch Aden's cheek. Before she could complete the motion, the setting, the hundred pairs of eyes, crashed back into her thoughts like an unwelcome nest of hornets, and she swiftly lowered her hand again. She couldn't help herself. After the first time he'd kissed her, she'd felt like a moth before a flame. "I trust you," she murmured, clenching her fingers. "But for heaven's sake, don't spare me from unpleasantness. I want to know the steps. I will take them with you."

His gaze searched hers for a moment before he nodded. "Then I'll tell ye Vale's looking at us right now. He's nae happy. If ye tell him that ye tried to be rid of me and I wouldnae take the hint, that would be helpful. Dividing his attention, turning some of it away from ye, is helpful. Now walk away, or he'll reckon ye're as reluctant as I am to part company."

Frowning, she took a step backward, the motion harder than she expected. In his presence she felt . . . not safe, but protected. Turning away from that wasn't pleasant. Or remotely easy. "If you want to avoid people gossiping about how you approached me twice and weren't granted a dance either time, I suggest you go find someone pretty and popular with whom to waltz. Patricia LeMere would suffice, as would Alice Hardy."

Aden narrowed one eye. "I'd rather shave a hungry bear than dance with Alice Hardy," he said, taking two steps away from her and then turning his back.

She nearly went after him. He'd more or less admitted to staging their conversation in order to tell the tale he wanted Vale to see, and he still hadn't promised to tell her what, precisely, he happened to be planning. And she couldn't even claim that it was her own common sense that stopped her. Rather, it was his mountain of a brother, Lord Glendarril, arriving in front of her for the quadrille.

"Ye ready, lass?"

"Yes." She put her hand around his forearm. "Your brother enjoys keeping people in the dark, doesn't he?"

"Aden? Aye. He specializes in nae telling

another soul what he's about," Coll agreed, walking with her onto the dance floor. "Half the time we dunnae ken whether he's even in the house or nae."

A quadrille wasn't the best opportunity for conversation, but it marked a definite improvement over a country dance — and Miranda decided this was an opportunity she couldn't let pass her by. Yes, rumors had set her against Aden before they'd ever met, but Coll was his older brother. If anyone had some insight into a MacTaggert brother it would be another MacTaggert.

"Aden is unreliable, then?" she began as they took their place around one of the five circles of dancers on the floor.

"I didnae say that," the viscount rumbled. "Aden keeps his thoughts and plans to himself, is all." As the music began, he bowed, and she curtsied. "I've nae been in a brawl when he wasnae there to bloody noses alongside me."

In Highlander terms, that was no doubt a high compliment. Her predicament, however, couldn't be solved by punching. "I heard that he once began wagering with a shilling and ended with a horse a day later."

Glendarril swung around behind her and back to the front again. "He didnae wager with the shilling. Our da was making a point about the value of a shilling. Aden wagered him he could *trade* nae but a shilling and end with a fine-quality horse. It took him an entire turn of the sun, but I can swear to it that that shilling became a pot of stew, a basket of trout, a chair, a goat, bagpipes, a sheep, some things I cannae remember, a pair of coos, and then Loki. And that chestnut is a damn fine animal. Aden's been riding him for three years, now."

Miranda did two turns about the circle as she pondered that bit of information. The very thing she'd flung at his face when they'd first met, the incident she'd seized on as proof that Aden was a deep-playing gambler and therefore untrustworthy, had only peripherally been about wagering. And he'd never bothered to correct her.

If circumstance hadn't forced her to seek out his help, she would more than likely have seen him at a few family dinners, at Matthew and Eloise's wedding, and nothing else. After all, he'd come to London expressly to find a bride. That was what he would have been spending his time doing, what he *should* be doing now. Tonight. And she would be nearly betrothed to Captain Robert Vale.

While the question of what he thought he was doing about his own matrimony while he found vacant rooms in which the two of them could meet and kiss sparked another set of imaginings entirely, she pushed them aside for later contemplation. Her plate at this moment was far too full for flights of fancy. If they were flights of fancy. If he was who she wanted.

As she pranced around her circle of dancers again, she caught sight of Captain Vale watching her. His expression, a horrid combination of avarice and smugness, chilled her to her heart. Aden wanted her, had told her so, but he'd also made it clear that the ultimate choice would be hers. Vale wouldn't bother with such niceties. He coveted her position in Society, and despite all her comments of disgust — or perhaps because of them — he now apparently coveted *her*. Or at least wanted offspring to carry on his legacy of stolen aristocracy.

The horror of that thought nearly stopped her heart. *Good God.* The thought of him kissing her as Aden did, of him . . . in bed and touching her . . . She shivered.

"Ye well, lass?" Coll MacTaggert asked, taking her hand for one last turn through the circle. "Ye've got a gray caste to ye."

"I'm fine," she lied, reaching for a smile. "Just a bit warm."

"Aye. Ye Sassenach think we Scots are

mad, but I reckon I'd be enjoying a cool breeze if I'd worn my damned kilt, tonight."

The ladies on either side of him gasped in almost theatrical unison, but Miranda only smiled. If that was their idea of scandal, which it was, they would fall dead after one glance at her thoughts. Of course, they would probably also find her present situation utterly romantic — a man so obsessed with her and her life that he was willing to stoop to ruining her brother to have her. As for herself, she was more taken with the other man, the one who claimed to find her bonny and desirable, and who had given his word to help her for no other discernible reason than the one he'd stated.

As the quadrille ended, she declined the viscount's offer to escort her to her parents. She knew quite well the waltz was next, and whether her mother and father had decided to invite Captain Vale to dinner or not, the less time they spent in each other's company, the better.

"I cannae leave ye standing here alone," Coll MacTaggert protested, scowling. "I'm nae a gentleman, but I am a man. And a man doesnae abandon a lass in distress."

Her smile flattened before she could catch it. "What in the world makes you think I'm in distress?" she twittered, too brightly. If he'd realized something was amiss, what hope did she have of fooling her friends? Staying away from them had been a wise decision, then, even if it did help Vale by leaving her more isolated. Or rather, making him think she had no allies at a —

"It's time for our waltz, Miranda."

Her back stiffened, her fingers clenching all on their own around Lord Glendarril's substantial forearm. Miranda took a deliberate breath, putting a smile back on her face before she turned to face the captain. "Is it? I lost count of the dances."

She couldn't thumb her nose at him, but that felt nearly as satisfying. Whether he believed or not that she'd been otherwise occupied and hadn't spared him a second thought, she'd made it sound that way. If he wanted to pretend this was a love match, he could damned well pretend to work to earn her pretend affection.

A large hand closed over hers before she could move away. "I reckon now would be a grand time for ye to tell me all about yer brother, before I hand my sister over to him," Lord Glendarril drawled, abruptly more lion than giant lamb.

A second MacTaggert willing to protect her. And from what she'd heard, Coll preferred fists to words. If only she hadn't already convinced herself that seeing Vale bloodied wouldn't solve any of her problems. She took a quick breath. "At our next family dinner, I will regale you with all — or most — of my tales about Matthew." She put her free hand over his large one. "You are waltzing with your sister anyway, I believe."

His green eyes narrowed, but he released her. "That'll do, then. I'll be close about in the event ye change yer mind, lass, and want to regale me now."

Her fellows called the MacTaggerts barbarians, and even Aden had decided he desperately required lessons in proper behavior. But Coll was the only person to realize something was amiss without her having first been told about it. Unless "barbarian" meant attentive to more than just his own appearance and standing, perhaps Society needed to find another adjective for these Highlanders. "Thank you, my lord."

"Miranda?" Vale prompted, holding one hand toward her.

She gave him her fingers. And Aden thought she couldn't hide her feelings. *Ha.* "Of course."

"Be very careful," the captain murmured as they found an open space on the dance

297

floor. "I will not be slighted."

"Only very nearly," she returned, putting on her brightest smile as the orchestra struck up the first note of the waltz.

"If he was anyone of significance, my next act would be to call on your father and explain to him precisely why you and I will be married. It doesn't matter if he knows, because he wouldn't dare tell anyone else."

She snapped her jaw shut over the response she wanted to make. "Eventually I may find you so intolerable that the poorhouse would be preferable to you. Do keep that in mind, Captain V—"

"I'll take the rest of this dance, if ye dunnae mind," Aden said, planting himself squarely in front of them.

Vale actually blinked. "You were supposed to be rid of him."

"I tried," she offered, under her breath.

"I *do* mind, MacTaggert. You're interfering."

"Miranda's dance card is full, and ye're the only man thick enough to claim two dances. Two waltzes, ye muttonhead. I've nae had one. Stand aside."

"I will not." The captain's hand tightened on hers, and he actually started pulling her around the formidably statured Highlander.

"Ye will, unless ye want me to introduce

298

yer arse to this polished floor." His expression still mild, Aden side-stepped to continue blocking their path. All around the floor other couples had to maneuver to avoid them, and Miranda could hear the muttering even over the music.

His narrow jaw clenched, Vale lowered his hands from her and took a step backward. "I won't cause a scene," he said tightly. "Miranda, I will see you Thursday at Harris House for dinner."

"She knows where she's eating," Aden said amiably, stepping up in front of her. "If ye need a reminder for yerself, ye should write it down, Admiral."

Before Miranda could complete the thought that Matthew had succeeded in delivering the invitation for dinner, Aden clasped her hand, placed his other palm on her waist, and drew her into the dance. She dug her fingers into his shoulder until she found her literal and figurative balance again.

"So this is how you put yourself into the middle of this mess," she finally said, torn between delight that she didn't have to dance with Vale any longer tonight, and dismay that Aden had made the captain more angry than she'd previously seen him, and by a good measure.

"Did I do someaught improper?" he asked, lifting an eyebrow. "Ye need to give me some more lessons, I reckon."

The lessons she had in mind had nothing to do with propriety, and she didn't think they had much to do with gratitude, either. The man in whose arms she danced was simply . . . mouthwatering. "Very improper," she returned, "but you sent your brothers to dance with me, so I cannot complain."

With a barely perceptible shrug, he grinned down at her. "Ye like to dance, and ye werenae dancing."

"But you didn't ask for a place on my dance card."

"I had my eye on this one, *boireannach gaisgeil,*" he returned, his voice a low, seductive murmur. "And I couldnae take it unless all the others were claimed."

"You might have said so," she whispered back.

Aden shook his head, his fingers flexing around hers. "Ye're nae one to hide what ye feel, Miranda. I reckoned ye'd be better off if ye were surprised."

"Teach me how to hide my silly feelings, then. I certainly don't want to go about shouting secrets with my eyes."

A grin cracked his expression. "I'll do what I can, but I reckon I like seeing the sunshine in yer smile and the thunder in yer frown."

Whatever disaster had led her to this point, whatever subsequent madness had seized her, nothing had ever made her feel what she felt right now as she waltzed with Aden MacTaggert. If that showed in her eyes, she *would* have to learn to conceal it, because she did not want to give up the sensation. A giddy, breathless excitement, a . . . rush of heat, the desire to always be touching him — if this was simple lust, it was very compelling. "Well, then."

"If I ever do keep someaught from ye, I promise ye now it's only because ye've enough weight on yer shoulders, and I've more practice being . . . evasive."

"So you expect me to trust you?"

His expression stilled. "Aye," he answered slowly. "I'd nae do a thing to cause ye harm. Ever. Ye have my word on that."

She believed him. "You can't expect me not to ask questions."

Aden's eyes crinkled at the corners. "I'd sooner expect my dog to turn into an elephant than I'd expect ye nae to ask questions, lass."

That made her grin in return. He was practically the only man she'd ever met that she couldn't dance circles around, and the only one who simply expected her to keep up with him.

"Whatever it is ye're smiling about now, I hope I'm the cause of it," Aden said in his low brogue, his stormy green gaze holding hers.

She finally had a simple answer to something, because of course he was the cause of her smile. But he wouldn't be the only man looking at her right now. "Even if you were," she returned, "and however angry this dance may be making someone else, I still have an axe against my neck."

His expression cooled just a little, and Miranda abruptly wondered if he hadn't been pondering that very thing. At least he'd put Vale out of her thoughts for a few minutes, but the captain had signed papers in his hands and plans that required a marriage to her, while Aden only spoke about naughty, tantalizing things that sent tingles down her spine.

"I finished reading yer *Tom Jones,*" he said, changing topics with dizzying speed.

"And?" she prompted.

His hand on her waist drew her a breath closer to him. "Ye've a nice selection of books in yer library. I reckon I've a mind to choose another one."

Where was he leading her now? "You're

welcome to come by anytime, of course, as long as you keep in mind that Matthew will likely be telling Vale."

Aden nodded. "I prefer reading at night, when I cannae sleep. Two, three o'clock in the morning ye'll find me awake, reading."

Before she could decipher why he'd decided to regale her with his sleeping schedule, the music rose to a glorious crescendo and then stopped. He held her for an additional few seconds beyond that, then with a visible breath released her to join in the applause.

"I'll see ye to yer parents," he said, offering her a forearm.

"Don't push Captain Vale too far," she returned, hesitating. Dancing with Aden had been one thing; with the way he'd walked into the middle of the waltz, refusing to allow him to cut in would have caused just the stir about which he'd taunted Vale. Even the captain had understood that. This, though, walking about on his arm, she could choose to avoid. And Vale would understand that, too.

"Trust me, lass," Aden murmured. "Take my arm."

"Tell me what that 'gazgeel' thing was you called me earlier."

"Ah. *Boireannach gaisgeil.* It means 'brave

woman.' "

Well. Miranda slid her hand around the dark-gray sleeve of his coat. It would have been lovely to stay that way, touching him and knowing not even Vale would be likely to approach, but it was only a very momentary respite.

Rather than head directly toward the window-surrounded alcove where her parents sat conversing with Aden's mother Lady Aldriss and a handful of other friends, he angled them toward the doorway of the gaming room. As she watched, feeling almost like a spectator in her own play, they crossed directly in front of Robert Vale. The captain narrowed his bird-of-prey eyes, and Aden grinned at him.

"I dunnae care what ye think I should call him, Miranda," Aden drawled, continuing on toward their parents, "the man does look like a damned vulture. I reckon I like my odds."

"What the devil was that, Aden?" she demanded as soon as they were out of earshot. "And why? Why would you de-liber—"

"Who do ye reckon he's plotting against right now?" he interrupted. "Me."

"That's not what I mean." *Men.* "You just declared — out loud — that you're pursuing me. Don't you realize what —"

"Miranda," he countered again, his mouth lifting in a slow smile. "I ken what I just did." He took a breath. "I'm hoping it's made him angry. Even more angry than me butting into his waltz did. Angry men make mistakes."

Either he was playing a game and had just made a wager, or he wanted her to think that. Considering the importance of finding the correct answer to that question, Miranda decided to reserve judgment and wait for further evidence. "Are you hoping he challenges you to a duel or something? You can't make him much angrier without risking fisticuffs."

That made him chuckle. "Fisticuffs sounds dainty. If he tried to flatten me — now, that would be interesting. I want him to be thinking he'd like to grind me into dust, lass. Dunnae lie to him for me. Ye warned me away, ye told me that I'll nae win because Vale has someaught he's holding over Matthew. Tell him that I told ye I like a challenge. Which I do. And which ye are, Miranda."

With that he lowered his arm, evaded his mother as she stood to intercept him, and vanished from the ballroom as if he'd never been there at all. But what he'd done remained. Now everyone knew she had two men courting her. Neither had asked her opinion on the matter, though at least Aden had reason to believe she liked him.

This all felt important and significant, but Aden had put more than simple — relatively simple — affection into play. The captain had set up a very complicated game of chess and had moved all the pieces precisely where he wanted them, and Aden had just sat down opposite Vale and dumped over the table.

He'd set everything in disarray and put Robert Vale's attention squarely on him. She knew she should be relieved that someone else had taken some of the weight from her shoulders, but mostly she felt worried. Aden *had* to be equal to the challenge, because now he'd stood up for her. In a sense he'd tied their fates together, whether by accident or, as she suspected, by design. And since she couldn't afford to lose, neither could he.

Captain Robert Vale watched Aden MacTaggert tilt his head toward Miranda Harris as the two of them spoke, watched Miranda lean in MacTaggert's direction even when she frowned at him. It wasn't a ruse, then. The Highlander was in pursuit, and she liked it. Liked him.

When MacTaggert slipped away into the gaming room, he made a point of avoiding a petite, brown- and gray-haired woman in a very tasteful, and very expensive-looking, burgundy gown. Robert took half a step closer, then turned to find Matthew Harris mooning over his pretty, naive fiancée. "A word," he said, not in the mood to be more polite than that.

Obediently Matthew begged Lady Eloise's forgiveness and left her side. That was what Robert liked to see: someone who knew how to show him the respect he deserved.

"What is it? I've only a minute until the next quadrille."

"Who is the woman seated beside your mother?"

Matthew looked. "That's Eloise's mother. The Countess Glendarril."

"Not 'of' Glendarril?"

"No. It's a Scottish title. 'Of' makes a title sound too English, I supposed. The e—"

"Why would Aden MacTaggert want to avoid his mother?" Robert interrupted, out of patience with the pup's good-natured yapping.

"Lady Glendarril ordered her sons down from Scotland and decreed they should marry proper English wives."

"She 'decreed'? How?"

Frowning, Matthew glanced over his shoulder. "I promised Eloise the quad—"

"Then speak, and you won't have to miss it."

"Everyone says Francesca Oswell-MacTaggert ordered it. She can be quite formidable. I nearly pissed myself when I asked her permission to wed El—"

"I don't care what everyone says, Matthew," Robert cut in again. "There's more to it or you wouldn't be rambling. Eloise told you something, I'd wager, and you will tell me. Now. I'm a busy man."

"She swore me to secrecy."

"Fifty thousand pounds, Matthew. Do not make me keep reminding you."

"When you do, I remind you that once you've married Miranda we'll be even."

"Yes." As even as they could be while one of them held fifty thousand pounds in promissory notes owed by the other. Because the majority of those weren't going anywhere. "Speak."

Matthew blew out his breath, petulant but still compliant. "Lady Glendarril has hold of the purse strings. When she left Scotland she made the earl sign an agreement that the sons had to marry before the daughter, and that they had to take English wives. If any of them fail, she cuts off all funding to Glendarril Park."

Well, now. That was both interesting and potentially extremely useful, though taking advantage of someone already being coerced by someone else could be tricky. "Go dance with Eloise. And then you and I will go somewhere quiet so you can tell me everything you know about Aden MacTaggert."

Matthew hurried away like a dog let off its leash. Still annoyed that everyone in the ballroom had seen him step back and let another man finish a dance he'd begun, Robert considered following MacTaggert into the gaming room and emptying the Highlander's pockets. He had to remind himself that he literally held the winning hand already. The Scotsman could pursue Miranda to his heart's content, and she would still inevitably become Mrs. Robert Vale.

It seemed far more likely that MacTaggert, who fancied himself a gambler, would be the one doing the challenging. Yes, Robert could imagine it now: the Highlander trying to win back Matthew's notes and thus set Miranda free. He allowed himself a slight smile. His weeks of plotting, preceded by years of planning his path into Society's upper reaches, couldn't be upended by some upstart barbarian who knew how to play faro. But watching MacTaggert try, catching him up in his own net, that could be interesting. And owning the brother of a viscount bound for an eventual earldom, even a Scottish one, could be extremely useful.

The clock in the foyer struck three o'clock as Miranda trudged up the stairs to her bedchamber. Kissing her far-too-merry mother and father good night and refusing to be baited into chatting about the two men now publicly pursuing her, she ducked into her room and closed the door.

Her maid slept in the chair set before the guttering hearth, and Miranda gently shook her awake. "Don't apologize," she said over Millie's sleepy-eyed protestations. "I'm dead on my feet, myself. Unbutton me and then go to bed, for heaven's sake. I can manage to pull a few pins from my own hair. I've done it before."

Thank goodness she did have a habit of readying herself for bed after a late night, because tonight she didn't feel up to answering questions about how horrid Vale had been or how relieved she'd felt when Aden had literally swooped in to rescue her, dancing with her so handily that her feet had barely seemed to touch the floor.

Once Millie left for her own bed downstairs, Miranda shrugged out of her pretty blue gown and pulled her much more comfortable cotton night rail over her head. With a sigh she submerged a cloth in the lemon-scented water of the washbasin and scrubbed the scent of cigars and men and sweat from her face and arms and legs.

She wished she could wash away the entirety of Captain Robert Vale as easily. The only good thing about him at all was that his threats had forced her to seek out Aden and look past the skin of the cynical aloof gambler he presented to the world.

A good portion of Mayfair now believed him to be courting her. Or rather, they believed she'd very nearly accepted Captain Vale only to be confronted by another at least as eligible suitor. Yes, she rather liked the heat between her and Aden, the feeling of being just a breath away from the next touch, and the craving for his presence when he was elsewhere. Every silly conversation she had these days she reimagined with Aden, because evidently he didn't care a whit that it was impolite to argue with a lady — and she very much enjoyed the challenge he presented.

Grimacing, she pulled the pins and ribbons from her hair and brushed out the unruly mass. She did like Aden MacTaggert. Quite a lot. The fact that he'd more or less declared himself . . . A slow, delicious shiver traveled down her spine. He might think what she felt was gratitude for a rescue, but for goodness' sake he hadn't rescued her yet.

At that troubling thought she set aside her brush and stood to tiptoe her way across the cold wooden floor so she could crawl beneath the blankets of her absurdly comfortable bed. Now she probably would never fall asleep. Captain Vale held Matthew's notes. As long as he did, any day- or night dreams she had about Aden would be just that — dreams.

It wasn't even a consolation that Aden seemed likely to be awake, as well. He'd made such a row about finishing *Tom Jones* and wanting a new book from the Harris House library and being awake reading at three o'clock in the morning — which he couldn't do without a book, anyway — that she'd begun to think he might be a little soft in the head. None of it made any sense, unless he meant to break into her house and read in her library in the middle of the night, so —

Miranda sat bolt-upright. Had Aden been

telling her precisely that? Was he in her library at this very moment? Was he . . . was he waiting for her? That made much more sense than him suddenly becoming a bed-lamite. Or was she being an idiot and overthinking a simple conversation meant to calm her nerves or something? And *that* made more sense than the brother of a viscount deciding to break into an occupied house for the purpose of bedding the home-owner's daughter.

She swung her legs over the side of the bed and slid her feet into her slippers. If he *was* down there, and if she didn't go look, would he think she'd been kissing him and flirting with him simply to get his assistance? Or worse, would he decide she was stupid for not being able to decipher his abysmally vague clues?

Slipping on her blue dressing robe, Miranda relit the bedside candle with a spill ignited from the fireplace coals. If someone saw her, she didn't want to look like she was sneaking. Being restless and searching for a book to read made perfect sense. She'd done it before, and on multiple occasions.

The candle in one hand, she slipped into the hallway and toward the main staircase. She wasn't trying to be unseen, she reminded herself. Only silent. As far as she knew Matthew hadn't yet returned home, and while she preferred not to run into him at all, at least she had an excuse in mind. Of course, her brother was likely out losing another ten thousand pounds to Captain Vale, but repaying those notes couldn't realistically be a part of any plan, anyway.

Matthew didn't arrive in the foyer as she reached the ground floor and then turned up the wide hallway leading past the library at the back of the house. No one appeared to keep her from going to see if she did indeed have a man waiting for her there in the dark, or if she was just hoping that would be the case.

Blowing out her breath, trying not to look like a wanton hoyden by bursting into the room, she pushed down on the door handle with her free hand.

The door opened silently, thanks to the butler and his obsession with eliminating squeaks. *Thank you, Billings.* Inside the large room the quartet of curtains masking the tall windows stood open, allowing in the light of a fog-dimmed three-quarter yellow moon. Her candle became the only other source of light in the library.

Aden MacTaggert was not in her library reading, at any rate. She felt abruptly ill that she'd put so much faith into such a silly notion, and that she'd wanted so badly for him to be there. And now she hoped he'd never been there at all; if he had been, and he'd left, he would not be thinking well of her.

"If ye mean to stay, lass, come in and close that door."

the door.

CHAPTER TWELVE

The low voice came from directly beside
her. Miranda jumped as Aden eased into
sight around the half-open door. The candle
wavered wildly in her hand, sending nightmare shadows up the walls and along the
floor. Aden caught hold of her hand before
she could drop it and set the entire house
on fire.

Shaking herself, she relinquished the
candle and closed the door behind her. "I
hope you know those were very poor hints
you gave. I nearly fell asleep before I realized you might possibly have been trying
to tell me —"

His mouth closed over hers. The fingers
of his free hand tangled into her loose hair,
the sensation nearly as intimate as the kiss.
Miranda slid her palms over his shoulders
and lifted on her toes, leaning her body
along the long, muscular length of him. He
was there. She hadn't imagined some silly

rendezvous simply because she craved his company. Aden had said he wanted her, but those had just been words. Except that they weren't just words, because this kiss would have most damsels swooning. Even she felt weak in the knees.

Pulling her away from the door, he blew out the candle and set it on an end table. "Those were poor hints, I reckon," he drawled, putting both of his hands on her hips and drawing her up against him again. "But then if ye hadnae come down here I could tell myself I was too cryptic or someaught. I wouldnae have to think ye were just batting yer eyes at me because I'm useful to ye."

She hit him on one shoulder. "I do not bat my eyes at anyone."

"Aye, but someaught about ye pulls at me, Miranda. I've an answer for nearly everything, but I cannae explain ye, or why the day seems brighter and the room warmer when I'm about ye."

That might well be the nicest thing she'd ever heard. He was a cynical, practical man, and yet he very nearly waxed poetical trying to explain how he felt about her. "You *are* useful to me," she stated, meeting his gaze in the moonlit gloom. "You're also infuriating and extremely annoying, with the way you refuse to tell me the details of things but expect me to catch up and go along with whatever it is you're up to."

"Ye're my partner," he returned, as if that explained everything. At her glare, his mouth softened into a grin. "I wouldnae throw things in yer path if I didnae think ye capable of climbing over 'em. Just as I wouldnae be here if ye didnae keep me on my toes."

"If I bored you, you mean?"

"Aye. And I reckon ye wouldnae be down here in yer library if I bored *ye.*" Amusement edged his voice. "But if ye're here tonight because ye do feel obligated, tell me so, Miranda. I'm nae some villain to force myself on ye because ye need an ally." He stopped, frowning. "I gave my word to help ye. That doesnae change, whether ye want me to stay or ye ask me to leave."

"For a man who prefers being called a barbarian to a gentleman," she whispered, trying to fend off the tears abruptly threatening to fill her eyes, "you appear to be rather honorable."

"*Boireannach gaisgeil,* if I were an honorable lad I'd nae be in yer damned library. Because I'm nae here for the conversation, and I'm nae here to plot. I want to take that bonny robe off ye and that damned night

318

rail ye're wearing, and I want to put my hands on ye." He narrowed one eye. "And nae just my hands."

With those same hands splayed around her waist, Miranda didn't doubt he felt her shiver. She could barely keep herself from tearing all his English-style clothes off before he'd even finished speaking. "I don't know what might happen tomorrow or when Captain Vale comes here for dinner on Thursday or at the end of all this," she said, plucking at his simple cravat with her fingers, "but I do know that I mean to have as much say in my life as possible."

"I'd expect nae less of ye, Miranda, and I reckon I like the way ye talk through a problem, but if ye dunnae tell me ye want me in the next minute or two I'm going to have to go climb back out the window behind me and go find myself a lot of drinks."

She snorted. "That's more direct than your usual conversation, Aden."

"Miranda, for God's sake. Say aye." He scowled. "Or say nae. I prefer aye."

"I do want you, Aden, even with the amount of trouble that could cause me. Yes. A —"

Before she could finish saying aye, he lowered his head to kiss her. Her breath, her senses, fled as he yanked her hips against his, their tongue tangling in a heated dance she felt all the way to her bones. Aden might look poetical with his too-long wavy hair and silent observations, but he kissed like a sensual hedonist.

She half expected to be tossed to the ground and ravished, and if that satisfied the keen yearning that had been coursing through her for the past days, she would have not a single objection. Instead he leaned in, tilting up her chin as his lips and tongue dipped to explore her throat, the base of her jaw, every touch sizzling through her like streaks of fire and lightning. She felt raw and naked, and yet neither of them had removed a single stitch of clothing. In the library. Her family's library. Where her father also wandered at night from time to time.

"We can't do this here," she panted, still clinging to his shoulders.

Aden straightened a little. "I'll lock the door," he said, freeing one hand to reach behind her.

"And invite someone to *un*lock it?"

"We could go out to the garden," he suggested, slipping a finger beneath one shoulder of her dressing gown and tugging it down her arm. "I dunnae want ye getting rose thorns in yer arse, though."

She shrugged back into the robe. "I don't want thorns, either." Cupping his face in her hands, feeling the beginnings of whiskers beneath her palms, she kissed him again.

"Miranda, I want ye. But I want all of ye. Leaving ye dressed and lifting yer skirt — that's nae enough for me. Or for ye, I reckon."

No, it wouldn't be. This was about them and trust and need, not about a quick — she assumed — impersonal urge either of them could satisfy with anyone. And given what could well happen later if Aden's ill-explained schemes didn't suffice to rid her and her family of that . . . man whose name she didn't even want to conjure, she wanted tonight to be something she could hold on to later. The memory might have to last her a very long time. An eternity.

Pushing out of the circle of his arms, she caught hold of his hand before he could lock the door. Deep satisfaction sank through her when his fingers curled around hers. She didn't think he was a man who followed anyone else's lead. "Come with me," she whispered, and opened the door with her free hand.

He didn't protest, but allowed her to lead the way out of the library and up the hallway toward the foyer and the main staircase. Lean and athletic as he looked, Aden was still broad-shouldered and over six feet tall. Despite that, it was her slippers she heard on the stairs, her robe rustling in the night's quiet as they climbed to the second floor. For all the noise he made, he might as well have been a shadow.

Upstairs she continued past Matthew's still-empty bedchamber, past the master bedchamber where her parents hopefully slept very soundly, and on to her own doorway. Hardly daring to breathe, she pushed open the door and slipped inside, Aden on her heels.

He closed the door himself and turned the key that rested in the lock. When he faced her again, she wondered what a young lady was supposed to do under the circumstances — offer him a beverage? Lead him to one of the cozy chairs by the fire? Strip off her clothes and lie on the bed? "I —"

In that same heartbeat his arms wrapped around her waist. Her feet left the floor, and she gripped his shoulders as he lifted her into the air. Miranda was fairly certain her feet hadn't been touching the floor, anyway, and the rush of her pulse made her feel giddy and giggly, neither of which she would ever have used to describe herself before.

Then with an apparently effortless flex of his arms, he slowly lowered her until she could catch his upturned mouth again.

They kissed, openmouthed and tongues tangling, every nerve in her body awake and shivery. Aden set her down onto her feet again, then, still kissing her, lifted her up under her shoulders and knees to carry her to the bed. "You're rather strong," she managed, between kisses.

"Ye're lighter than a sheep," he returned, lowering her onto the bed.

"So now you're comparing me to a sheep?"

He snorted. "Nae. I haul sheep about when it's time for shearing. This" — he climbed up over her, using a forefinger to tug down the front of her night rail and lowering his head to kiss her exposed breastbone — "is much more fun."

Her eyes rolled back in her head when his mouth strayed over the mound of her left breast. "Well," she rasped, "I'm glad I'm more fun than sheep shearing."

"Aye," he replied, his voice muffled. "I prefer ye to sheep shearing, a pint of beer at The Thistle — that's the tavern close by Aldriss Park — and a game of vingt-et-un."

"Oh, my, even more fun than wagering?"

He lifted his head to eye her. "If ye still

have enough wind for sarcasm, I'm doing someaught wrong. I'll see to that now, shall I?" Taking the neck of her night rail in both hands, he tore it open all the way down her front. The trio of buttons popped off and plinked onto the floor.

"Aden!" she gasped, then slapped a hand over her mouth too late to hold in the sound.

"Hush, lass. We're being improper," he said, grinning, and bent to take her right breast in his mouth.

Good heavens. He hadn't given her any time to think, but perhaps he'd done that intentionally. She had spent a great deal of time thinking, lately. The sensation of his very capable tongue flicking across her aroused nipple drove everything but want and need out of her mind.

Moaning again, writhing beneath him, she wanted . . . more. Since they were partners, she would take his lead in being — what had he said? — improper. Unable to keep her hands from shaking, she dug her fingers beneath the lapels of his dark gray coat and shoved. Rather obligingly he freed one arm and then the other so she could get it off him and drop it to the floor.

She tugged off his cravat next, while he pulled aside the ragged edges of her night rail, leaving the entire length of her exposed and naked except for a bit of her shoulders and upper arms. Then he reached a hand down to her ankle, slowly sliding his hand up her leg, his fingers drawing toward her inner thighs until they brushed against her *there.* She jumped, but didn't have much time for startlement as his teeth and tongue captured her nipple again.

"I don't think proper men do that at all, Aden," she said shakily, arching her back when his fingers returned to her intimate place and opened her to slide inside. The sensation made her tense, and she fought to keep from clamping her knees together.

"I hope that's nae true, Miranda," his response came, reverberating into her chest. "Because unless ye have an objection, I reckon I'm doing it the right way. Now that I can see and touch all of ye, that is."

He shifted, sitting up to kneel with his thighs on either side of hers. Putting his weight on one hand he leaned over her, dipping the forefinger of his other hand inside her as he did so.

"What do ye think, Miranda?" he murmured, studying her face with an intensity that all in itself made her breathless. "Do ye have any objection?"

His finger inside her curled, pressing . . .

"Oh. *Oh!*" She convulsed around his finger, every inch of her centered on that one touch. Grabbing onto his shirt, she dragged him back down for another kiss. As he obliged, she shakily pulled his long-tailed shirt from his trousers and yanked it up toward his shoulders.

"I'm assuming ye've nae objection, then," he drawled, his voice sounding not quite as composed as she'd become accustomed to hearing. Straightening for a moment, he finished pulling the shirt off over his head and tossed it aside.

"Whatever that . . . was, I want you to do it again."

"That is my intention, lass. But I'm nae going to use my damned finger." Aden tilted his head. "Ye ken?"

That made her look down at the rather impressive bulge straining at the front of his trousers. In the very back of her thoughts she realized, very belatedly, that he still wore his attire from the Darlington ball, that he must have come straight from there to break into her family's house in order to . . . claim her. And she very much wanted to be claimed. She very much wanted it to be someone she liked and respected rather than someone she feared and loathed. Miranda nodded. "I understand."

Turning onto his back beside her, he grabbed off his boots and set them fairly quietly onto the floor beside the bed, before he lifted his hips and started unfastening buttons. "I should've worn a bloody kilt," he grunted. "Whoever invented trousers needs to be hanged by his nethers."

Despite his complaining, he had them down his hips quickly, and kicked them aside as he rolled back onto his hands and knees over her. Long, sinewy ribbons of muscle flexed beneath his skin, hard, strong and warm beneath her questing hands. His great cock and testicles — as her father's well-hidden illustrated anatomy book deemed them — moved large and hot between her thighs.

With one hand he parted her legs further, drawing a bent knee up over his hip. She felt very exposed and very vulnerable, and very, very aroused. This was desire, she realized. This was how it felt to want something so badly she couldn't even speak a coherent word.

"There's pain and there's pleasure, lass," he rumbled, his voice tight. "Much more pleasure, but bear with me, because the pain comes first. And just this once."

She nodded, and he pushed his hips forward. Pausing at her nether lips, he said something in Gaelic and then slid slow and hot and tight inside her. Deeper and deeper he penetrated her, until with a sharp bite he buried himself in her to the hilt.

Miranda squeezed her eyes closed and dug her fingers into his broad back, refusing to utter as much as a squeak. When Aden kissed her forehead, her eyelids, the tip of her nose, and her chin, she opened her eyes again. "I'm fine," she stated, even though she still wasn't quite certain of that.

"Ye're still a terrible liar," he whispered. "I hope ye nae need to ever be otherwise." Running a finger down her cheek, he bent down again, this time kissing her on the mouth.

It took a moment before she wanted to move again. She began by relaxing her fingers, moving her hands from his back to tangle them into his lanky black hair, guiding his mouth back to hers and then down to her throat and lower. With a muffled chuckle he licked and nipped her breasts until she moaned again.

That seemed to unleash him, because he made a low sound and slowly canted his hips away from her and then forward again. Miranda opened her eyes wide, wanting to memorize the exquisite sensation, the weight of his hips on hers as he entered her deeply again, the wanton . . . craving she felt for him.

As he increased his tempo she locked her ankles around his thighs, unable to help panting and mewling like a kitten. And there she lay, on her back with her legs spread, her shredded night rail and her dressing gown still beneath her. One by one she shrugged her arms free, shifting her grip between his shoulders, his back, and his fine, muscular arse as he continued pumping into her. The bed rocked, the footboard bumping against the trunk sitting at its base. Openmouthed kisses, his fingers teasing at her breasts as he rested his weight on his elbows, touching and caressing until she wanted to scream with ecstasy.

She drew taut again inside, her fingers flexing helplessly. Aden kissed her as her entire body shook loose. He thrust fast and hard into her, grunting with a shiver she felt beneath her hands and all the way inside her to her very center.

"Sweet Saint Andrew," he breathed, sliding onto his right side and drawing her left leg up over his hip as he did so.

They lay there for a moment, facing each other, touching but not conjoined. She wished that they were; her skin felt cold where his body didn't cover hers. Her breath came hard and ragged, as if she'd just run all the way from Marathon. Aden panted as well, a fine sheen of sweat on his chest and brow. His right arm lay outstretched beneath her head, his fingers playing idly with her hair and sending goose bumps along her scalp.

"What do ye think of being improper, lass?" he murmured, shifting a little to kiss her again, his caress gentle and intimate and achingly tender.

That kiss alone might have made her fall for him, if she hadn't been halfway there already. Her, with a Highlander. It was nearly as absurd as her marrying a sea captain. These MacTaggerts had upended all of London, and she, for one, found that fascinating. "I would say," she whispered back, "that being improper in private is quite . . . exhilarating."

"That's a grand word for it. Ye do make my heart beat faster, Miranda Grace."

"And how do you know my middle name?" she asked, actually not surprised he'd found it out. She knew his, after all.

"I asked Eloise."

That made her smile. "So did I, Aden Domnhall MacTaggert. She said you and your brothers are all named after Scottish kings of old."

"Aye. Niall Douglas, after James the Black Douglas — because our da thought James sounded too English. Coll has Arthurius, whom I reckon ye know as King Arthur, the lad with the round table. There were at least three Domnhalls, but with the spelling of mine I reckon I'm actually called after my great-great, who was made the first Earl of Aldriss Park by yer Henry the Eighth for agreeing that a man should keep after finding a wife who could bear him a son."

Miranda snorted. "You're teasing me."

"Nae. Ask any MacTaggert, and they'll tell ye the same. But who is Grace to ye, *boireannach gaisgeil*? A mighty queen? A bonny warrior lass?"

Her smile deepened, even as it occurred to her that she'd never thought to have a conversation like this, lying cozily in bed with the man who'd just taken — plundered — her virginity without first being made her husband. "Grace Harris was my father's grandmother. From the stories I've heard she was very fond of cats, and owned at least two dozen of them."

"Aye? Did she ever milk them to make cheeses?"

"Cheeses? Cat milk cheeses? What are you —"

"Och, nae ye mind. I know an old man on

331

our land in the Highlands who makes cat cheeses."

She had no idea whether he was jesting or not. "How does he milk them?"

"I've nae seen it. Coll has, and he says it's a wee bit disturbing." Aden slid his arm around her back, pulling her closer against his chest. "I dunnae want to talk about cats, Miranda. If Vale has any sense at all, he will-nae give ye up, nae out of kindness. I will set ye free from him, lass. I swear it, by Saint Andrew."

Miranda frowned. Did he want her free, or free to be with him? Perhaps that was a silly question under the circumstances, but it mattered to her. "You shouldn't swear something when you can't be certain of the outcome, however noble your intentions."

"Noble, are they?" he returned, cupping one of her breasts. "But that doesnae signify. I swore by Saint Andrew, so that's that. I'd nae be a Highlander if I took back an oath to the patron saint of Scotland."

His touch was making it difficult to con-centrate. "Aden, you've asked me to trust you, and I do. I think I just proved that. But thus far all you've done is let Vale know you're a rival, belittle him in public, and break into my house. None of those things rescue me from his . . . . his dastardly clutches. You could ruin me a hundred times, and while I would certainly enjoy it, my problem remains."

"A hundred times isnae enough."

Her cheeks warmed. "What is your plan? Do you have one? How am I a part of it? What should I be doing? What happens if he arrives on my doorstep tomorrow with a special license from the Archbishop of Canterbury?"

Aden turned onto his back, pulling her up over his chest so they were eye-to-eye, with her looking down at him. "If I had the time, I'd twist Captain Vale about like a windmill, until he didnae ken up from down. But we dunnae have time, so I reckon I'll go at him head-on. I'm nae certain yet of the details, but I've got nearly seventy percent of a plan. And because ye're a horrid liar, my lass, there are parts of it I dunnae wish to tell ye."

"So I'm to put everything into your hands and trust you with my life. With my family's future."

His gaze held hers, no trace of humor in his eyes at all. "I lost a card trick to ye. I made ye a promise. Now I've sworn an oath to ye. I've tasted ye, taken ye, and I'm still here, unwilling to part from ye. So tell me what else ye require of me, Miranda Grace

Harris, and I'll give it to ye." He took a slow breath. "I ken it's all just words, and since I'm being honest, I'll tell ye that I prefer to avoid trouble. I slip away, no one the wiser. And I ken that ye came to find me because ye thought me a villain. Th—"

"I didn't think you were a villain," she interrupted, unwilling to let that pass by without comment. "I thought you were heartless, as all gamblers must be. But I don't think I could like anyone heartless. And I do like you."

That made him grin, before his serious face reappeared. "I hope ye mean that, lass, because I'm nae here for . . ." He paused, a brief frown furrowing his brow. "A gambler's reputation is everything to him. A reputation means when ye sit at a table the other players lose just because they cannae concentrate with either trying to figure ye out, or worrying how much they're about to lose. A reputation is more important than skill, in the end. Ye ken?"

She nodded. Though she wasn't quite certain what his point might be, the information felt . . . invaluable. On her own, without him as her partner, something like a man's reputation all on its own affecting his success at the table wouldn't have occurred to her. "We're going to destroy Vale's reputation, I presume?"

"Aye. Someaught like that. I'll tell ye when I've enough facts to face the argument ye'll give me. Will ye trust me that far?"

At this moment, with him in her bed, she would trust him with anything. Miranda kissed his cheek. "I will."

"Good. I reckon I need ye to poke as many holes in my plan as possible. That's the only way to be sure it's seaworthy." He stroked a hand down, between her legs, and she arched against his hand before she even realized she was doing it. "But I'm nae there yet, and it seems a shame to waste the rest of the night, doesnae?"

"Oh yes, it does," she agreed, and then couldn't speak as his fingers dipped into her. No, she didn't want to waste any of this. Or any time with him. Because however much trust she had, Vale had at least as much of a reputation as Aden did, and at the moment the captain held every single card. Every card except her heart.

"Mia! Damn it, Mia, I need to talk to you!"

Aden started upright. Miranda, draped across his chest, slid down to his lap and rolled to look up at him, sleepy-eyed. *Christ.* What the devil time was it? The edges of the lass's curtains were well lit, and as sense

335

returned he could hear the house about them well past stirring. He'd fallen asleep. Soundly. In a lass's bedchamber. In Miranda's bedchamber.

"Mia, you can't ignore me forever," came through the door, which thudded again.

Her chocolate eyes widened, her face paling to ashes. "Matthew," she hissed, sitting up and knocking Aden in the chin. "You have to hide! Oh, dear Lord!"

Rubbing his face, Aden slid from beneath her and rose. He grabbed a spare blanket off the bed and tied it around his waist as he strode for the door. Behind him Miranda gasped and hurried after him to grab his arm. "Leave off, woman," he grunted, continuing forward with her dragging at him.

"Aden, you can't," she whispered, her voice sharp.

"This isnae how I had planned it, but aye, I can. I need a word with yer damned brother. Now is better than later." He glanced back at her, taking a moment to appreciate just how bonny she was in nothing but her long, dark hair. "And ye're naked. I appreciate it, but I dunnae ken if Matthew will."

"Damnation!" Slapping him across his

bare back, she retreated to dive behind her bed.

Making certain she was where she wanted to be, he turned back to the door, unlocked it, and pulled it open. Before Matthew could do more than open his mouth, Aden grabbed him by the cravat and hauled him inside the room, closing and locking the door again before he released his grip.

He could see immediately why the lad had proven such an easy target for Captain Vale. Every emotion took a turn on Matthew's pretty face, shock to disbelief to rage to confusion. Good God, a blind man could read the young Mr. Harris. "Shut yer damned mouth," he grunted before Matthew could say something to ruin everyone's plans.

Matthew snapped his gaping jaw closed, squared his shoulders, and opened his mouth again. "Where is my sister, MacTaggert? What have y—"

"Ye worried she'll nae suffice any longer to pay yer debt to Captain Vale?" Aden interrupted, stalking forward as Matthew retreated. "Ye troubled that he may nae get all he's paid for?"

"I—"

"Sit down, and keep quiet."

He wasn't surprised when Matthew seated

himself in one of the chairs by the cold hearth. While he didn't generally approach trouble head-on, he also generally didn't care whether he won or lost a particular hand. This time, he did. And he knew what he looked like, half naked and over six feet tall and accustomed to a hard day's work.

While Matthew watched, Aden went over to Miranda's wardrobe and found a clean shift and a pretty blue walking dress. Keeping his gaze on her brother, he walked to the corner of the bed and set them in front of where she crouched, naked and clearly extremely annoyed with him.

He wanted a minute to contemplate where he was, and what it meant that he'd not only relaxed enough in her presence to fall asleep, but that he'd evidently slept well into midmorning. That conversation with himself would have to wait, though, because he had several things to set into motion, and most of them would depend on the other angry person in the room.

"Ye set aside what ye think I'm doing here for a minute and what that means to the plans ye've hidden from yer ma and da," he said, taking the seat opposite Matthew. "Vale took ye for a fool, and ye didnae disappoint him."

"George introduced us," Matthew said,

his voice clipped. "I had no reason not to trust either of them. They're cousins, and George is a good sort, so —"

"They're nae cousins. Vale dug into Humphries's pockets first, and used him to get to ye. Ye ken?"

"He's n . . ." Young Mr. Harris sat back in the chair, his eyes losing focus. He was no doubt running through his first encounters with Vale all over again with new eyes. "Why w—"

"I reckon he's been in London longer than the seven weeks he claims," Aden interrupted. Proper young ladies had maids, and simply because Miranda's hadn't yet tried to enter the room didn't mean she wouldn't do it any second now. "He's been watching and chatting with people here and there, and whatever he learned pointed him to yer sister. Everything else has been part of his road to her."

"But I beat him several times at the tables. How could he have planned ahead of time that I would lose . . . such a substantial amount to him?"

"Because he let ye win, so he could see the face ye show, so he'd learn which bets ye'd take and which ones ye'd shy away from. He was leading ye about the paddock like a buyer trying out a horse's paces before he plunks down the blunt to buy him."

"He couldn't be that certain," Matthew insisted. "I'm a fair gambler, I'll have you know."

A faint feminine growl came to Aden's ears in response to that. "Ye're nae a fair gambler," he stated. "Ye're a horrid one. It's nae yer fault; ye and yer sister both show yer every feeling clear as glass on yer faces. What ye did wrong was listen to someone who told ye otherwise and then likely took ye for all ye had in yer pockets and then some."

"That is not so. I refuse to believe you. Especially with you sitting, naked, in my sister's bloody room, you bas—"

"Dunnae finish that insult, or I'll be forced to punch ye," Aden warned, rising. He found his coat crumpled up on the floor, and freed a deck of cards from one pocket. As he returned to the chair he shuffled it, then handed the deck to Matthew. "Pick any card, and put it on top of the deck. Keep the deck."

Scowling, Matthew did as he was told. Sliding a card from the deck, he examined it with absurd caution, looked at all the other cards in turn because evidently everyone thought Aden kept decks of single-denomination cards in every pocket, then set his on top of the deck. "Now what?"

"Look at me." Once the lad had reluctantly met his gaze, Aden took a slow breath. "Ace," he said, then, "one, two, three," and on, slowly, until he'd gone through every possible number a card could be. "Club," he continued, "heart, spade, diamond."

"What does —"

"Yer card is the nine of clubs," Aden cut in.

Before he could reach forward and turn it, a graceful female arm reached past him to do so. "Nine of clubs," Miranda said, turning the card so the three of them could all see it.

"Bloody . . . How did you do that?" Matthew demanded.

"I read it on yer face, lad. The same way Vale did, every time he placed a wager with ye." Taking the card from Miranda, he looked up at her.

She'd donned the gown he'd selected for her, her hair in a careless knot and the dress's buttons still open at the nape of her neck. *Mesmerizing.* No tears from her last night, no lamenting the loss of her virginity, no fretting over her very uncertain future. Rather, she'd been an enthusiastic if inexperienced delight who made him more randy than he could ever recall being, and who had thrice pushed him over the edge before he'd been ready to give up the game.

"Lass," he drawled, taking her hand and pulling her down to sit on the arm of the chair beside him.

He'd clearly overset Matthew, because her brother didn't even make a squawk at the appearance of his half-dressed sister. Rather, the lad sat where he was, staring at the remaining deck of cards and wearing an expression on his face that would have saddened a professional mourner.

Finally Matthew cleared his throat. "How did you . . . find out about all this?"

"I told him," Miranda supplied. "After you informed me that you'd sold me to Captain Vale, I went to find another competent wagerer who could provide me with some insight."

"Seems to me he gave you more than insight."

"And if you say a word about it to anyone, I will wring your neck," she retorted. "I've kept your secret. You will keep mine."

"But . . ." Matthew's face reddened. "But he just told me that Vale reads my every expression like a book. What if he asks about you and Aden?"

"I imagine he will," Aden put in. "And

ye'll say ye can't imagine Miranda would allow me near her bed, and Vale will know ye're lying."

"And then I'll still owe him fifty thousand quid, and I'll be ruined."

"As ye should be, ye nodcock. Ye couldnae help losing to him, but ye might have stopped wagering with him. That's on yer head. But nae, he'll nae call in yer notes. He would have wanted to be Miranda's first, but as long as Society's opinion of her doesnae change, he's nae going to alter his plans. He may even decide punishing her will be more fun than breaking her in."

"Aden," she whispered, and he tightened his grip around her hand.

"I cannae stop him from imagining, but I can stop him from acting. If he's dead he cannae harm ye, Miranda."

"But then you'll —"

"I swore ye an oath. I'm nae going back on it. One way or the other, he's lost ye."

"You can't beat him," Matthew supplied, his shoulders slumping. "Believe me, I've tried. And even if you could, I'll still be destroyed. My entire family's name will be ruined."

"Do ye want Eloise?" Aden asked.

Matthew's face grayed even further. "Of course I want Eloise. She's my soul, my heart, my —"

"Aye, I ken. Do ye reckon I'll allow her to marry a man who's sold away his own younger sister?"

"Aden," Miranda murmured.

"So that's it, Mia?" her brother snapped. "I've hurt you, and so you'll hurt me? I thought —"

"This isnae yer sister's idea. It's mine. And if ye want Eloise, ye need to prove to me that this was just a moment of weakness, that ye lost yer head this one time and it'll nae happen again. In order to prove that to me, I've a few tasks for ye. And ye'll do them exactly as I set them out. For yer sake, for Eloise's sake, and mostly for Miranda's sake. Do ye ken that, Matthew?"

He slumped again. "It seems I'm a slave to two masters, then. Thank you so very much, Miranda."

"Thank her later," Aden stated, wondering if the lad knew just how precariously he was holding on to his temper. "This master has a mind to set the two of ye free." And to claim one of them forever, but he wasn't about to say that aloud now. Not while someone else held her chains.

CHAPTER THIRTEEN

"Is her ladyship home?" Aden asked, brushing from his shoulders the last of the rose petals he'd acquired climbing out of Miranda's window.

The butler bent down to pick up one of the petals and crush it in his fingers. "Lady Aldriss is in her rooms. She has a luncheon this afternoon."

He'd forgotten about that. Francesca and Eloise were about to hie themselves over to Harris House to dine with Miranda and her mother. Well, his timing continued to leave something to be desired, but he'd already begun the hunt. No time now to call back the dogs. With a short nod he trotted up the stairs.

"Master Aden, your cravat is untied," Smythe called up after him.

"Aye." Slipping it off, he hung it over one of Rory the stuffed deer's antlers. Somewhere the stag had now acquired a red dancing slipper with one lace broken off, but it looked rather fine tied about his front left hoof.

His mother's bedchamber door stood open, but he stopped short of the doorway and knocked on the heavy oak frame anyway. He and his brothers barreled in on each other all the time, but he didn't feel nearly as familiar with Francesca — which made the conversation he was about to have even more awkward and pride-pricking.

"Enter," the countess called, and squaring his shoulders, resisting the urge to tug on the front of his coat, he stepped inside.

Even without her standing before the dressing mirror, her maid holding a pair of bonnets, he would have known the space belonged to a lass with a great deal of blunt. The light-green curtains had been embroidered throughout with wee gold-threaded birds, warblers or swallows or the like. Fresh flowers, mostly white and yellow roses, sat in an identical pair of vases on either windowsill overlooking the garden, and oddly enough a Highlands landscape painting of the Falls of Clyde that looked like it had been done by Jacob More himself, hung on the near wall.

"Ye've a Scottish painting?" he asked, moving closer to look at it.

"Yes. The Scottish landscape is beautiful beyond words," she said, facing the painting as well. "And it should always be painted by Scotsmen."

"I'm a wee bit baffled, then," he commented.

"Why? Because I fled Scotland?"

"Aye, that would cover it."

"I never said it wasn't lovely. It was also lonely and desolate."

"And full of Highlanders."

"Not full enough."

At that he turned around. "Ye've lost me now."

"You may have noticed that your father isn't one to . . . socialize."

"Ye mean he's nae fond of going about prancing in other people's parlors when there's work to be done?"

"Nor was he one to invite a neighbor over for dinner or luncheon or breakfast, or to take a stroll about the village and stop in the bakery for tea, or to do anything social at all unless it involved drinking."

Aden narrowed one eye. "Ye did marry him, ye ken."

"Yes, after he danced me off my feet and charmed all resistance out of me with one damned smile." Her brow furrowed. "That is neither here nor there. As you didn't know I had a Jacob More painting in here, I presume you came for another reason."

"Aye." Good. He disliked the idea of chatting about nonsense and past deeds with her, anyway.

"Does it have something to do with why you're coming home at nearly midday and still wearing the clothes you had on at the Darlington ball? Or most of them, anyway."

He ignored that. She likely had a good idea where he'd been after that waltz last night, but she would have known that whatever he'd decided to wear. "I'd like to borrow a thousand quid."

Francesca drew a breath in through her nose. "Hannah, I changed my mind. I'd like to take the barouche to luncheon."

Behind her the maid set aside the bonnets, bobbed, and hurried out the door, pulling it closed behind her. The countess took a seat in one of the green overstuffed chairs by the window, but didn't offer him the seat opposite her. He wouldn't have taken it, but she'd read him well enough to know that. Lady Aldriss would have made a fine card player, herself, Aden reflected.

"Now, where were we?" she asked, her dark-green eyes very like Coll's in color, but far more sly than the oldest MacTaggert brother's.

"I'm asking ye for a loan of a thousand pounds," Aden said, keeping his voice cool and level.

"Ah. No. Is there anything else, my dear?"

Aden tilted his head, a bit surprised, but not willing to let her know that. She'd practically moved heaven and earth to aid Niall in his quest for Amelia-Rose Baxter, after all. The question became deciphering whether she was bluffing, or questing for more information and looking for a way to slip into his life — or if she wasn't doing any of that and simply wasn't interested in handing out any of her money to him.

He could get the money himself; it would simply take him longer. And there his mother sat, clearly attempting to remind him that she was not content with being relegated to his personal bank. "How confident are ye that I'll tell ye anything of my private woes?" he asked aloud, sitting in the matching green chair without being asked. He was a card player, too, after all.

"I didn't ask you to tell me anything," she responded coolly, only the curved hand stretched out along the arm of the chair saying that she had more interest in this conversation than she cared to reveal. "You requested a great deal of money, and I refused."

"Nae to give me; to lend me."

"I do not 'lend' things to my children, Aden. I give, or I do not."

"So ye reckon that now I'll ask ye to *give* me the blunt, and ye'll say nae again, and then expect me to have a conversation with ye so that I earn it. But I dunnae owe ye any conversation, or any explanation. Ye've nae been a participant in my life for seventeen years. I dunnae need ye to be one, now."

Her eyes narrowed just a touch. He'd scored a hit, then. "But you do need a thousand pounds from me."

Abruptly this chat wasn't so much interesting as it was stifling. Aden rose. "I dunnae need it enough to give ye whatever it is ye want in return." He turned for the door. "I'll likely nae be about for the next couple of days. I have some things to attend to." Time was the one thing he couldn't control, but he would have been willing to wager that he didn't have much of it. And once Matthew spoke with Vale, he would likely have even less.

"I'm going to say a few things," she stated, to his back. "For every one I get wrong, I will give you a hundred pounds. How does that sound to an accomplished wagerer?"

There it was, her demand for information

350

in exchange for the money, couched in a way that would make it a game he would want to play — wagering her conjectures against his hopefully well-hidden facts. And having the damned money to hand would make things so much easier. "Aye. I'll give ye a go. And aye, I'll answer ye honestly, if ye had that on yer mind."

"I did not." She sat up straighter, both hands folding into her lap. "The money involves Miranda Harris."

Aden nodded. "Aye." The simplest of observations could have told her that.

"You've asked her to marry you."

"That's a hundred pounds to me."

"The money is so you can ask her to marry you."

Indirectly, but he would agree in principle. "Aye."

A brief smile touched her face before she smothered it again. "The money is for a betrothal gift."

"Two hundred pounds."

"You're trying to demonstrate to Miranda that you don't rely on me for your every need."

That sounded like a bit of a jab, but other than noting it, he let it pass. "Three hundred."

Francesca sat where she was, silent, for a

long moment. "Are you attempting to buy off your rival? What's his name? Captain Vale?"

Her description made him frown. In a sense, yes, he supposed the money was the beginning of him making an attempt to convince Vale to go away. But then again, it wasn't. And Vale wasn't so much a rival as he was a crook and a blackmailer. "I reckon that one's worth fifty quid to me."

This time she nodded. "I'll allow that." Taking a breath, she sat back again. "You are difficult, my middle son."

"This is yer game. I was about to leave," he responded, leaning sideways against the closed door.

"So it is." She studied his face for a few seconds, though he doubted she would see anything he didn't wish her to. "Miranda is in trouble of some sort."

Hmm. Perhaps he needed to work a bit harder, if she'd seen that. "Aye."

"She asked you for money."

"Four hundred fifty quid."

"She asked you to get something for her."

That wasn't close enough to anything to qualify except in the broadest of interpretations. "Five hundred fifty."

"Miranda can't or won't go to her parents regarding this trouble."

"Aye." That was interesting; Francesca kept flirting about the correct path, but couldn't quite find it in the forest — likely because she was an only child and couldn't fathom a brother or a sister causing such upset.

"Matthew has been gambling again."

Or mayhap she *could* imagine it. "Aye."

At that, the countess scowled. "You're giving him the money so Elizabeth and Albert won't know that he's strayed again. Aden, I will not h—"

"Six hundred fifty."

She closed her mouth. "You are helping him repay his debt."

It would have been closer to say that Matthew was helping him repay the lad's debt. "Seven hundred."

"I'm close, then. Is . . . what you're doing illegal?"

"That's nae a statement."

His mother blew out her breath. "What you're doing is illegal."

Not yet, it wasn't. Gambling wasn't illegal, and even Vale likely hadn't cheated as much as he'd chosen the perfect bird to pluck. Eventually, well, he'd cross that bridge when he rode up on it. "Eight hundred."

"Thank God for that. Your brothers are assisting you, at least."

"Nine hundred."

She stood up. "I will give you the last hundred if you will make certain you're not in this alone, whatever it is. Tell Niall. Tell Coll. I know you trust them, at least."

He contemplated that. Generally, he slipped out of his messes alone; three MacTaggerts caused a stir, where one of them — him, at least — by himself could be more subtle. But fifty damned thousand pounds wasn't subtle. They knew the most important part of this already — that he was after Miranda Harris. "Ye've a deal. A thousand pounds. I'll need it by this evening."

"You'll have it."

Aden pulled open her door. "Da always said I reminded him of ye. I reckon I can see why, now."

Francesca collapsed into the chair again as the door clicked shut behind her middle son. Aden Domnhall MacTaggert, twenty-seven years old and more mysterious than the Sphinx. After all that, she'd discovered almost nothing, with one very important exception: He meant to marry Miranda Harris.

That should have been enough. A second son had plans to wed an English bride, and before the deadline she'd set of their sister's own wedding. That was what she'd asked, and when they'd first arrived, she'd had serious doubts that any of them would bend that far.

But she'd learned tantalizing bits of other things. He hadn't asked her yet, and something about the thousand pounds stood between them. She was in some sort of trouble, and while Aden hadn't directly admitted that this was something that had been kept from the Harris parents, she thought it had been. Or rather, the trouble with Matthew's wagering wasn't the main issue.

Drat. She was generally much more proficient at deciphering the comings and goings — and needs and wants — of the people around her. Aden was clever, and tricky. Even his brothers, on the rare occasions she managed a chat of any length with them, adored him but kept to generalities such as "likes wagering" and "always has some lass or other after him."

His admission that he'd found a lass therefore seemed especially significant, and that increased her frustration. She knew almost nothing of the how or why or where of it all, and even less about the circumstances surrounding the trouble in which

Miranda seemed to be embroiled. Had Aden caused the trouble? That actually seemed likely, given that Miranda Harris was highly admired for her grace and poise and her cool, calm demeanor.

Francesca stood to collect one of the hats Hannah had set aside for her approval. She couldn't inquire of Miranda's mother without overturning the apple cart, or so Aden had hinted — unless that had been done precisely for the purpose of keeping her at bay. Oh, this, he, was maddening. And he'd said that Angus saw *her* in their middle son. Had Angus found her maddening, then?

That thought made her pause in the doorway. She wasn't like Aden. Certainly she didn't go about screaming her feelings and emotions and thoughts for all the world, but that was just common sense. It did no good to complain unless she could also find a remedy. Half the things she *had* attempted to discuss with the great nodcock of a man had flown straight past him, unnoticed, anyway.

Perhaps she could concede that not everyone was as observant and . . . . intuitive as she was. As Aden was, rather. But everyone *should* be, which would make every interaction much less complicated, and would also entail many fewer explanations, apologies, and excuses. The —

Hannah appeared in front of her. "My lady, the barouche is being brought around, and Lady Eloise awaits you in the foyer."

Francesca opened her mouth to point out that the barouche had only been a ploy to give her a few moments to think before she began fencing with her son, but she abruptly decided against it. She'd asked for a task to be completed, and Hannah had seen to it. Her underlying thoughts were hers alone. How could they be otherwise? And now she had several new things to contemplate later. The next two hours were reserved for dining with her daughter and Elizabeth and Miranda Harris, and figuring out how she could help when no one would tell her what in the world was going on.

"Don't be a spendthrift, George," Captain Robert Vale said, lifting a hand to acknowledge young Matthew Harris approaching from across the main paddock. "I've an idea that fox hunting might be a splendid hobby for me to take up."

"Then borrow a hunter and go fox hunting," Lord George Humphries grunted, making notes on his Tattersall's auction sheet.

"That bay, Steadfast, should do me

nicely," Vale went on, ignoring the protest. "He's out of Sullivan Waring's stable. And his other brother is owned by Wellington."

"Do you expect that makes you a relation to Wellington? That damned hunter is going to go for four hundred quid, at the least."

"And you owe me twelve thousand quid."

"By my reckoning, I owe you two thousand now, taking into consideration your living at my home, meals, parties, clothes, sundry expenses, and all the introductions I've made for you — in addition to a probationary membership at Boodle's."

"And yet not one for White's."

"Yet."

"Our bargain is not yet completed, George. I am not a married man." He shifted, making room for his second drudge. "Good morning, Matthew. Any news?"

That put a frown, quickly stifled, on Mr. Harris's face. "Just my usual request that you leave Miranda out of this and allow me to work off the debt I've incurred."

"As I've said, Miranda is *the* reason for all this. Did you discuss Aden MacTaggert with your dear sister?"

A nervous twitch of Matthew's mouth. "She likes him."

"Yes, he's quite large and muscular and pretty, I suppose, as if any of that signifies.

George, do buy me that horse, cousin."

Muttering beneath his breath, Lord George waved his paper in the air, placing a bid for Steadfast. Good. A proper man should have a proper mount for a proper hunting of small, skittish beasts.

"He's also Eloise's brother, Robert. Neither she nor I can simply tell him to go away."

Vale dug his nails into the wood beneath his fingers. Yes, MacTaggert had slipped through the only crack in his entire plan — one that hadn't even existed when he'd begun this two months ago. Yes, Matthew had just become engaged to Eloise, but that young lady had been the doted-upon only child of Lady Aldriss. The damned trio of giant Scottish brothers hadn't made an appearance until well after he'd seen Miranda Harris and begun putting a rope around her brother's neck.

"A woman may only marry one man, Matthew. That's the law in England, anyway. She's marrying me. What's so difficult about making him understand that?"

"Scotsmen are stubborn," George put in, flicking his paper again as the bidding continued.

"They are that," Matthew agreed.

Good God, it was like standing between

two parrots, both mindlessly repeating everything they'd heard while understanding none of it. "I don't want commentary. I want him gone. Is that clear?"

Matthew shifted his stance to focus on a very small mouse hiding beneath a very small weed at the base of the paddock railing. Not even a place with the reputation of Tattersall's could entirely eliminate its vermin. But Matthew wasn't sharing that thought, Vale knew. Matthew was attempting to conjure an excuse, or a lie — neither of which was acceptable.

"I am growing tired of reminding you that I didn't force you to make any of those wagers, Matthew," Vale pointed out, even if he had coerced the majority of them. Encouraging a sin in someone else didn't make him guilty of sinning, himself. "Presenting a single one of the notes you owe me would see you cut off from your family, and you would still be in debt to me for the remainder of your life."

"Damn it all," Matthew swore, and kicked at the mouse. The thing scurried toward one of the stable buildings and dove out of sight. "She'll never forgive me, you know."

"Very likely. Not my concern. What is it you're hesitating to tell me?"

"Aden knows. About my debt, and about

you. She told him everything, while . . . while they chatted last night." He moved closer, lowering his voice. "I went into her room this morning to tell her what you'd said, and he was in there. *With her.*"

Vale clenched his jaw, his fists, every part of him that could still feel fury. He wanted to think he'd heard wrong, to demand a repeat of Matthew's statement, but that would have been both pointless and a useless waste of time. That damned Highlander thought he'd won, then. MacTaggert thought that by taking Miranda's virginity, he'd saved her from some villain's clutches. "And no doubt he called *me* a blackguard," he said aloud, keeping his voice level and cool.

"I don't know what they called you, Rob —"

"And I don't care. It doesn't signify. *I* didn't despoil her. I will make her a greater paragon of Society than she could possibly have dreamed. The grandest of the grand will beg for invitations to our soirees, and our dinners will be the most exclusive in Mayfair. No one else will know that some Highlander once led her astray, and she will be grateful to me for that fact. George, buy me that damned horse!"

He took a breath, pulling his temper back

in again. Yes, he'd indulged in fantasies of taking Miranda Harris's virginity. Yes, in them she'd been initially resistant and her eyes had widened in surprise when he'd shoved his cock into her and rammed her again and again until he filled her high Society cunt with his dirty common seed. Well, he could still do that. Because he still owned her. And now every time he fucked her, he could remind her that pretty Highlanders with aristocratic families might turn *her* head, but they would never beat *him*.

"I'll go collect your damned horse for you then, shall I, cousin?" George commented, stepping back from the railing. "Five hundred fifty bloody pounds."

There. Everything remained on the path he'd carved. A few pebbles were easily kicked aside, once they had been identified. "MacTaggert has a plan to take your sister back from me, I presume?"

Matthew flinched like a puppet whose string had been pulled. "I don't — I mean, we didn't actually discuss anything in particular."

Vale put an arm around the younger man's shoulders. "You don't want to take a side. I understand."

"Good, because —"

"And yet, you've already chosen where

362

you stand. The point where you had a choice was fifty thousand pounds ago. You owe me your sister. What, then, is the barbarian's plan?" He took half a step back. "Wait. Allow me to guess. He intends to win your debt back from me at the table."

Matthew blinked. "How —"

"You've told me several times that he's a wagerer. You've carried some impressive tales, and yet you're the only one who seems to know them. These stories, therefore, came from either his admiring younger sister or from the man himself, neither of which source overly impresses me. So. Am I to be surprised, or does he want me to know I'm about to be challenged?"

"I . . ." His shoulders slumped. "He said I should tell you that he's coming for you."

"Ah, Matthew, don't look so dejected. You've done as he asked, and you've more or less done as I asked. Now. Come see my new hunter, and then you may purchase me luncheon at Boodle's. I am quite looking forward to dinner with your family tomorrow evening."

Hopefully Aden MacTaggert would come after him soon; he could be exceedingly patient, of course, but he'd never owned a Highlander before, much less destroyed one. He did look forward to it.

■ ■ ■ ■

"Miss Harris," Billings said, stepping into the morning room, "I thought you might wish to know that Mr. MacTaggert is in the kitchen."

Miranda put a hole through the middle of her embroidery. Well, the red blooming rose would now have to sport a strategically placed thorn. The electricity shooting through her at the very sound of the word "MacTaggert" surprised her a little; after all, she'd been hearing it in connection with Eloise MacTaggert for months. Setting aside her hoop, she stood.

Then the rest of what the butler had said sank in. "Why is Aden MacTaggert in our kitchen?"

"Perhaps he's emptied the Oswell House pantry," Millie suggested, putting aside her own mending, "and he's come here looking for food."

"He's brought us a treat," Billings returned with an uncharacteristic smile, then cleared his throat and bowed. "If you'll excuse me, I still have some preparations for dinner this evening."

With that sentence, the cold claws that had been digging at Miranda tightened their grip again. Her mother, at least, had chatted all during breakfast about how delighted she was to finally have an opportunity to exchange more than a sentence or two with Captain Vale.

Miranda managed a nod, and then, barely, to keep from running down the hallway to the servants' quarters and the kitchen. In the narrow corridor just outside, she stopped at the sound of Aden's deep-voiced brogue and took a breath, her tense shoulders lowering again. She wasn't alone in this. She had an ally. A partner.

She knew his plans now, or at least the part he'd risked telling Matthew yesterday, but he'd dressed and slipped out the window before she could tell him just how little she liked the idea of yet another man wagering his future against the formidable skills of Captain Vale. And she knew — she *knew* — that he hadn't told her everything.

"I reckon if I'd meant these only for the shiny folk tonight, I'd nae have brought three baskets, lass," he drawled, and Mrs. Landry, their longtime cook, giggled in return.

That very unlikely sound all in itself would have been enough to pique her curiosity. Squaring her shoulders, she moved into the middle of the hallway and then stepped into

365

the kitchen. The cook continued tittering over three large baskets of what had to be hothouse strawberries, since the weather had been too cloudy and cool for anything but scrawny, pale berries in the house garden. These were bright red and plump and juicy looking — and almost as mouthwatering as the tall, lean man presently standing beside the old, scarred kitchen table.

At that moment he looked up and his gaze met hers. He took half a step in her direction before he smoothly altered course and continued with his conversation about wild berries in Scotland. That motion, though — it was the first time she'd seen him make a misstep in . . . well, in anything. And it had been in reaction to her. *Delicious.*

"Did I hear that you've brought us strawberries, Aden?" she said, sweeping into the room amid bows and curtsies from the kitchen staff and half the house staff. "My goodness! I doubt there's another strawberry to be found in all of London today!"

"He said he wanted to be sure he had enough for your dinner and for the entire household, miss," Meg, the cook's young assistant, chirped. Immediately she flushed bright red and ducked behind Mrs. Landry's sizable shoulders.

"I should think he accomplished that," Miranda agreed. "In fact, I vote that we all have one immediately." With a grin she picked up a berry, noting that everyone else crowded into the room dove in after her, and took a big, juicy bite. *Heaven.*

"God's sake, lass," Aden murmured, somehow directly in front of her, "ye make me wish to be a strawberry."

The place between her legs, the place where he'd spent a great deal of time night before last, went damp. "I found another book about London life for you," she said aloud. "Come along and I'll fetch it for you, as long as you're here." Miranda glanced over her shoulder at Millie, to see the maid looking longingly at the strawberries. "Millie, stay here and eat strawberries, for heaven's sake. It's just a book. I'll be back in a trice."

"If you insist, Miss Miranda."

"Aye, she does insist," Aden whispered as he trailed her back into the main part of the house.

She could practically feel his warm, solid presence behind her, tugging at her senses, her emotions, and making her want to reach back and touch him. "Strawberries?" she queried, stepping into the library.

Aden moved past her, searching the nooks

and crannies of the long room, before he returned and closed the door behind her. In the same motion he turned, swept her into his arms, and kissed her. "Hello, lass," he murmured, before claiming her mouth again.

The way he said those two simple words . . . She'd never heard anything so seductive and full of longing and promises. Miranda wrapped her arms around his shoulders, holding him as close as she could. Oh, she wanted more, especially now that she knew what that entailed. Her, longing for a man. *This* man. Six months ago — six weeks ago — she would have laughed at the notion.

With a regretful sigh she tore her mouth from his. "Everyone in the house knows you're courting me. We can't remain here alone."

"Nae, that'd leave ye compromised, aye? And yer da would point a weapon at me and force me to wed ye. We cannae have that."

His tone was so dry that she had no idea whether he was jesting or not. She had every reason to believe he cared for her, enjoyed her company, but then he'd also suggested she spend more time being improper, at least in private. Well, he'd certainly been a splendid instructor. If there was more to it than that . . . This was more than likely not the time for her to be considering forever afters. Not when the man trying to force a forever after on her would be dining tonight with her and her family.

"Why would you bring fresh strawberries for a table where my family will be dining with . . . that man?" she asked, as the lunacy of that idea belatedly occurred to her.

"They're nae for him. He just happens to be dining here tonight."

They were for her? She did adore strawberries, but gifting them now, today, seemed ill timed. Vale would be impressed by the opulence, and even less likely — if that were possible — to give her up. In fact, even if her family owned orchards or fields or whatever they were of strawberries, or even if they didn't, Vale's plans wouldn't alter.

"They're for the servants," she said aloud. "You want them on your side."

At that, his mouth curved in a faint grin. "Ye're learning to be sly, lass."

"Yes, I think your lessons to me are going much more swimmingly than mine to you on proper behavior."

"Well, I'm a Highlands barbarian, so ye've quite a task before ye."

She grinned back at him. "You want my

369

mother to gush over the lovely strawberries you brought us, and have her urge Vale to try one because Aden MacTaggert is so generous." She poked him in the chest. "I may not be naturally sly, but I have navigated the drawing rooms of Mayfair for the past five years. I know just how cutting even a compliment can be, when it's delivered at the right time."

Aden flicked a finger down her cheek. "Ye've nae idea how much I want ye lass, here and now."

A swift look down at the front of his kilt backed up that statement quite nicely. "Put that away, Aden, before someone walks in on us," she said beneath her breath, reaching out to smooth down the front of his tartan.

He took a quick step backward, batting at her hand. "Dunnae touch it, woman. Ye'd be setting it loose, and all sorts of mayhem could result."

That made her laugh, and he slid his arms around her waist, pulling her closer. Miranda lifted up on her toes and kissed him again. Whatever lay between them, whatever word she'd been avoiding whenever it danced through her thoughts over the past few days because it was horribly ill timed and inconvenient and would make things even more difficult under the likely circumstance that their resistance was unsuccessful, she did enjoy him. Immensely. Enjoyment was much easier, and much safer, to acknowledge than that other pesky, danger-fraught word.

Aden kissed her throat, with that soft, slow touch that made her inner thighs want to melt. Her body certainly remembered the pleasures of two nights ago. *Goodness gracious.* "Aden . . ."

With a sigh he lifted his head again, wavy dark hair framing his face and brushing his shoulders. "I know. We cannae. I need to see to a few things tonight, anyway. If ye need a word with me, though, send a note to Eloise. I'll see that it comes to me."

She nodded, unable to keep from plucking at his lapels. "My one fear is that he'll produce a special license tonight and announce to my parents that we're to marry."

"He'll nae do that, Miranda. He wants a grand Society wedding with all the trimmings. A special license stinks like bad gossip. That's according to Eloise, anyway." He took her hand, twining her fingers with his. "My worry is that he'll propose to ye tonight, in front of yer parents."

Her heart shivered. "That's almost worse. I can't precisely turn him down, Aden."

"Dunnae allow it, then. When he first comes in, if ye get the chance to introduce him, ye call him Matthew's friend. Ye call him a retired boat captain, and nae a ship's captain."

"Damn him with faint praise, you mean. So if he were to propose, it would sound like he's too eager, or that he's infatuated while I'm not."

It might be enough to stop him this once, but it wouldn't work twice. Vale would make certain she knew not to insult him in public again. But she did have a little leverage: He wanted a certain appearance of propriety, and she knew it. It would be a delicate balance between pushing too hard and not doing enough, but luckily she was a practiced and skilled dancer.

"What 'things' will you be seeing to tonight, then?" She pursued.

"He might ask ye where I am, so I'll be earning a bit of blunt, hopefully. But only from those who can afford it, *boireannach gaisgeil,* I swear. And if ye need a distraction, mention that my older brother, Coll, took himself down to Cornwall to have a look about, likely for property or someaught, even though he's supposed to be in London finding himself a bride."

Miranda put a hand over her mouth. "You

sent him to look for Vale's family."

"I asked him to go, and he agreed. I doubt there's a thing for him to find, but the fact of him looking might shake Vale's spine a wee bit."

The door bumped open behind her. In the same heartbeat Aden took a long step sideways, turned away from her, and lifted a book off one of the shelves he'd perused . . . goodness, how long ago had it been? A week? Two weeks? It seemed like both yesterday and ages ago, all at the same time.

"Miss Miranda," Millie said, eyeing the two of them suspiciously, "Mrs. Harris inquires what color you mean to wear tonight, so she won't clash."

"I dunnae, lass," Aden drawled, the book held loosely half across the front of his kilt, "but if ye say Samuel Johnson's got a good eye for more than dictionary words, I'll believe ye."

Of course he'd already figured out which book would be appropriate. He likely re-membered the title of every book on that shelf. And she'd once thought Highlanders thickheaded and dull. On at least one count, and with at least one man, she'd been very wrong. And under any other circumstances, that would have made her exceedingly happy.

CHAPTER FOURTEEN

"Ye dunnae need to come with me," Aden rumbled from Loki's back. "Ye let Coll go off on his own."

"Ye sent him on the safer trip," Niall returned.

Aden finished off the last strawberry he'd tucked away in a pocket. Whatever he thought of soft Sassenach, he had to give them credit for one thing: They built fine roads. Rutted and muddy in places, aye, but they had them aplenty, and leading everywhere a man could want. Even directly south of London all the way to Portsmouth.

"I ken ye dunnae like the idea of leaving yer lass unprotected," his brother went on, "but *I* dunnae like the idea of ye being killed and yer corpse dumped in the ocean."

"I reckon Miranda can defend herself at a dinner table as well as I could. She's safer there in her own house than she would be out at a soiree where Vale could make a grand gesture and propose before all the *haute ton.* And she's nae my lass. Nae yet."

His younger brother sent him a sideways glance. "Ye've thought it through, at least, nae that I'm surprised by that. It still doesnae answer why ye dunnae want me heading south with ye. Ye ken I'm going to keep asking until ye answer me."

The conversation reminded Aden forcefully that he frequently had a damned good reason for keeping his own counsel. His brothers could be helpful, but they weren't the sort to follow orders without question. At the same time, he couldn't be everywhere at once. And he had a lass to save, and a shrinking amount of time in which to do it.

"Coll's impressive, and he'll be chatting with farmers and shopkeepers who've likely nae seen a Highlander before, much less one who's a viscount."

"And I'm nae impressive enough for Portsmouth?"

"For Saint Andrew's sake, Niall, aye. Ye're impressive. I dunnae need impressive for sailors or officers of His Majesty's Navy. They've seen the world. They've had cannons shot at 'em. I need charm, nae fists. I need subtle. Ye're a might more subtle than Coll, I'll admit, but ye're nae as subtle as I am."

"That might be, but Portsmouth's nae just a few farmers and shopkeepers, either. I reckon two of us can cover more ground than the one of ye, however subtle ye are. That's why I'm here with ye. Because I'm nae staying in London while ye do someaught heroic."

"Fine. I'm glad ye're here, then."

"As ye should be, Aden."

"But I'd rather at least one of us was in London making certain that bastard doesnae lay a single scabby finger on my woman."

Niall closed his mouth over whatever it was he'd been about to say. "I'm glad ye decided to tell us yer troubles," he finally ventured.

"Francesca made me."

"*She* knows?"

"Nae." Aden frowned. Gauging by the sun, it was past noon already. By the time they reached the harbor at Portsmouth they'd be pushing against evening, with an unknown number of conversations and the ride back to London still ahead of them. "She wouldnae lend me any blunt unless I at least told the two of ye, so that's what I did."

They — he — needed to be back in Mayfair before Vale knew he'd left. He'd told both his brothers that Coll's trip to Cornwall was mostly a distraction, a chance for them to rattle Vale a bit, and perhaps come up with something useful. The navy anchored at Portsmouth, and that was where he would find any more recent tales about Robert Vale — short of sailing to India, of course.

"So ye only told us because she forced ye?" Niall grunted a fairly imaginative curse in Gaelic. "What, did ye reckon we'd tromp all over yer delicate plans like a great pair of oxen?"

"Dunnae be a nodcock," Aden retorted. "Aye, at first I reckoned I could rescue a lass in distress and nae have to ask ye for help. This is complicated, Niall. It's nae a simple kidnapping or two. Vale holds papers proving Matthew's debt. It's nae only Miranda I need to rescue, and the Harris parents dunnae even ken they're in jeopardy."

"Coll will flatten Matthew the first chance he gets. Ye know that, aye?"

"He willnae, because Vale's a soulless devil who preys on naive, friendly young lads, and our *piuthar* loves the boy. *I'll* manage Matthew Harris."

They rode in silence for a mile or so. "Aden, are ye in this for a bride who's grateful to ye, or for one ye can love?"

"Those two things arenae mutually exclusive, I reckon."

"Ye know what I'm saying," Niall insisted. "When Amy and I —"

"Nae." Aden cut him off with a slash of his hand. "Ye dunnae get to advise me because ye were lucky enough to find a woman who thinks yer annoying charm is . . . well, charming. I'll find my own path, thank ye very much. And aye, I know *my* heart. I dunnae yet know hers. I cannae, until she's free."

"Well, that sounds wise enough, but ye've nae twisted yerself into knots for any other lass that I recall."

No, he hadn't. And whatever reasonable, logical story he tried to spin for himself, deep down he knew the truth. He'd found his forever, and he would do anything necessary to rescue and protect her whether it ultimately benefited him or not. "Mayhap I did, and I just nae told ye," he quipped, mostly to turn the subject to his past romantic escapades and away from the one that actually mattered.

The sun brushed the tops of the old, rolling hills to the west as they trotted into Portsmouth. He could smell the ocean just to the south, wet and salt and cold, but less

378

wild than its Highlands self. This part of the Atlantic had been tamed a very long time ago, and only dared raise its head when it had the might of winter at its back.

Ignoring the rows of wee houses and shops, they continued toward the port and its accompanying warehouses, taverns, inns, and whores. Finally he slowed, gesturing with his chin toward a well-lit tavern resting on a wide, well-traveled lane. "The Briny Deep," he said aloud. "I reckon that looks to be a place for a naval lieutenant or two. Ye remember what I need to know?"

Niall swung out of the saddle and tied Kelpie to the nearest hitching post. "Aye. I'll see ye back here at two o'clock. Dunnae get knocked over the head and end up on some ship bound for the Orient."

Aden nodded. "I'll start at the other end and work my way back toward ye. Six hours is all we have; I need to be back in London before the gossips are awake."

He continued east and south, closer to the water. Niall would look for officers, equals of Vale whether the captain had seen them as such or not. As for himself, he wanted to chat with some common sailors, the ones who would have had to follow Captain Vale's orders. His father had always said that to know a man's character, speak to those whose lives he's responsible for. Or something close to that, but with more profanity.

With the piers and docks and the ocean — gray and flat at twilight — in sight, he stopped in front of the Mizzenmast tavern. It wasn't even fully dark, yet, but the tavern already spewed fiddle music and loud men's voices and a few female ones amid the clutter of sound. Wrapping Loki's reins around a hitching post, he patted the chestnut on the neck. "Dunnae let anyone make off with ye, lad. We've a busy night ahead."

At the Mizzenmast he received only blank stares, even after he purchased a round of drinks, at the mention of Captain Robert Vale. It made sense; Vale had served in India, while the royal navy had men stationed all over the world. This lot seemed to have bonded over their travels to the southern Americas and the Caribbean tobacco plantations. When he inquired where he might find lads who sailed Indian waters, they gave him the names of three additional taverns — the Public House, the Punjabi, and the Water Buffalo.

The latter two taverns, he subsequently discovered, were owned by former sailors who'd each been in the employ of the East India Company. Finding one of them, though, took him nearly an hour amid the maze of building and shipbuilding yards, supply wagons, piers, and broken old sailors lurking in doorways and ready to pounce for enough coin to purchase just one more drink.

Finally he rounded yet another corner, beginning to wonder whom he could bribe to guide him without worry over whether they'd try to murder him in some alley, and a dingy sign with a very large, fierce-looking black cow came into view ahead.

As he drew closer, faded lettering beneath the malformed bovine proclaimed that he'd found the Water Buffalo. It reminded him of some of the worst gaming hells in London, but even more run-down looking. Thank the devil he'd come himself to this one, instead of asking it of his newly married younger brother. Aye, Niall could charm the stinger off a bee, but the inhabitants here weren't honeybees. They were more likely to be drunk, angry wasps.

Making a quick check to see that his *sgian-dubh* remained sharp and hidden in his boot, he pushed open the door and walked inside. No one played music here, except for the cymbals between the fingers of the old woman standing on a chair in the corner, her middle bared and brown, intricate tattoos winding up both forearms to vanish beneath the faded red and gold silk she wore above and below her belly. Her feet were bare beneath the calf-length skirt, and decorated in more of the same ink as was on her arms. The old, gray-haired woman rolled her hips to the left and swayed to the right, then the opposite, in a slow, rocking dance accompanied only by the tinny chink of the cymbals. With every sway of her hips she lifted one foot a few inches above the seat of the chair.

"My wife," the short, bald man behind the counter grunted, and pulled a cork from a barrel to pour a stream of brown liquid into a tin cup. "You looked at her dancing, so you owe me a shilling and I owe you a mug of Indian cider."

Aden flipped a shilling onto the counter, and it disappeared before it could finish moving. "What's Indian cider?" he asked, lifting the mug and taking a sniff. Apple, cinnamon, and something musty smelling. Not unpleasant, but not something he'd scented before.

"Apples, cinnamon, blackcurrant vinegar, and ginger. And a dab or two of whisky. I make it myself."

Elsewhere Aden might have downed the entire cupful, but even up in Scotland he'd heard the tales of men being drugged in taverns and waking up halfway across the Atlantic where they would be declared a stowaway and given the choice of either being tossed overboard or signing on as a member of the crew. Keeping his gaze on the tavern keeper, he lifted the tin and took one tentative swallow. "Hmm. Nae half bad. Ye werenae jesting about the whisky, either. That's a Scottish dab, nice and potent. Ye dunnae water down yer brew."

The old man chuckled, clearly flattered. "You're a brave man, Highlander. And I haven't helped the merchants or His Majesty recruit crew in a decade. You keep putting coins on my bar top, and you've nothing to fear from me."

"Just don't eat any of that stew he'll be peddling next," one of the dozen men scattered about the dark tavern called out, and the others laughed.

"Just for that, Weatherly, I'm giving your supper to Duke."

"Heh. I thought you liked that dog."

Amid the continued laughter, Aden stuck out his hand. "Aden MacTaggert."

The old man shook it. "David Newborn."

"I'm looking to hear some tales about a particular man," Aden went on. "And I have a bit of coin if the stories turn out to be true."

"Which man's made you so curious, then?"

"He goes by Vale. Robert Vale. Calls himself a captain, late of the *Merry Widow* out of India."

"Vulture Vale?" asked one of the men seated at the long wooden table dominating the center of the space.

"From what I've seen, aye, that would be him." Taking his mug, Aden strolled over to take a seat on one of the worn benches. "Are ye acquainted with him, or just his name?"

"How much coin is it worth to you if I answer that?" the tall, skeletal man with a startling shock of ginger hair asked.

"That depends on how much ye actually know."

"I'll tell you he's a right bastard for free," a second, red-faced man seated toward the end of the table stated.

"I reckoned he was that, all on my own," Aden returned. "Tell me someaught more interesting. More personal."

The ginger snorted. "It's interesting to me that he'd likely pay me to tell him some big Scot's looking for stories about him."

"Aye. But then ye'd have to find him, talk to him, and get the blunt from him."

384

"That's the truth, Billy," the ruddy man put in. "That fucking vulture would listen, smile, give you a shilling, then slit your throat the minute you turned your back."

"I, on the other hand, dunnae slit throats," Aden added, not at all surprised by the description.

"So you say. You look like you could beat a man to death with but one hand, though."

"Dunnae cross me and dunnae lie to me, and ye'll nae need to discover if that's so. Are any of ye willing to tell me a true tale?"

Billy grimaced. "If it gets back to him that I talked, I'll be on some scow drudging up mud to widen the Port Jackson harbor alongside the convicts."

That would be Port Jackson in Australia. Was Vale that powerful, though, or did he simply give that impression? By rising to captain as quickly as he had, he'd at least proven that he had influence — but was it real, lasting influence, or the kind that had been bartered for with losses at the table and could be quickly disposed of?

"He's retired from the navy and he's in London chasing after a Society lass," he said aloud. "Unless ye tell him yerself, he'll nae ken a thing about this conversation."

"A Society lady, eh?" Billy took a swig of Newborn's potent cider. "Makes sense. He

385

was always going on about grand mansions and dining with dukes. Every time we went ashore, he would head for officers' clubs and win the shirt off some admiral's up-jumped son without a brain twixt his ears, and suddenly Vale had another promotion or another medal. And then he'd lecture those of us bunking in hammocks below-decks about how we was animals bred to feed the wealthy and powerful, and how none of us had the spleen to turn predator ourselves."

"And if ye so much as twitched or grumbled," the ruddy-faced man added, "it was up into the rigging you went until he saw fit to allow you down again."

"Danny Pierce was up there for near two days once," Billy said, nodding. "Fell out of the rigging, finally, but got tangled up on the way down or he'd have opened his skull like a ripe melon on the deck. He was odd and scared of high places after that, and whenever the cap'n saw him on deck, up the bastard would make him go. Danny finally vanished one day. They said he'd gone ashore and fled his duties, but we weren't anywhere near land the last I seen him."

"Do ye reckon Vale killed him?" Aden asked, memorizing every name and anecdote for later use.

"Nah. I think poor Danny got tired of being scared and jumped overboard. There should've been an inquiry, but Vulture Vale knew who would bend over for him, and nothing ever came of it."

The rest of the stories were equally disturbing, and all followed a similar pattern: Vale wanted something to happen, and he either went out and arranged for someone to owe him a favor, or he called in one of the favors he'd already secured. All of the favors involved forgiving debts his victims had mysteriously accrued in his presence. They said a leopard couldn't change his spots, and while Vale's ultimate plan might have been to don a lion's pelt, he was still a leopard.

A common-born leopard, at that, and one who told himself he was better or more worthy than his fellows, but at the same time tricked and cheated because deep down he knew he couldn't earn a better life on his own merits — because he had none. Vale knew what he was, and spent all his efforts convincing himself otherwise, likely terrified that someone he couldn't catch beneath his thumb would point out the fact of his monstrosity.

Once Aden had purchased a few rounds

of drinks, two more men came forward with their own tales about Vulture Vale. Nothing more about Cornwall or Vale's origins, though the bulk of tales continued to suggest that he'd come from very ordinary stock. Every bit of it at least clarified Aden's view of the man he'd set himself to face across the table. It said something that even far away from Vale and India and assigned to different ships under different captains, the sailors still hesitated to come forward. Vale scared them, in a way that rough seas and cutthroat pirates did not.

That was how Vale worked, though: He found the vulnerable, the frightened, the desperate, and he took advantage. It was damned time someone fought back. The fact that it was a woman who'd chosen to do so, a lass with manners and propriety and kindness and a barbarian Highlander on her side, made it all the sweeter. Now he only needed to make certain she won.

When he met up with Niall again, he had fifty fewer pounds and a priceless amount of information. And his brother had a tale or two of his own, including one from an officer who'd known Vale back when he'd first purchased his junior lieutenancy, and had described younger Vale as being cunning, heartless, and utterly focused on

388

achieving a captaincy. He'd claimed to come from a family who hadn't appreciated his "gifts," while he'd certainly understood their limitations.

That bit of information had cost another twenty quid. The thousand pounds Francesca had given him seemed to be shrinking before his eyes, but strawberries, bribes, and rounds of drinks were expensive.

He had a few more things to secure when he returned to London, but two or three hundred pounds in his pockets when he finally sat down should be all he required. His mother might believe he meant to use all the money at the tables, and she was welcome to think so. But attempting to win fifty thousand pounds with one thousand, and doing it in a matter of days, would be a fool's errand. And he did try not to be foolish.

"Is yer hurry to be back in London because ye reckon ye're the only obstacle between Captain Vale and a marriage license?" Niall asked, kneeing Kelpie in the ribs to keep the gelding apace with the long-legged Loki.

"I want to get back so I can put a ball through him if he *does* try someaught," Aden retorted.

He'd kept a firm rein on his temper all

night, but now that they were galloping north every tale of cruelty and callousness thrummed into him like a drumbeat. That . . . *man* had his gaze set on Miranda. Had danced with her, and while Aden had been miles away Vale had dined with her family in her house. Robert Vale wanted to use her as a stepping-stone, and the bastard wouldn't hesitate to grind her into the dirt once he'd done so.

"Aden!"

Aden started, looking sideways at his younger brother. "What is it?"

"I said, ye cannae gallop all the way back to London," Niall commented. "Slow down and ye'll get there without killing Loki and Kelpie — unless ye care to change horses at every inn we pass by."

Cursing under his breath, Aden drew the chestnut back to a canter. Aye, he did want to change up horses at every inn, but that would eat away at the money in his pockets, too — not to mention the embarrassment Loki would feel at being left behind to walk back to London later in the company of some stable boy. He'd figured the pace — walk a mile and canter for two — would have them back in Mayfair by midmorning, and that would simply have to do.

"If ye want someaught to ponder other

than what peril yer lass could be in at just past two o'clock in the morning, why dunnae ye tell me what, exactly, ye do mean to do about her brother? Ye may nae have said exactly how Vale came to have so much paper of Matthew's, but I reckon it was because the lad's a poor gambler with nae any common sense."

His brothers weren't idiots, and Niall made a good point — if he'd filled in the empty bits of the story with some logic and imagination, Coll would have no difficulty doing the same. "It was wagering, and it was him being hunted by a man who spits venom. Dunnae ye fret about Eloise. If I ever catch him wagering again, I'll break both his arms. We dunnae need ye or Coll breaking his neck. Eloise chose him for his good heart, and nae because he can tell a friend from a foe at fifty paces."

"*Ye* can do that."

Aden sent his brother a grim smile. "Aye, but I've nae a good heart."

"Och, *bràthair,* I do hope I'm about when ye realize just how wrong ye are about that."

Considering he'd lacked the self-control to keep from ruining a lass who needed his help and that he was now having deadly serious thoughts about killing a man who planned to marry her, Aden wasn't so certain he had any heart at all, much less a good one. All he *did* know was that he meant to rescue Miranda Harris, that he wanted her for himself, and that he didn't care about the cost.

Captain Vale knew which fork went with which dish. He knew how to chat politely about the weather and the attractions of London, as well, but to Miranda's eyes it all sounded rehearsed, as if someone — George or Matthew, no doubt — had told him which topics to pursue and which to avoid, and so he'd perused the newspapers to find as much banality as he could.

She wouldn't say her parents had been charmed, but they certainly hadn't been alarmed — which was undoubtedly all he'd aimed for. At the same time *she'd* seen a few moments where he clenched his jaw or gripped his proper fork too tightly, because she'd been looking for them. Aden might as well have been seated at the dinner table last night as well, because the Highlander had seen to it that he was very much a topic of conversation.

In fact, if Aden's goal had been to infuriate Robert Vale, he'd thus far been doing quite well. Whether angering a heartless villain and blackmailer would accomplish anything useful, Miranda had no idea. All she *did* have, actually, was a rather alarming amount of trust in — and infatuation with — Aden MacTaggert.

She rose early, half expecting him to climb through her window before dawn, whatever mysterious wagering task he'd assigned to himself overnight. When no one but a blackbird came knocking at her windowsill, she summoned Millie and dressed, and then decided Aden would come calling by breakfast so she could tell him how her evening had gone. Or rather, to select a new book from the library. As she stirred her soft-boiled eggs into mush, he continued his absence, and she resentfully tried to ignore the chiming of the clock in the foyer — which nevertheless insisted on sounding off nine times.

"What are you doing up so early?" her father asked, strolling into the breakfast room to select a stack of sliced ham and toast before he sat at the head of the table where the ironed morning newspaper awaited his perusal.

"I thought I would risk calling on Eloise and Amy unannounced," she improvised. "I need to go to the milliners, and hoped we might make a morning of it."

"Calling without first making an appoint-

393

ment?" Her father put a hand to his chest. "That's deuced daring of you." He glanced toward the doorway. "Don't tell your mother I said 'deuced.' "

Miranda grinned. "Your secret is safe with me, Papa."

She adored the way her parents adored each other, and once she'd reached marriageable age, she'd determined that she would have that for herself, or nothing at all. But now, when under other circumstances she might think she'd found that very thing, people owed people debts, and one man demanded her hand while the other declined to ask for it. Perhaps Aden meant to be honorable, to not make her choose when she was trapped, but she wanted to hear the words, to have him say aloud what she thought she saw in his eyes.

Or was that just what she *wanted* to see in his eyes? Eloise had called her middle brother "elusive" back before she'd even met him. Did that mean he would never declare himself? He'd promised he would free her from Vale, and thus far, nothing else. Could that be enough for her? Miranda frowned. What if that had to be enough?

"Well, you look very serious, suddenly," Albert Harris commented around his cup of tea. "But then you've got two men pursuing you. That's a subject for some serious thought, I would imagine."

"I have been pursued before," she quipped, trying to look amused rather than horrified at the conversation. After all, one of the men was blackmailing her, and the other had ruined her.

"That, you have, and more times than I can count. This is the first time you've allowed it to be known that two men are pursuing you, however. And it's also the first time I can recall that one of them managed to make it as far as a private dinner with the family." He slathered butter on his bread. "Is it to be him, then? Captain Robert Vale? Your mother swears that you prefer the Highlander, but Mr. MacTaggert doesn't seem to have received a dinner invitation. He did send some delightful strawberries, though. Those must have cost him a pretty penny."

She wanted to shut her eyes for just a moment and think. Eventually, if Aden's plans didn't succeed, she would have to agree to Vale's terms. Therefore, she couldn't simply dismiss his so-called suit out of hand, however much she wanted to do so. But neither was she ready, yet, to let her parents think she'd made her choice. Not until all hope was gone. "I haven't decided anything yet, Papa. And *you're* the one who wanted the captain to call for dinner, if you'll recall."

He smiled. "I do recall. Very well, my dear. Keep your own counsel, then. Just know that if you ever do want my opinion, I have several of them."

Now she didn't know what would be worse — if her father approved more highly of Vale, or of Aden. For heaven's sake, what if her preference for Aden disappointed her father? Or what if he disliked Vale, told her so, and then she had to marry the man without telling her father the true reason why?

Oh, she needed someone with whom she could talk. Someone she could trust. Not a parent, or a maid, or a lover. She needed a friend, one who would not repeat any of the secrets she carried, and who wouldn't judge her for them. One who could help her untangle the mess of her thoughts and hopes and fears.

"I hope I haven't distressed you, my sweet. You know your mother and I will support whatever choice you make — including spinsterhood. I'm not so very anxious to see your smile gone from my table." He sighed. "Alas, I know not even my silly doting can come between you and a new hat. I'm off

396

to meet Tom Blaisdale and look at a steer he fancies. I'll drop you at Oswell House if you'll give me but a moment."

"Of course I will." And now her imaginary destination had just become real. Hopefully her prayer for a friend — or a pair of them — had, as well.

Once she'd disembarked from her father's phaeton at Oswell House and waved goodbye to him, she took a deep breath. She hadn't decided yet. She could still make this about nothing more than hats — if Lady Eloise and Mrs. MacTaggert were even home and available for an outing this morning. That in itself would be something of a surprise with the Season now in full swing.

"I shall inquire," Smythe the butler said when she conveyed her request and he'd shown her into the morning room to wait.

Inquiring meant that at least one of the young ladies was still home, but not that either of them didn't have previous plans. It would no doubt be better if their time *was* already spoken for this morning. How could she tell her friends something she hadn't even dared tell her own parents? How could she tell Eloise that one of her adored older brothers had ruined her — even if it had been at her own request? She couldn't. Silence was better. Silence and perhaps some hat shopping.

The morning room door swung open. "What very good timing you have, Miranda," Eloise exclaimed, sweeping into the room and arm in arm with her new sister-in-law, pretty, blond-haired Amy. "We were just debating whether to go shop for hats, or take a morning stroll in the park to show off Amy's lovely new walking dress. It's embroidered with hummingbirds!"

Miranda stood and tried to add her vote for shopping, but instead only managed a strangled sob. Then tears began running down her face willy-nilly, so she plunked back down onto the couch and covered her face with her hands. All the tired, frightened bits of her broke loose at the same time. *Wonderful.* Now she was a weepy, soggy lump.

"My goodness!" Arms went around her shoulders. "Whatever is the matter, Mia?"

"Nothing," she wailed, her voice broken now, too.

More arms surrounded her from the other side. "Tell us or don't," Amy soothed. "We are here for you."

More frustrated, worried bits softened into mush. "It's a secret," she managed thickly.

"A sad secret?" Eloise asked, rocking her

398

now like a babe. "Did Aden do something horrid? I'll box his ears."

"Not Aden," Miranda sobbed, though of course Aden was directly at the center of it all. "I'm in . . . so much . . . trouble!"

"Smythe, fetch my mother and some peppermint tea, and close the door, please," Eloise stated.

By the time Miranda had enough control of her voice to protest that she didn't need either tea or Lady Aldriss, one was cupped in her hands and the other stood in front of her, a gorgeous multicolored dressing robe knotted around her and her always-perfect salt-and-pepper hair loose down her back. The countess still managed to look elegant, competent, and, for her, very curious.

"I . . . don't . . ." Miranda sniffed.

"Have a sip of tea, dear," Lady Aldriss urged, pulling a chair close to sit a few feet in front of her.

Miranda sipped the hot tea and tried to gather in her thoughts and her scattered broken bits. She couldn't tell them anything — if they knew what sort of debt Matthew was in, the countess would definitely call off the wedding. Eloise and Matthew would be heartbroken, and while it wasn't her fault, they would both blame her for it.

The countess regarded her with cool green

eyes. "Your brother has been wagering, and it has caused you some difficulties," she said after a moment.

Eloise gasped. "Matthew wouldn't! He knows —"

"My dear," her mother interrupted, "Matthew is an amiable young man who joins in rather than standing back and observing. And I don't know if you've noticed, but that Captain Vale he's befriended is rather . . . how shall I put it? Self-absorbed. And insistent on being so."

"But Mama, he's courting Miranda. You shouldn't —"

"Aden is also courting Miranda. I believe I'm supposed to be prejudiced in his favor." She clasped her hands in her lap. "But that isn't presently the point, is it? Or shall I continue to speculate?"

Shaking her head, Miranda took another gulp of tea before she set it aside. Everything she knew screamed at her not to tell anyone, not to risk damaging her family's reputation by gossiping about it. But she also remembered what Aden had said, that Vale knew the rules, too, and that he used them against her. She liked the idea of playing by her own rules; she certainly enjoyed where it had led with Aden. This, though, was different. This was telling people who could ruin her

400

without any effort at all. People Aden hadn't told . . . Except that he'd told the countess something, enough for her to know that her troubles had something to do with Matthew and Captain Vale.

Could she trust them? Or was it that she wanted to so badly? Miranda made herself take a deep, slow breath. "What I'm about to tell you, you cannot tell *anyone.* My parents — they don't even know. They would be so . . . mortified."

Eloise clasped her hand and squeezed it. "We're MacTaggerts, Miranda. You and Matthew are part of our clan. And clan comes before everything."

If that statement surprised Lady Aldriss, she didn't show it. In her own mind, it explained some things about Aden: If he considered Matthew, and by extension her, part of his clan, she imagined he would go to some length to protect what he considered his. Did he think of her as his, or was she a pleasant diversion in his quest to aid Eloise and the man his sister loved?

That thought became entirely too painful to contemplate further, so instead she began speaking. She told them about Vale being Lord George Humphries's cousin and then not being his cousin, about how Vale had lured amiable Matthew into owing more than he could possibly repay, about Vale's actual plan to become an instant fixture within the *ton* by marrying her and using her reputation to shape his own. She told them about going to Aden for advice and that he'd agreed to help her, though she did leave out the main intimate details of their relationship.

When she'd finished, she sat back, drained — and Eloise began to cry. *Oh, dear.* "What is it?" she asked, squeezing her friend's hand. "Aden says he has a plan."

Eloise shook her head. "They're going to murder Matthew," she wailed.

"Who is?"

"My brothers! He panicked, and he was so stupid, but they won't — they won't care that I love him! Only that he made a horrid, wretched mistake!"

Across from them, Lady Aldriss lifted an eyebrow. "It would seem, my darling, that he does rather deserve a thrashing."

"I know, but they're very large! I know they'll murder him. And I shall be . . ." She hiccuped. "I shall be widowed before I'm ever married!"

Amy opened her mouth at that quite impossible scenario, but the countess gave a subtle shake of her head. "I believe Miranda said that Aden spoke to Matthew about his lapse in judgment, and that Matthew agreed to help extricate himself. Aden most certainly did not attempt to murder Matthew — which we know for a fact because if he had, Matthew would be dead."

"That's true," Eloise admitted, swiping at her tears as she looked over at Miranda. "And killing your brother would make you cross, so of course Aden wouldn't allow it. He wouldn't want you to be cross."

While Aden seemed to delight in aggravating her, Miranda couldn't recall him ever, by either his actions or his inaction, doing anything that would frighten or harm her, or allowing any such thing around her — other than the large ghoul that was Captain Vale, who'd dug in his claws well before Aden had become involved. Of course none of this was finished yet, but just the idea that Aden acted as he did to keep her safe felt warm and comfortable and . . . irresistible. She cleared her throat. "Aden did seem to think that Matthew could be redeemed."

"Oh, thank heavens."

"Niall rode out with him yesterday," Amy added, "with the explanation that Aden needed help resolving a problem. I would imagine Aden told him something about it, or he wouldn't have gone. Wherever they were headed, they still haven't returned."

Aden had gone somewhere? That didn't sound like the evening of gambling he'd vaguely described. Of course he'd also said, once again, that he didn't want her to have to attempt to lie. No, he'd simply given her a few suggestions for conversation, ones that seemed to have proved deeply annoying to Vale, and then he'd taken a handful of strawberries and left. "I'm glad he took help with him, but I don't know where he's gone, either."

"Has anyone seen Captain Vale?" Eloise piped in, apparently untroubled by the idea of bloodshed as long as the victim wasn't her betrothed.

"He was sound when he left my house at midnight," she returned.

"He still is, as far as I ken."

The low-pitched drawl came from the doorway, and Miranda whipped her head around to see Aden standing there and stripping off riding gloves, his brother Niall in the foyer behind him. "Aden," she breathed, every ounce of her wanting to run into his arms. Vale hadn't killed him and left him in an alley somewhere. At least she could tell herself that was the feeling flooding through her like mulled cider on a winter night. Relief. Yes, that was it.

"Ye decided to share yer story then, did

ye, lass?"

Jealousy? Was that what the flash in his eyes, the sharp tone beneath his easy words, had been? Jealousy that he wasn't the only one who knew her secret, any longer?

"She didn't intend to," Lady Aldriss commented, rising. "I have no idea how she managed to go so long without even the slightest hint of the weight on her shoulders, but evidently your sister being kind to her made her cry. We needled the rest out of her after that."

"Nae doubt. As ye're here and have saved me a ride over to Harris House later, Miranda, might I have a word with ye? In private?"

Miranda waited a beat for someone to protest. Apparently all the females in the room could read his expression as well as she could, though, because no one so much as let out a peep. Nodding, she stood. "Of course."

"The breakfast room, I reckon," he said once she'd joined him in the doorway. "I'm hungry."

"As am I," Niall interjected.

"Ye can wait a bloody minute."

"Aye. I can do that."

Niall stepped out of the way, and she followed Aden's long stride into the breakfast room. The lone footman inside scooted out a side door and shut it after one look at Aden, who let her pass him and then closed the door behind her. *Wonderful.* Six-feet-plus of angry Highlander whose help she still needed. "I *did* want to tell someone I could trust about all this," she stated, lifting her chin and unwilling either to prevaricate or to apologize. "You suggested I abide by my own rules."

He picked up a slice of beef in his fingers and stuffed it into his mouth.

"I did not, however, mean to tell your mother. Eloise called for her, and I was . . . I didn't wish to leave."

Aden took someone's half-empty cup of tea from the table and used it to wash down the beef.

"Are you not going to say anything?" she prompted. "I am not going to apologize for wanting to talk to someone who isn't —"

"Me?" he cut in.

"Someone who isn't already tangled up in this mess. Don't be an ass, Aden."

Narrowing one eye, he went after the bread, tearing off a hunk with his fingers. "Did ye just call me an arse?"

"If you're the one standing there glaring at me while you attack innocent bits of food, then yes, I called you an ass."

406

"Good." He finished off someone else's tea.

Miranda blinked. " 'Good'?"

"I've been on horseback for fourteen of the past twenty hours. For the last seven I've been imagining ye being forced into marrying Vulture Vale this morning before I made it back here, and wondering whether they would hang or transport the second son of a Highlands earl for murder."

"A —"

He held up one finger. "But ye're here, and ye're in high enough spirits to curse at me, and I reckon that's a good thing. Now come over here and kiss me before I knock the table over to get at ye."

CHAPTER FIFTEEN

The lass was sure of herself, so it didn't surprise Aden when she marched up to him, took the bread out of his hand, and dragged herself up by his lapels to kiss him on the mouth. For some damned reason she tasted like peppermint. It, she, intoxicated him.

Taking Miranda around the waist, he lifted her to sit on the edge of the breakfast table. She'd told someone else — three someones, actually — about her troubles, and while the idiot white-knight part of him wanted to be the only one to know, the only one who could save her, the more sane and logical bits of his brain realized quite well that she'd be better off if at least one other person had an inkling about her troubles. He'd been gone from London for nearly a day, after all, and if something had gone wrong, only her brother would have known to step in, if he'd had the spleen to do so.

Now that she had more support, however,

he wasn't entirely certain where he stood. Aye, she kissed with enough passion to arouse even a jaded cynic like himself, but everything she did aroused him. Her appearance, her voice, the biting, direct things she said, the swish of her skirts when she turned, the violet scent of her hair.

He wanted to ask her if she'd told her friends about Vale because she was bloody brilliant, or if it had been because she still didn't entirely trust him. And however much he could tell himself that it didn't matter, that he'd resolved to aid her whether she proved to be using him or not, he knew the truth. It *did* matter, and she mattered, and the way she felt about him mattered.

"Where did you go?" she asked, when he lifted his head to take a ragged breath. "You took your brother, and you've been riding for fourteen hours, you said. That does not sound like an excursion to go wagering at Jezebel's or Boodle's."

"First tell me ye're still unmarried and unbetrothed, lass."

"I am still unspoken for," she returned. "Your suggestions for conversation and the strawberries nearly gave Captain Vale an apoplexy last night, though."

"Damned shame that they didnae. That would've solved some problems."

"I would have to agree with you."

Aden looked down into her chocolate-colored eyes, and time simply . . . stopped. *Sweet Saint Andrew.* It would be wiser to keep his thoughts to himself, to do what he'd sworn and just wait. And yet he was always wise and logical, and this time it was tearing at his insides like an angry wildcat. "I promised myself I'd nae put any more weight on yer shoulders, Miranda Grace," he murmured.

Her brows furrowed. "Where in the world were you? Is something amiss? Something more, I mean?"

"Nae for me. For ye, well, it could be. I meant to wait until ye had yer life free from Vale, until ye had choices, real choices, in front of ye again. But I love ye, and I have for some time now. If I dunnae tell ye how I feel right now, then I'm liable to shout it out loud the next time I set eyes on ye."

Miranda's sweet mouth opened and then closed again. "You —"

"I dunnae expect ye to say anything in return, *boireannach gaisgeil.* And I'll help ye whether ye want me about or nae. I just realized that yer being in trouble or nae has naught to do with how I feel about ye."

"Say it again, Aden," she whispered after a too-long moment.

410

"All of that?"

"I will punch you, you know."

That made him grin. Remarkable, this lass. "I love ye, Miranda. I like ye, I admire ye, and I love ye."

She looked down at her hand as she tugged on the top button of his waistcoat. And aye, he wanted to hear her say the words back to him. But then he'd just told her that she didn't need to do any such thing. And he'd made it clear that her feelings wouldn't affect whether he continued to aid her or not — though he would have liked to know whether he was risking ruining his own life for more than a passing smile. If he was a fool, at least he was aware of that fact.

"I went to Portsmouth," he said, trying to give her room to maneuver if she wanted it. "I decided that short of sailing to India, finding a sailor or two who served with Vale would give me the best chance at getting some answers about his character."

No response. Just more carnage to his waistcoat buttons.

"We had the right of it. He's lied and cheated and manipulated his betters at every corner. He especially liked bleeding the sons of admirals dry, and then asking their das for medals and assignments and promotions. I doubt he's ever had a man challenge him to his face, and I reckon he's nae lost a wager he wanted to win."

"I insulted you the first moment we met," she stated.

"So ye did."

"The first words I spoke to you."

Deep down he'd hoped for a slightly more romantic exchange. But then, conventional, sugary-sweet romance was damned dull. "Ye spoke yer piece. I've nae had any trouble figuring out where ye stand."

"Don't make excuses for me," Miranda retorted. "I was rude, when I'm almost never rude to anyone. And I kept asking myself why I said what I did."

"Ye thought me a gambler, and ye'd at least two good reasons to nae like wagering. Ye still do."

Miranda put a hand over his mouth, and he just barely resisted the temptation to kiss her palm. "Yes, I still have several good reasons to dislike wagering. Even more now than I did then. I thought . . . You're a striking man, Aden. You walked into that room with a dog you'd just rescued and your shirt dirty and wet and . . . clinging to your muscles, and a kilt and boots and your poetical hair, and . . . my mouth went dry."

" 'Poetical hair'?" he repeated behind her

412

hand, lifting an eyebrow. She'd get around to making her point when she was good and ready to do so, but thus far it all seemed to be shifting in his direction — which lent him a touch more patience.

With her free fingers she tugged a lock of his so-called poetical hair down over one of his eyes. "Oh, please. I think you know exactly the effect you have on women. Half of them at luncheon were practically drooling over you." She freed his mouth. "You made me angry, strolling in there and being so grimy and not even caring. And yes, I do have reason to dislike wagering. And wagerers."

And now this didn't sound so positive. "We've established, then, that ye dunnae like my hobby and that I'm too uncivilized for ye. Anything else ye'd care to stab me with?"

She tugged on one of his ears. "I'm not finished. There's one thing — one only — for which I'm grateful to Captain Robert Vale. He made me seek out someone uncivilized — unscrupulous, I thought — who was proficient at wagering. I did not expect to like you, Aden MacTaggert. I did not expect to trust you. And I certainly did not expect to fall in love with you."

His breath stopped for a good dozen beats

413

of his heart. "But ye did, aye?"

She lifted up on her tiptoes and kissed him, achingly soft, on the mouth. "Aye," she whispered.

Aden kissed her back, putting his palms flat on the table on either side of her thighs. "That's more like it," he murmured. "Now as long as everyone knows what's afoot, I'd like ye to stay here today while I get a bit of sleep."

"I can do that. But first I need to know what you're planning."

"I've told ye w—"

"No, you haven't. You've said you'll take care of things, and I'm assuming you mean to wager against him, but fifty thousand pounds, Aden? If you mean to tell me that number is in your reach, I will call you a liar."

"Dunnae call me a liar."

"Then tell me what is going on, for God's sake!"

He could damned well understand why she didn't want to be kept in the dark. The men in her life hadn't done so well at protecting her, thus far. Aden shifted to sit on the edge of the table beside her. That way he could hold her hand. "I reckon it doesnae matter if I'm a better gambler than he is, however much my pride wants me to

414

prove that I am."

"That's a fair beginning," she commented.

"Thank ye for that. So I've been considering, and we only need one thing from Vale. The papers."

"The papers worth fifty thousand pounds."

"Aye, partner. We can win them, which isnae likely given that at any minute he could refuse to put them on the table or, worse, go get a special license and wed ye to keep me from interfering."

"That is not acceptable." Her fingers tightened around his.

"I agree. And I'll nae allow it. Which leaves me one other way to get the papers."

Her fair face paled. "Aden, you are *not* going to kill him. As much as I want him to go away, you would be throwing away your own life, as well. And that . . . And that is not acceptable."

"Because ye'd miss me, lass?"

A tear ran down her cheek, and he immediately regretted teasing her. Before he could apologize, though, she sighed. "I didn't expect any of this, you know. I don't need to marry; my parents have seen to that. I thought I might marry, if I found someone I could love, but I never felt any great urgency. I certainly didn't mean to like you, much less love you. All of this" — she gestured around the breakfast room with her free hand — "is so far from anything I could have imagined that it doesn't even seem real sometimes, except for the shivers running down my spine whenever anyone says his name."

"I dunnae have a plan to kill him." That wasn't exactly a promise not to do so, but it would have to suffice for now. Because if everything else failed, he *had* made a promise to save her. And he would do so. Regardless.

"Then what?"

"Lass, he's spent his entire adult life luring men into disaster and then offering them a hand up — in exchange for becoming his man, doing his bidding. He's broken men and left 'em gasping and desperate for air. But I reckon in all that time he's nae sat across from a MacTaggert. From me."

"Considering that you just said you're not likely to win, I hope your skill matches your confidence. You're not the only one who pays a price if you lose."

"Dunnae ye fret, Miranda. I know what the true prize is. And it's nae the fifty thousand pounds." He smiled at her exasperated expression. "Winning's nae the only way to win."

"I am going to punch you, Aden. Right now."

"Well, I've nae wish to be punched." Taking a breath, he told her what he meant to do, and how he meant to go about it. While he did gloss over a few of the details, from her expression and the alarming paleness of her face she'd caught enough to fill in the spaces he'd left empty.

"Aden, you can't do that."

He tilted his head at her. "Do ye see a hole in my logic, then?"

"Y . . . Well, no, but don't you realize what it will mean?"

"Aye. I realize."

"I won't allow you to do that for m—"

"Excuse me," his mother said, pushing open the door and shifting sideways to allow Brògan into the room before her. "Your dog, it seems, missed you so much last night that in her despair she saw fit to disassemble the blue footstool."

Aden hopped down from his seat on the table and crouched to ruffle Brògan's ears. She'd gained weight in the few weeks since they'd found each other, and her bedraggled coat had taken on a much healthier sheen. "Sorry, lass," he said, straightening again.

"Aden," Miranda said through clenched teeth, a smile on her face, "do not leave me sitting up here on your mother's breakfast table."

He lifted her down, then bent his head and kissed her for good measure. "Ye're a fine, bonny lass, ye are," he whispered, his forehead tipped against hers. "I didnae expect ye, either. Nae much surprises me. Ye have. And the only thing that scares me is that when ye realize ye're free, ye'll nae wish to be caught again."

With that he put her in his mother's care even though he would have preferred to take her with him, and instead went upstairs with Bròan to try to get some sleep. Wagering took a clear mind, even when one of the players meant to lose. Especially then, because Vale couldn't know that was the plan.

But he did. And he knew what the real prize was. A lass, a lifetime, and a love he'd never expected to find at all, much less in London. He had her in sight, in touching distance. And he did not mean to lose this war, because doing so would cost him far more than he was prepared to give.

"But yer majesty, he'll throw someaught at ye," the odd young man the three brothers shared as their valet whispered, blocking Francesca from approaching Aden's closed bedchamber door. "And he's got good aim."

"He will not throw anything at me," she countered.

"But —"

"That will be all, Oscar."

"Aye, yer majesty. Do duck, though, for Saint Andrew's sake."

As the valet backed away from the door, Francesca stepped forward, rapped her knuckles against the hard, old oak, and then pushed it open. "Aden?"

He sat up from the middle of a pile of pillows and sheets. "What's amiss?"

"You've received a note. From Captain Vale."

Cursing, her middle son slid to his feet. Bare-chested, naked in fact but for an old kilt, only traces of the skinny young boy he'd been remained. In that lad's stead stood a tall, well-muscled young man of twenty-seven years with a mop of unruly black hair even longer than he'd demanded to wear it as a boy.

"How long was I asleep?" he demanded, crossing the floor to her and taking the folded note out of her hand.

"Not even thirty minutes, I'm afraid."

"I can believe that." He broke the wax seal and opened the paper. "Bloody damnation," he muttered, followed by a few words in

Scots Gaelic that sounded very familiar and very colorful.

"May I ask what it is?"

He handed her the note, turned on his heel, and dove into his wardrobe. "Is Miranda still here?"

"Yes. I've sent over a note asking her parents to allow her to spend the night."

She looked down at the missive. In plain, unadorned lettering, it said, *Aden MacTaggert. I'm at Boodle's, and I'm tired of waiting for you to screw up enough courage to face me. Do so now, in the next thirty minutes, or I will call you a coward and a bounder. Whatever you're planning has already failed. Meet me across the table, or slink back to Scotland like the craven you are. Captain R. Vale.*

"Well, that's quite pointed," she commented, folding it again. "You're going, I presume?"

"Of course I'm going."

As he unbelted his kilt she turned her back. There were some things a mother simply didn't want to see. "You were going to meet him anyway, yes?"

"Aye. I meant to call him out tonight. No doubt one of his lackeys told him I'd been gone all night, and he reckoned to catch me while I'm tired." Material rustled. "My nethers are covered again, my lady."

"So you're going to challenge him — or accept his challenge, rather — to a game of cards?"

Aden pulled a shirt over his head and tucked it into his trousers. "I did as ye asked. Coll and Niall know what I'm about. I keep my word, *màthair,* but I dunnae owe ye anything else."

Her heart had very nearly melted when the first of them had called her "mother." She'd waited so long to hear it again from her boys. Aden, though, used the word like a weapon. "Are you implying that I don't keep my word, son?"

"I'm nae implying. I'm saying it straight out." He slipped into a waistcoat and buttoned the trio of buttons up over his chest, then picked up a starched cravat and slung it around his neck.

"You've insulted me. Please explain."

He scowled at his twin image in the dressing mirror as he began knotting the cravat. " 'This year for your birthday, Aden,' " he said, in a quite remarkable imitation of her London-raised accent, " 'you and I are going to York. And whatever your father says, I am purchasing you that saddle.' "

Memories flooded back, scented with moors and pines and fresh-cut lavender. "And I left three weeks before your birthday.

You resent me still because of that?"

"Nae. I resent that Da told me I couldnae trust the word of a Sassenach woman, and I believed him. And so I nearly didnae see Miranda with her standing right in front of me. I nearly didnae trust that she wasnae using her wiles on me to get me to help her. I was wrong. Da was wrong. And ye were wrong to promise a ten-year-old boy someaught ye knew ye couldnae deliver."

"Aden, I —"

"I dunnae need to hear an explanation or an apology. But if ye're going to warn me now nae to make a stir when Miranda's troubles dunnae concern the MacTaggerts — or the Oswell-MacTaggerts, rather — ye may as well save yer breath."

"Oh, stop that," she said, walking forward to pull the ruined cravat out of his fingers and toss it to the floor. She picked up a fresh, crisp one and pulled it around his neck. "How much debt is Matthew in? Miranda studiously avoided mentioning a number." Twisting the ends of the cloth, she put in a knot and pulled the middle into an understated cascade of ruffles. She had to reach up to tie it; Aden might be the shortest of the brothers, but that was akin to being the third highest peak in a range of mountains.

"I'll nae be responsible for stepping between Eloise and her beau."

"Despite the fact that doing so would mean you and Coll will have an indefinite reprieve in your task to find an English bride?" From what she'd learned and deciphered, Aden had been plotting with Miranda for at least a fortnight. From the first moment he'd learned of Matthew's losses he could have stopped his sister's engagement. He could have freed himself from the agreement between Angus and herself — at least for a time. If he'd returned to Scotland and found some bonny Highlands lass to wed, she wasn't certain she would have had the nerve to declare the agreement broken.

"Was Matthew unlucky, then? Or unwise?"

"He was foolish. He crossed paths with a snake and didnae realize it until he'd already been bitten."

"And he traded his sister to cover his debt." She finished his cravat, but continued tugging at it to give herself an excuse to remain standing there. "I find that much more troubling than the debt itself."

"Miranda was the prize all along," he returned, lifting his chin a little to accommodate her. "Vale pushed at the lad till he had nae other way to go."

"So you're not angry with him? I got the distinct impression that you're rather fond of Miranda Harris."

Aden put his hands over hers and gently removed her fingers from his neck. "Ye're sly, Lady Aldriss, but I'll keep my own counsel. If ye've misgivings about Matthew Harris, *ye* break Eloise's heart. I'll nae do so."

"I cannot make that decision without all the necessary information."

"I gave ye the necessary information. And I'll give ye a wee bit more. I'm off to Boodle's, and I mean to make a ruckus. A large ruckus. Feel free to tell all yer blue-blooded Sassenach friends that ye strongly disapprove of me."

Pulling on a dark-green coat and picking up a matching beaver hat and a pair of gloves, Aden moved around her to the bed-chamber door. *Highlanders.* He made her want to stomp her feet. "If you gave me a few more damned details, I might be able to assist you, Aden Domnhall MacTaggert."

That earned her a raised eyebrow. "That would require me trusting ye now, would-nae?" He set the hat over his longish hair, the very image of a handsome English gentleman until he opened his mouth and spoke. "Keep my lass safe, and then I'll consider it."

Francesca waited a beat before she followed him downstairs and watched him out the front door. He had perhaps a thousand pounds with him, and she presumed he meant to win enough money to pay off Matthew's debt. But it somehow involved making a ruckus at one of the most prestigious gentlemen's clubs in London, one to which he hadn't even yet been granted full membership.

"Smythe, alert me the moment Lord Glendarril returns from wherever he went off to," she instructed, and the butler nodded. "And we'll all be staying in today. They know better, but under *no* circumstances are Eloise, Amy, or Miranda Harris to leave this house."

"Are we in for some trouble again, my lady?"

"I believe we may well be. Arrange to send one of the footmen to lurk about outside of Boodle's. I wish to be informed immediately if anything untoward happens."

"I'll see to it, my lady."

In the meantime, she would try squeezing some additional information out of Niall. The MacTaggert brothers, though, tended to become a veritable wall of stone whenever she attempted to cajole one of them to

425

speak about another. It made her proud to see them so close and so loyal, but at the same time their stubbornness was absolutely maddening. And whether they'd been apart for seventeen years or not, she still worried about them — and about the one who supposedly most resembled herself, in particular.

Chapter Sixteen

Aden brushed street dust from the shoulders of his coat and stepped into the Boodle's gaming room — half a dozen tables with a fair amount of space between them and no windows to speak of. Determined gamers didn't always wish to know how late an evening had gotten. This afternoon only half the tables were occupied, with Vale sitting by himself at the very center. The captain wanted to make a show of this, then. Well, he was going to have one, even if it likely wasn't the spectacle he expected.

Without preamble he took the seat opposite Vale. "Generally when a man calls me a coward and a bounder, or whatever it was ye wrote out and had someone else deliver to me, it means I'm about to be in a fight. Ye seem to want to play cards, though, so let's get to it."

"You've been busy, I hear," Robert Vale said. "From what I've been able to determine, you have what, eight hundred quid left in your pockets with which to win back what Matthew Harris owes me? Unless you were very lucky wherever it was you were last night, that is."

The vulture didn't know everything, then. And Aden had only five hundred twenty quid left to his name. "Oh, I was lucky. Just nae playing cards."

Vale sat forward a little, placing a crisp, fresh deck on the table between them. "Good for you. That is your goal, though, is it not? To purchase Matthew's debt and set him and his lovely sister free?"

"Mayhap," Aden returned, gesturing for a plate of roast chicken and a glass of whisky. The bits he'd eaten before his five minutes of sleep hadn't been enough to keep a mosquito alive.

"Not maybe," Vale corrected. "It's a fact. Matthew told me that you're . . . what was it? 'Coming for me.' " He lowered his voice beneath the hearing of the men seated around them. "He also told me that you despoiled my bride-to-be. A cowardly way to attempt to win a game, but an unsuccessful one."

"Ye talk a lot," Aden drawled, and rapped his knuckles on the deck of cards. "What's yer game?"

428

"What isn't my game? I enjoy faro, hazard, vingt-et-un, and whist, though it's difficult to find a competent partner for the latter. Piquet is good, and it has the benefit of not requiring a dealer or a banker."

"Aye. Just ye and me. Piquet it is, then. Low card deals."

"Not so fast, MacTaggert. You are an eager brute, aren't you? A hundred quid that I draw the low hand."

Pure chance didn't much appeal to Aden; he preferred relying on his skill. In the end it likely didn't much matter, except that if Vale truly meant to rely on nothing but chance and happenstance, winning — or losing — might take some time. "From the size of the deck it looks like ye've already pulled out the cards we'll nae be using, aye?"

"Of course I did." The vulture lifted one arched brow. "Thirty-two cards. It didn't take much insight to know you would choose to play piquet."

Robert Vale didn't lack confidence. "Cribbage would work, but I reckoned ye're anxious to prove yerself, and piquet is a wee bit faster-paced. A wee bit. A hundred quid for the low card, then." His gaze on the captain's raptor eyes, Aden reached over and cut the deck, turning over the stack over in his hand.

It was Vale who looked down at it first. "A ten. Well picked." Once Aden set all the cards back into the stack, the captain in his crisp blue uniform cut even deeper and turned a seven. "Ah, the low card," he said. "You couldn't beat that even if I gave you another chance at it."

Aden reckoned it had more to do with Vale prearranging the deck than with good fortune, but he kept that to himself. They had a long way to go yet, and he needed to pay attention, not get caught up in trying to prove some simple trick. "As ye say." He produced a hundred quid and set the money on the table.

"No argument? Hmm. I'd heard that Scotsmen were poor losers."

"We're nae accustomed to losing, so aye, I reckon some of us are bad at it. But I'm nae some Danny Pierce to get a whiff of trouble and jump overboard."

A muscle in Vale's cheek jumped, though his fingers didn't falter as he shuffled. "That's an odd saying," he noted. "Wherever did you pick it up?"

"Ye've nae heard it before? It's used to describe a lad who gets picked on by his betters and pays dearly because he doesnae fight back. Nae a man wants to be called a

Danny Pierce and get bullied by some smug bastard who can do as he chooses and nae face a consequence."

Vale dealt them each twelve cards. He'd won first deal, which meant Aden would have the last — not a good position in which to be. With six deals in the first *partie,* Aden would have to be well ahead to have a chance to take the game. "I should ask what stakes we're playing for," the captain said conversationally, arranging the leftover cards into two stacks and sliding the more generous one in front of Aden. "I do hope it's not a penny a point. This is not some cheap gaming hell, and I am not a clerk in some warehouse."

"Twenty quid a point?" Aden suggested.

"Promising. Let's make it fifty, shall we? To be settled at the end of each *partie*? Or it might be more fun to settle at the end of our contest. Then the meager amount in your pocket won't send you home too early."

That was Vale's plan, then, to push him into debt and make him keep playing in an attempt to win back points before they settled up. A quick road to ruin, that was. And an obvious one. "I reckon I'd prefer to settle up at the end of each *partie.* I've nae idea when ye'll decide to turn tail and run."

"As you wish, then."

431

Halfway through the third *partie,* with Aden ahead by some forty points and twenty-five hundred quid on top of that, Matthew and Lord George Humphries appeared. Both of them looking like beaten dogs, they took seats behind their master.

"So ye had a chat with Vale, did ye, Matthew?" Aden commented, countering the captain's queen of diamonds with her king and taking a point.

"I think it's more interesting," Vale cut in, before Matthew could respond, "that very soon both you and I, MacTaggert, will be brothers-in-law to Matthew. You through your dear sister Eloise, and me through *his* ravishing sister Miranda. You'll be surrounded, won't you, Mr. Harris?"

Matthew frowned. "Apparently."

"Aye, he *will* be surrounded," a low drawl sounded behind Aden. "By three MacTaggert men and their wee sister."

A large hand clamped down on Aden's shoulder, and he twisted his neck to see Coll, Niall close behind him. "How did ye get in here?"

Niall sidestepped, and his father-in-law, Charles Baxter, came into view. "Turns out I *do* know someone who's a member of the club," the youngest MacTaggert said with a slight grin.

"And I dressed like a damned Sassenach for the occasion," Coll added.

"Why are ye here at all?" Aden asked, discarding the two of clubs and giving a point back to Vale.

"To make certain everything here stays honest," Coll answered, dragging up a chair and dropping into it. He swiped a chicken leg off Aden's plate and bit off a generous chunk of it. "I nae made it to Cornwall," he went on conversationally, chewing. "Found a wee place in Taunton that might suit, and got distracted. Just got myself back to Oswell House thirty minutes ago."

Everyone else except perhaps for Niall would likely believe Coll. He was big and tended to be blunt, and people translated that into stupidity. But Coll was far from stupid; he'd simply never bothered to correct anyone else's perception because he didn't give a damn what any Sassenach thought of him.

Aden saw it quite plainly, though — his older brother was lying. More than that, Coll should have been in Cornwall for at least another day or two. It all led him down one path: Coll had found something significant.

"Aye?" he said aloud. "Let me finish this deal, and ye can tell me about it while I get

433

myself some more food." He played his last card, taking one more point. "Ye can add it all up, but ye seem to be behind in this round by two thousand fifty pounds, Vulture Vale."

Some of the men around them, their numbers having increased as the afternoon wore on, took up the epithet in a growing wave of amused murmurs. Vale's face lost a bit of its wan color. "I concur. Are you surrendering, then? Halfway through a round? Very gauche."

"Nae, but I am going to stretch my legs. Niall, keep yer eye on the table. And the cards. And the captain."

"I am not going to sit here and wait for you, MacTaggert."

"Four damned minutes, Sassenach."

Vale pulled out a fine-quality pocket watch and clicked it open. At the sight of it, Lord George frowned and sank lower in his chair. "I'm counting. You'll owe me a thousand pounds for every minute you're late."

Rather than arguing with that, Aden pushed away from the table and stood. With Coll on his heels asking about where to get more of the roast chicken, he left the gaming room for the much more sparsely populated library. "What did ye find?"

"I cannae be entirely certain it's the same

434

man, but the time and description fits."

"What, then? I've only three thousand quid in my pocket."

Coll scowled. "If ye'd put that brain of yers to serious wagering, we'd nae need Francesca and her blunt at all. We could go home still bachelors."

"Coll. Tell me yer tale."

"Fine." The big Highlander shifted a step closer. "I started down the southern coast, figuring to work my way around and then through the middle. The fifth or sixth village — I lost count because they all look so bloody similar — was called Polperro. I asked for any interesting tales about a man with a face like a hawk's, and at a tavern called Naughts and Crosses a man said that sounded like old Tom Potter's boy, young Tom."

"Tom Potter," Aden repeated. "And who is he?"

"Glad ye asked. It's nae often, ye ken, that I know more of someaught than ye, Aden."

"Gloat later. If I'm three minutes late getting back to the table I've nae blunt to wager with."

"Oh, aye. Tom Potter, the elder one, was a smuggler. On board a ship called the *Lottery* loaded with smuggled lace and brandy, he murdered a customs officer who was row-

435

ing out to confiscate the cargo. Another smuggler, one Roger Tom, informed on him, and they dragged him off to the Old Bailey and tried and hanged him."

Aden absorbed that bit of information. "That's the da, then. What of the boy, young Tom?"

"Vanished when the redcoats came after his da. Some say he took money to hang a lantern outside when his da had drunk enough brandy and fallen asleep, but nae a thing for certain. Rumors that he went on to rob a coach or two, took to cheating at cards for money, may even have killed a man and used the navy commission in the lad's pockets for himself."

"That would explain the name change," Aden mused.

"Aye, but it's still naught but stories told in exchange for a shilling or a beer. I tried nae to lead a tale in the direction I wanted, but I'm nae certain it didnae happen."

The odds said that they might have eventually found some information about the hawk-faced man in Cornwall. The stories in Polperro could therefore be true, and Coll had just lucked into finding Vale's — Potter's — birthplace sooner rather than later. It seemed Aden would have to trust in luck a little, after all. "I'll risk it."

436

"So ye mean to sit there and play for yer lass? That's yer grand plan? To win her back?"

Aden scowled. "Nae. But I need to make a good fight of it."

"Ye've lost me."

"I need to be angry enough that he doesnae feel safe."

"Then hit him."

Shaking his head, Aden turned back toward the gaming room. "I dunnae have time to explain, Coll, but he needs to reckon that he beat me, that I cannae come after him again at the table — but that I do mean to come after him."

Coll put a hand on his shoulder again, stopping him. "I dunnae ken everything ye have in that head of yers, but if ye lose and then threaten his hide ye're going to have the devil of a time finding a gaming hell anywhere in London that'll allow ye through its doors."

Aden shrugged. "I realized that some time ago, *bràthair.* My lass doesnae like wagering."

"Now ye're putting me off the idea of falling in love, after ye and Niall nearly convinced me." The viscount gave a shudder. "If I find a lass who doesnae approve of brawls or horseback riding, I reckon I'll

437

walk away."

"I hope ye get the chance to see that the choice isnae all that difficult, when it comes down to it. Now let's get back, aye?"

"So ye're going to sit there for hours and hours, working yer strategy to get close to winning and then lose and make some pointed threats?"

"That's what I said, ye lummox."

"And ye being tired and in a foul mood, anyway?"

"Aye. What's yer damned point?"

"As far as London is concerned, ye're a fucking Highlands barbarian. Like I said before, ye *could* just hit him."

Coll brushed past him and on into Boodle's gaming room. Aden stayed where he was. There were times when his brothers and his father had declared that he was too clever for his own good. He understood that; he liked intricacy and minutiae, and was good at them. His older brother was a fighter; if it came to a choice between solving something with his fists or his words, Coll would choose his fists every time.

Here Aden needed to consider the end result. With the tremendous money advantage Vale had, it would literally take hours of precise, careful play to turn this into an actual fight. And that was unless Vale realized he was being outplayed and Aden wasn't going to become his cowed dog, and he walked away from the table.

Neither was he entirely at his sharpest, which Vale had known when he sent over his note. And then there was that misleading gambler's confidence, that voice inside his head that knew he could win it all, win Miranda's freedom, without any tricks or alternative plans. But he'd made his plan, put all his pieces on the chessboard where they needed to be. He didn't need to win. He just needed to make a fight of it.

Rolling his shoulders, he walked back into the gaming room. At least a dozen more men, evidently sensing that this wasn't just a friendly game, had gathered to watch the play. Ignoring them, Aden took his seat.

"Before we continue," Captain Vale said, his hawk's eyes assessing, "you owe me one thousand pounds. You were away for five minutes and twelve seconds. I'll forgive the twelve seconds."

Aden nodded. "As we agreed, then." Willing his hands to stay steady, he deducted the amount from the paper in front of him he'd been using to keep score. Twenty-five hundred left, then. And forty-seven thousand five hundred left to go.

"That's it? No argument?" One eyebrow

dipped, giving the captain the quizzical countenance of an owl. "You're aware, I hope, that I'm about to marry the woman you've been pursuing, and in a matter of hours I'm going to own you, MacTaggert."

"So ye say. I disagree."

Vale flipped a card back and forth in one hand. "Was she wet for you?" he murmured.

He'd kept his voice below the hearing of the onlookers, because of course he wouldn't want anyone else to know that the lass he meant to use to buy his propriety had been taken by another man, but Aden heard it. Loud and clear. "Deal the cards."

"I've asked myself, you know," the captain went on, returning the stray card to the deck and shuffling, "what use I could make of you. Certainly you would be a good inducement to make certain my repayable debts are properly collected. I'm thinking, though, that perhaps having you watch while I fuck her might be truly satisfying."

Aden tilted his head, briefly wondering if the red he was seeing would be visible to anyone looking him in the eye. "Ye're trying to rattle me, aye? To make me falter, miss a declaration of cards, drop a few points here? Get ye to extend me the favor of some credit so I can continue play until I've lost far more than I can afford?"

440

Vale shrugged. "I don't care that you know. You still have to play."

Nodding to himself, Aden picked up his cards. "Thank ye."

The captain snorted. "Why, for the devil's sake, are you thanking me?"

"I was thanking *him.*" Aden cocked a thumb in Coll's direction. Then he coiled his fist and punched Robert Vale squarely in the beak.

Neat uniform and all, the captain went over backward, crashing to the floor. Aden overturned the table, cards, paper, pencils, whisky, and chicken flying as he shoved it out of his way. He landed another blow as Vale tried to roll free of his chair. Insults to himself didn't trouble him. Insults to Miranda didn't overly concern him when whispered for effect. No, what made him clench his teeth and dive into a tangle of bastard and chair was the idea that this man *meant* his threats. If he could manage it, he would do exactly as he said. To her. To Miranda.

When the captain hooked his leg, Aden made sure to fall elbow-first onto the bastard's rib cage before he took a quick dig through his pockets. No damned promissory notes, damn it all. That would have made things much simpler. "I'm a damned

Highlander," he snarled, taking a punch to the jaw and lifting Vale by the front of his coat before he slammed the captain down again. "Ye dunnae insult a lass in my presence. Nae that one, ye beaky bastard."

"I'll . . . ruin you, you, MacTaggert," Vale rasped, scrambling onto his hands and knees and trying to crawl away. "And you will . . . never set eyes on Miranda Harris again! Do . . . you hear me?"

Aden shoved him over and grabbed him by the shirt with one hand to punch him with the other. He had to make this work. He'd given his word. "Ye delusional wee man," he growled. "All ye have is some bits of paper. Paper burns. Houses burn. I know where ye live. And a corpse cannae collect on any debts."

"Enough!"

A burly man in Boodle's livery shoved them apart. Immediately another half a dozen footmen and waiters stepped between them, grabbing arms and legs. "You're going to have to leave the premises, Mr. MacTaggert. Our members do not engage in fisticuffs inside the club."

"You heard him!" Vale shouted, struggling to his feet and falling again. "He threatened my life! I won't have him a member of this club! He should be locked up!"

"I'll nae be a member of any club that would have *him.*" Pulling free, Aden landed another kick at the retreating Vale. "Dunnae make any bloody plans for tomorrow, Vulture. Ye dunnae have another sunrise coming to ye."

"Nor will you be a member of this club. Or any club, I'd warrant," the big Boodle's enforcer went on. "Leave now, sir, or we will be forced to summon Bow Street."

Aden shrugged out of the grip of the men holding him as Lord George and Matthew belatedly helped Vale to his feet. He jabbed a forefinger in the navy man's direction. "I ken where ye fucking live, ye bastard," he snarled. "Dunnae go home tonight, Humphries. Ye may find it a wee bit warm."

Grabbing his beaver hat away from one of the footmen, he jammed it on his head and stalked for the door. He kept walking until he reached Loki outside.

"That was . . . unexpected," Niall said from behind him.

Aden kept his back turned to his brothers. "Grab me and yell at me that I cannae be serious," he whispered as loudly as he dared, "then meet me around the corner." Only then did he turn around to face his brothers and Boodle's bow window beyond them. "I know exactly how to stop Vale!"

Niall looked unhelpfully puzzled, but Coll strode forward and dug fingers into Aden's labels, yanking him practically off his feet. "Ye cannae be serious!" he bellowed.

"I've nae been more serious in my damned life!" Aden returned, and broke free to swing up on Loki and gallop away.

As soon as he turned the corner out of sight of Boodle's he reined in the chestnut and patted him on the withers. Straightening, he wiped a string of blood from his chin. He wouldn't be wagering anywhere in London again. Not after that. The flash of regret he expected, though, didn't come. Instead, far too many of his thoughts centered on imagining dark-brown eyes and a soft mouth that tasted of strawberries, rather than the dozen next possible steps that lay ahead. This was all for her, and that all by itself made it worthwhile.

"What the devil are ye about?" Niall demanded, drawing up beside him. "Ye ken ye just . . . Are ye mad? Ye'll nae be welcomed at any club in London now, Aden."

"He kens," Coll put in from the back of his big Friesian, Nuckelavee.

"But —"

"Coll gave me an idea. I meant to make this a battle of nerves and skill, a chess match, but then Vale had to gloat before he

444

had any right to do so, and I . . . Well, Coll suggested fists."

"Of course he did. Why'd ye listen to him?"

"Because Vale said things about Miranda that ye dunnae say about any lass. And then I reckoned Vale's accustomed to battles of nerve and skill, which is what I'd planned to give him. He's heard threats and warnings aplenty, too. But from what Coll discovered and what we found in Portsmouth, I doubt he's been bloodied before. Men have likely said they wanted him dead, but how many have proven their willingness to actually kill him? They were likely too busy with giving in, and giving him what he wanted so they could buy back their debt. And who in their right mind would publicly threaten to burn another man's house down just to put a dent in the bastard's plans?"

"Nae a one," Niall supplied. "But how does this help ye? And Miranda?"

Aden shook out his bruised fingers. This was the part that worried him the most, the bits over which he had no control, the bits where he hoped that indulging himself in losing his temper might actually have benefited them. "A bit of patience and a pint of luck, and we'll see."

"So ye planned on being blackballed?"

445

He shrugged. "Aye. Eventually. Vale being a foulmouthed pig altered the way I meant to go about it, though."

"Aden."

"I gave that lass my word. Do ye reckon for a second that I would go back on it?"

"Nae. What are we waiting for, then?"

"A note. It'll be delivered to Oswell House, though, so we need to get back. I dunnae ken how much time we'll have."

And if this all ended up going to the devil, he wanted at least one more moment with Miranda Harris before he went to stop Vale permanently.

"You should eat something," Eloise urged, pushing a plate of biscuits closer to the middle of the breakfast table. "Something sweet. That always makes me feel more optimistic."

Miranda looked up from the tart she'd been stabbing to death. "Hmm?"

"Eat something," her brother's betrothed repeated, with a sympathetic smile. "Coll and Niall are with Aden now; everything will be fine."

"I wish Coll had told us why he rushed in like a fox after a chicken," Amy put in, her own luncheon half uneaten. "Niall wouldn't take the time to say before they both ran

446

out again. It seemed serious, though. Coll didn't even stop to eat."

Eloise pushed to her feet. "I'm going to see if Mama's heard anything. I think she sent a spy to follow Aden."

Once she was gone, Amy broke a biscuit in half and gave one piece to Miranda. "Niall saved my life, you know," she said conversationally. "Not from anything as horrible as what you're facing, but he did save me." She ate a bite of biscuit. "Mm. These are good. I think Mrs. Gordon added a dash of cinnamon."

"How did Niall save you?" Miranda asked. Being saved seemed to be a good thing, but then Amy had waited to speak until Eloise was elsewhere. If this was more intrigue, Miranda didn't think her heart would be able to stand it. She'd already been fretting for three hours while Aden faced Vale. To lose? Thank goodness he'd told her about his plan, but losing on purpose, relying on a man's poor character to save her . . . As much as she trusted Aden, it all made her feel very vulnerable. Whatever happened, it would shape the remainder of her life. And lately she'd had a few thoughts of her own on that very topic.

"You've met my mother," Amy said, lowering her voice further. "She wanted me to marry a title, and she settled on Viscount Glendarril."

"Aden's brother? Where was I when all this happened?"

"Tending your aunt and cousins, I think. Anyway, I spent the first part of this Season trying to be someone a viscount — or an earl or a marquis — would consider a proper wife. It was awful. But then Niall stepped in, and he liked that I sometimes speak my mind. He liked . . . me." She smiled, a small, intimate smile that Miranda understood very well, even if it made her a little jealous. "And that's why I go by Amy now, and not the dreadful mouthful of Amelia-Rose Hyacinth my mother insisted was better. However miserable it made me."

"I'm very happy for you, Amy."

"Yes, so am I. My point I suppose, is that once Niall knew that he loved me, and I loved him, nothing stopped him. Not another beau, not my mother, not England." She edged even closer. "You mustn't tell anyone, but he and his brothers kidnapped Lord West and stole his coach, and then he kidnapped me and took us all the way to Gretna Green. Nothing stops a MacTaggert." She straightened again. "Which I suppose is my way of saying that given the way Aden looks at you, he's going to do whatever he has to in order to keep you for himself."

Since Vale had made his appearance known, she'd spent more time thinking about being free than anything else. Lately, though, the image in her head had altered a little. It was about conversations with Aden, about hearing his voice reading one of those books he so loved aloud to her, it was about his kiss and his touch and the weight of him on her and sex.

If he did help free her, she could go back to the way it had been before Vale — her, saving dances for the silly late-arriving young men who needed a partner, worrying over nothing more serious than someone wearing the same colors as she to a soiree, being her parents' adored daughter who had been told multiple times she didn't need to marry if she didn't wish to. Her family was well-enough respected, their status enough admired, that whoever she did eventually marry, *if* she did eventually marry, would more than likely overlook her less-than-virginal status.

But if she did go back to pretending none of the past weeks had happened, Aden would marry someone else. He *had* to; everyone knew that his mother had decreed her sons should wed before their sister. She suspected it had to do with money, though

449

no one had been able to confirm that. Whatever the incentive, Niall had married Amy, Lord Glendarril had lately been seen dancing country dances despite his dislike of hopping about, and Aden . . . Aden had just hours ago told her that he loved her. The sound of those words still wrapped warm and comforting and safe around her.

It helped a little to realize that if indeed all he had needed was a wife, there were a plethora of possibilities all around him that would have all taken less effort than she. Of course, he hadn't proposed to her, hadn't said anything about ever afters, but then she couldn't have answered the way she wanted to. Not while she had another man's chains around her neck.

"I have not heard anything," Lady Aldriss said, gliding into the breakfast room, Eloise on her heels. "Further, I think we should all repair to more comfortable chairs, and perhaps have a glass of wine. I think that would be eminently more helpful than fretting over tea and biscuits."

That did sound more pleasant, especially if she could have several glasses of wine, Miranda decided. She was halfway through her first when Lady Aldriss sat on the deep couch beside her. "How are you, my dear?"

"Worried," she answered, rather grateful

that she'd made the formidable woman's acquaintance weeks ago, before Matthew had officially offered for Eloise. Francesca Oswell-MacTaggert preferred direct talk, though she was a consummate expert at speaking around any given subject and still acquiring precisely the information she was after. Up until now her most digging questions had been about Matthew's character — and that had been before Robert Vale, or at least before *she'd* known anything about the awful captain and about Matthew's debts.

"As am I. When one of my sons says he means to make a ruckus, especially one who's slipped through life avoiding them, it does rather concern me."

Miranda took another sip of wine. "If you don't wish me to speak of it please say so, but I . . . Your sons have only lately come to London. How do you know Aden has 'slipped through life'?"

"Ah." The countess regarded her with dark-green eyes. "I am a woman of great wealth and greater determination. Aside from the letters Eloise's father has written her about her brothers, I have . . . listened. For trouble, for stories, for anything I could grasp that might bring me an inch closer to their lives." Her voice tightened a little

451

around the words, but Miranda could only imagine what it would be like to be so far away from her own children, and for so long. Seventeen years, according to the conventional rumors.

"That was insufficient, I take it?" she pursued.

"Extremely so. It's one thing hearing and seeing Aden described as 'stealthy' or 'keeping his own counsel,' and quite another to realize he's fallen in love only after he told me so. Not in so many words, but I believe you know of what I speak."

Warmth crept up her cheeks. "I believe I do," Miranda conceded.

Lady Aldriss smiled. "If you ever have the opportunity, purchase him a saddle." She patted Miranda on the knee. "Don't ask me why."

The front door opened. "Miranda?" Aden called, his low brogue echoing into the grand house.

"We're in the morning room," Eloise returned, before she could do so.

Miranda stood as the three brothers entered the room. They had all dressed like proper English aristocrats, no doubt to accommodate Boodle's rules, but while the oldest and the youngest might have fooled anyone watching, the middle MacTaggert didn't look at all gentlemanly. One sleeve of his coat had split a seam, his cravat hung limp and untied around his neck, and red drips stained both it and his white shirt beneath. She gasped. "What in the world happened?"

He crossed the room, bent his head, and kissed her — right there, in front of everyone. "I willnae be getting an invitation to join Boodle's," he drawled, keeping an arm looped around her waist as he took the seat beside her, on the far side from where his mother still sat.

"You're bleeding." She brushed a hand along his mouth, feeling the lump of a bruise forming beneath the skin.

"I walloped Captain Robert Vale. Bent his beak nearly back into human shape."

That sounded very satisfying, until she recalled what an angry Robert Vale could do to her and her family. "Aden, how does that help anything?"

"Well, firstly he deserved it, and secondly it was damned satisfying," he returned. "The rest of ye might as well ken now that I had a plan to lose to him, reveal my desperation, and then stage a failed break-in at Lord George's house to convince Vale to move yer brother's promissory notes somewhere a might safer. I reckon this saved me some time sitting across the table from the rat."

"And he got to threaten to burn down Lord George Humphries's house with Vale and his notes inside it, *after* Aden dug through his pockets to be certain the vulture wasnae carrying them." Niall sat on the arm of the chair occupied by his bride and took her hand in his. "Trying to lose doesnae seem at all Scottish, but at least ye set him on his arse."

Miranda looked from one brother to the next, and finally back at Aden. "You threatened him after you hit him?" she asked, her insides twisting a little. "Inside Boodle's? With witnesses, I presume?"

"Aye. All of that."

"That's . . . not good. Unless you're kicked out of a club for politics or something more frivolous, being banned by one generally means you won't be welcomed at any of the others. Not if you aren't already a member everywhere. I mean, I know you meant to lose to him, but I had no idea you meant to ruin your own reputation to do so."

"Och," Aden returned softly. "Who wants to have to dress up to play a hand of cards?"

"That sounds very . . . heroic, but you, well . . ."

454

"Out with it, lass. Ye're to tell me if I've a hole in my trousers."

Miranda would have preferred to sit in the circle of his arms, to simply enjoy the fact that he'd punched a man she'd wanted to punch from the moment she'd met him. But she and Aden were partners, and if he did have a hole in his trousers — his plans — he needed to know about it. "You didn't get the notes. Vale will very likely go to my father now, and tell him exactly why I am going to marry him." She shuddered.

"Aye, he'll have that on his shopping list. Nae doubt about it. But first he's going to make certain that all his wee promissory notes are safe. He's wagered his entire future on what they can bring him. He's owned admirals, and shareholders of the East India Trading Company, I reckon, and now he has Matthew and Lord George, and the devil knows who else. If I burn his house down, he wants to be certain he can call in enough favors and notes to see me jailed for it. Or worse."

The matter-of-fact way he spoke to describe just how much trouble he'd voluntarily made for himself chilled her to her bones. "Somehow I'm not reassured. You trading fates with me doesn't serve anyone but Vale, and those odds you delight in don't seem very much in my favor, either."

"I'd wager he has those notes somewhere in George's house, so hidden nae even George kens where they could be. But now he'll be moving them. Since he's nae a voluntary ally to speak of, nae other place to lay his head but an inn or a hotel where he doesnae own the loyalty of the staff, and he cannae carry them about with him without risking me taking them, he has to tuck them away somewhere safe."

"A bank?" she supplied, frowning. "So now you mean to burn down a bank?"

Aden grinned. "Nae. I mean to rob a bank. I've a particular one in mind."

Miranda abruptly wished she'd been a woman who fainted. She could close her eyes, sink to the floor, and when she woke again everything would be resolved. She wouldn't have to worry or watch Aden be arrested, or see Captain Robert Vale gloat because he'd won.

But Aden wasn't foolish. Far from it. He'd made her a promise, and thus far he'd gone to great lengths to keep it. Above all of that, she trusted him. She trusted his instincts, his capabilities, and his heart. "Then I suppose if you bring the black powder, I'll bring the fuse."

"*Boireannach gaisgeil,*" he whispered.

456

"Ye're a bonny, brave lass, Miranda Harris."

"Just a moment," Lady Aldriss said, rising. "While previously you three boys — men — have flouted the conventions of polite Society and I've condoned it, this is . . . a bit much, even for me."

"Then dunnae condone it," Aden returned. "I dunnae need yer permission." He climbed to his feet, pulling Miranda up with him. "I could eat a sheep," he drawled. "Smythe, do ye reckon Mrs. Gordon could make me a sandwich or two?"

"I will have dinner set out early," the butler said. "With your permission, Lady Aldriss."

The countess waved her hand at him. "Evidently no one requires my permission any longer. By all means, serve dinner early. Perhaps we should begin with dessert."

They actually began with potatoes, while Mrs. Gordon, according to Smythe, wept and threw more wood on the stove to speed the roasting of the chicken she'd meant to serve with a delicate sauce of cheese and pine nuts and garlic, but now had no time to make.

Lord Glendarril seemed to be the only one with an appetite anyway, but Miranda did her best to eat a few bites. She thought Aden was eating — until she caught him passing bits of chicken beneath the table to Bròagan. Despite everything, despite being half out of her mind waiting for the mysterious note Aden had them all waiting for, the sight made her smile. Yes, he'd knocked Captain Vale on his arse and threatened him, but he'd also rescued a dog, and he was doing his damnedest to save her.

When a footman stepped into the room, every pair of eyes watched him deliver a note on a silver salver to Smythe and whisper something in the butler's ear. Immediately Smythe took charge of the tray and walked it around the table to deliver it to . . . her.

"A note, Miss Harris," he intoned, and held out the salver.

She took the note. "Is this it?" she asked Aden, who shrugged.

"It could be."

"Who delivered it, Smythe?" Eloise asked, leaning forward to look.

"It came by messenger, Lady Eloise. The man didn't say who'd dispatched him."

Aden's sister looked over at him. "Are you going to tell us?"

"Open it, lass, and tell all of us."

Miranda broke the wax seal, unfolded the paper, and frowned. "It's from . . . Basil Jones, Lord George Humphries's butler."

458

"A butler?" the countess repeated, lifting a curved eyebrow. "How unusual."

"Yes. It says, and I shall quote, 'Lord George requests the honor of your presence at a small breakfast gathering tomorrow at eight o'clock.' Basil Jones, his butler." She looked up. "What in the world?"

"What's wrong with it?" Aden asked, his expression perhaps a bit more intense than it should be.

"Well, to begin, a bachelor does not invite an unmarried lady to his home without detailing precisely who will be there, and he certainly doesn't have his butler write out the invitation."

"This far into the Season, an invitation should never be sent out in the evening for an event the next morning," Eloise added. "Everyone's calendar is full to bursting."

"Vale wouldnae know all those rules though, I reckon, would he?"

She looked at the missive again. A servant sending an invitation on behalf of his master, an assumption that she would be available and would appear — it actually seemed rather like something of which Vale would approve. "No, I don't think he would. But George certainly does."

"There it is, then." He pushed away from the table. "That's one thing fallen into place. If ye'll excuse me, I've a note of my own to write."

"Just a moment," Miranda countered, handing the note to Coll when he gestured for it. "*That* is what you've been waiting for? A note from *Basil Jones?*"

"Nae. I asked Humphries if he cared to get out from under all this, and if he did, for him to send me a note about someaught peculiar if Vale should make a visit to the bank today — or go anywhere without wanting his shadows to prop him up. From what ye said, a letter from a butler asking ye to breakfast is peculiar."

"So now you're rescuing Lord George Humphries, as well?"

"I'd rescue the devil from hell if it helped ye, lass," he returned, steel beneath his easy tone. "I'll be back here by dawn. The rest of ye stay indoors. Vale's likely to have somebody watching this house."

"And how are you getting to this bank you're robbing?" his mother demanded.

He sent her a brief, grim smile. "Nae by the front door."

CHAPTER SEVENTEEN

It was odd, having what felt like half of London know his plans. Back up at Aldriss both his brothers and their father had complained more than once that they never knew whether he was coming, going, or drowned in a loch somewhere. He'd liked it that way, or so he'd thought, though lately the idea of being answerable to someone else had taken on a certain, unexpected appeal.

Aden ducked into Francesca's office and found a piece of paper. Dipping a quill into ink he wrote out *nine o'clock* and folded it again before he summoned Gavin from the stables.

Trotting up to his bedchamber, he stopped the maid from setting the fire in his hearth, and turned the single lamp down to a flickering sputter. Once he'd pulled the curtains closed, he shed his English clothes in exchange for his old, worn kilt, work

461

boots, shirt, and black coat. He didn't mean to be seen much tonight, but he did need to move fast. This way he felt much more . . . himself.

Once Gavin appeared, Aden handed over the note and recited the address. "I need ye to deliver this for me. Ye'll need to slip out of the stables without anyone seeing ye, and hire either a hack or a pair of horses. When ye've done it, wait for me in the park with the old, split oak."

The groom nodded. "I'll need a bit of coin for that."

Aden handed over a few pounds. "Dunnae be seen by anyone watching the house, Gavin."

"I reckon that's why ye sent for me, and nae some Sassenach boy in pretty livery."

Aden pulled out his pocket watch and checked the time. He wanted to leave immediately, go see this finished once and for all. But Gavin needed time, and he needed to be certain no one lingered late at the bank doing the books or whatever it was bankers did at the end of the day.

It was odd; generally, he was an exceedingly patient man. Gambling required patience, and so did coaxing wallflowers out to dance and encouraging them to talk, to hand out the little dabs of information he enjoyed collecting for its own sake. Now, though, he wanted to gallop through the middle of London and slay Miranda's dragons. *Him.*

But now he needed to wait, and for at least thirty minutes. The less time he spent out where one of Vale's so-called friends could see him and note where he happened to be, the better. He paced to the curtained window and back. Dinner was likely still sitting on the table, but he didn't want more polite conversation. He didn't want to hear the speculating, and he didn't want his brothers picking apart his plans and trying to force him to reveal the bits he hadn't yet deciphered.

Brògan scratched at his door, and he walked over to open it for her. Just beyond the spaniel stood Miranda, her hand upraised to knock. Well, this seemed a much better way to spend half an hour. "Come on in, lass," he said, holding out his hand as Brògan scooted in between his legs and dove under the bed.

"Thank you, Aden," she returned, angling a finger to point over her shoulder.

He looked where she indicated, to see Eloise standing well within earshot and apparently engrossed by a painting of a mad-haired Oswell ancestor. "Ye've brought a chaperone, I see."

"Not my idea," she whispered as she moved past him.

"I'm protecting her reputation," Eloise called out. "Mama's making me. And she's worried about *you,* too."

So Lady Aldriss had her fingers in this pie, as well. "I'm a man grown, Eloise. Some of the things I've done would turn yer hair white. It's too late to be worrying about me, now."

"But I'm worried, too," Miranda put in. "Punching a man who certainly deserves it is one thing. I wish I'd been there to see it. But this is risking you being arrested, or worse. I don't like it."

"I'm nae baying at the moon, lass. I've a plan."

"Yes, taking Vale's notes from a bank. You've been a bit light on the particulars, partner."

He cocked his head at her. "That, I have. And that, I am." Moving her farther into the room and out of his sister's earshot, he told her, as briefly as he could, how he expected the next few hours to proceed.

She didn't like it; he could see that in her tight-pressed lips and the nervous tapping of her fingers in his. "Aden," she said when he'd finished, "I didn't ask for your help to see you in jail. Or dead."

"Not even at first, when ye didnae like me?"

"I liked you. Far more than I ever wanted to admit. And don't change the subject. You're relying on luck, here."

He scowled. "I'd nae do such a thing. Ever. If the wind chooses to be at my back, though, I'll nae complain about it. If ye've a better idea, I'll listen to it."

"I'm beginning to think simply running away might be the easiest solution."

Aden wanted to ask if she meant to flee on her own, or if she'd prefer to have a certain Highlander by her side, but she would only accuse him of trying to distract her again, which he would have been doing. "Sitting about and waiting is harder than what I have before me, lass. But I'll nae fail ye."

"Just this afternoon you got yourself banned from every proper gentlemen's club in London to save me, so I have no doubt about your intentions. I don't want you to be hurt while you're going about rescuing me. I . . . I love you, you know."

He brushed his fingers down her arm, taking her hand in his. "And I love ye, lass. Nae a thing will ever change that. But if ye dunnae feel the same way about me tomor-

465

row morning, I want ye to tell me so. I could stand being wrong, but nae being wrong and nae knowing it."

She frowned. "Aden, how many —"

"Nae," he cut in. "At this moment ye cannae talk to me honestly about forevers, because yers is still being held by someone else. So afterward, when ye're free, ye can decide if ye're grateful to me, or feel obliged, or that I'm just . . . convenient. After."

Miranda looked at him for a long moment. "They say that sometimes the brightest men are also the stupidest, but have it your way."

Not many things genuinely surprised Aden, but Miranda did, almost constantly. "Could ye repeat that?"

"You heard me. You're being honorable, and stupid. I'm slightly insulted, but I understand."

"Ye're a sharp-tongued woman, Miranda. I like that about ye." He adored it about her, but this definitely wasn't the time for those sorts of declarations.

"Good. I don't intend to change."

For Saint Andrew's sake, he hoped not. Even with Vale after her for weeks, she'd kept her sense of humor. She hadn't crawled under the covers and decided to hide until all the unpleasantness went away, which is precisely what he would have expected from one of the delicate English lasses his father had gone to great lengths to describe. That definitely was not Miranda Grace Harris. He hoped, after all this was finished, that he would still have the privilege of facing her indignation. "Might I kiss ye, then?" he asked.

Her mouth twitched. "I would be amenable to that."

Drawing her up against him, he lowered his head to capture her mouth. Sharptongued and sweet tasting. What a conundrum she was. And he delighted in it. In her.

"I've counted to thirty," Eloise announced a moment later, "and I'm sorry, but I'm going to have to separate you now."

That made two lasses, then, who had him twisted about their wee fingers. With a sigh and a last nibble at Miranda's lower lip, he took half a step backward. "I'd argue with ye, *piuthar,* but if I caught ye kissing Matthew for a count of thirty, I reckon I'd have to put him in a trunk and ship him off to the Orient."

"I'm going with you," Miranda said abruptly.

That stopped him in mid-thought. "Nae. Ye arenae."

"Oh, dear," Eloise muttered, and vanished in the direction of the stairs.

"Och, she's going to tell Coll and Niall," he muttered.

"You're doing this for me, Aden," Miranda persisted. "You shouldn't be the only one taking a risk."

"I —"

"Ye're nae going alone," Coll said from the doorway, Eloise a slender shadow behind him.

Aden glared at the giant blocking all the light from the hall. Beside him Miranda looked from one MacTaggert brother to the other. He could see the sense in not going alone, but he also knew who stood to gain or lose the most from this plan of his. "Ye're right," he returned. "I'm nae going alone. Miranda's coming with me."

"Y—"

"I've nae more time to argue." Walking to the bedside table, he lowered the lantern still further, till it barely managed any light at all. "We're going out the window," he said, moving over to the opening and pulling open the curtains again. "The idea is to be unnoticed. Ye and Niall and the lasses go into the front room and make some noise. We're all home, and we're celebrating me setting Vale on his arse."

With a muttered curse, Coll reached back for Eloise's hand and wrapped it around his arm. "Ye heard him, *piuthar.* Come sing us a song."

With a glare that told Aden he'd best know what he was about, the viscount closed the door to leave Aden and Miranda alone in his bedchamber. "On another day, I wouldnae be using this moment to climb out a window," Aden muttered, catching her mouth for a quick kiss. "Now. Let me climb down first," he went on, releasing her and taking the old knife out of his bed stand to shove it into his boot. "Watch how I do it. If ye fall, I'll catch ye."

"Thank you," Miranda said, her voice catching.

"Well, we're partners. Aye, lass?"

She smiled, a tear running down one cheek before she wiped it away. "Aye."

Shaking himself loose of thoughts of Miranda and forever, Aden walked over and ducked out the window, using the trellis and drainpipe to climb to the ground and taking more care than he generally did since Miranda was watching and would be using his descent as her example.

"Come along, lass," he whispered. "One foot at a time."

"I should have put on trousers," came

floating down to him as she found her footing on the trellis.

"But then I couldnae look at yer legs."

"Aden."

"A little to the left lass, and dunnae catch up yer skirt," he countered, positioning himself below her and not feeling the least bit of guilt at looking up to see those long, pretty legs. The idea that he had the slightest chance of waking up every morning with her warm, lithe body in his arms . . . He shook those soft thoughts out of his head — he hadn't won this game yet.

When she was close enough, he reached up and caught hold of one slender ankle to guide her down to the ground. "My da warned me about falling for a soft, hothouse flower of a Sassenach lass," he murmured when she stepped back and turned around to face him. He plucked a flower petal from her dark hair. "All delicate and fainting and helpless."

She grinned up at him, a smudge of dirt across her nose. "Did he, now?" she returned, tangling her fingers into his lanky hair and pulling his face down for a kiss.

He could drown in her smile, he decided. "Aye," he whispered, lifting his head. "Now let's go rescue ye."

■ ■ ■ ■

In her wildest dreams Miranda couldn't have conjured anything remotely like this. Hand in hand with a tall, kilt-wearing Highlander, slipping from shadow to shadow along the streets of Mayfair with only the moonlight and the scattered, flickering glow of oil lamps to light the way.

She couldn't detect anyone watching Oswell House, but she didn't doubt that Vale had someone lurking there. He'd known the moment Aden had returned from Portsmouth, and he'd known her to be dining at Oswell House.

Three streets away from the grand house they approached a small park dominated by a grand old oak tree, one of the huge branches split from the trunk and hanging almost to the ground. Aden let out a low whistle, making her jump.

Three shadows, two of them horse-shaped, separated from the tree. "Bloody stable master tried to rob me," a deep Scottish voice said in the dimness. "Said he reckoned if I needed two horses at this time of night it wasnae for anything good, and I could pay him double or go elsewhere."

"Did ye convince him otherwise?" Aden

asked, ducking beneath the hanging branches.

"Aye, but we'll nae be able to rent horses from him again." A stout man in a groom's jacket and worn boots, together with a kilt in the MacTaggert plaid, stepped into the moonlight. He looked over at her and stopped. "Ye didnae tell me ye'd have a proper lass with ye. I shouldnae have said 'bloody,' I reckon. Begging yer pardon, miss."

"I wasn't offended," she returned. "There's no need to apologize."

"Well, I only fetched two mounts, as Master Aden asked, and nae one trained for the sidesaddle, so I *do* need to apologize, even though I wasnae told ye'd be here."

"She'll ride with me," Aden put in, his tone amused. "Miranda, this is Gavin. He came south with us to make certain our horses were properly seen to. Gavin, Miss Harris."

"Miss Harris," the groom said, tugging on his forelock.

Aden moved past her and swung into the saddle of the bay mare. Once aboard he kicked his left foot out of its stirrup and held a hand down to her. "I'll have ye in my arms after all, it seems."

With Gavin boosting her up, she stepped

472

into the stirrup and then practically flew through the air to sit sideways across Aden's thighs.

"Cozy?"

That wasn't quite the word she would use, not with her heart pounding practically out of her chest, but she nodded, anyway. Once the groom had mounted a short-chested gray, they set off at a canter that would have had pedestrians frowning at them if they'd attempted it in daylight. As it was they nearly ran one hack off the road, and the driver of a grand, black coach gave them the two-fingered salute as they hurried by.

"Which bank are we burgling?" she asked, turning her head to look up at Aden's lean face.

He glanced down at her, then back to the streets. She thought she saw brief humor in his eyes, but it could have been the moonlight. "The big one," he returned.

" 'The big one'? Could you narrow it down a bit?"

"What do ye Sassenach call it? The Old Lady of Threadneedle Street, aye?"

"The . . . The Bank of England?" she croaked. "*The* bank?"

"Well, aye. Where else would a man take his most precious possessions to make certain they stay safe?"

"Good heavens. I thought you meant some out-of-the-way private little bank that has favorable lending terms for criminals or something."

She felt his responding laugh all the way to her bones, and that made her consider the other things she could feel, as she sat on his thighs and the horse rocketed down the lane. When she deliberately shifted a little, he gave a muttered curse.

"Here I am trying to be a bloody hero," he murmured, "and all I can think of is that I want ye again, and now that I've had ye, I reckon no one else will ever do for me."

She kissed his jaw. "I was beginning to think there was something wrong with me, because even with Vale breathing down my neck, being with you is all I can think about."

"Mayhap we're both wicked, lass."

Miranda liked that. Wicked. A few weeks ago being called "nearly scandalous" had satisfied her, but she was finished with being "nearly" anything. And she was finished with frivolous evenings where the most serious discussion she was likely to have was whether the long-lost Lady Temperance Hartwood would finally reappear as the wife of a butcher or a tanner or something, six pudgy children in tow.

"We could keep riding all the way to the coast and board a ship bound for Portugal," she suggested.

"I'm rescuing ye whether ye want it or nae," he returned with a brief grin. "If ye want to flee after, well, the Highlands are a fine a place as any to get lost." His smile flattened a little. "Or wherever ye wish. Ye'll be free to call on Prussians or Egyptians or even Americans, if ye care to do so."

There he went again, sidestepping any mention of a future they might share. Stubborn, stubborn Highlander. He would tell her that he loved her and melt her heart, tell her that he wanted her and heat her from the inside out, but he rode miles away from any mention of the word "marriage," for fear that she might be answering out of gratitude or a sense of obligation or even a last, desperate effort to free herself from Vale's grasp. And he doubted his own sense of honor.

When they reached Threadneedle Street, the massive Bank of England looming dark and imposing to their left, Aden slowed to a walk. "Northeast corner," he muttered, turning them up Bartholomew Lane along the bank's broad backside.

"You trust this fellow we're meeting?" she whispered, shivering as she looked up at the

475

building. "Not to disparage you, but he *is* a gambler. Vale *could* own him."

"I was a gambler, too, until a few hours ago. I reckon we'll find out shortly if I read him rightly or nae."

Half of her hoped Aden had been wrong, that they weren't just about to burgle the Bank of England. But if he *was* wrong, she would be paying a horrible price, anyway, and he would have been blackballed for no blasted reason at all.

"Gavin," he called, his voice barely audible, "keep an eye on that lad in the blue coat. He's a guard, I reckon. Let me know when he turns the corner."

Keeping them at a walk, the two horses headed up toward Lothbury. If he didn't decide what he was about soon, they would have to circle the entire building again.

"Go," Gavin hissed. An instant later, Aden had his hands around Miranda's waist as he lifted her to the ground. He followed her a second later and tossed the bay's reins to the groom.

"Keep going up the street and around, in a big circle," he instructed. "Look for us."

Nodding, Gavin continued up to the cross street and headed left on Lothbury. "He seems very comfortable with this," Miranda noted, hardly daring to breathe.

"He's done worse in our company," Aden agreed, and took her hand. Hurrying her into a brisk walk, they headed directly for the small employee's door at the northeast corner of the building. Ducking them into the shadows, he made a fist and knocked.

"That's rather anticlimactic," she muttered.

He chuckled. "If nobody answers I'll have to start breaking things."

The door opened with an abruptness that startled her, dim lantern light flooding into the street. "This way," a thin, older man with a cloud of brown and white hair whispered. "No lingering."

She stepped past him, Aden on her heels. As she watched, the man shut and locked the door again, then picked up the lamp to lead the way down a long hallway lined with doors.

"Stay close. It gets very dark in here at night." He half faced her. "Peter Crowley," he said in a low voice. "You would be Miss Harris, I presume?"

"Yes, I would be. So you and Aden have played at cards?"

"I'd say he's bought me a few beers over the course of the Season," Mr. Crowley returned. "And lost many a penny."

"Crowley nae wagers more than a shilling," Aden commented, warm and solid behind her. "Claims his wife, Mary, would crack him over the head if he ever lost more than that."

"That is very good incentive, then. But why are you helping us, Mr. Crowley? You're risking your employment."

"I've worked in this bank for most of my adult life," he said. "I've seen men come in to empty their accounts and hand them over to some stranger because of an unlucky turn of the cards. Lately I've seen several account holders arrive with the very same man in tow. When Aden told me your troubles, I realized we were all dismayed by the very same man. Legally I can't do anything to stop this cheating and double dealing. But tonight, here in the dark, I can."

"Ye're a good man, Peter."

"As are you. If you weren't, I wouldn't be here. I *am* risking a great deal. Not to mention my wife cracking me on the head."

He stopped them somewhere close to the bank's middle, a place with cabinets and counters and still more doors and walls. It was a labyrinth. Even if there had been a hundred lamps, she didn't think she would have been able to find her way out again.

"The private rooms where customers store their items in need of protection are down the hall over there." Mr. Crowley gestured into the darkness. "I can't in good conscience allow you in there, and I don't have another lamp. So please, don't move. We have a very limited amount of time."

Mr. Crowley and his lantern retreated, the small circle of light receding until he turned a corner, leaving them in the dark. In the distance something rattled, followed by the sound of a door opening and closing.

"You might have told Lady Aldriss that this isn't quite a burglary," Miranda whispered, reaching out and finding Aden's sleeve, then working her way down to his hand.

"It is a burglary. We're just nae breaking a door to get inside. If we get caught, ye're to faint and claim I kidnapped ye. And I'm nae jesting about that, Miranda. Ye ken?"

"So you go to prison for even worse crimes than burglary and I get to marry Vale?" she retorted, sotto voce. "I would rather join you in a cell at the Old Bailey."

"I dunnae reckon they'd let us share."

It still sounded better than marrying Vale. "Did you make Peter Crowley's acquaintance because you knew he worked here, and you knew Lord George and Matthew banked here?"

"I met Crowley before I met ye. Once ye

asked for my help I did query if he'd ever seen a hawk-faced man wagering, and he said nae but that he'd seen him here at the bank with a lad who sounded like George Humphries. The rest came together later."

"I imagine I'm supposed to deliver another lesson in polite Society to you now, and tell you that sons of earls and brothers of viscounts do not go wagering at establishments where bank clerks and tradesmen spend their coin," she mused, squeezing his hand. "And that aristocrats do not call commoners 'friend.'"

"Ye can if ye'd like, but I'd be disap—"

"I'm not going to do any such thing," she interrupted. "By breaking those rules, you very likely saved my life — or at least my sanity."

"Ye broke a few for me, as well, lass," he returned in his low brogue. "And I hope ye'll break a few more."

That made a shiver run down her spine, one not entirely caused by the looming darkness around them. The idea of being with him again left her feeling nearly euphoric.

The flood of light as Mr. Crowley reentered the main space was nearly blinding. Despite all the conversation about why they'd come here, it wasn't until she saw the wooden box in the bank clerk's hands that the worry of it all hit her. If Vale's papers weren't in that box, one of two things would likely happen tomorrow: Either Vale would arrive at her house and tell her parents why she would be marrying him; or Aden would kill him. There didn't seem to be a third choice, however desperately she wished for one.

"Captain Robert Vale did *not* want anyone looking at his possessions," Mr. Crowley said, putting the box on the counter. It made a heavy thud, not at all like something that held a few very valuable pieces of paper. "It's nailed shut. And before you ask, I cannot let this box leave the bank."

Indeed, the box was stamped with the bank's seal and several notations indicating its ownership, location, and the date it had been deposited. As Miranda began to lament all over again why no one had brought a hammer or an iron pry bar, Aden bent down and freed the knife from his boot.

Crowley didn't look at all pleased, but before he could protest Aden flipped the knife in his hand and jammed the blade beneath the lid. He shoved downward, using his weight, and with an earsplitting squeak it lifted. "Well, that's just poor workmanship, the way that lid fell off there,"

Aden noted, pulling it free to set it aside.

Holding her breath and half expecting spiders to be inside, Miranda lifted the lantern and peered inside. Dull metal gleamed back at her. "There's another box inside."

The banker pulled it free, setting a smaller metal box, its lid secured by a latch with a keyhole, onto the counter. "We don't have the key. And this box can't —"

"Leave the premises," Aden finished. Taking hold of the metal container, he set it carefully on the floor, then stomped on it. Hard. "I'm finished with being subtle," he growled, stomping again.

After a few more blows with the hard heel of his boot and backed by the impressive strength of a frustrated Scotsman, the box collapsed on one side, the latch bowing outward. Aden crouched again, using his knife to wrench off the entire latch. Forcing open the lid, he looked inside. And stilled.

"Aden?" she queried, her heart freezing. Spiders or biscuits, if it wasn't Matthew's debts inside, she was done for.

A long string of soft Scots-Gaelic curses answered her. "Come down here," he said finally, settling onto the floor. "Ye need to see this."

Still barely breathing, she sank onto her

knees. She couldn't marry Vale. She *couldn't.* the idea had been repulsive before, but now . . . now she had something she wanted, with all her heart. Anything else — her mind refused to even form the words.

"It's nae just Matthew and Lord George," Aden said, lifting a short stack of mismatched papers and handing them to her.

Her fingers shaking, she looked at them while Aden pulled still more out of the misshapen box. Paper after paper, all with the amount of the debt, the date incurred, and the signature of the debtor, plus a careful set of notations on the back of each one listing the "favors" the signatory had delivered, and additional notes about what further deeds they could do in exchange for the forgiveness of their debt. "He never returns them," she said, a different kind of dread creeping through her.

"Nae. Some of these are a decade old. Older."

"He keeps these people the way a farmer keeps cattle. Matthew, Lord George, they would never have been free of him. *I* would never have been free of him, of bowing to his every demand. I —"

Aden grabbed her hand. "Ye're free of him now, Miranda. Ye hear me? Ye beat him." He pressed a dozen papers into her palm.

"Fifty thousand quid worth of promissory notes, all in Matthew's name. Dunnae read the notations. Just burn them."

He'd read the notations. She could hear the fury, barely restrained, in his voice. Miranda clenched her fist around the notes. "We beat him," she said fiercely.

"And those papers of your brother, you can take with you," Mr. Crowley said. "But do it quickly. I need to put this back together so no one knows it's been moved."

"Not just my brother's papers," she said, grabbing handfuls of notes and stuffing them into the pocket of her pelisse, the pockets of Aden's coat, and his sporran. "All of them."

"Aye," Aden echoed, finding a cloth bag from somewhere and emptying the rest of the box.

"Aden," Crowley said, a scowl in his voice. "That wasn't —"

"Nae. We're stopping him. But if ye dunnae want the box empty, I've an idea of someaught we can put in there." Handing her the bag and standing, he walked to the nearest desk, found a paper, ink, and a pen, and wrote out a few lines before he folded it and put it inside the mangled metal box. They set it back inside its wooden nest, and using the butt of his knife he hammered the lid back on.

"Once again, don't move," Mr. Crowley warned them, hefting the box and lantern and disappearing again.

"What did you say in the note?" Miranda asked, holding the bag and its contents tight to her chest. She held dozens of lives, dozens of futures, in there, hers included.

"I pointed out that the odds werenae in his favor any longer, and suggested he try his luck elsewhere."

"Will he, though?"

Aden put an arm around her shoulders. "If he wants to continue breathing, aye." His muscles flexed. "I'd best get ye back to Oswell House before our turn of luck runs dry. We've some things to consider, *boireannach gaisgeil.*"

Yes, they did. He'd actually found a way to set her free. And even more important to her heart, *she'd* had a hand in saving herself. Now she needed to enjoy the moment, to think, and to perhaps deliver a lesson to a barbarian that he should believe a woman when she'd declared she knew her own mind.

CHAPTER EIGHTEEN

Aden sent Miranda up the trellis before him. As she reached the window she gasped and with a rush disappeared inside.

Cursing, Aden swarmed up the trellis after her. If Vale had made his way there in the dark to put a knife through someone, the bastard was going to have to go through a damned Highlander first. And the naval captain was going to find out if he could fly when Aden pitched him out the window.

With a last upward lunge he dove inside, pulling the knife from his boot as he rolled to his feet. "Dunnae . . ." he began, then closed his mouth, breath returning to his body all in a rush. "Coll."

Lord Glendarril settled Miranda back onto her feet before he sank into the chair he'd dragged over to the window. "Ten more minutes and ye'd have found me pounding on the door of every bank in London," he rumbled. "Next time ye go do a burglary, ye tell me where."

In a very short time Aden had gone from being the mysterious brother who went his own way with no one being the wiser, to being the one without any damned secrets at all. Oddly enough, though, the idea didn't even trouble him. "Agreed. Now get out of my bedchamber, giant."

With a sigh Coll rose, a book clutched in one hand. "Aye, but I'm taking this with me. This Tom Jones is a *sgat.* Ye didnae tell me any of the books ye read were actually interesting."

"Take it, then."

The oldest MacTaggert brother reached the door and pulled it open, then looked back with a lifted eyebrow. "Might I show ye to yer room, Miss Harris?"

Miranda looked from the giant to him. Aden wanted to catch hold of her, make her stay, but he'd spent weeks telling her he'd set her free, and telling himself not to try to put more ropes around her when she'd only just escaped. Clenching his fist to keep from reaching out to this stubborn, exasperating, impossibly irresistible woman, he shrugged. "Do as ye think best, lass."

With a sour look that felt like a dagger in his heart, she nodded and joined Coll at the door. "Good night, then," she said quietly, and turned away — to shut the door on the giant's backside.

"Miranda?" Aden whispered.

Facing him, she leaned back against the door, reaching down one hand to turn the key and lock it. Aden was fairly certain he heard Coll's low chuckle, then the sound of the door across the hallway closing.

Slowly she straightened and took a gliding step toward him. Both her hands went up, and a moment later her hair came down in a dark, curling tumble. "The way I see it, Mr. MacTaggert," she murmured as she continued her approach, unbuttoning the front of her pelisse and dropping it to the wood floor, "I am a free woman."

"So ye are," he made himself say, wondering that he didn't burst into flames from just being close to this sultry goddess disrobing in the dimness before him.

"So I am."

"Ye just said that."

She paused, her gown down around her waist and only a shift shielding her fine breasts from his view. "Do you really want to argue right now, Aden Domnhall MacTaggert?"

"Nae. I do not." He enunciated the last word clearly. "But we've a sack of notes to burn."

She looked at his hand, where the sack still hung from his fingers. "If we burn them," she said, meeting his gaze again, "how would the people Vale has caught know that they're free?"

"They wouldnae, I suppose. He could claim he still has the papers. Or rather, just nae admit he lost them."

"Then we need the names and addresses first, so we can let them know they're free. *Then* we burn them."

Aden nodded. He wasn't about to argue with her. She'd nearly been caught by Vale. If she wanted to see the rest of the unfortunates set free as well, by God they would do it.

Aden set the sack into his wardrobe, put a coat over it, and closed the doors again. "That'll do for now, I reckon."

Whatever came next, he wanted this damned bonny woman in his arms tonight. Crossing the room he kissed her, reveling in the way she leaned into the embrace, the way her arms swept around his neck to pull herself closer against him. A swift tug of the ribbon at her waist dropped her gown to the floor, and he lifted her out of it.

This wasn't a lass looking for a pleasant night to hold in her memory against a future of possibly awful ones. Nor was she a lass determined to give her virginity where she would instead of having it taken against her will. Tonight she was a lass who wanted . . . him. And that was intoxicating.

Crouching, he let her lean against his shoulders while he removed her shoes one by one. Then, gathering the hem of her shift in his hands, he lifted, kissing every inch of the skin he laid bare. At the apex of her thighs he slowed further, dipping in for a taste of her. Sweet Saint Andrew, she was wet for him. This wasn't a ploy, and it wasn't some payment in exchange for a completed task. This was desire, and he felt it through every inch of his body.

When he straightened, lifting the shift off over her head, she was smiling at him. "Amused, are ye?" he quipped, cupping her warm breasts in his hands, feeling her nipples peak beneath his fingers.

"Happy," she returned breathlessly, and yanked the coat off his shoulders.

"Free," he added, pulling off his own shirt and leaving her to fumble with the buckles of his kilt. "Ye live yer life however ye choose, bonny lass. Give a few curtsies to Society, and do as pleases ye."

"I mean to do exactly that," she returned, straightening and evidently giving up on the kilt. Instead she pushed him in the chest, and he allowed himself to drop into the chair behind him.

He took off one of his boots while she wrenched off the other. Aden showed her how to unfasten his kilt, hoping that it was knowledge she would care to make use of in the future, and often. This bit was new, where he craved a particular woman, wanted her always in his life, but he knew that trapping her there would be wrong. He was the one who fled a lass's bed at the first sign of fawning or forever afters, and yet that was what he wanted most with Miranda.

It was a nice, big chair he had, and with a grin he took her hand. "Care to join me here?"

She looked down at his cock. "Right here? Yes."

Aden half lifted her, settling her over him with her knees on either side of his thighs. "I do adore ye, Miranda," he murmured, lifting up a little to reach her mouth as she looked down at him.

Wide-eyed, smiling in clear anticipation, she sank down over him. He wanted to meet her there, take her, claim her, empty himself into her so she would be his forever. Instead he waited, unable to stifle a moan as she took in the length of him, tight and hot and for tonight, at least, his.

491

"Oh," she breathed, bouncing experimentally. "This is . . . Oh."

Christ. Aden took her breasts again, pinching her nipples as she moved on him. With a gasp she came, pulsing around him, digging her fingers into his shoulders. He held her as she trembled, using every ounce of willpower not to succumb, as well.

When her fingers loosened a little and she raised her head, he kissed her. "Wicked, bonny lass," he breathed.

She shifted again, nearly sending him over the edge. "But you're —"

"Aye. Ye make me feel like a green boy, Miranda, but are ye ready for a bit more?"

The grin she gave him was something he would remember forever. "Oh, yes."

Holding her where she was, still impaled, he slid to the edge of the chair and then onto the expensive-looking rug spread before the hearth. Putting her on her back he withdrew and then entered her deeply, holding her gaze as he took her over and over again.

He'd never wished more that he was the barbarian the Sassenach thought him, so that he could put her over a horse and ride off with her, take her into the Highlands where no one else would be able to harm her or frighten her or take her away from him.

With every stroke he claimed her body, memorizing every gasp and moan and deep sigh, every motion and the warm, soft feel of her skin against his. She tightened around him again, and as she came, he let himself ride over the edge with her, emptying himself deep inside her.

When he could breathe again he rose, sweeping her up into his arms, and carried her over to his bed. She fell asleep with her head on his shoulder, her hands wrapped around his arm. Aden had never been one for praying, but as he watched her sleep, a slight smile on her sweet face, he did so, praying that he was the man she'd declared him to be, and that he'd done enough good in his life to perhaps deserve her.

Miranda woke to the sound of papers rustling. Stretching, she reached down toward the foot of the bed, feeling Aden sitting there. "It's not morning already, is it?" she asked.

"Barely. Seven o'clock, maybe," he returned. "How did ye sleep?"

"Better than I have in quite a long while," she admitted, pushing aside the heavy covers and sitting up.

Aden sat cross-legged on the foot of the bed, dozens of small stacks of papers around him. From the look of it, he'd been at it for a while. Hours, more than likely. "How many people did he do this to?"

"I made a list," he said, nudging a paper toward her. "Thirty-seven, by my count. He's written *deceased* on five of them, but he has addresses for the rest. Nae doubt he kept track of them so he could keep making use of them, but his diligence makes yer plan to let 'em know they're free a whole acre easier."

She watched him for a few moments as he read each of the half a dozen papers left in his hand and then sorted them into the existing piles. "You didn't need to read them," she said as he shoved all but a single stack of them back into the sack. "We know how horrible he is."

"I reckon I did need to read every one of them. Somebody should know exactly who he is."

It wasn't how she'd wanted to begin the day, especially after such a spectacular, invigorating night, but she did understand it. Last night they'd taken away Robert Vale's means of supporting himself, and she was glad of it. But she knew Aden saw some parallels between himself and Vale — to her regret, she'd pointed out some of them to him, herself. "You like to wager. That doesn't make you his twin, you know."

He looked up at her, the intensity of his gaze reminding her all over again of last night, not that it would ever drift far from her thoughts. Heavens, she'd begun to feel like two separate people, almost. One who smiled and curtsied and played charades at parties, and another who delighted in having sex with a poetical-haired Highlander and found nothing more entertaining than bantering words with him.

"It doesn't," she repeated firmly.

"There are similarities," he said finally. "I *could* have made my way through life by gambling. Coll's suggested it a few times, to break us free of Francesca. To keep the three of us — or two of us, anyway — from being obligated to follow her orders."

"Obligated? And unwilling to do as she says?" Miranda prompted.

"Willing or unwilling, my . . . Any lass I ask would know I'd been ordered to domesticate myself."

Stubborn, impossible man. "So yes, you *could* have become a gambler, and I *could* have become a nun, but knowing what I know now, I certainly wouldn't have enjoyed it."

"Och, lass." Grinning, he leaned over and kissed her.

Miranda wrapped her arms around his shoulders, kissing him back. "Forget about the odious things he wrote," she murmured, resting her forehead against his. "Just write down the rest of the addresses and burn them. All of them."

"Aye."

He hesitated, the second time he'd done so in the past four minutes. This time it made her heart shiver a little. "What is it?"

"Ye should know, he bought other debts, too. Or won them, more likely."

She frowned. "So he took over the debts of other gamblers?" When he didn't answer she looked at the stack of papers still in his hands, then up to his face again. *No. It couldn't be.* "He has Uncle John's debts, doesn't he?"

"Damnation, ye're quick," he commented. "Aye. He *did* have them. He doesnae have them now. Ye do." He handed them to her. "No notes scribbled on them, other than *Miranda's uncle* written on the back. A bit of additional leverage against ye, I reckon."

A few more chains with which to bind her. And freedom for John Temple to return to his family, if he was still alive. *Good heavens.* It was both horrible that Vale saw a man's life as nothing more than leverage against her, and wonderful that Aden's actions had set someone else dear to her free. As soon as she could arrange it, every newspaper in America would be carrying an advertisement to Uncle John, notifying him that he was free and could come home.

"Ye're pleased, aye?" he asked, making one more notation before he set aside his pencil.

"Oh, yes." She kissed him again. How could she not? "When you perform a rescue, you don't muck about with it, do you?"

Putting the rest of the papers back into the sack, he stood up. He'd put on his kilt, though he was still bare-chested and barefoot. "Ye're the one who wanted to bring all these back with ye. I would've burned them on the spot."

"That's why we make such a sound partnership," she said. "We catch the leaks in each other's boats."

"That, we do." He took her hand, helping her off his bed and handing her the shift she'd discarded earlier. "I have all the names, now. And I wrote out notes to Lord George and yer brother; the sooner they know what's happened, the better." Scowling, he handed her the bulging sack. "Ye should do this, Miranda."

She pulled on the thin muslin shift, then, her heart hammering, added Uncle John's notes to the sack. With Aden behind her, she carried it over to the fireplace. The fire still crackled; he must have stoked it when he got up earlier to retrieve the notes.

"Part of me wants to perform some sort of ceremony," she mused, crouching, "but I rather think they just need to go away before they can do more harm." With that she leaned forward and set the sack into the middle of the fire.

"Well done, lass," Aden breathed, squatting down beside her to watch the cloth begin to smoke and then darken into flame. "He's finished, and ye're free."

One man's livelihood destroyed and thirty-seven men and women set free, all in the space of five minutes full of smoke and fire. Simple and swift, and oh, so momentous all at the same time. Once nothing remained but ash and a few blackened edges of paper, Aden straightened and drew her to her feet beside him.

"Ye need to get yerself into the bedchamber Lady Aldriss gave over to ye, Miranda Harris. Coll willnae say anything, but Eloise will faint if she sees ye leaving my room with yer hair loose and still wearing yesterday's clothes."

Yes, they couldn't have that. If someone found her in Aden's room, she would be compelled to marry him. Heaven forfend.

"Someaught on yer mind, lass?" he queried, narrowing one eye. "Ye've a look about ye. Nae a somber, contemplative look, either. Something a bit more devilish."

"Just last night you were advising me to do as I pleased," she returned. "But now you're suddenly worried about propriety?"

"I reckon this should be the part where ye curtsy to Society, is all. Unless ye want everyone to know we're lovers, ye and me."

"Oh, no, we can't have that," she retorted, knowing she sounded flippant, and not caring if he heard it. He was so blasted determined not to step on her freedom that it would have been amusing if it wasn't so aggravating.

"I'll show ye to where ye've spent the night, then."

While he shook out her gown, Miranda knotted her hair in a loose ponytail. "And then I'll go home, I assume?"

He paused his motion. "I imagine it would look odd if ye stayed on, yer own house being so close by."

Now she wanted to punch him again. Part of what he'd been telling her all along *did* make sense, though, whether she cared to admit it or not. All these things — Vale, Matthew's debt, meeting Aden, her . . . exploration and enjoyment of her carnal side — had flown by at breakneck speed. She needed time and quiet to sort through them.

At the same time, there were things she *knew,* things that no amount of contemplation could alter. Things like how she felt about Aden. Now she just needed a way to convince him.

Once she looked nearly put back together, he pulled on his own shirt and stomped into his boots. "Ready, lass?"

"Yes. I'm already awake, though, and will be heading downstairs very soon to find some breakfast."

"I'm famished, myself." So abruptly it made her gasp, Aden yanked her against his chest and bent his head to take her mouth in a hot, toe-curling kiss. "There," he said after a moment, straightening again. "That should do me for a few minutes."

Before she could protest that now *she* needed a moment, he favored her with a wicked grin, inched open the door to peek out, and then led her down the hallway just past Eloise's door. He motioned for her to wait there and then slipped inside the neighboring bedchamber. Emerging a moment later, he motioned her inside.

"Eloise put one of her gowns in there for ye, it looks like," he whispered, stepping around her back into the hallway and pulling the door shut between them. "I'll see ye shortly."

Once she was alone, Miranda walked across the small bedchamber to push open the curtains, then she sank into a chair. Vale didn't know yet that his reign of terror was finished. No doubt he expected her to appear at Lord George's house for breakfast at precisely eight o'clock, as she'd been bidden by the butler. If someone still watched Oswell House, Vale would know she remained here.

At that thought a tremor ran through her. The captain didn't know yet that he'd lost his teeth. He might well arrive at the front door of Oswell House, demanding to know why she hadn't accepted his improper, outrageous invitation.

Miranda blew out her breath and stood again. She was so tired of sparing Vale any thought at all. But toothless or not, he was still in London. He was still in Mayfair, less than half a mile away. Would he try again to control her? Or to hurt her, once he realized she was out of his grasp?

"Stop it, Miranda," she muttered, shaking

out her hands.

Eloise had draped a pretty green muslin across the foot of the bed, its skirt embroidered with yellow and blue flowers. She'd also provided a simple night rail for Miranda to sleep in. Moving quickly, Miranda slipped out of her gown, unmade the bed and rolled across it a few times to properly rumple it, then wadded the night rail and left it at the foot of the bed.

The green gown was an inch or two too short and a little snug around her hips, but it would certainly suffice until she could return home and change. Of course, she preferred to remain at Oswell House. Aden lived there. And back at Harris House she would have to explain why Vale was no longer a suitor, and she would have to tell her parents something about what had happened. Matthew had helped; he'd given Vale exactly the information Aden had asked him to pass along, and he'd done it cleverly enough that the captain had believed it and called Aden out. But he'd also caused all this mess in the first place.

As she brushed out her hair and put it up in a coiled bun, she heard footsteps hurrying up and down the hallway, and Aden's low voice issuing instructions. The first of the letters were going out, then. Good. The more people who knew they'd been freed, and the more quickly they knew it, the better. As far as she could tell, all of Vale's allies were unwilling ones. Strip away their reason for being in his company, and he would find himself very much alone.

A knock sounded at her door. Tucking in a last hairpin, she went and pulled it open. She expected Eloise, or perhaps Aden, but instead Lady Aldriss stood in the hallway. "Good morning," the countess said.

Oh, dear. "Good morning, my lady. It seems I'm not the only one to have risen early today," Miranda replied with a smile.

The countess didn't return the expression. "Accompany me down to breakfast," she said without further preamble, stepping back from the door.

"Certainly."

"You went burgling with Aden last night."

"It wasn't as dangerous as it sounds."

"Hm. Nevertheless, he took you with him."

The last thing Miranda wanted was more tension between Aden and his mother. "I insisted. It wasn't my fault all this mess happened, but it certainly wasn't Aden's, either. And we were successful. Captain Vale might not realize it yet, but he's been stopped."

Lady Aldriss nodded. "Thank heavens. I

surmised as much, given the string of comings and goings this morning." She paused on the stair landing, taking a moment to glance into the foyer below. "I was quite worried about you," she said, lowering her voice further. "In fact, I knocked on your door a bit after midnight."

"Oh, I'm quite a sound sleeper, I fear," Miranda improvised, inwardly flinching.

"Mm-hm. I know who my sons are, my dear. Has he asked for your hand, or am I to pretend none of this ever happened?"

Miranda scowled. "He won't propose."

The countess blinked, real surprise crossing her features for the first time. "Really?"

"He kept promising to set me free, and then went on about how I couldn't make a proper choice with my head on a chopping block, and *then* how I could never know if I was merely feeling gratitude or if I felt a sense of obligation toward him. And also something about him having to marry, which meant that he couldn't know his own motives, and neither could whichever lass he asked. It's very aggravating."

"You love him, yes?"

She nodded. "I do. And he's said more than once that he loves me. I just can't — it's as if he's walled himself into a room and now he can't or won't admit that he forgot

504

to add a window."

Lady Aldriss looked at her for a long moment. "Well, with you being so shackled to manners and propriety," she said, sighing, "I don't suppose there's anything to be done about it."

The countess continued on down to the foyer. Miranda, though, stood where she was. Whether Lady Aldriss knew more than she claimed or whether she was simply a very good judge of character, she'd just said some very pertinent things. Some very interesting things.

Shaking herself, Miranda resumed her way down the stairs and up the hallway to the open breakfast room door — where she froze again.

"Mama?" she quavered, taking in the sight of the three people sitting at the table with the countess. "Papa? *Matthew?*"

"Sit down, darling," her mother said, patting the seat of the chair beside her. "Evidently we have a few things to discuss. It's been a very busy morning."

"I'm merely pointing out, Master Aden," Smythe intoned, "that there are no footmen left in the house, or grooms in the stable. If you want more missives to go out now, I will have to hire messengers." He fidgeted a little, his neck flushing. "And you should know —"

Aden took the pen from between his teeth, glad he'd moved downstairs to the library with his list of names and addresses. He waved a fistful of letters at the butler. "All of these can go by post. I'm nae sending anyone to India."

The butler nodded. "The mail will be arriving shortly. Might I hand them over then?"

As impatient as Aden was for this to be finished, twenty minutes wouldn't make any difference for letters sailing halfway around the world. "Aye. That'll suffice." He dipped the pen and started another note. Now that he'd settled on the wording, writing them out was a fairly quick process. "Has Miranda come downstairs yet?"

"I have not seen Miss Harris come downstairs, no."

That sounded a bit . . . precise. Aden sent the butler a sideways glance, uneasiness trickling up his spine. He'd checked the bedchamber before he'd allowed her inside, and it had been free of possible angry navy men or henchmen or nosy MacTaggert females. Perhaps she'd fallen asleep, though. They devil knew they'd been awake most of the night. "Let me know when she does."

"I shall do so. And there's something else you should —"

The brass door knocker thundered up the hallway, slamming against the front door at least half a dozen times in rapid succession. Hmm. It was early for callers, and he hadn't put his name or address on any of the notes. Lord George would know where any missive came from, though, as would Matthew Harris.

"If you'll excuse me," Smythe said, leaving the library as the loud rapping repeated.

The front door opened, followed by a loud exclamation and what sounded like a scuffle. Aden shoved to his feet and was halfway to the library door when the butler stumbled through it and fell to his knees, a pistol and then the blue-clothed arm of Captain Robert Vale directly behind him. Aden helped the butler to his feet, then stepped between him and the captain. No one else was going to be hurt.

"Where are they?" Vale snarled, the pistol moving to aim squarely at Aden's head.

"If ye shoot me ye'll nae find out, will ye?"

"A ball in the leg will persuade you. Give them back. I'm not asking again."

This was the way Aden had wanted it, with Vale's anger turned on him. Thank the devil Miranda was still upstairs. "Ye look a bit disheveled this morning," he noted, taking in the poorly knotted cravat and missing regal captain's hat. "Did ye get booted out of bed or someaught?" If that was how it had happened, he would have loved being there to see Lord George toss out his unwanted houseguest.

"Do I look like I'm playing?" Vale enunciated, waving the pistol a little for emphasis.

"Nae. Ye look like a man who's nae thought through his next couple of moves. Mayhap this'll help ye." Moving slowly on the chance the captain might panic and fire, Aden reached over to the table and retrieved the letter he'd just written out. "I'll read it to ye, so ye dunnae have to look down." He lifted the paper. " 'Admiral Jonathan Kenny, Bombay, India. This missive is to inform ye that the promissory notes in yer name and possessed by Captain Robert Vale, née Tom Potter of Polperro, Cornwall, have been destroyed. Ye may be interested to know that while I'm nae aware of his current location, Vale was last seen in Mayfair, London, on the ninth of June. He nae longer possesses any promissory notes at all, and nae any friends, either. Best of luck in yer future endeavors. A friend.' "

Vale stared at him, his face pale and a vein pulsing visibly at his temple. "Give me that."

"Nae. I willnae. I've already had seventeen or so of them delivered — which ye already know, since I reckon Lord George bade ye goodbye — and this one looks quite proper. My ma would be proud of my penmanship, I reckon."

"I am going to . . . kill you, and then I will kill Miranda Harris."

Something cold and hard settled in Aden's chest, and he altered what he'd been about to say. The time for baiting and jests was over with. Vale had just put a stop to it. "Ah. Now ye have two choices, Tom Potter," he said, noting that his voice sounded perfectly calm despite the black fury in his heart. "Ye —"

" 'Two choices'?" the captain repeated, snarling. "I'm giving you none at all, you bastard."

"I'm talking now," Aden cut in sharply. "If ye interrupt me again, we'll be down to one choice. Now. As I was saying, ye can put that pistol on the floor and leave, leave London, leave England before I catch a whiff of where ye've gone. Or ye can go with yer second choice, and fire that pistol and pray to God ye kill me. Because if ye flinch, if ye miss me or but wound me, I am going to put a knife through yer chin and up through yer brain and ye'll be dead before

509

ye hit the floor. And if ye don't miss, one of my brothers will see ye dead before ye get ten feet out the front door. Those are your two and only choices. You, alive, or dead by a MacTaggert's hand."

Aden took a slow breath, giving what he'd said time to sink in past Vale's desperation, time for the man to consider where he was and whether he had the spleen to shoot a man who stood there looking him in the eye. Because Vale was a man who prided himself on being roundabout, who made other men dirty their hands so he wouldn't have to. Except that this time he'd put the pistol into his own hands. "Now choose which one it's to be."

"You —"

"I said, *choose*, ye mealymouthed coward!" Aden bellowed. "You, alive, or dead?"

Vale flinched, opened his mouth, and shut it again. After six loud ticks from the clock on the mantel the pistol fell to the floor with a dull thud, and Robert Vale turned on his heel and fled the house.

"My . . . Thank you, Master Aden," Smythe said faintly behind him.

A door opened to his right, and he turned just as Miranda slammed into him. "Aden!" she sobbed, flinging her arms around him like a woman drowning.

He held her close. If he'd known she was in the next room, that a stray shot might have . . . *God's sake.* Aden lowered his face into her hair. "It's over," he whispered, his voice only now beginning to shake.

His mother and the Harris parents and Matthew piled out of the adjoining sitting room behind Miranda, but other than noting that someone — Francesca — had been maneuvering behind his back, he ignored them. Miranda was safe. Now she was safe.

Coll thundered in from the direction of the stairs, a claymore in one hand and wearing nothing but a scowl. "Where is the bastard? I'll cut him in half!" he roared.

"He's gone," Francesca answered, one hand over her heart. "He . . . Your brother threatened him, and he fled." She sat down hard in the nearest chair.

"Fuck. Mayhap I can catch him." Coll ducked back into the hallway, calling for his horse.

"He's . . . he's naked," Elizabeth Harris said faintly.

Amusement began to crack through fury and relief. "He'll realize that before he gets too far down the street," Aden commented, holding Miranda a little away from himself so he could get a better look at her. "Ye're nae hurt, are ye, lass?"

She wiped tears from her cheeks. "Me? *Me?* You were the one with a pistol pointed at you." Miranda clutched at his arms. "Are you certain you're all in one piece? We were headed in here to talk to you, and I heard . . . I heard everything. Your mother wouldn't let me open the door."

Aden looked over her head at Francesca, still seated and the gray caste slowly leaving her face. She'd been genuinely worried, he realized. Over him. It wasn't just a show for her guests. "Thank ye for keeping her safe, *màthair,*" he intoned.

Dark-green eyes met his. "Of course. I cherish what and whom you cherish."

Miranda shifted a little and took hold of his hand. "Come with me for a moment," she said, and tried to pull him toward the sitting room doorway.

"Aye. Excuse us. Smythe, I need those letters to go out."

"They will, Master Aden, if I have to take them to the nearest ship myself."

Aden allowed Miranda to lead him into the sitting room, and only lifted an eyebrow when she let him go and moved away to shut the door behind them. If she wanted to kiss him a few more times he wasn't about to protest, but he'd allowed her to be put in danger, and he needed to answer for

512

that. "I didnae reckon he'd dare show his face here, Miranda, or I'd have posted a guard. I guessed wrong, and it . . . Ye might have been hurt. It'll nae happen again."

She faced him, putting her back against the door. "You didn't guess wrong. For heaven's sake, Aden, *you're not like him.* You didn't anticipate an attempted murder because you're not a murderer."

"I'd have killed him just now, if he hadnae run."

"So I heard. In very graphic detail."

"Well, if I'd known ye were there, listening, mayhap I'd have been more polite."

Out in the hallway Coll bellowed for someone to bring him a damned kilt, and her mouth twitched. "At least he's returned," she commented.

"Aye. He generally does, though on occasion Niall or I have to go out and fetch him. Are yer parents here to take ye home?"

"Someone saw me in the street last night riding through London on your lap, and informed them," she said, clasping her hands in front of her waist. "They came to find out what in the world was going on."

He should have been there to help her with that conversation. "Ye told 'em, then?"

"Yes. Matthew and I did. He told them everything, and took complete responsibility for Vale, gambling, and the entire nightmare."

That impressed him, more than he would have expected. "Good lad. Is he disowned?"

She shook her head. "No. He *is* surrendering his membership to every gentlemen's club of which he's a member, though."

"That's wise. He and I can play Beggar My Neighbour over punch in the evenings. Out in the garden, mayhap, so the womenfolk willnae hear us weeping."

Miranda lifted on her toes, then sank down again, but didn't move from her spot in front of the door. "I'm grateful to you," she said.

"Ye dunnae have to be. We're partners."

"Yes, and I appreciate that. At the same time, I think it's fair to say that I've received more benefit from our partnership than you have." When he opened his mouth to argue with that, she scowled at him. "I'm not finished."

"Go on, then."

"I'm not just grateful because of your assistance with Vale. You . . . opened my eyes to some things, and —"

"Miranda," he broke in, frowning, "dunnae thank me for that, for Saint Andrew's sake. It was a genuine pleasure."

514

It occurred to him that she was likely trying to find the softest way to bid him farewell, and he straightened despite the fact that he felt like he'd just been punched in the chest. He couldn't pull in a solid breath, and his heart felt hollow and pinched.

"I wasn't . . ." She blushed. "Yes, the sex was — is — a genuine pleasure for me, as well," she whispered, then cleared her throat. "I didn't mean that, either, though."

"Then what —"

"I've always followed the rules," she cut back in. "I've enjoyed being good at them. The idea of breaking them to suit me . . . I don't know that it ever would have occurred to me, if I'd been on my own in this mess. But it's rather delightful, really."

"Good. I'm glad it makes ye happy." Even if the idea of her being with another man, smiling at him, kissing him, killed him inside.

"It does. In fact, I broke a few rules not ten minutes ago."

Curious despite himself, he tilted his head. "Aye?"

"Aye. I, um, asked your mother's permission to request your hand in marriage."

Everything stopped. Time, his breath, his heart. "I beg yer pardon?"

She walked back up to him finally, taking his hands. Hers shook. "I love you, Aden MacTaggert. I love your cleverness, and your heart, and the way you have Smythe so twisted about that he couldn't figure out this morning how to tell you that not only is Brògan a girl, but she had pups on his bed last night."

A laugh burst unbidden from his chest. Everything seemed to be breaking free, letting him breathe again. "She *what*?"

"Yes. Five of them. He's very attached, already."

"Saint Andrew's sake," he mused. "I saw she was putting on weight, but —"

"Aden," she interrupted. "I'm trying to tell you that I want to spend forever with you. Will you marry me?"

"Aye." His heart resumed beating again, in a fast, hard tattoo. Aden lifted her in his arms, kissing her as he lowered her into reach of his mouth again. "Yes, Miranda Harris. I will marry ye." He grinned. "I thought ye'd never ask me."

She laughed, kissing him back with a passion that delighted him beyond words. Her lessons about being a proper gentleman hadn't been even remotely successful, Aden reflected, but she'd taught him something even more useful — how to trust his heart again.

It wasn't about being a Highlander or a Sassenach, or where they chose to live, or even whether someone had ordered him to find London to find a wife. None of that mattered in the least. All he needed was his hope, his joy, his sharp-tongued, bonny lass. And now he was hers, and she was his. No more wagering was necessary; he'd just been dealt the perfect hand.

ABOUT THE AUTHOR

A native and current resident of Southern California, **Suzanne Enoch** loves movies almost as much as she loves books, with a special place in her heart for anything Star Wars. She has written more than forty Regency novels and historical romances, which are regularly found on the New York Times bestseller list. When she is not busily working on her next book, Suzanne likes to contemplate interesting phenomena, like how the three guppies in her aquarium became 161 guppies in five months. Some of Suzanne's books include *Barefoot in the Dark, It's Getting Scot in Here, Lady Whistledown Strikes Back,* and *The Legend of Nimway Hall.*

The employees of Thorndike Press hope you have enjoyed this Large Print book. All our Thorndike, Wheeler, and Kennebec Large Print titles are designed for easy reading, and all our books are made to last. Other Thorndike Press Large Print books are available at your library, through selected bookstores, or directly from us.

For information about titles, please call:
(800) 223-1244

or visit our website at:
gale.com/thorndike

To share your comments, please write:
Publisher
Thorndike Press
10 Water St., Suite 310
Waterville, ME 04901